The Secrets Sisters Keep

The Secrets Sisters Keep

Sinéad Moriarty

W F HOWES LTD

This large print edition published in 2015 by
W F Howes Ltd
Unit 4, Rearsby Business Park, Gaddesby Lane,
Rearsby, Leicester LE7 4YH

1 3 5 7 9 10 8 6 4 2

First published in the United Kingdom in 2014
by Penguin Group

A CIP catalogue record for this book is available
from the British Library

ISBN 978 1 47129 601 7

Typeset by Palimpsest Book Production Limited,
Falkirk, Stirlingshire

Printed and bound by
www.printondemand-worldwide.com in Peterborough, England

This book is made entirely of chain-of-custody materials

To my godsons: James, Sam and Max

Once upon a time there were three sisters,
and a brother who went to work naked . . .

'Shit!' he exclaimed, rushing to the woman. 'She was looking for the loo.'

'Sorry!' the girl said, trying desperately to cover her breasts and nether regions with her hands.

'No problem, easy mistake to make,' George said. To his wife, he added, 'You can put that down now – we're not in any danger. Good thinking, though! A plastic toilet brush would have provided great protection.'

'This is Amelia,' Gavin said.

'Annalise,' she corrected him.

'Christ,' George muttered.

'Really?' Gavin frowned. 'I was sure it was Amelia.'

'No, Annalise.'

'Right, sorry.'

'When you two have finished having your little catch-up, perhaps you might consider putting some bloody clothes on!' Anne suggested.

'There's no need to be rude, Mum.' Gavin looked offended.

He pulled Annalise from the bedroom. As she left, she gave them a wave. 'Nice to meet you.'

'You too.' George smiled.

As they watched the naked lovebirds scamper across the landing, Anne turned to her husband. 'You can stop staring at her bottom now, George.'

'I was just keeping an eye on the poor girl to make sure she didn't get lost again.'

'Poor girl? She's the most brazen hussy I ever met. The cheek of her saying, "Nice to meet you," while she's bare-arsed in our bedroom!'

'How does Gavin get these girls? He's a complete idiot.'

Anne bristled. 'He is not. He's handsome and charming and—'

George cut across her. 'Unemployed and penniless and going nowhere fast.'

'You're too hard on him. He's just finding his way.'

'He's not going to find it having sex with women whose names he can't remember.'

'Keep your voice down,' Anne said. 'The poor boy hasn't figured out what his path in life is yet.'

'How long is it going to take? He left university five years ago!'

'He'll get there soon enough.'

'You have him ruined,' George muttered. 'Spoilt rotten. The girls were never this lazy. It's ridiculous. I was running my own company at his age.'

'These are different times.'

'His sisters all had jobs at his age too!' George pointed out. 'He needs a kick up the arse.'

'Don't get all het up. If you have a heart attack you'll have to make your own way to hospital. I'm not missing Julie's lunch. I'm dying to see the new house. Apparently it's stunning.'

Three hours later

George parked beside the brand new Jaguar in the driveway.

'Is that Harry's new car?' Gavin asked.

'Yes.' Anne sniffed, 'It's very flashy. I think the money's gone a bit to his head.'

'It's awesome!' Gavin exclaimed.

They walked up the huge stone steps to Julie and Harry's new house. Gavin whistled. 'It's a bloody mansion.'

They rang the bell and heard a commotion inside. It was the triplets fighting over who would open the door. Losing patience, Anne bent down and shouted through the letterbox, 'Stop bickering and let us in.'

The door swung open as the three boys continued to wrestle. While Gavin and his father tried to prise them apart, Anne stepped over them and walked into the vast kitchen where her three daughters were sitting up at the marble counter.

Harry rushed over to greet his mother-in-law, then handed her a glass into which he made a big show of pouring Dom Pérignon.

'Oh, this is very decadent. Thank you, Harry.'

'Well, we're celebrating so I wanted to push the boat out.'

'I'd forgotten how good it tastes.' Sophie savoured it. 'I miss great champagne.'

'I don't see the difference. Prosecco would have been fine.' Julie looked cross.

Sophie placed a hand on her sister's arm. 'Relax and enjoy it, Julie.'

Gavin came in. 'Dude, this gaff is like something on MTV Cribs. I need an old aunt to die and leave me money like yours did. Harry, you are one lucky guy.'

George followed his son. 'Nice place, Julie. You'd need a map to find your way around.'

'A bit like Gavin's friend this morning, who got lost,' Anne said.

Louise rolled her eyes. 'What's Gavin done now?'

'Unbeknown to your father and me, he brought a fast girl home last night. This morning, she lost her way and ended up in our bedroom – naked.'

'Oh, my God! What did you do?' Julie tried not to laugh.

'Well, your mother thought it was a robber and came thundering out of the bathroom to fight him with a toilet brush.'

They all laughed.

'What did you do, Dad?' Louise asked.

'He stared a lot,' Anne huffed.

'Was she hot?' Sophie wondered.

'Well, I couldn't say. I tried to avert my eyes,' George protested.

'He was totally checking her out, the old perv.' Gavin chuckled.

'His eyes were out on sticks,' Anne added.

'Not a bad sight to wake up to.' Harry laughed. 'Better than Julie's fleecy pyjamas.'

'You don't actually wear those, do you?' Louise asked.

'They're comfortable.' Julie shrugged.

'You have to ditch them. You need fabulous new gear for your new bedroom suite. I'll take you shopping,' Sophie offered. 'La Perla do amazing pieces.'

'That stuff costs a fortune,' Julie said.

'Julie, you're loaded. You can buy anything you want,' Sophie reminded her.

Julie blushed and changed the subject. 'Is anyone hungry? Harry insisted on ordering a ridiculous amount of food from some posh caterer so we have tons.'

While the others made their way to the table, Louise pulled Julie aside. 'Look, I know having money is new to you, but you need to enjoy it. Stop being so defensive – we're all thrilled for you.'

Julie's eyes filled. 'I just feel . . . embarrassed about all this. It seems so over the top.'

'Julie, you of all people deserve it. Besides,' Louise said, watching as the triplets started a water fight, 'the boys will trash it and make it feel like home in no time.'

Julie squeezed her sister's arm. 'You're right. Is Clara OK?'

Louise turned to look at her little daughter, who was curled up on the couch with her fingers in her ears, reading a book. 'She's not used to so much noise.'

There was an almighty crash as one of the triplets rugby-tackled his brother and knocked over a platter of food.

Julie ushered them out into the garden.

Anne shook her head. 'They are pure wild. They need a firm hand.'

'They're just high-spirited,' Harry said. 'Besides,

they'll be calmer once school starts tomorrow. You know, Castle Academy's considered the best in the country – the sports facilities are second to none.'

'I think that's the tenth time he's mentioned it,' George whispered.

'Are the triplets excited?' Sophie asked Harry, trying to cover her father's mumblings.

'Not as excited as their father,' Julie muttered.

'Incredibly excited. They can't wait,' Harry enthused. 'The best thing about coming into money is being able to give the boys the best education.'

'I want to go to Castle Academy with the boys,' Tom said, pulling at his mother's leg.

Julie picked up her youngest son and kissed him. 'I know, pet, but you can't go until you're seven.'

Sophie's phone beeped. She read the message and her face fell.

'What's wrong?' Julie asked.

'Jess wants to stay with Jack and Pippa tonight. She's supposed to come home at six. I always do a movie night on Sunday and get her to bed early for school. But now she's begging to stay. If I say no, I'll be the worst mother in the world. I'm sick of it – she never wants to be with me any more. It's all about Jack and Pippa.'

'Oh, Sophie, that's rotten.'

She sighed. 'Yes, it bloody is. I need to meet someone so I can move on with my life.'

Julie patted her shoulder. 'You will, you're gorgeous.'

Harry clinked his glass. 'I just want to make a toast. Welcome, all of you, to our new home. Julie and I are starting a very exciting chapter in our lives and I know it's going to be a lot better than before.'

Julie looked down into her glass of expensive champagne. She'd liked her old life. She'd been very happy. All this change frightened her. What was this next chapter going to bring?

CHAPTER 1

Julie

I swirled my porridge around the bowl and breathed deeply to try to calm my thumping heart. It was ridiculous. I had no reason to be so nervous. It wasn't a big deal. I needed to get a grip and try not to be intimidated.

The triplets tumbled into the kitchen, kicking a football to each other. Luke picked up the ball and sat with it on his lap. God forbid he'd let it out of his sight for even a minute. Leo's polyester Ronaldo football jersey was sticking out from under his uniform and Liam was spouting football statistics.

'Did you know that Alan Shearer is the top Premier League goal scorer since 1992? He scored 260 goals.'

'Wow!' Tom said, following them into the kitchen. At five years of age, he thought everything his brothers said and did was wonderful. 'Who's the second best?' he asked.

'How would I know, squirt? Do I look like a computer?' Liam dismissed his younger brother and concentrated on pouring a huge mound of Cheerios into his bowl.

'So, boys, are you excited about school?' I asked.

'I hate this stupid uniform,' Leo complained. 'It's really scratchy.'

'Maybe if you took your football jersey off it would fit better,' I said. 'Come on, off with it.'

'No way!' he exclaimed. 'You're already forcing us to go to a new school where we have no friends. You can't make me take my Ronaldo off, too.'

I glanced at Harry, who had his nose stuck, as usual, in his iPad, peering at swirly graphs about stocks and option prices or whatever they were called. 'Harry? Feel free to chip in here.'

He looked up reluctantly. 'Leo, we've decided to send you to the top school in the country. All of the boys there will be properly dressed. You can wear the football jersey when you get home.'

'Some of them will probably be in tuxedos,' I muttered.

'What's a tuxedo?' Liam asked, his mouth stuffed with cereal.

'It's obviously something that geeks wear,' Leo said.

'Yeah, because all the kids in this school are morons,' Luke added, pulling at his navy-and-white-striped tie.

'Great, Julie, thanks a lot,' Harry said angrily. 'Very supportive of you.'

I glared at him. 'You know I think it's completely over the top.'

I wanted to poke my husband's eye out with my spoon. Harry had insisted on using some of the money to send the boys to the poshest school in Dublin. I was all for my children getting a good education, but the national school nearby was excellent. They had been happy there and had made lots of friends. As had I, the other mums had become a little network for me. I wanted to use the money wisely and send them to a good private school for their secondary education when they were twelve. But Harry had heard about Castle Academy from one of his new 'friends' in the golf club he had recently joined and had insisted the boys go there.

Luke threw the football into the air. It landed in the middle of his cereal, sending Cheerios and milk flying everywhere. I counted to ten. I was trying really hard not to shout so much. So far, the longest I had lasted on any given day was fifteen minutes.

'Clean it up.' I handed him a roll of kitchen paper.

I turned to put my bowl in the dishwasher and felt a thump on the side of my head as the football whacked me.

I spun around. 'Ouch! That really hurt.'

'Sorry.' Leo giggled.

'It's not funny.'

'Yes, it is,' Liam said, snorting with laughter.

'Good shot.' Luke was impressed.

I picked up the ball, opened the back door and flung it out into the garden. 'Harry!' I shouted. 'Can you please take your nose out of that bloody iPad and control your children while I get dressed?'

'You lasted thirteen minutes,' Harry said drily, tapping his watch without looking up.

'Being walloped in the head is grounds for losing my temper. I'm entitled to shout. I could be concussed!'

Harry stood up. 'Right, boys, do you fancy a quick game before school?'

'No!' I exclaimed. 'They can't get all muddy now! Come on, Harry, it's their first day.'

Harry came over to me. 'Go and get dressed in peace. I promise not to let them dive or slide-tackle in the mud.'

'Fat chance.'

Harry laid a hand on my shoulder and looked at me properly for the first time that morning. 'Julie, I know you're nervous about their first day and about meeting all those posh mums, but you need to relax. It'll be fine. This school is going to guarantee that our boys turn into geniuses and world leaders.'

I rolled my eyes. I somehow doubted that our troublesome three would ever be geniuses. Harry was right about my nerves, though. I was worried about meeting the other parents. I was hoping to make friends. To be honest, as the mother of triplets, people tended to avoid me. Other mothers

She switched off her electric toothbrush and listened. She could hear her husband shouting. He sounded panicked. Oh, my God, they were being robbed. She looked around the bathroom for a weapon. The only thing she could see was the toilet brush. She crept over to the door, opened it slowly and jumped out, shouting, 'Leave him alone!'

Instead of coming face to face with a balaclava-wearing thief, Anne found herself in front of a naked woman. She stared over at George, who was sitting bolt upright in bed, eyes wide with shock.

The young woman let out a bloodcurdling scream.

'What the hell is going on?' Anne shrieked.

'For the love of God, will you get her a towel or something?' George hissed.

'Who is she?' Anne snapped.

'I've no bloody idea. I woke up and found her stumbling around at the end of the bed.'

The bedroom door burst open and their son, Gavin, charged in, naked and dishevelled.

'I'm up to my eyes here, Julie. I really have to go.'

'Please, Sophie – I'll be quick.'

'OK – but hurry.'

I put the phone on loudspeaker and tried on her suggestions.

'Can you believe Gavin and the naked girl? He gets away with murder. Mum would have killed us if we'd brought a guy home to stay the night,' Sophie said.

'I know – he's completely indulged. He really needs to get a job.'

I looked in the mirror and sent a photo to Sophie.

'Got it. Perfect. You look great.'

'Thanks, sis.'

'Anytime. Even though I hardly get to buy clothes any more, I still love them.'

'I can't believe I have nice clothes. Me, Julie, in outfits that weren't purchased in Primark!'

Sophie laughed. 'Enjoy it. You deserve it. Now, don't be nervous, and if you see Victoria, duck.'

Oh, God, I'd forgotten about Victoria. Her son, Sebastian, went to Castle Academy. He was in the same form the triplets were joining. There were two classes of twenty boys in each year and I was praying Sebastian would be in the other one. Victoria had been one of Sophie's friends in the Celtic Tiger days, when Sophie was married to Jack and lived the high life. Victoria might have been beautiful and stylish, but she was shallow and nasty underneath her perfect year-round tan.

6

The minute Jack and Sophie had lost everything, Sophie hadn't seen her for dust.

'I won't be on Victoria's radar,' I said. 'I'm far too dowdy for her.'

'You never know,' Sophie replied. 'Now that you're a millionaire, she might take a shine to you.'

'After that time I bumped into her and told her I thought she was a low-life for treating you so badly, I don't think she'll be rushing over to me.'

'True. But I was thrilled you did it.'

'To be honest, I'd say Victoria will have a heart attack when she sees me and the boys, lowering the tone at Castle Academy.' I giggled.

'Well, if you're talking to her and she's being her usual condescending self, ask her how Gerry is. Her beloved husband is currently shagging one of my models – Amber.'

'Really?'

'Yes, and he's not even bothering to be discreet. He took her to Le Jardin last week, on a busy Friday night.'

'What age is Amber?'

'Twenty. He's a creep.'

'Poor Victoria,' I said, feeling a tiny bit sorry for the snobby cow.

'Don't pity her too much. Remember what a weapon she was to me.'

'Don't worry, Sophie. Me and "Vicky" are not going to be bosom buddies. Somehow I don't see her inviting me and the boys over for playdates so they can trash her immaculate house.'

Sophie laughed. 'What a lovely thought! Now, go and do your makeup. Use that new eye shadow you bought last week – it's really flattering. And you're just as gorgeous as any of those other mothers.'

'I am not, but thanks anyway.'

'Gotta run. I'll call you later. Good luck.' Sophie hung up and I went to put on my face.

When I got back downstairs to call the boys, I looked out of the window to see Harry, the triplets and Tom all running about with muddy knees. Having grown up a lonely only child, Harry was thrilled to have four boys to wrestle and play football with. He was in his element. I often felt very left out. As the boys got older, they needed me less. It was all about Harry now. They wanted him to play football, wrestle and play the Wii with them.

I secretly hoped Tom was gay. I needed someone to hang out with. There was so much testosterone in the house that I sometimes felt suffocated. I loved my boys, but I did envy my sisters, who had daughters they could go shopping and watch *Tangled* with.

I called them all in, and while Harry went to change his trousers for work, I tried to get the mud out of the triplets' brand-new school uniforms with a wet cloth.

Eventually we got into the car. I was delivering the older boys while Harry was dropping Tom to his old school. Thankfully Tom would have a couple more years of 'normal' school before going to Castle Academy.

'Good luck today, boys,' Harry said, sticking his head through the car window. 'Sorry I can't be there for your first day, but I have a very important meeting with a fund manager. I'll see you later. Be good and enjoy this wonderful opportunity. Castle Academy is a school for champions.'

'Is it a school for Premier League footballers?' Luke asked.

'Did Ronaldo go there?' Leo wanted to know.

'No, you idiot, he's from Portugal,' Liam said.

I started the car and drove off, waving to Harry as we went.

The triplets pinched, thumped, flicked, kicked and poked each other for the twenty minutes it took us to get to the school. I turned up the volume on the radio so I wouldn't shout and tried to let the music calm my nerves.

I had recently upgraded the battered family van I used to drive, which I'd hated, to a Hyundai Santa Fe and was very proud of my new car. It was only three years old, red, and had a leather interior. It quickly lost its appeal when I drove through the tall iron gates of Castle Academy: BMW, Porsche and Land Rover jeeps were *de rigueur*. It was like a little oasis in the middle of the economic desert that was recession Ireland.

As I stared up at the imposing castle in front of

me, I could feel my hands getting clammy on the steering-wheel. This school was way out of my league – I'd never fit in here. All around us were acres of grounds. It was like something out of *Downton Abbey*. OK, not quite, but close enough.

I took deep breaths. The boys were quiet now in the back. They were intimidated too. I prayed they'd get on all right. I wanted them to be happy.

I parked the car beside a shiny black Land Rover and turned to them. Faking a smile, I said, 'OK, guys, this is it, your new school. Now, don't be nervous. You're going to have a great time and they're lucky to have you. I want you to go in there and be yourselves – well, not your crazy selves, your good selves. OK?'

They nodded. I'd never seen them so still and silent. We got out of the car and I watched as yummy-mummies greeted each other warmly, air-kissing and shrieking like teenagers. I gripped my handbag and stood close to the boys.

My stomach lurched when I saw Victoria climbing delicately down from a powder blue Porsche Cayenne. She was wearing a tightly fitted silver-grey dress with sky-high strappy silver sandals. A huddle of women rushed over to her. She was clearly the queen bee. Most of her minions looked like clones of her – glossy blonde high-lighted hair, stick-thin bodies, expensive clothes and manicured nails.

I looked down at my nails. I'd painted them while I was watching *Mad Men* last night, but then

Tom had wet his bed so I'd had to change the sheets and smudged most of them. I felt like a kid on her first day in school, watching the cool girls and knowing I'd never be one of them. I was always going to be an outsider here.

Thankfully, I recognized one of the mums, Emily. I'd met her at a fashion show Sophie had organized. Her niece had been one of the models. Emily was slightly less well dressed than the others. I imagine she shopped in House of Fraser rather than Harvey Nichols. Buying clothes in House of Fraser was something I used to aspire to, but now it wasn't good enough. I hated this, hated feeling inferior, and I didn't want my kids feeling this way. I shepherded the boys over to where Emily was standing and reintroduced myself to her. She was staring at Victoria and her posse.

'Look, it's Victoria Carter-Mills.' Emily sounded awed.

'The one and only,' I said, unable to keep the edge out of my voice.

'Wow! She's so stylish. She always looks gorgeous in the social pages of magazines, and she's even more stunning in the flesh. I wonder where she got those shoes – they're incredible.'

The triplets had started to play football beside me with a ball they had grabbed from my car. A few other kids joined in and soon there was a gang of them. I smiled to myself. My boys would be fine: they had each other.

Victoria and her group passed in front of us.

11

I turned to look at the boys and avoid her. Just as I did, Leo kicked the ball hard. It zinged past me and smacked Victoria's leg. Damn!

She staggered. Emily rushed to grab her. They both turned to stare at Leo who, sensing Victoria's rage, stood very close to me.

'How dare you?' Victoria screeched. 'You horrible child. You almost knocked me over. Look at my leg! I'm going to have a huge bruise.' Then, glaring at me, she demanded, 'Are you his mother?'

Victoria's clones fussed over her, asking if she was all right. I was surrounded and outnumbered. I thought – for a split second only – about denying that Leo was mine, but then I decided to stand my ground. 'Yes, I am.'

'He's just attacked me with that wretched ball. Have you nothing to say?'

'I do, actually,' I said, my blood beginning to boil. I could feel all eyes on me, judging me, but suddenly I didn't care. 'It was an accident, and Leo is very sorry. There's no need to call him names.'

'I beg your pardon?' she spluttered. 'Is that it? Is that all you have to say? Your son has scarred me.'

I looked at her leg. 'No, he hasn't. It's a tiny bruise.' I kept my voice as even as possible.

She tried to frown, but her Botoxed face remained stiff. 'You're obviously new to the school.'

'Yes, we are.'

'Well, let me tell you that such behaviour is not

tolerated. Boys are not allowed to behave like wild animals.'

I'd had enough. 'Chill out. They were only playing football.'

'*Chill out?* Who do you think you are?'

'Julie Devlin. Sophie Devlin's sister. You remember my sister Sophie? You were best friends for a while. We've met before. In fact, we had an interesting little chat in Starbucks a while ago.'

Victoria looked shocked. 'What on earth are *you* doing here?'

'The triplets are starting in the third form.'

'But you can't possibly be sending your children to Castle Academy.'

'Actually, I can, and I am. They might even be in your son's class. Anyway, I'm sure you'll be delighted to hear that your old pal Sophie is doing really well. She's a partner now in the Beauty Spot.'

Victoria narrowed her eyes and gave me a sickly smile. 'Poor Sophie. I did feel for her when Jack divorced her and took up with Pippa Collins. Pippa is so young, beautiful and successful. It must have been hard for Sophie to be cast aside like that.'

The hairs on the back of my neck were now at right angles to the ground. How dare she belittle my sister? 'Actually, Sophie divorced Jack. She's really happy and fulfilled now. All that lunching and shopping was boring her to death.'

Victoria turned to her posse. 'Sophie was married to Jack Wells. You must have heard about them. So tragic. He lost everything in a Ponzi scheme. He even tried to get Gerry involved, but Gerry was much too clever to fall for that.'

I was very tempted to ask her if Gerry had enjoyed his dinner in Le Jardin on Friday night, but decided not to stoop to her level. It was my first day: I was supposed to be making friends, not mortal enemies.

Victoria flicked back her wavy, honey-coloured hair and tottered off in her high heels with her adoring fans. Emily followed them, so I found myself alone.

The bell rang, calling the boys into class.

I fought back tears. My first day was a disaster. I'd alienated about half the bloody school.

Leo looked up at me. 'Sorry, Mum. I didn't mean to hit her.'

I bent down and hugged him. 'I know, pet. She's just a stuck-up cow. Don't you mind her. Now, off you go and have a great day.'

I watched the triplets lining up behind their teacher. They were the only ones with Tesco backpacks and I was proud of that. Some of the boys had leather ones with their initials embossed on the back. More money than sense, as Mum would say.

My heart sank as I saw Victoria's son standing in line behind the triplets. They were in the same class. Could this day get any worse?

14

As I stood there, waving, fake-smiling, standing alone, I longed for my old life at the school gates, with Marian at my side, laughing and joking. Here, I was an outcast already.

CHAPTER 2

Louise

I snapped my laptop shut and cursed under my breath. Wendy just wasn't on point. I'd have to talk to her next week. I really didn't want her sending me annoying emails on Sunday morning about things she'd forgotten to tell me.

Women like her got up my nose. Why the hell couldn't she be more professional? She had been late twice last week and had arrived at a client meeting with a soother sticking out from the breast pocket of her blouse. It had distracted me, and everyone else, for the entire meeting.

I'd have to talk to her. She was letting the department down. I ran a tight ship and I wanted everyone on my team to be efficient, competent professionals at all times. Clients came to me because of my reputation. Wendy was not going to tarnish it.

I put my laptop on the counter and watched Clara counting raisins into her porridge. I knew she'd stop at twenty. She was just like me: she

16

didn't want their kids befriending mine because a playdate meant having to invite the three of them. No one really wants three boisterous boys bouncing off their walls after school. So I was worried about being isolated. That was the great thing about my old neighbour, Marian: she had four kids and was very laid back about her house, mess and noise. I really missed having her next door.

For the first day of school, I had planned to wear my new Seven jeans with a cream silk T-shirt and a beige jacket, but suddenly I wasn't so sure. I rang my younger sister, Sophie, who knew everything there was to know about fashion and style.

'Hi, it's me. I've got First-Day-at-New-School-Outfit Syndrome.'

'OK, what were you thinking?' These days, Sophie always got straight to the point. Before, she used to spend ages on the phone analysing this and that, but now that she was working full-time, she was all about efficiency and time management.

I filled her in on my outfit choice.

'Sounds good, although maybe you should wear the navy Donna Karan jacket you bought. It's smart, stylish and would look great with those jeans. Also, the navy Marc Jacobs wedges – they'll finish the look off nicely.'

'Good idea. Can you hang on while I try it on so I can send you a selfie?'

loved order and routine. I shuddered as I imagined breakfast at Julie's house. It was a zoo over there.

While Clara finished her breakfast I sent a text to Christelle, to tell her I needed her in early tomorrow because I had an eight o'clock meeting.

No prob, c u then, she replied.

Hope Galway good fun, I added.

Gr8 fun, xcpt Harry texting evry 5 mins to chek up on me!

I smiled. Poor Harry. He'd been completely thrown when he found out he had a grown-up daughter he'd never known existed. Julie was far more relaxed about it. In the past four years, Harry had tried to make up for the eighteen he'd missed. He was ridiculously over-protective and it drove Christelle nuts.

Give H a break, he wants to b a good dad.

I no but he's suffocating.

Want me to say smthg at lunch today?

Yes pls!

Clara and I were the first to arrive at my parents' house for lunch. Mum opened the door and bent down to hug Clara.

'Squeeze tighter, Granny,' Clara said, and Mum obliged.

We went into the lounge, where Dad was watching rugby. He waved at us and I sat down beside him. Clara sat on the floor and opened her book.

'What are you reading about this week?' Dad asked her.

Not looking up, Clara said, 'Birds of prey.'

'Does she ever read anything except books about birds?'

I shrugged. 'She has a huge interest in them, so I'm encouraging her. I was always reading at her age, too.'

Dad rolled his eyes. 'You never had your nose out of a book. You barely said a word to anyone.'

I patted his arm. 'Well, it didn't do me any harm.'

'Fewer books and more lipstick might have got you a nice husband,' Mum said, coming in with a platter of nibbles, which she placed on the table in front of the fire.

'I presume she had lipstick on the night she met Clara's father,' Dad muttered, under his breath. Mum tutted behind us.

Clara was the result of a one-night stand, which was still a sore point with Mum, especially as it had happened in Italy and I didn't even know his name. I had simply told Clara that some kids had no dads and that I loved her enough for two parents. She had accepted it. I'd eventually have to tell her the truth but for now she was happy.

I glared at Dad and mouthed, 'Shut up!'

Clearly Clara hadn't heard anything: 'Granddad, did you know that birds of prey hunt for food using their keen senses, especially vision?'

'Very interesting, pet.' Dad turned to me. 'My

18

God, Louise, they're very big words for a small girl. Can she honestly read that? She's only four and a half.'

I felt a rush of pride. 'She's way ahead for her age, Dad. I think she's genuinely in the genius category.'

'Like mother, like daughter,' Dad said. 'I bet she'll end up in Mensa, like you.'

'Their talons and beaks are large, powerful and adapted for tearing flesh,' Clara continued.

Dad looked at me. 'Is that really suitable reading for a four-year-old? Tearing flesh?'

Before I could answer, Gavin arrived with a tall, thin, blonde girl in low-slung jeans and a tight vest T-shirt. 'Hey, guys, this is Shania.'

'Are you sure?' Dad snorted. 'It could be Shandy.'

'It's Shania, Dad.' Gavin glared at him.

'Nice to see she has her clothes on, anyway.'

Shania grinned. 'Gavin told me about that other girl. How mortifying for everyone. Don't worry, Mr Devlin, I have my own place so you won't be seeing my bare arse anytime.'

'Very reassuring to know. Thank you.' Dad grinned.

'It's super nice of you to have me over,' she gushed.

'We had no idea you were coming, but you're very welcome.'

'Shania works in Stars and Stripes. She's the one who got me an interview with them,' Gavin explained.

'When is it?' I asked.

'Tuesday,' Gavin said.

'It would be, like, so awesome if Gavin got a job there. We'd have so much fun together. Gavin is the funniest guy ever.'

'Really?' Dad and I were both surprised.

'OMG, totally.'

'Where are you from, Shania?' Dad asked.

She looked puzzled. 'Killiney.'

'As in, Killiney up the road?' Dad spluttered.

'Totally.'

'I thought you were American.'

'I wish.' She smiled, showing a perfect set of pearly white teeth.

Sophie and Jess walked into the room. Sophie was wearing a dress that was far too short. It wouldn't even have looked good on Shania. Since Jack had met Pippa, Sophie had been wearing clothes that were too young for her. I'd have to say something, she looked ridiculous.

'Hi, Gavin. Nice top. Is that Stars and Stripes?' Sophie asked.

'Yeah, Shania gave it to me.'

'I think he looks hot in it,' Shania said.

'Sorry, who are you?' Sophie asked, looking her up and down.

'This is Shania, Gavin's "friend",' Dad said, winking.

'Very subtle, Dad.' Sophie grinned. She proffered a hand to Shania. 'I'm Sophie, and this is my daughter, Jess.'

'Hi,' Jess said. 'I like your jeans.'

Shania's jeans had pink hearts stitched down the side of each leg.

'Thanks, they're Stars and Stripes too. You should come into the store. I can help you pick some out.'

Sophie butted in: 'Jess is too young for that shop.'

'Oh, no, honestly, we do really cute jeans for teenagers.'

'She's nine,' Sophie said firmly.

'Wow, you look older, probably because you're tall, like your mum. You could definitely be a model.'

'Really? Do you think so?' Jess's face lit up.

'Totally.'

'Pippa thinks so, too.'

I saw Sophie's face darken. Pippa was a sore subject. I felt sorry for my sister. Pippa was like a slap in the face, she looked like a younger version of Sophie and was Jack's first serious girlfriend since they had broken up. The fact that Pippa was living with Jack and spending time with Jess was hard on Sophie.

'Who's Pippa?' Shania asked.

'My dad's girlfriend. She's a TV presenter and she's amazing,' Jess gabbled. 'She's beautiful and so much fun. I love my weekends with her and Dad. My other weekends are so boring.'

Ouch, poor Sophie. I walked over to her and took her arm. 'I think Mum needs help in the kitchen,' I said, leading her away. Once we were outside the room, I said, 'Jess doesn't mean it.'

Sophie sighed. 'Yes, she does. She worships Pippa and hates me. Honestly, Louise, since Pippa came on the scene, Jess has been a nightmare. It's bad enough that Jack is going out with someone half my age, but to have my daughter obsessed with her, too, is really hard to take.'

'Pippa's still a novelty. It'll wear off. You're Jess's mum and she adores you.'

'She used to, but not any more.'

The doorbell rang and I went to answer it. The triplets tumbled into the house, Julie, Harry and Tom following. Julie was wearing a cute navy shift dress with navy-and-white ballet pumps. She looked great.

'Hi, Harry, how's things?'

'Good, thanks,' Harry said. 'Is the game on inside?' He nodded at the door to the lounge.

I stepped aside. 'Be my guest.' He headed straight in.

'You look lovely, Julie,' Sophie said.

'Thanks. You told me to buy this – remember?'

'Oh, yeah! Well, it suits you.'

It's a pity Sophie doesn't buy similar clothes for herself, I thought. She'd look so much better.

'I have to admit, having money to buy decent clothes makes such a difference,' Julie said. 'I never knew how much tailored clothes could enhance your shape. They hide all my bad bits.

22

I'm not like you two, with your skinny frames. You can wear anything and look good.'

'Harry's had a make-over, too,' Sophie noted. 'That was all Hugo Boss, wasn't it?'

Julie nodded. 'One of the men in the golf club told him it was the "only place to shop". So Harry went in and bought almost everything in there. He came home with a car full of clothes. I was shocked. He never cared about clothes before. I know he's a lot smarter, but I kind of miss his cord jackets and crumpled chinos.'

'He looks way better now,' Sophie assured her.

'Which golf club did he join?' I asked.

'The Royal Marine.'

'Wow! That's the most expensive club in Ireland. Very fancy!' I said.

Julie shrugged. 'It costs a fortune to be a member. Harry spends half his time worrying about money and the other half spending it. But he says he only makes investments, including the boys' new school and the golf club, which he says is great for networking. The amount of time he devotes to meeting people to discuss how to make the money grow and last for our future is ridiculous.'

'Hang on! He's right to be cautious. You came into a large sum, but it disappears quickly. Harry's wise to be thinking about investment plans and pensions,' I reminded her.

'Damn right! Look at me,' Sophie said. 'One day we were millionaires, the next we were home-less. You need to mind your cash.'

'I understand that, but I wish we didn't have to talk about it all the time,' Julie said. 'I spent years budgeting every single day. I just want to enjoy not having to worry about money.'

'You should treat yourself – just don't go mad like Jack and I did.'

'There's no fear of that. I'm never going to wear designer clothes. I'm still too intimidated to go into Harvey Nichols.'

'Julie!' Sophie laughed. 'It's just a shop.'

'I find it really daunting. I'm not comfortable there. I don't feel like I belong, and I keep expecting someone to ask me to leave because I'm not glamorous enough.'

Sophie and I roared laughing. 'That's insane,' I said. 'You're one of the only people in Ireland who has money at the moment. They'll be welcoming you with open arms.'

'I used to spend half my life there, shopping or having coffee or lunch. Now I only ever go there for work.' Sophie smiled ruefully.

'Well, I'd be happy to go with you and treat you to new clothes,' Julie offered.

Sophie put an arm around her. 'Thanks, Julie, but you need to spend your money on yourself and enjoy it. By the way, I keep meaning to ask you how the boys are getting on at Castle Academy.'

Julie filled us in. Sophie laughed wickedly when she heard about Victoria getting smacked by the football. I didn't think it was so funny, though.

Julie needed the triplets to start behaving. They were wild, and if they got expelled from Castle Academy, she might find it difficult to get them accepted elsewhere. She needed to be firmer with them. Harry was far too easy on them, too. He hardly ever gave out to them. He thought all of his children were wonderful. That was fine, but the triplets needed a firm hand. Tom was the opposite, an incredibly calm, sweet child. How had Harry and Julie ended up with such polar opposites?

Gavin's head appeared around the door of the lounge. 'The witches are in conclave, I see,' he said, grinning at us. 'What are you three whispering about out here?'

'We're putting bets on as to how long Shania will be around,' Sophie said, teasing him. 'The previous girl only lasted a night, didn't she?'

Julie and I burst out laughing. Gavin's love life was a constant source of fascination to us. Why so many girls fell for him was beyond us, but he seemed to have the magic touch.

'You'd better get used to her,' Gavin said, shaking his finger at Sophie. 'This one's a keeper, I swear.'

'If she lasts a month, I might start believing you,' Sophie said. 'How are you anyway? What's happening? Any interviews lined up?'

'One at Stars and Stripes on Tuesday.'

'Cool store.' Sophie seemed impressed.

'Isn't that the place where the guys stand outside

on the street shirtless, covered with fake tan and baby oil?' Julie asked.

Sophie laughed. 'It gets people into the shop.'

'Really? Are you seriously going to work with no top on?' It sounded ridiculous to me.

Gavin glanced towards the kitchen door, then shushed us. 'Keep your voice down. Mum and Dad don't know about that.'

'What?' I was shocked.

'Don't get all judgemental. The dudes in the shop don't wear shirts.'

'Are you honestly telling me that you're considering working half naked?' I know I sounded like a granny, but come on! We didn't live in Santa Monica: this was cold, grey Dublin.

'Shania said it gets the ladies in. And, apparently, it's the old birds, like you lot, who always cop a feel,' Gavin said.

'Do they proposition them?' Julie asked.

Gavin grinned. 'One or two of the really fit guys have had phone numbers slipped into their jeans by cougars.'

'Well, if they're single, why not?' Sophie said.

Gavin crinkled his nose. 'It's a bit desperate.'

'Do you think you'll be propositioned?' Julie asked, trying not to laugh.

'I'm working on my six-pack in the gym, so I reckon I probably will.' Gavin patted his thin frame. He didn't even have a one-pack.

'If you actually get this job, aside from being mauled by older women, are you going to try to get into management or are you going to spend your time in the stockroom with Shania?' I asked. Gavin had a long history of getting distracted by girlfriends.

'No, I'm totally focused this time. The company is really cool and I definitely see my future there.'

We all laughed.

'What?' Gavin snapped.

'Come on, you always say that and then something or someone turns your head and it all goes pear-shaped,' Sophie said.

'Well, I'm serious this time. Stars and Stripes rocks and the clothes are amazing.'

'What about Shania? Does she rock too?' Julie asked, with a knowing smile.

'She's a very cool girl.'

'With a weird fake American accent,' I noted.

'That's the way all the young girls speak now,' Sophie said. 'You should hear the models at the agency – you'd swear they were all from LA.'

'She's very pretty, great figure,' Julie said, sounding envious. Julie had lost weight in the last few years, but she was big-busted and would always be curvy. She had always envied Sophie and me for being taller and slimmer. Mind you, we both worked hard at staying slim. I ran five miles every day and Sophie had been starving herself since she'd started modelling at eighteen.

Mum came out of the kitchen and clapped her hands. 'Right, lunch is ready. Julie, we'll leave the boys outside playing football so we can eat in peace. I'll give them pizza later on.'

'Fine with me,' Julie said.

We went in to take our places at the table, and Shania brought Clara's book in for her. 'Louise, your daughter is awesome,' she said, smiling widely at me. Her teeth were scarily perfect. 'I was reading her book with her and she's, like, super-bright. I cannot believe how much she knows about birds. She's just like my little brother – he was obsessed with animals when he was young.'

I smiled at her. 'Thank you. Clara is pretty amazing, even if I say so myself.'

Harry was sitting beside me, checking Bloomberg on his phone.

'What are you into these days?' I asked.

'Donald at the golf club told me to buy Ardvarnid and I made a killing last week. I got out and bought some Janson shares. They're up and down, so I'm keen to keep an eye on it.'

'Harry!' Julie snapped. 'Put your phone away.'

He stuffed it reluctantly into his pocket.

'I was on to Christelle this morning,' I said. 'She's having a great time in Galway.'

Harry shook his head. 'I don't even know who she went with. She was very vague – she just said pals from college. I hope she's not hanging out with a wild bunch.'

Julie snorted. 'Christelle has more sense than all of us put together. Stop fussing, Harry.'

'I can't help worrying about her.'

'Of course you can't. That's what good fathers do,' Mum said.

partner in the business. That kind of outfit is hardly business-like.'

Sophie's mouth fell open in surprise. Then she dropped her knife and fork with a clatter. 'Get off your high horse, you judgemental cow. We can't all be as perfect as you.'

'Jesus, Sophie, calm down, I'm just trying to help.'

Julie interrupted us: 'Guys, stop, please. You have different styles. Leave it at that.'

Sophie shook a finger in my face. 'You're not helping me, Louise, just kicking me when I'm down.' With that, Sophie stood up, grabbed her coat and Jess and stormed out.

'Well done, Louise, very sisterly of you.' Mum glared at me.

'Someone needed to say it to her,' I snapped. 'I'm the only one who had the balls to do it.'

'You shouldn't have said it here, in front of everyone,' Mum said.

'It wasn't the right time,' Julie agreed.

'Fine. I'll just say nothing and let my sister go around looking like a desperate divorcée, shall I?'

'Let's not spoil lunch altogether,' Dad said quietly. It was his fault – he'd mentioned it in the first place. 'Your mother's made us a lovely meal so we should settle down and enjoy it.'

But I couldn't eat because I knew I'd handled it badly. The last thing I wanted to do was hurt Sophie. I'd only tried to help her. Why did everyone have to be so sensitive?

CHAPTER 3

Sophie

I reapplied some lipstick and examined myself in the mirror. Was my dress too short? Bloody Louise had made me paranoid. I was questioning all of my clothes now. To Hell with her. I looked good and the date was going well.

I sashayed out of the Ladies and back into the restaurant. At the table, I sat back down opposite Julian. He was good-looking, successful and kind – the first date I'd really connected with since I'd broken up with Jack. Tick, tick, tick. All the things I wanted in a man.

I sipped my wine and smiled as I listened to him talking about his years living in Hong Kong. I felt good. I felt attractive. I felt like a real person for once. Not just a mother or career woman or sister or daughter – an actual woman.

Julian smiled at me. 'Enough about me. Let's talk about you. So, what happened with your ex, if you don't mind me asking about it?'

'No, it's OK, all water under the bridge now. Well, when we lost everything our lives were turned upside-down. He was at home with Jess while I went out to work. It took him a while to get a new job and back on his feet. When he did get a job, it was in London, and those two years when he was commuting back and forth, we grew further apart. As break-ups go, it was pretty amicable. We get on quite well and Jess is our priority.'

'Was it difficult to lose everything?'

'Awful, really traumatic, but we've built our lives back up and I've learnt a lot.'

'Like what?'

'Like making sure that my daughter studies hard and has her own career and money.'

Julian smiled. God, he was sexy. 'I prefer women who work. They're more interesting and less needy,' he said.

'So,' I was keen to change the subject and get back to more flirty chat, 'I'm really glad we met up. I'm having a lovely time.'

He nodded. 'Me too. I'll have to call Grace in the morning and thank her for setting this up.' He was referring to our friend-in-common who had played Cupid.

'She was very keen for us to meet. She was positive we'd get on well, and she was right.' I winked at him playfully.

Julian glanced at his watch. 'Gosh, look at the time. I didn't realize it was so late. The evening flew. I'd better get the bill.'

I wasn't normally so forward, but I really liked

him and I hadn't had sex in ages, so I took a deep breath and said, 'Would you like to come back to my place for a nightcap?'

Julian handed his credit card to the waiter. Then, turning to me, he said, 'Sophie, I've really enjoyed dinner. You look great for your age, you're good company and good fun, but to be honest, you're a little older than I thought. I'm looking for someone younger. Sorry.'

My lip began to wobble uncontrollably. I pushed my wine glass against it to stop it and pretended to take a sip. I managed to say, 'No problem,' then bent down to busy myself with my bag and try to stop myself crying.

Somehow I was able to walk to the door on shaky legs, accept a kiss on the cheek and climb into a taxi before I buried my head in my hands and sobbed.

It was utterly crushing. At forty-two I was too old for a forty-eight-year-old man. Would I have to go on dates with sixty-year-olds? Was that it? God, it was so humiliating. I wanted to crawl into bed and never get up. I was a fool, a complete and utter fool.

I sat up, looked out of the taxi window and wiped my eyes with a tissue the taxi driver had handed me. He was completely unperturbed by my embarrassing outburst. You'd think he had weeping forty-something women in his car every night of the week. He gave me the well-worn line that it couldn't be that bad, and I smiled gratefully and pretended he was right. But he was wrong. Things were that bad. The thought of being on my own for the next thirty or forty years was terrifying. It made me feel physically ill.

The next morning I dragged myself out of bed, dropped Jess at school and went into work. I made myself a strong cup of black coffee, picked up my diary and walked into Quentin's office for our morning briefing. He was sitting in his throne-like chair with Stella on his knee. The poor dog was so fat from being overfed and over-pampered that she could barely walk.

'Morning, darling,' Quentin said. 'Loving the suit, but you look exhausted.'

I was wearing the only designer trouser suit I had left. I'd sold almost all of my clothes and jewellery on eBay to make some money when Jack lost everything. But I'd kept this suit, an Armani in midnight-blue. Even Louise would have approved of it. 'I dressed up today because we have that Style Central department store account review.'

Quentin rolled his eyes. 'Oh, God, I forgot. We mustn't let Frankie railroad us. She can be so aggressive.'

'She'll try to screw us on our rates.'

'I know.' Quentin frowned.

We had already cut back our model rates for that account twice in the last two years. We had to roll with the times, but our profit margins were being squeezed. The company was still in profit, but only just. The Style Central account was important.

'Don't worry, we'll just have to be firm but charming,' Quentin said. 'Now, darling, what is up with you? You look like I did after Ramón dumped me.'

Quentin had broken up with his partner six months ago and had been devastated. I'd nursed him through it.

'Bad date. Well, actually a great date, but it ended abruptly when I propositioned him and he turned me down because I'm too old,' I said, desperately trying not to cry.

'Oh, sweetie . . .'

'I just find it all so hard. I hate being on my own, but I hate having to go on stupid dates too.'

'I know how you feel. I'm sixty next year and I want to find someone to grow old with. I don't want to be a sad old queen who's found dead in his apartment when the smell of the decomposing body finally draws attention to his fate.'

'Stop that,' I told him. 'You'll meet someone wonderful. You always do. I've never known you to be alone for long.'

'So will you, my lovely Sophie.'

'I don't believe it any more, Quentin,' I said sadly. 'And I don't want to put myself through it. It's so humiliating having to sell yourself. I'm sick of it. I feel like going home and curling up on the couch with a glass of wine and a good box set.'

'You mustn't give up.'

I sighed. 'I guess I'm finding it harder now – now that Jack has found someone. It makes my aloneness more acute. He seems so happy. He's got his old swagger back and he looks great, all upbeat and confident. I'm jealous of his happiness. I want that too.'

Quentin wagged a finger at me. 'Well, then, you have to get back out there. If you stop going out, you'll never meet anyone. You have to force yourself, Sophie. You're a gorgeous woman and any man would be lucky to have you.'

I smiled at him. 'Thanks, Quentin. If only you weren't gay, I'd go out with you.'

Quentin and I ran through the rest of the day's events. Amber, our top model, was shooting a commercial for a new health bar; we had eight models booked for a lunchtime fashion show in Style Central and six out on various press calls.

I went back to my desk and sat down. Quentin was sweet to say it, but I certainly didn't feel gorgeous. In the good old days, when I'd had all the time and money in the world, I'd looked good. I was toned, tanned, Botoxed, blow-dried, manicured, pedicured, massaged and designer-clad. Now I shopped mostly in TK Maxx.

I opened my email and saw another message from Louise, apologizing. She'd left two voice-mails as well, but I was still too cross to talk to her. There was also an email from Jack.

36

Morning Sophie, Pippa has to go to London on Friday to tape a piece for her show so I'm going to go with her. We're taking Jess. Pippa wants her to model some of the kids' clothes for the show. I'm going to tell her tonight, she'll be so excited.

London? Modelling clothes on TV? Had Jack lost his mind? I *ran* a modelling agency and I never, ever used Jess for photo shoots or TV slots. I didn't want her anywhere near that world. She was too young and impressionable. I wanted to protect her innocence for as long as possible. He knew that.

I picked up the phone and rang him.

He answered straight away. 'Hi, did you get my email?'

'Yes, Jack, and the answer is no.'

'What do you mean, no?' He sounded irritated. But, then, so was I.

'You're not taking Jess to London to model for some TV show.'

'Come on, Sophie, it's no big deal. Pippa thought it would be fun for Jess to model a couple of outfits.'

'I'm sure she did, but I'm not having my nine-year-old daughter on TV. I have never used her for any of my agency campaigns, so I'm not about to let someone else use her. I don't want her head turned.'

'Jess would love it.'

'I said no, Jack. I don't want my daughter modelling.'

'Our daughter,' he said sharply.

'I want her to remain grounded.'

'You're being ridiculous.'

'Protecting Jess isn't ridiculous.'

'Let her live a little.'

'She's perfectly happy.'

'Lighten up, it's just a bit of fun.'

'She doesn't need that kind of fun.'

'So that's it, she can't do it?'

'No, she can't.'

There was a pause and I could nearly see the expression on his face. Jack was not a man who liked being told what he could and could not do. 'When did you turn into such a killjoy, Sophie?'

'When your greed left us destitute,' I said, and slammed down the phone.

It took me the whole drive to Amber's health-bar ad campaign to calm down. In the old days, I would have loved Jess to model. I used to dress her up like a mini version of me. She was always in designer clothes. She looked like an angel, all blonde curls and big blue eyes. I thought it was fun for us to dress alike and spend our days shopping, buying more clothes. I never took her to the playground: it was far too boring. I took her to expensive restaurants, but only let her eat non-fat food. Also, if I'm being honest, I often left her with Mimi, our Filipina housekeeper, while I travelled with Jack. I felt terrible about that now. Jess had always hated it when I went away. She'd cry when she saw my suitcase.

But then we found ourselves with nothing and I ended up sharing a bed with my little girl in a small apartment. During those long, dark days, we'd become really close. We'd snuggle up and watch Disney movies on rainy afternoons or go to feed the ducks in the park, which turned out not to be boring. We went for walks along the seafront, cooked and read books together.

My other self, rich Sophie, suddenly seemed like a monster. I couldn't believe how stupid and blind I'd been, and for so long. Now, instead of filling her head with rubbish, like, 'You'll meet a prince who will buy you diamonds and sparkly dresses and take care of you,' the new me began to tell her how important it was to be clever and have a great career, like her aunt Louise. I told her she needed to work hard in school, then find a job she loved and never, ever give up working and earning her own money.

'But, Mummy, you said you felt sorry for the mummies who work,' she had reminded me, at only five years of age.

I was wrong, I had told her firmly, very wrong. I assured her that the mummies who worked were the smart ones. Over the last four years I'd told her every day it was imperative that she could always support herself and her family, and the only way to be sure of that was to work.

At first she was a bit taken aback by my complete

turn-around. But I could see that over the years my advice had begun to sink in. Jess had gone from a very princessy girl, obsessed with sparkles and pink frills, to a thoughtful and considerate nine-year-old. Well, she had been until Pippa turned up six months ago.

I wanted Jess to remain unblemished by the fickle world of modelling and fashion, and I was determined to protect her, regardless of what her father and his vacuous girlfriend thought.

When I picked Jess up from school, she slammed the car door, threw her bag into the back and glared at me. 'I hate you.'

'Well, hello to you, too.'

'Pippa told me you won't let me be on her TV show.'

What did she mean, Pippa told her? 'When were you talking to her?'

'She called me at lunchtime.'

'You know you're only allowed to use your phone to talk to me or Dad, no one else.'

'Why won't you let me do it?'

'Because you're too young.'

'Pippa said I'd be amazing. She said the clothes are really cool and I might even get to keep some. She said to tell you to chill out and let me do it.'

I gripped the steering-wheel so hard my knuckles ached. 'I don't give a damn what Pippa said. I am your mother and I said no.'

'I told Pippa you wouldn't let me. She said she

feels sorry for me. She wants to have kids young so she's a cool mum and not a grumpy old mum who hasn't a clue about anything.'

There was nothing I could think of to say that wasn't full of swear words, so I clamped my mouth shut and thought of all the different ways I'd like to tell Pippa exactly what I thought of her.

CHAPTER 4

Julie

The triplets had managed three weeks at school without getting into trouble. Maybe it was worth paying huge fees if it meant I wasn't being called in on a weekly basis to be told about food fights, wrestling matches during class, climbing out of windows, mooning at teachers . . . I could actually drop them to school without avoiding eye contact with anyone in authority. It felt good.

'Mum!' Liam shouted, from the back of the car, on the way to school.

'Yes?'

'How many goals did Messi score in 2012?'

'I have no idea.'

'Guess.'

'Twenty?'

'Mum, you're such a loser. Twenty is a stupid guess.'

'Thanks a lot. How many did he score, then?'

'Ninety-one.'

'Mum?' Leo asked.

42

'Yes.'

'What did you put in my sandwich?'

'Tuna.'

'WHAT?' Leo shrieked.

'You cannot eat ham sandwiches every day of your life.'

'Why not?' Luke demanded.

'Because it's bad for you to eat the same thing all the time.'

'I hate tuna. It's gross,' Leo grumbled.

'No, it isn't. Stop your drama.'

'It tastes like puke,' Luke said.

'I'm not eating it,' Leo huffed.

'I like tuna,' Liam said.

'You're a moron,' Leo shouted.

'You're a dork,' Liam retorted.

'You're a big hairy-arse gorilla,' Leo said.

'You're a dickhe—'

'STOP!' I shouted. 'Don't you dare use that word.'

'Why not? Dad said it last night when Suárez scored against Man U,' Liam protested.

'Well, he shouldn't have. You know I hate bad language.'

'Then how come you're friends with Marian? She says bad words all the time,' Luke said.

He had a point there. Marian swore like a trooper. She had no edit button. But somehow it didn't bother me with her. It was just the way she was. I'd have to remind Harry that the boys were now repeating everything we said at home. I'd overheard Liam telling a boy in the school playground, 'My mum said that people who only have one kid and buy big jeeps are ridiculous.'

What made it worse was that the boy was Sebastian, an only child, and he was walking towards his mother, Victoria, in her giant Porsche jeep. Thankfully, Victoria was bellowing into her mobile phone at the time so she didn't hear my son's pearl of wisdom. I'd have to watch my mouth.

After I'd dropped off the boys, I called over to Marian for a catch-up. She opened the door in her pyjamas with a raincoat over them.

'How the fuck do you look so good this early?'

'Nice to see you too.' I grinned.

'Money suits you.' Marian hugged me. 'You look great.'

I was just wearing jeans and a shirt, but good-quality jeans that fitted perfectly and the shirt was green silk.

'Thanks. I'm making more of an effort in the morning now that the boys are at Castle Academy. You should see some of the gear the mums wear. I suppose they're like Sophie was in the old days, completely overdressed.'

'I don't think I'd fit in,' Marian said, laughing. She took off her raincoat and switched on the kettle.

'I don't fit in either,' I admitted. 'So how are things?'

'Shite. I've just found out that Greg is staying in Dubai for another year.'

Marian's husband, Greg, had lost his job in the recession. He was an engineer and, with the construction industry in tatters, he hadn't been able to find a job in Ireland, so he had gone to Dubai. He'd been there for almost a year already and now he'd be gone for another. It was hard on Marian, with four children to manage – the eldest was nine and the youngest four.

'I'm sorry. That's going to be really tough on you.'

She shrugged. 'What can you do? We need the money. It's bloody hard going on my own all the time, though. Sometimes I just want to kill my kids.'

'Have you told them that Greg's going to be away for longer?'

She handed me a coffee, then added a glug of brandy to hers and a little to mine.

'Marian! We can't have brandy at this hour of the day.' I looked at the clock. It was twenty past nine.

'Well, I need it, and I only put a tiny nip in yours. It won't kill you. So, Greg told the kids last night on Skype and they started crying and bawling about "Daaaaaddy". I wouldn't mind but when he's here he does shag-all with them. He's always jet-lagged. I'm stuck here, killing myself, raising our kids alone, doing everything for them, and they couldn't give a toss about me. They

45

wouldn't give a damn if I was in Dubai. It's all about Daddy.'

'Come on, your kids love you and they know how much you do for them.'

'Bollox.'

'They do. Children just don't show appreciation. Half the time the triplets don't even know I exist.' It was true. I often thought that if I replaced myself with a robot, the boys wouldn't notice. Tom would, though: he was still young enough to need me. 'Did you manage to console them?' I asked.

Marian nodded. 'You know how fickle kids are. I gave them a box of Celebrations and told them they could eat the whole shagging lot because of the bad news. Two minutes later they barely remembered they had a father.'

I threw back my head and laughed. Marian was such a tonic. She said what lots of women thought but were afraid to say. She was always in trouble for being so blunt and honest, but I loved it about her.

'It must be hard on your relationship with Greg, though, only seeing each other for a week every three months.'

She sipped her coffee. 'At least I don't have to shag him regularly. Mind you, we tried Skype sex.'

'What?' I almost choked on my coffee.

Marian smiled. 'He was banging on about how lonely he was and I was afraid he was going to end up shagging some young one from the office, so I said, "Come on, let's try it." And we did.'

'And?'

'Disaster. No one looks good naked on Skype, especially not a forty-something couple with lumpy bits. He started talking dirty to try to get me going.'

I giggled. 'What did he say?'

Marian grinned. '"I know you want it, you dirty bitch," and "I want to make you scream."'

I roared laughing. 'What did you say to him?'

'I told him I couldn't take him seriously. He was talking in this fake American accent, pacing up and down in front of the computer, his penis swinging about, and it was all just ridiculous.'

I wiped tears from my eyes. 'Oh, Marian, that's hilarious.'

'Maybe for you, but I haven't had sex in three months and I'm horny as hell.'

'Really?' I was surprised. Marian had always said having sex with Greg was something she did as little as possible because she was so tired all the time.

'When you can have it, you don't want it. But when it's taken away from you, you want it. Besides, I'm finally getting my mojo back. After nine years of having kids, I'm getting some sleep and I'm definitely more up for it.'

'Good for you.'

'Maybe we should try phone sex – it might be easier. If I'm not looking at Greg's hairy arse on a computer screen, I can pretend I'm having sex with Don Draper.'

'Sounds like a better plan,' I said, although I

couldn't imagine having phone sex with Harry. It would be so strange and awkward, but I suppose if we only saw each other every three months it would be worth a shot.

'Have you ever tried it with Harry?'

'Phone sex?'

'Yeah.' Marian grinned.

I shook my head. 'No. The only phone sex Harry wants is with his broker. Honestly, it's ridiculous how consumed he is by making money. He's obsessed!'

'Well, he's spent most of his life with very little. Let him enjoy it.' Marian shook a chocolate digestive out of the packet and took a bite. 'Now, tell me about you. Are you still missing the column?'

My weekly column in the *Herald* newspaper had been cut three months ago, after almost four years. I'd been gutted. It was my little lifeline. I'd written about kids and parenting every week and had enjoyed it so much. It was only five hundred words and it brought in very little money but it was my thing, my small piece of identity outside the home, and I'd cherished it. But the newspaper had made cutbacks and I was one of the victims.

'I'm OK. It's a pity, but it's over now, so that's that.' I didn't want to complain about it in front of Marian. She was struggling with so many things that I didn't feel I had the right to moan.

'I'm sure you'll find something else at a different paper.'

I knew I wouldn't. I didn't want to admit it,

because I was embarrassed, but I'd approached three other newspapers, all of whom had turned me down. My confidence was shot. I wasn't a journalist. I was just a mum who wrote little stories about her kids. I knew now that I'd never get another job like it. My writing life was over.

'It's fine – it was just a hobby. It's no big deal,' I lied.

'Well, you certainly don't need the money now. So, tell me, have you met your new neighbours? I hope none of them is going to take my place as your best mate!'

I took a sip of coffee – the brandy was actually very soothing. 'I called over to the people on the left, the right and opposite. To be honest, they weren't that friendly. They were polite but distant. No inviting me in for coffee, no suggestion of playdates or a glass of wine some evening. None of them was like you. I was very lucky to find you. I knew the first time I called over to you that we'd be friends. I recognized a kindred spirit when I saw one and we were in the same predicament.'

'Knee deep in shitty nappies and trying to live on tiny budgets,' Marian said.

I nodded. 'Exactly. You got me through those baby years.'

'Right back at you. I'd have gone mad without your support.'

'I miss living here,' I admitted. 'I miss having you next door to pop into any time, day or night.'

Marian glared at me. 'Are you mentally unstable?

Are you seriously telling me you miss having to count every penny, being stuck in a small house with four boys running wild and a washing-machine that's always on the blink? Come on, Julie, enjoy your good luck. I'd give anything to move into a bigger house with a boiler that didn't pack up every two months.'

'Look, I'm not complaining. It is lovely not to have to worry constantly about bills, but I miss having you next door.'

'So go shopping, have massages – go to yoga classes and do all the things you dreamt of doing when you were broke. I can tell you, if I ever come into money, I'll be at the beautician's morning, noon and night. I'd have all the fat sucked out of my thighs, I'd have an eye lift and hair extensions and designer clothes – and I'd dump Greg and the kids and run off into the sunset with Don Draper.'

'You do know that Don isn't real? He's a character in a TV series.'

'Don't ruin my buzz. Besides, Don is real to me. In the last year I've spent far more time with him than I have with my husband. Speaking of husbands, how's Harry getting on at that posh new golf club?'

I paused. 'I hardly see him. He spends half of his life there getting tons of lessons and playing with all of these high-flying businessmen. He's certainly enjoying having a nicer lifestyle.'

'You can't blame him for that.'

'True. But when he's not playing golf he's with lawyers or fund managers . . . He seems to worry more about money now that we have some than he ever did before. He's obsessed with investments and long-term returns and pension schemes. He keeps saying, "Look at Jack and Sophie. We have to plan for our future."'

'To Hell with that. Jack sounds like he was a greedy idiot. Money is there to be enjoyed. Spend it.'

She was right. We should have been enjoying it more, but it was all we seemed to talk about now. We'd hardly ever discussed money when we had none. Now it was a constant source of arguments. Harry was worried that it would run out. He was spending half his days researching the best way to manage it. I just wanted to enjoy it and stop talking about it. But Harry was different. He kept meeting people at the golf club who told him about this investment and that fund, and he was so impressed by their success that he was listening to every word they said and tying himself up in knots. But I didn't want to bore Marian with all that. She was still struggling financially and the last thing she needed was me droning on about how our sudden money seemed to be causing Harry more worry than happiness.

'On a completely different note, what do you give your kids for lunch? The boys will only eat ham sandwiches. I want to try to give them healthier options.'

Marian snorted. 'Beef Wellington! Julie, you know me. I give them whatever's in the house. Yesterday I went to make sandwiches and the bread looked like it had been attacked by green aliens. Mould everywhere. So Brian had a tin of sweetcorn and a bag of popcorn, Oscar had half a packet of Tuc crackers, Molly had a slice of cold pizza and Ben had a yoghurt that was only one day out of date and a knackered banana. A ham sandwich is a bloody Cordon Bleu meal in this house.'

We both laughed. Marian always made me feel better about my parenting. It was another of the things I loved about her. You never felt judged or bad about yourself around Marian.

Marian looked at her watch. 'I'm sorry about this but I have to get a couple of hours' work in before I pick up the kids.'

'Oh, sorry, I didn't mean to keep you.' I stood and picked up my bag.

Marian had gone back to work when Ben started at playschool last year. She worked from home, doing telesales for an insurance company, and was good at it – she was very hard to say no to. The basic salary was low, but the commission was good and she was focused on getting high sales figures.

'You know I could talk to you all day, Julie. But this job is vital for my sanity, and for the extra cash. Hopefully, we'll be out of debt and able to breathe financially by the end of the year, with the two salaries coming in.'

'I understand that, but she is a very mature and sensible girl. You probably need to give her a bit of space,' I suggested.

Harry sighed. 'I know, but I'm trying to make up for all that time we missed.'

'Of course, but try to remember she's twenty-two. She's an adult,' I reminded him.

'I like Christelle. She's really cool,' Jess said.

'Jess thinks everyone's cool except me,' Sophie said.

Jess rolled her eyes. 'You're my mother. Of course I don't think you're cool.'

'Compared to a lot of your friends' mothers, I am actually quite cool. I never wear frumpy clothes.'

'You could do with a longer skirt,' Dad said.

'I agree,' I said, seizing my moment. 'It's way too short, Sophie. It doesn't look good. It looks a bit . . . well . . .'

'What? Desperate? Come on, Louise, spit it out.' Sophie's face was bright red.

'It's just not age-appropriate,' I said.

'So what should I wear? Boring suits like you?'

'I'm not saying that, but going around in a bum-skimming mini-skirt at forty-two is ridiculous.'

'I work in fashion, Louise.' The rest of the table had gone quiet and, out of the corner of my eye, I could see Gavin drawing his finger across his throat, obviously telling me to quit while I was ahead.

'I know that, but you're not a model, you're a

29

I hugged her. 'That's great. Good for you.'

'I'll call you later. We'll do coffee again soon.'

'I'd love that.'

Outside, I got into my car and looked at the clock. Nine forty-five. I didn't have to pick Tom up until one and the triplets at three. What would I do? I decided to kill an hour grocery shopping, then maybe I'd go for a walk.

Sod the walk. I'd go home and finish my book. It was strange: I usually read two books a week, but lately I'd been struggling to get through one in a month. For some reason I just couldn't concentrate, my mind kept wandering. I worried constantly about everything, much more now than I had when we were broke.

My phone rang. The screen said 'Principal'. It was the headmaster from Castle Academy. My heart sank.

In his fake English accent, Mr Henderson said, 'I'm afraid there has been an incident.' I put my head against the steering-wheel in despair, already sure I wouldn't like what he was about to tell me. 'Liam, Luke and Leo hung Sebastian Carter-Mills by his underpants from a clothes hook in the changing rooms. He was there for quite some time before one of the teachers heard him shouting.'

Oh, God! Why did it have to be Sebastian? I took a deep breath. 'That's terrible. Did they say why they did it?'

'They claim to have been provoked.'

'In what way?' I asked.

53

Mr Henderson cleared his throat. 'Apparently Sebastian called them "scumbag lottery winners".'

I went from ashamed to raging in a split second. How dare the little brat say that to my boys? No wonder they'd hung him up.

'That's obnoxious,' I said.

'If it's true, it certainly is rude,' admitted Mr Henderson, 'but regardless of what Sebastian said, we cannot allow boys to retaliate with violence.'

'It's not exactly violent, though, is it?' For once I was going to defend my triplets.

'Sebastian was very upset. Mrs Carter-Mills is traumatized, and I have to inform you she was pushing for the boys to be expelled.'

'What?' How dare that cow try to get my kids kicked out of the school? 'But that's ridiculous. It was just a prank that Sebastian provoked in the first place.'

'I understand, Mrs Hayes, but the boys did cause Sebastian physical and emotional distress.'

'What about my sons' distress at being called horrible names?'

'I can assure you that Sebastian will be spoken to about his unpleasant behaviour. But I've had to give your sons an official warning. They must learn to control their tempers. We cannot allow students to lash out at each other.'

'What does an official warning mean?'

'If a boy gets three warnings, he is asked to leave the school.'

Oh, God, they'd been there only three weeks. I

knew how much Harry wanted them to be in the school. I just wanted them to settle down and learn something. I decided not to say anything else. I was angry and emotional: I didn't want to get into an argument with the headmaster and make things worse. 'I'll speak to the boys when I pick them up,' I said.

'That would be wise,' Mr Henderson said.

I drove home, fuming. There was nothing I'd like more right now than to hang Victoria Carter-bloody-Mills up by her La Perla G-string.

I collected the boys five minutes early and was rushing them towards the car, hoping to escape without bumping into anyone, when I heard a loud voice.

'You there. Sophie's sister. Stop.'

I ignored her and pushed the boys into the car. But as I went around to climb into the driver's seat, a thin hand clamped my arm. 'I'm talking to you,' a furious Victoria snapped.

'Really? I didn't hear my name.'

'Yes, well, I can't remember it.'

'It's Julie.'

'It's really not important. Do you know what your brutish boys did to Sebastian today?'

I stared into her perfectly made-up eyes. 'I heard that Sebastian said something incredibly rude to them and that they reacted.'

She dug a bony index finger into my chest. 'Your children are wild animals. They traumatized my son today. They're nothing but common bullies and I will do everything in my power to have them removed from this school.'

Rage fuelled me. Shaking, I grabbed her finger and pushed it away. 'Your son needs to wash his mouth out with soap. If he ever speaks to my boys like that again, he'll end up with a lot worse than a wedgie!'

'How dare you—'

This time I did the poking. 'No! How dare you try to intimidate me with your bullshit threats? Why don't you just go home and paint your nails?'

I pushed her aside and climbed into the car. Turning to the boys, I said, 'If Sebastian ever calls you horrible names again, you have my full permission to thump him.'

CHAPTER 5

Louise

Christelle came in and took off her coat. '*Bonjour, Clara, ça va? Tu as mangé le petit déjeuner?*'
I had insisted she speak French to Clara. I wanted Clara to be stimulated at all times. She was also doing Mandarin, piano, violin and chess. My sisters thought I was over the top, but I remembered being bored as a child because I wasn't challenged enough in school.

Clara showed Christelle her empty bowl.

'Thanks for coming in early,' I said, putting the dirty bowls in the dishwasher. 'I'll be home by six.'

'No problem. The guy in the flat next door was up at six blaring his music, so I was awake anyway.'

I put on my coat. 'Maybe you should reconsider Julie and Harry's offer to live with them. They have plenty of room in the new house.'

Christelle grinned. 'Much as I love my dad, Julie and my little brothers, the house is like a zoo. I'd never get any study done.'

'Fair point.' I bent down to hug Clara.

'Harder, Mummy,' she urged me.

I squeezed her tight. 'I'll see you later, sweetheart.'

'Bye-bye, Mummy, have a good day at the office,' Clara said.

Christelle took her by the hand. '*Viens, chérie, on va t'habiller.*'

I was on my way to a meeting when my phone rang.

It was Gavin. 'Hey, sis, I need some advice.'

No surprise there, Gavin always needed advice. We three sisters had been supporting him, funding him, giving him shelter and advice since the day he was born. I felt more like a mother to him than a sister. With a nineteen-year age gap between us, I could have been his mother. Poor Mum thought she was getting the menopause when she discovered she was pregnant with Gavin – it had almost killed her. With the big age gap between him and us girls, he had been raised like an only child and spoilt rotten. The upshot of this was that he was very immature.

'What's up?' I asked.

'After three interviews, Stars and Stripes have finally offered me a job.'

'What kind of a job?'

'It's a Manager in Training programme. But I have to start off by working in the shop so they can see I'm not a total gimp.'

Here we go again, I thought. Since leaving college Gavin had done the eco-warrior thing, when he lived up a tree in our parents' golf club for a few weeks; a stint with the National Wildlife Federation in Washington; set up his own company selling fake designer watches from China, which told the time backwards, then a sandwich business from Mum's kitchen. I got him a contract to sell his wares in my office block. There were 120 employees at the Price Jackson law firm and Gavin had done well selling sandwiches to them . . . until someone found mould in their bread.

'What are the terms of the programme?' I asked, glancing at my watch.

I heard a rustling of paper and then Gavin began reading: 'It says here, "The Manager in Training (MIT) programme is a ten-week course that immerses a manager in all aspects of running a successful business for Stars and Stripes. Training takes place in our store locations, blah-blah-blah." And then it says, "The MIT must successfully complete the training programme to be moved into an Assistant Manager role." And then it says that the vice president of the company, who earns, like, a billion dollars a year, started out doing the MIT programme.'

At least it was a job with a good company and not some pie-in-the-sky scheme. I'd looked into Stars and Stripes and they were a solid business. 'OK. Well, it sounds promising, and with

59

big companies, there's always the potential for promotion, if you work hard and impress them.'

'That's what I thought. I just wanted to check you hadn't heard they were about to go bust or something.'

'You can never be sure, but they seem solid. You do realize the hours will be long, Gavin? Retail is a tough industry.'

'Duh, obviously I know that. But it's a really cool company and I think I'll totally fit in. I'm ready for a new challenge.'

'All right. Well, call into me at lunchtime with a copy of the employment contract and we can look over it before you sign anything.'

'Cool, I owe you one. I'd love to chat, but I have to go to the gym to buff up. The dudes that work there are very fit.'

'OK – I won't keep you from your busy schedule.'

As I walked into my office I wondered if my little brother would ever grow up.

Nine thirty. She'd better have been run over by a bus or struck down by a heart attack.

The doors of the lift opened and Wendy came panting down the corridor towards the conference room. 'Sorry!' she said.

I grabbed the file from her and glared at her. 'The meeting was supposed to begin half an hour ago. I've been plying our clients with coffee and pastries waiting for you to turn up with the files. This is inexcusable.'

She blinked. 'I'm sorry, Louise, but Freddy was up all night with croup.'

I held up my hand. 'It's not good enough. You've been late nine times in the last six weeks. We could lose this account because of you.'

Her face flushed. 'It's not my fault my child has croup.'

I really didn't have the time or patience for this. 'Neither is it mine. Having a child does not give you an excuse to be unprofessional. Five of the senior partners and ten of the junior partners have children and they do not repeatedly arrive late for work.'

Wendy's eyes welled. 'I'm on my own, Louise. Freddy's dad isn't around to help out. You know what it's like being a single mum.'

I never discussed motherhood in the office and I never used it as an excuse to be late. I certainly wasn't about to become her bosom buddy and bond over our shared lot. She could forget that. 'Lots of career women raise their children alone. It does not excuse your consistent lateness. Sort out your childcare or we'll have to look at your future here. Now go to the Ladies and freshen up.'

I turned to walk back into the meeting. 'Bitch,' I heard Wendy whisper behind me.

I pretended not to hear her. She was wrong: I wasn't a bitch. Before I'd had Clara, I'd been a lot tougher. But having Clara and raising her on my own had forced me to admit how difficult it was for working mothers. I had made a mistake on a huge deal shortly after she was born. It had made me realize that I couldn't keep going at the same pace and level at Higgins, Cooper and Gray, the firm I'd worked for in London. I'd had to reassess everything and had moved back to Dublin, for Clara's sake. In career terms I had taken a step back, but not a big one, and I was happy with my set-up in Dublin. I had support so I was able to work full-time and enjoyed my job.

None of the other partners with children came to work late. Wendy, a junior partner, was not entitled to special treatment because she was a single mother. There were mornings when Clara woke up feeling sick and she would cling to me, begging me not to go to work. At times I had had to peel her off my leg and hand her to the child-minder. I had often fought back tears on the way to work, but I had chosen to work in a demanding profession and I knew that meant sacrifices. On those difficult days I was extra loving to her when I got home. Did I feel guilty? Of course I did. But I had to work to support my child and I also happened to like what I did. I loved the high energy of the corporate world. Having specialized in securitization, I had carved a niche for myself and things were going very well. But there was always a price to be paid for success.

How could women expect to break glass ceilings

if they turned up late for work, complaining about sick children, bringing all their personal issues into the office? Women like Wendy felt the world owed them something. She'd never make it. I had seen lots of Wendys come and go. The stress would get to her and she'd resign or take a less demanding position within the firm.

Not every woman was ready for a serious career with all its demands, but I was and I wanted Clara to be as well. It would give her more choices in life and a wider set of career options. I wanted Clara to have the world at her feet. She was so clever and had such amazing concentration for such a young child. I knew she'd be a huge success and I'd be cheering her on every step of the way.

While Wendy fixed herself up in the bathroom, I went in to salvage the meeting and try to placate my client.

After the meeting ended and we had walked the clients out, Wendy followed me into my office.

'That went well,' she said.

I looked at her. She was completely dishevelled. Her skirt was twisted around, her shirt was crumpled and her jacket had a stain on the shoulder. Her hair was unbrushed. She was not representative of the image I wanted for my team.

She'd also given the client misinformation during the meeting. She'd got her figures mixed up and I could see Ross raising his eyebrow when she did.

I'd smoothed it over, but it had been one more mistake and I was fed up.

I sat down behind my tidy desk. Wendy flopped into the chair opposite me.

'Actually, Wendy, it didn't go well. The mistake you made with the profit-margin figures reflected badly on us.'

She shrugged. 'Come on, it's no big deal. I'll change it now and send him a clean copy of the figures.'

Was she stupid or just careless? Where was the Wendy I'd hired two years ago, the ambitious, hard-working, focused young woman?

'I'd appreciate it if you were not casual with details. I pride myself on this department always being on top of our portfolios and I do not want anyone dropping the ball.'

Wendy flinched. 'I'm not dropping the ball, Louise. Stop trying to make me feel bad. I work very hard.'

'No, Wendy, you used to work very hard. But lately you've been unpunctual, you've made mistakes and your attitude is very . . . casual. You need to pull up your socks, Wendy.'

She stood up, her eyes filling. Oh, God, she was going to cry. I really didn't want to deal with tears. 'I'm doing my best. Could you just cut me some slack? God, Louise, you're a single mother too – don't you ever have bad days? Or is your child just perfect like you?'

How dare she speak to me like that?

'Listen, Wendy, I'm sick and tired of you using your child as an excuse. As I said earlier, you need to organize your life and your childcare so that you can get to work on time. If your child doesn't sleep, get a sleep expert in to fix it. You cannot continue to come into work late, half asleep and half dressed.'

'Not everyone has a perfect life, Louise!' Her voice was rising. 'Some of us are mere mortals whose children get sick, puke and cry.'

'Am I interrupting?' Sophie stood in the doorway, holding two cups of coffee.

I'd never been so glad to see anyone. 'Not at all. Wendy was just leaving,' I said coldly.

Wendy stormed out of the office, almost knocking Sophie down.

'Someone else you were hard on?' Sophie asked.

'No. I was hard on you and I'm sorry, but Wendy is just a mess.'

'She was upset.'

'If you look at her sideways, she gets upset.'

'Go easy on her, Louise. She looked like a woman on the edge.'

'She's letting the department down.'

'OK, but everyone has bad days. Even you.'

'Rarely. Anyway, forget my work woes, it's great to see you.'

Sophie smiled. 'I had a meeting nearby so I thought I'd call in. I got all of your messages and your apologies are accepted. Just don't ever criticize me again.'

'I was trying to help.'

'I understand, but you came at me like a bulldozer – and in front of everyone.'

'I'm sorry. I completely mishandled it. What I was trying to say is that you're a gorgeous woman with an incredible figure. You don't need to wear mini-skirts. You look great in everything and there does come a stage when women have to lower their hemlines a little.'

Sophie sighed. 'Thanks, and I know you meant well, but you need to work on your approach.'

'I will. How—'

My office door flew open. It was Wendy. 'I have to go home. Freddy has a raging temperature. I know, if it was you, you'd stay and continue working but I need to be with my son.'

God, she was annoying. 'Go home, Wendy. If you decide to come in tomorrow, please be on time.'

'Ice Queen,' she muttered, loudly enough for me to hear.

'Yikes!' Sophie said. 'She really doesn't like you.' She looked thoughtfully at the door Wendy had just slammed behind her. 'I'd be careful there, Louise. You don't want an employee who hates you. They can cause you a world of trouble. Wendy seems very tightly wound. She could go to HR and complain that you're being unfair to her, causing her emotional distress. Things could get tricky.'

'I'm running a department, Sophie, not a crèche.'

'Running a department requires people skills, Louise. You need to remember that. You're not just a lawyer, you're also a boss. You don't want to alienate your staff.'

'My staff are fine, except Wendy.'

'She's a mum with a sick child. Cut her some slack.'

'I've often had to leave Clara at home with a nanny when she's had a temperature. I just check in every hour and ninety-nine per cent of the time she's fine after a spoonful of paracetamol. There've been plenty of times when I'd have liked to rush home to her, and many more times when I've felt like a bad mother, riddled with guilt. But if you choose to work in a professional corporate environment then you have to step up to the plate.'

'I know what it's like – I've left Jess at home feeling ill and gone to meetings. I understand where you're coming from, but you can seem a bit hard at times, Louise.'

'I'm very fair. Michael's son had to have a heart operation and I gave him two weeks off. When he came back, he just got on with his job like everyone else. When Clara was small I went to work after two hours' sleep and did my job. If you choose to have a child and work in a client-facing role, you have to be professional.'

Sophie put her hands up. 'Look, I don't want to argue about it. I'm just saying you should tread lightly, for your own sake, to avoid complaints.'

She was wrong. Mollycoddling your employees achieved nothing. I ran a successful and profitable department. I led by example and my employees just had to follow suit.

CHAPTER 6

Sophie

'Jess, I need you to be polite to me in front of your grand-parents. I don't want them to see how rude you're being or it will reflect badly on both of us.'

'Yeah, well, if you weren't so mean and let me do fun stuff, I'd be happy.'

Jess was still furious with me because I hadn't allowed her to wear a tarty dress Pippa had bought her in London. She was being really difficult. We drove on in silence, Jess staring out of her window with her shoulders hunched. On days like this, being a mother was a big fat pain in the arse. Sometimes I had to sit on my hands to stop myself slapping her sulky face.

The annoying truth was that she hero-worshipped Pippa. Everything Pippa did, wore and said was amazing. I was just her old mum. She was completely smitten with Pippa and kept telling me how fabulous her figure was, her clothes, her hair and her job . . . I'd been biting my tongue almost in half, trying not to snap.

I was tempted to get out my old photos and say, 'Look! I was young and beautiful, too.' In fact, I'd looked great until Jack lost all our money. I'd aged ten years overnight when it happened. Between that, selling my designer clothes on eBay and not being able to afford Botox, I was nothing like I used to be. I was like an older, faded, jaded version of the girl who used to be Sophie Wells, the socialite.

To be honest, I missed my old life. I knew I was a better person now – stronger, more rounded, more empathetic – but I remembered those carefree days fondly. I could see now that my life had been shallow but I wasn't aware of it then, so I was happy. Now it was all about bills, work, dealing with Jess's moods, fighting with Jack about parenting and hearing how Pippa did everything better than me.

Truth be told, I was jealous of Jack. He seemed really happy with Pippa. I wanted that. I wanted to meet someone and be happy, too. I wanted someone to talk to at night. Someone to take me out to dinner. Someone to cuddle up to. Someone who actually gave a damn about me. Someone who thought I was amazing. I was lonely. I'd never been on my own. I'd had a steady stream of boyfriends all my life. I hated sitting in night after night when Jess was asleep or, worse, when she was with Jack and the apartment was empty.

I didn't want to tell my sisters how lonely I was because they had their own lives to lead and their own issues to deal with. Besides, they'd been so good to me when everything had fallen apart that I had no intention of burdening them with something silly like loneliness. And I didn't have any single friends I could call on either. Everyone I knew was married with young kids. When Jess was with Jack, the weekend stretched out endlessly and I'd no idea how to fill it. By four o'clock on Saturday afternoons, I was ready to give up. It was just so lonely.

I glanced over at Jess. Thanks to Pippa, I felt lonely even when my daughter was with me.

I rang the doorbell and Mum ushered us in. She kissed Jess, and led us into the kitchen where she had tea and Jess's favourite brownies ready.

I sat back and watched as Jess chatted easily with her grandmother about school and her friends, then gushed about Pippa. Mum caught my eye as Jess was in mid-flow and winked. When she finally paused for breath, Mum suggested she went to watch TV for ten minutes while she talked to me. Jess obediently went into the lounge.

'Well,' Mum said, pouring me another cup of tea, 'she certainly seems very enamoured of this Pippa.'

'She thinks she's a goddess,' I said.

Mum patted my hand. 'Don't worry, pet. It'll wear off.'

'I'm not so sure.' I suddenly felt weepy. There was something about being in my childhood kitchen with Mum pouring tea and fussing over me that made me want to wail. I brushed away a tear. 'Sorry, it's just that it's harder than I'd thought it would be. I knew Jack would meet someone, but I didn't think Jess would adore her so much.'

'Is she a nice person?' Mum asked.

'I don't know, but the things she says to Jess really bug me, and the way she pushed for Jess to be in her show in London a few weeks ago put me right off her. I'm Jess's mother and she needs to remember that.'

'Of course you are, and you always will be. And you're dead right not to have your nine-year-old prancing about on the television.'

'I know, but I'm always the bad cop. Jess never wants to be with me any more. She's nine, Mum. Surely I'm not going to lose her already. She's all I've got.' Tears now began to flow.

Mum fished up her sleeve and pulled out a tissue.

'Thanks,' I said, mopping my face.

'Now listen to me. You are not losing Jess. She's just excited by this young, glamorous girl. The shine will soon wear off. You continue being the wonderful mother that you are to Jess and she'll come out of this phase. That is all it is, a phase. Jess loves you. The two of you have been as thick as thieves since she was a baby.'

'That's just it. We used to be so close and now we're not at all. I miss her.'

'Welcome to motherhood. You and your sisters

went through different phases. Mind you, you were the easiest and Louise was the most difficult. But you all had times when you were sulky. And, remember, Jess has had a lot to deal with and adjust to, what with the divorce and everything. It's normal that she's acting out a bit. Just stay firm and steady with her.'

I blew my nose and nibbled at a brownie. 'Thanks, Mum. What do you think I should do about Pippa, though? Just ignore her?'

'In so far as you can, yes. But if she starts filling Jess's head with silly notions, you might have to step in. My advice is to keep communicating with Jack and make sure you're on the same page. As long as you and Jack are in agreement about how to raise Jess, Pippa won't matter.'

'Generally we are, but I'm worried Pippa will influence him badly.'

Mum clicked her tongue. 'Jack's a grown man and he's a great father. You just keep talking to him, and if you don't agree with something Pippa does, don't make a scene, just calmly tell Jack why it's not OK. You have to play it cool. If Jack thinks you're criticizing her, he'll take her side.'

I was impressed with Mum's wisdom. 'You're a wise woman.'

She grinned. 'I've been around a long time.'

I hugged her. 'Thanks, Mum.'

'You're welcome. Now go home and have a nice time with your daughter.'

★   ★   ★

As we were driving home, I asked Jess if she wanted to go ice-skating on Saturday. I had taken her once before and she'd loved it.

'Really? Cool.' She smiled at me for the first time in days.

'And let's make popcorn and watch a movie tonight.'

'Seriously? On a school night?' She looked surprised.

'Why not? It's Thursday, so you've only one day left before the weekend. Once you've finished your homework we'll make the popcorn.'

Jess grinned.

My heart sang. It would be lovely to sit on the couch with my little girl and be together.

Jess's phone beeped. 'Oh, my God!' she squealed.

'What?' I asked.

'Pippa has . . . Oh, my God, Mum . . . She's got VIP tickets for the One Direction concert on Saturday. I'm going to the concert and then back-stage to meet them after.' She screamed and hugged her phone. 'This is the coolest thing ever. Pippa rocks!'

'But it's my weekend with you,' I reminded her.

She looked at me in disbelief. 'Are you crazy? Who cares? Mum, this is the most amazing thing that's ever happened to me. I can't wait to tell all my friends – they're going to be so jealous. Pippa is just so amazing.'

I wanted to cry. I wanted to take her phone and

smash it into a thousand pieces. But instead I plastered a smile on my face and pretended I was happy for her. Because that's what a good mum does . . . until her jaw breaks.

CHAPTER 7

Julie

I changed for the sixth time. 'How do I look?' I asked Harry, who was shaving in the en-suite. 'Julie, you looked good in all of the outfits you've shown me. What's going on? Why are you so nervous about a cake sale? Come on, you're only selling a few buns.'

I sat down on the edge of the Jacuzzi. 'You don't understand. It's not easy for me. I don't fit in.'

'What are you talking about? You fit in every-where – every-one loves you.'

I shook my head. 'Not at Castle Academy. The women are very glamorous and confident. I find them intimidating. They all seem to know each other and that awful Victoria is the queen bee.'

Harry wiped the last bits of shaving foam from his chin. 'Julie, you're worth ten of any of those women. Just go in there and be yourself.'

'It's not that easy. I'm doing this stupid cake sale because I really want this school to work. I want the triplets to have a good education. They'll never be speaking ten different languages, like

76

Clara, but I want them to have the best shot in life.'

Harry grinned. 'I reckon by the time poor Clara is nine she'll be speaking ten languages, playing ten instruments and be the world chess champion.'

'I feel sorry for her sometimes. She's so quiet. I think Louise overdoes it.' Much as I admired Louise's determination to stimulate Clara, she was completely over the top.

'Maybe you should say so to her.'

I stared at Harry. 'Have you met my sister?'

He walked into the bedroom to get dressed. I followed him. 'I know Louise mightn't react well initially, but Clara is very introverted,' he said. 'I think as her sister you should say something to her.'

'There is no way I'm going to tell Louise how to raise her child. She'd rip my head off. Besides, Louise always felt *she* was under-stimulated when she was young. She's overcompensating with Clara.'

Harry sat on the bed and put on his socks. 'Well, I'm glad you're not like that. I want our boys to be well rounded.'

We could hear them thundering around down-stairs. 'Do you think they'll ever calm down?' I asked.

Harry buttoned his shirt. 'Of course they will. In the blink of an eye they'll be moody teenagers who never want to get out of bed.'

That sounded great to me. The boys, without

fail, woke up at six. I hadn't had a lie-in for nine years.

I handed Harry one of his new silk ties. As he knotted it, he said, 'To be fair, they've been really well behaved since they moved to Castle Academy. I know you were against it because of the fees, but I think now you'll admit I was right. The school really does suit them.'

I still hadn't told Harry about the Sebastian 'incident' and the official warning. He was so happy, so sure that Castle Academy was the right school for the boys, that I didn't want anything to ruin it.

He put on his suit jacket. 'Maybe the other mothers aren't so bad when you get to know them. Sophie used to be friendly with one of them, didn't she?'

I flicked through the rails of clothes and fished around for something else to try on. '"Used to be" are the key words. Victoria dropped Sophie like a hot potato as soon as she lost her money.'

I pulled on a pair of cream Capri pants and a pink chiffon shirt with little cream daisies on it. I twirled. 'Well?'

Harry kissed me. 'You look gorgeous. Now go and knock 'em dead.'

'Can you meet me for lunch later so I can tell you how it went?'

'Sorry. I've got a day of meetings about a new computer program we're working on that could really help to speed up internal communication.'

Harry set off for work and I stomped down to the kitchen to get the boys ready for school. As I opened the door I heard, 'Run for your life.' The triplets tore out of the back door into the garden. I surveyed the scene. The two chocolate roulades I had spent ages making the night before were in tatters on the table. They both had big chunks cut out of them. Not content with eating lumps from one, they had attacked the other, too.

Tom was sitting in the middle of the chaos with a spoon in his hand and crumbs all over his face.

'What the HELL is going on?' I shouted.

Tom blinked. 'Sorry, Mummy. The boys said we were allowed to eat cake for breakfast for a special treat.'

I charged outside. The triplets were hiding in their tree-house. 'How could you do that?' I roared. 'I spent ages making those bloody cakes for your stupid school cake sale and now they're ruined. Why do you always have to make a mess of everything?' My voice shook. I had really wanted to make a good impression. I'd placed the roulades on my best plates, surrounded by fresh berries. I knew none of the other mothers was remotely interested in me, but I was pleased that at least my cakes would impress people.

But now everything was ruined and I didn't have time to make anything else. The triplets climbed down and shuffled into the kitchen, where Tom was trying to stick bits of cake back together.

'Look, Mummy, I fixed this one,' he said, pointing to a mound of mushed cake.

'Thanks, Tom, but it's ruined.'

'Sorry, Mum,' Leo said.

'We only meant to take a bit, but it was really delicious,' Liam added.

'Your best cake ever,' Luke said, 'like, by miles. We just couldn't stop eating it.'

'It was *soooooooooo* yum.' Leo was trying to get round me.

'I feel sick,' Tom moaned, and threw up all over my trousers.

I tried not to cry as I changed into a pair of jeans and a plain blue jumper. What was the point in trying to impress the other mothers? I was just boring old Julie. Expensive clothes weren't going to make me fit in. The triplets would always be in trouble and no one would ever want to invite them or me to their house. I might as well give up now.

I dropped Tom to school. After vomiting all the cake he had eaten, he felt much better. Then I headed for Castle Academy. I stopped at a garage on the way and bought a coffee cake.

'Well, thanks to you three, all the other mums are going to think I made no effort at all,' I huffed.

'We said sorry,' Leo reminded me.

'I'll tell them that we ate the cakes,' Luke offered.

'Why don't you take that cake out and put it on

a plate and pretend you made it?' Liam pointed to the box.

'Because it's too late for that. I just wish that once in a while you could be good. Really good, like Jess and Clara and Tom.'

'What? Tom just puked all over you, remember?' Liam was incredulous.

'Yeah, he spewed on you,' Leo agreed, warming to the theme.

'It was, like, alien vomit,' Luke said.

'It came flying out like—'

'STOP!' I shouted. 'That's enough.'

'All Jess does is play on her phone and Clara just reads and talks about boring birds. What's so great about that?' Leo demanded.

'And Tom's Mr Perfect. You always say he's great and we're terrible,' Luke said.

'Yeah, Tom's never in trouble. You never shout at him and get all red in the face with crazy eyes.' Liam imitated my eyes bulging.

'That is because he doesn't break things and answer back and get into trouble at school. If you behaved properly, I wouldn't have to give out to you and my eyes wouldn't bulge and we'd all be a lot happier and calmer. I'm begging you to be good this term. I do not want the headmaster to call me. If you get into trouble again, I'm going to give your Ronaldo football tops to the kids in Africa.'

The triplets were clearly shocked. 'You wouldn't dare,' Leo said.

'She would.' Liam knew me better than his brother.

'Dad wouldn't let you,' Luke said.

'I'll do it while he's at work.' I had all the angles covered.

'You're mean,' Leo said.

'No, I'm not. If I was mean, you'd be in boarding-school.'

'I'd love to go to Hogwarts,' Liam said.

'Duh, it's a made-up school in a book,' Luke told him. 'You're such a dork.'

'You're a moron,' Liam retorted.

Luke hit him. Liam thumped him back. A fight ensued, just as I was pulling into the gates of Castle Academy.

'STOP IT!' I roared, trying to park as Luke's foot smacked the side of my head.

I narrowly missed crashing into Victoria's Porsche. She got out of it and glared at me. She was wearing a camel-coloured wrap dress with an amazing gold necklace and nude stiletto court shoes, and she was carrying a cake that looked as if it had been made by the Queen of England's baker. It had two tiers, for goodness' sake!

We clambered out of the car and I tucked my garage-bought cake under my arm.

'Hey, Sebastian,' Leo called.

Sebastian looked terrified. 'Hi,' he said, giving the boys a shaky wave.

Ignoring me, Victoria hissed at the triplets, 'If you ever upset my son again, I will have you expelled from this school. The headmaster is a very good friend of Sebastian's father, and he's watching you three.'

'Good morning, Victoria.' I moved to stand between her and the boys. Much as I would have loved to shove her perfectly made-up face into her cake, I decided to take the higher ground. Besides, I didn't want the boys to see or hear me being rude. 'The boys apologized to Sebastian and it's all in the past now. We don't need to rehash it.'

She flushed. She clearly wasn't used to being stood up to. Spotting my cake, she asked, 'Is that your contribution?'

I had two options: be embarrassed, which I was, or ballsy, which I pretended to be.

'Yes. I just picked it up in the Texaco garage.'

'The mothers are supposed to make the cakes,' Victoria drawled.

'So you're telling me you made that.' I pointed to her elaborate cake.

'Of course I did. I make one every year. It's the headmaster's favourite.'

'Does he really need two tiers?'

She smirked. 'Well, I've surpassed myself this time. The second tier is new.'

Another mother came over, carrying a large tray of perfectly symmetrical cupcakes with different-coloured icing. 'Oh, Victoria, that's not a cake, it's a work of art,' she brayed.

Out of the corner of my eye I saw Liam reach over and stick his finger into the side of Victoria's cake. As he pulled his finger out, covered with cream and sponge, the second tier wobbled. I held my breath and prayed it wouldn't fall. Thankfully, Victoria was so busy basking in praise that she was oblivious to the potential disaster. By some miracle the cake didn't collapse and I was able to grab Liam and drag him away before he made a second raid.

With the boys in class, we volunteer mums went into the main hall and set up the cake stands. As head of the parents' association, Victoria was in charge, and she proceeded to boss everyone around. I was the only mother who hadn't baked her cake or buns. Well, I was the only one admitting it. One or two of the cakes seemed a little too perfect to me. I was sure they were also shop-bought, but no one was going to admit it and lose face.

'You're very brave bringing that,' Emily whispered to me, as she placed her chocolate cake on the table. It was decorated with little red icing flowers.

'I actually made two roulades last night, but the boys ate them for breakfast.'

'Oh, no. Poor you.' Emily looked genuinely upset for me.

'It's fine. Your cake's amazing.'

She smiled proudly. 'It took me ages, but I'm really pleased with how it turned out.'

'Victoria must have been up all night making hers.' I jerked a thumb at Victoria's creation.

Emily didn't reply. She was normally so eager to compliment Victoria that I was surprised.

'Do you think it's over the top?' I prodded her for a reaction.

Emily began to fold paper napkins. 'No it's just . . . well . . . I just think that . . . I . . .'

'Spit it out,' I said.

'I've seen it before,' she whispered.

'Where?'

'In Le Beau Gâteau.'

'What's that?'

'A very fancy patisserie in town. I went there yesterday to buy ingredients for my cake and I saw Victoria's on the counter.'

Yeeeesss! Victoria was the lying, conniving cow I'd had her pegged to be. 'Did you say anything to her?'

'No!' Emily looked shocked.

'Are you sure it's the same one?'

Emily nodded. 'It had a card on it with Victoria's name and it said, "For collection at seven p.m."'

Before I had time to whoop and cheer, Victoria sashayed over to us, followed by one of her fans, a looky-likey called Heidi. 'Nice cake, Emily,' Victoria said, adjusting its position slightly. 'It's so nice to see that *almost* all of the mums made such an effort to bake for today.'

'You're probably very busy with the triplets,' Carol said, looking at my coffee cake, still in its box.

'We're all busy,' Victoria snapped. 'It's about

86

prioritizing. I was up until three a.m. finishing mine. I literally had to drag myself out of bed this morning.'

'Wow, you don't look tired at all.' I beamed at her.

'Crème de la Mer and good genes,' she lied.

'Speaking of cakes, do any of you know Le Beau Gâteau?'

Victoria's eyes widened. It was almost imperceptible, but I noticed. Emily froze. Only Carol answered: 'No – is it good?'

'It's amazing. You know it, don't you, Victoria?' I stared at her. She looked away. 'They do cakes almost identical to yours. Isn't that strange? In fact, if I didn't know you'd been up all night slaving away, I'd actually wonder if your cake wasn't the one I saw in Le Beau Gâteau yesterday.'

Victoria's face went bright red, although I'm not sure if it was from shame or rage. She sneered at me: 'I would think that someone who turned up to a cake sale with a cheap, nasty cake would refrain from commenting on anyone else's.' She turned on her fabulous heels and walked off, with Heidi at her shoulder.

Emily grabbed my arm. 'I can't believe you did that!' she gasped. 'Why would you antagonize her?'

I shrugged. 'Because she's full of shit and a complete phoney.'

'But, Julie, don't you get it? If Victoria hates you, she'll turn everyone else against you.'

'Come on, Emily – what are we? Twelve? I'm a forty-four-year-old mother of four boys. I'm not going to be intimidated by some fake idiot.'

'Well, I just want to get on with everyone. I don't need any hassle in my life. I want to arrive into the playground and not feel any tension.' Emily walked away from me and went to where all the other mothers had gathered around Victoria and her cake.

She was obviously telling them what a bitch I was. I heard an audible gasp and they all turned to stare at me. My bravado vanished. It *was* like being twelve again: I was the class outsider, the loser, the one no one wanted to be friends with.

All my life I'd had lots of friends and never had a problem getting on with people. I was considered easy-going and friendly. But now I was an outcast and it did not feel good. It felt very lonely.

Two long hours later, the cake sale was over. I ended up buying my own cake because no one else wanted it. As I was tidying my table, I heard Victoria inviting the other six mums back to her house for coffee. She didn't ask me. I was embarrassed in front of the others. I finished cleaning up, then sprinted out of the hall, back to the safety of my car, and drove away from the tense, uncomfortable environment. I was now officially a pariah among these women.

I went home and poured myself a large glass of wine. It was only midday, but I needed it badly.

I knocked it back and felt the alcohol calm me down. Then I decided to call Marian. 'Are you busy?'

'I've just made two sales so I'm due a coffee break. You sound stressed. What's up?'

I poured myself another half-glass of wine, settled down on the couch and filled Marian in on the morning's events. 'The really stupid thing is that I mind. I didn't think I'd care about those empty-headed women blanking me, but it was embarrassing and I was upset.'

'That Victoria needs a good slap. The lying bitch. As for Emily, she's just weak and wants an easy life. I hate people who sit on the fence. Pick a side and get on with it. Don't sit there trying to please everyone – it's the coward's way. Seriously, Julie, don't waste your energy on these people. They're pathetic.'

'I know, but I'm probably going to have to deal with them for the next ten years. Their boys are in the triplets' class. I may have just shot myself in the foot.'

'You can't please everyone and you don't want to be friends with those witches anyway. They're a pack of privileged, shallow losers. If it makes you feel better, most of the mothers in my kids' school think I'm certifiable. They dive into bushes when they see me coming. Molly had a playdate over the other day, some drippy kid called Rebecca. She was one of those kids who kept saying she was thirsty and hungry and bored, and that Molly's toys were crap. I could see she was making Molly feel bad. So, eventually I lost it. "Rebecca," I said, "the only reason you're here is to entertain Molly and make my life easier. So shut your moany trap, get out of my face and start playing with my daughter."'

I burst out laughing. 'What did she say?'

'Nothing. She didn't open her mouth for the next hour until her mother came to pick her up. So obviously she told her mother about our little chat and the mother rang me.'

'Oh, no, what happened?' I picked up my wine glass.

'She said her daughter was traumatized and that I was a terrible mother. She told me that Rebecca would never darken my door again. So I said, "I never want your pain-in-the-arse kid in my house again anyway, so you'll be doing me a favour."'

'Oh, my God, Marian! You *are* certifiable.'

'I'm just honest and I speak my mind – and you know what, Julie? If people don't like it, they can shag off. I'm too old to walk on eggshells. If Molly was behaving badly in someone's house and the mother gave out to her, I'd have no problem with it. People are so bloody precious about their kids. It's ridiculous.'

She had a point. Parents had become very over-protective of their children.

Marian was on a roll now. 'I was ten when my dad walked out and my mother had a nervous break-down. I shopped, cooked, cleaned and raised my

90

brother alone. I didn't have playdates because my mother didn't know what day it was. There's all this bullshit nowadays about talking softly to your kids when they're behaving like brats. If I didn't shout, my kids would never put their shoes on, get dressed or do anything.'

'I agree. The boys only ever listen when I shout.' I took a sip of my wine. Thank God for Marian. I could already feel my shoulders dropping down from my ears as the tension of the day began to loosen.

'I'm sick of these psychologists making us mothers feel guilty. We're all just trying to get through the day without killing our kids. As for positive affirmation, what does that even mean?'

'It's saying things like "I know you can learn this poem because you're a fast learner."'

'Bullshit. Brian had to learn a six-line poem last night. I swear to you, Julie, I nearly hit him. He wriggled around in the chair, messing and refusing to concentrate for an hour. We went over it and over it. The whole bloody family knew the shagging poem – even Ben could recite it – but not Brian, because he wouldn't even try. So eventually I lost it. I ripped the poem out of the book and Sellotaped it to his forehead.'

'I might need to try that. Can you imagine what it's like getting three nine-year-olds to learn a poem at the same time?'

'I always say it, you're a saint. I don't know how you do it.'

I stifled a yawn. After fifteen years of marriage I still had no idea what Harry did. I knew he was a computer programmer, but after that it got a bit hazy. I'd thought he might give up work when he inherited the money from his aunt but he said he wanted to keep working. I was glad because, with the golf club and all of the fund-manager chat, Harry needed something of his old life to keep his feet on the ground.

'OK. I'll tell you all about it tonight.' I was disappointed he couldn't meet me. I had already rung Sophie, Louise and Marian to see if any of them were free for lunch, but none of them was. Everyone was so busy all the time. Everyone except me.

'I'm not around tonight. I'm meeting Donald McGreegan for dinner at the club.'

'Again?' I was exasperated: it was the eighth time Harry had met Donald or one of his other golf cronies for dinner that month. I didn't like the sound of Donald McGreegan. From what Harry had told me about him, he sounded like a pompous old git, but Harry was mesmerized by him and his success in business. He hung on Donald's every word. It was Donald who had persuaded Harry to send the boys to Castle Academy – he had been a pupil there.

Another night in by myself, then. I was fed up with Harry ditching me for his new friends. I seemed to have been on my own all the time recently.

'Actually, now that we have all this extra space in the new house, I've divided and conquered. They all do their homework in different rooms. It works so much better. It's still a total nightmare getting them to finish it, especially Liam, who has the concentration span of a gnat, but it's much easier than having them all at the same table, fighting and winding each other up.'

'Who says money can't buy you happiness?' Marian laughed.

'Apart from homework, any news?' I asked. 'How's Greg?'

'Who cares? He told me last night he's not coming home next week. He's too busy, apparently. It'll be another three weeks. The kids are devastated. Anyway, forget about Greg. I've been very distracted by something else.'

'By what?'

Marian lowered her voice to a whisper. 'My Polish roof guy, Lew.'

'Define "distracted".'

'I'm in lust. He's so hot. I swear my hormones are all over the place. Maybe I'm getting early menopause, but I'm dreaming about sex with this guy all the time. We get on really well, even though his English isn't great. I think he was flirting with me yesterday.'

I was a bit worried. Marian and Greg had always had a tumultuous relationship, but they made it work. But just as they were coming out of the nappy stage with their kids, getting their life back and arguing less, Greg had lost his job and had had to go to Dubai. His being away so much had definitely put a strain on their relationship.

'Marian,' I said, in my hang-on-a-minute-here voice.

'Don't start lecturing me. You're the only person I can talk to.'

'I know how hard it is, with Greg away so much, but don't do anything silly because you're angry with him.'

'So far it's just flirting, but I haven't felt this horny since college. Lew is so sexy.'

'How old is he?'

'About thirty, I'd say. He had his top off yesterday and I swear he has a better body than David Beckham. I almost swooned.'

This was not good. I'd never heard Marian talk about a man like that and she was very impulsive. I'd need to keep an eye on her. 'How much longer will he be there? Is the roof nearly fixed?'

'Yes, but I have a few other things I need attended to around the house.' Marian snorted down the phone.

'You can look, but don't touch,' I warned her.

'I'll try. Anyway, I have to go now and put on some lipstick. It's time for his lunch break.' She was laughing as she hung up.

CHAPTER 8

Louise

At work the next day I got landed with a last-minute conference call and couldn't collect Clara from school. Christelle was in Paris for two days, and Mum was out, so I rang Dad. He agreed to collect Clara and take her home for her violin lesson.

As soon as the conference call ended, two hours later, I rushed home. When I walked into the apartment, Dad was sitting on the couch, snoring, as Clara read to him from her bird book.

When she saw me, she got up and ran over. I gave her a hug and a kiss. 'I see Granddad's having a sleepy,' I said.

'Is he?' She was surprised. 'I didn't know.'

I went over. 'Dad!' I said loudly.

He sat bolt upright. 'What the hell?'

'Did you have a good snooze?'

He smoothed back his hair. 'I wasn't asleep. I was only resting my eyes.'

'You were snoring.'

'I was not.' He looked affronted. 'I was listening

to Clara reading about the birds over and over again. By God, she's very fond of that book.'

'It's her favourite.' I smiled. 'How did her violin lesson go?'

Dad stood up and stretched his back. 'Lookit, I know you're very keen for her to do lots of things but, to be honest, Louise, it was like listening to a cat being tortured.'

'Dad!' I glanced over to see if Clara was listening, but she was immersed in her book.

'She's no Yehudi whatshisname.'

'Yehudi Menuhin. She's four and a half, Dad. Menuhin began playing at four and I'm sure he wasn't perfect after a few lessons either.'

'Well, according to the teacher, she's doing really well, much better than last week. God only knows what last week sounded like. Would you not let the poor child go to the park and run about?'

'Learning the violin is known to improve children's co-ordination skills, develop their brains and give them confidence. Clara can be a bit clumsy and she's shy, so the violin will help with that.'

Dad shook his head. 'I've no doubt you've researched it all. I'm just saying that children need a balance.'

'They actually don't. I hated those Irish-dancing classes you sent me to and the sports camps in the summer. I'd much rather have been at home reading. I'm going to encourage Clara in what she's good at. I'm not going to waste her time with pointless activities.'

Dad put his hands in the air. 'I wish I'd known how miserable you were. I could have saved myself a fortune on all those lessons and camps. I'm sorry to hear you had such a traumatic childhood. You should report your parents for abuse.' He grinned.

'Thankfully, I managed to turn out well despite it all.'

'That's debatable,' Dad said, giving me a wink.

I punched his arm playfully. 'You know I'm the sanest of your children.'

'You're certainly saner than your brother. Your mother called into the shop he's working in today while I was here. I missed ten calls from her because the violin was so loud I couldn't hear my phone. And then I got this message.' Dad took out his phone and showed me: *Gavin has LOST his mind. I'm devastated. Where in God's name are u???*

This was not good. I'd have to call her and try to calm her down.

'She's on her way over,' Dad said.

'Now?' I began to panic. I really didn't want Mum storming into my apartment, hysterical. It would upset Clara. As I was thinking of a way to stop her, there was a pounding on the door.

'Open up!' It was Mum. Dad and I glanced at each other, then at Clara, whose eyes were wide with fright. I went over to her and gently persuaded her to go into her bedroom and read in there.

Dad opened the door and Mum came storming in, dragging Gavin behind her. He was wearing Mum's lilac golf jumper, which was far too small for him.

'Nice jumper.' Dad chuckled.

Gavin flopped down in a chair, arms folded, clearly furious.

'Never in all my life! Never! I'm telling you, George, never.' Mum was beside herself. I went to her and led her to the couch. She was shaking her head and muttering under her breath. I poured her a large glass of wine and sat down beside Gavin.

'What happened?' I whispered to him.

'She made a complete show of me. I'll never live this down.'

'You two can stop whispering,' Mum said. 'I hold you responsible, by the way.' She pointed at me.

'How is it my fault?'

'Because you knew and you never told me.'

'I'll have a glass of wine too, please,' Dad said. 'I think I'll need it.'

'I'm mortified,' Mum said, getting emotional. 'I'll never be able to show my face in the golf club again. You've really done it this time, Gavin.'

'For the love of God, woman, tell me what happened.' Dad was getting exasperated.

Mum pointed over at Gavin. 'I decided to surprise him with a visit, to see where he worked and show my support.' She paused and had a large gulp of wine. 'So I went into the Stripes and Stars shop. It looked very fancy from the outside, but when I got closer, I realized that there were men with no tops on standing outside. Like strippers they were!'

If only she had told me she was going to surprise him, I could have stopped her.

'I presumed they were just low-life boys hanging about with no feel for the cold. But then they said, "Welcome to Stripes and Stars"!'

'It's Stars and Stripes.' Gavin groaned.

'Gavin!' Mum slammed her glass down on the coffee-table. 'The name of the shop is really not the issue here.'

'Let her tell the story,' I said to Gavin. Mum clearly needed to get this off her chest.

'"Where are your shirts?" I asked the boys. "We don't wear shirts," they told me. "Why not?" I asked. "Company policy," they said. So I told them I wanted to speak to whoever was in charge immediately. They told me to go inside and ask for the manager.'

'Company policy to wear no shirts?' Even Dad, who was rarely fazed, was taken aback. 'Nonsense. It's nine degrees outside. Were they not frozen?'

'Of course they were. One fellow's lips were nearly blue, and sure you could see goose-bumps all over his body,' Mum told him. 'And his false tan was all streaked. He looked ridiculous.'

Gavin rolled his eyes.

'Anyway, I went into the shop to find Gavin,

but the lights were out. I was stumbling around in the pitch dark and I saw people shopping! They must be desperate, I thought. They're buying things and they can't even see what colour they are. Sure you couldn't tell black from green. So I bumped into a girl who said she worked there and I told her to call the ESB and get a man out to fix the lights.'

I stifled a giggle. The idea of Mum lurching around Stars and Stripes telling them to get their electricity fixed was too funny.

'She told me it was normal! Normal? She said that was the way the shop was always lit. "But it's not lit at all," I pointed out. She just shrugged and said that was the way it was. So I asked her if she knew Gavin and she said he was up at the till.'

'Did she lend you a torch?' Dad asked, and I started to laugh. Gavin was looking thunderous.

Mum glared at us. 'I finally made it up to the counter, knocking into people and clothes in the dark, and I peered up, but I couldn't see Gavin. So I called out his name and saw a man duck.'

Oh, God. I'd say Gavin nearly had a heart attack.

'I peered over the counter and there was our son, crouched on the floor. "Hello, Gavin," I said. So he stood up, and I could see, even though it was almost pitch dark, that he was going red in the face. And I could see why. Because he was NAKED! Naked, George! Our son was naked! What kind of a place hires men to work with no

99

clothes on?' Mum wagged a finger at Gavin. 'A place of ill-repute, that's what.'

'Jesus, Mum, I wasn't naked, I had jeans on and shoes and socks and a watch.'

'You were doing well until the watch.' Dad chuckled.

'It's actually a very successful company,' I said. I wanted Mum to stop freaking out.

Mum swung around to face me. 'No son of mine is going to work in a company that gets its staff to work with no clothes on.'

'He did have clothes on, just not a lot of them apparently,' Dad said.

'She caused a huge scene. I'll probably get fired and I really liked working there,' Gavin grumbled.

'I don't want to hear one word out of you. You've humiliated me and made a fool of yourself.' Mum took another glug of her wine. 'Why can't you just get a normal job? Why can't you work in the bank, like your cousin Victor? He's never caused his mother a day's worry. I've had it, Gavin. No more. This is the last straw.'

'What did you do when you saw him?' I asked.

Gavin punched the side of the chair in exasperation. 'She freaked out and started roaring and shouting, and then she dragged me out of the shop hitting me over the head with her handbag.'

'Did your boss see?' I was really hoping his boss hadn't witnessed the drama.

Gavin shook his head. 'Thankfully he's in LA

at the annual conference. He left me and another guy in charge of the store.'

'It shows he trusts you even though you've only worked there six weeks. That's a good sign,' I said.

Gavin glared at Mum. 'Yeah, until Psycho here ruined everything, I was doing really well. I'm totally into the company. I actually suggested a few changes to the layout of the shop three weeks ago and sales are up ten per cent. They love me in there.'

'Good for you.' It was great to see Gavin being enthusiastic about work and doing well.

'*Good for you?* What in God's name are you talking about? It's obviously a cover for a strip joint or a brothel!' Mum shouted.

I put my hand up to stop her. 'Sssh, you'll frighten Clara. Mum, you need to calm down.'

'Don't tell me to calm down,' she hissed. 'Just you wait until you find Clara working topless in a shop and see how calm you are.'

Dad perked up. 'Do the girls have no shirts on either?'

'Of course they do.' Gavin was getting frustrated. 'They wear vest tops. It's not Hooters!'

'I'm so ashamed.' Mum's voice shook. 'After all that education, this is where you end up.'

It was time for me to step in. 'Mum,' I said firmly, 'I want you to listen to me. Stars and Stripes is one of the most successful clothing firms in the US at the moment. Last year they had sales revenues of 3.72 billion dollars. It's not a cover for a brothel. I looked into the company before Gavin started working there. It's a very successful business selling good-quality casual wear to kids and students. When they opened their first store in LA they hired the best-looking models they could find to work there so that people would talk about the store. It was very effective and it's become an integral part of their brand. They only hire good-looking people and they get the guys on the shop floor to take off their tops. It's a gimmick, but it gets people in the door.'

'When you're promoted to manager, do you get to keep your top on?' Dad asked.

'Totally,' Gavin said, trying to pull the lilac jumper down over his stomach. 'Once you get to assistant manager you wear a shirt. I've been fast-tracked for the assistant manager job because they've been impressed by me. I'm due to have a six-week review on Monday, but after the scene Mum caused, I'd say I'll be fired. Thanks a lot, by the way.' He glowered at her.

'I don't care what sales figures they have. A company that exploits its employees like that is no better than a sweat shop in Bangladesh.'

Gavin stood up, the jumper exposing half of his stomach. He waved his hands in the air. 'For God's sake, no one's being exploited. The dudes who work there love having their tops off. They want to show off their six-packs. There's a waiting list of three hundred people who want to work in the Dublin shop. It's the coolest company around. The staff have great fun together, the opportunities to do well are really good. I was happy there, Mum, until you ruined it.'

I saw Mum poke Dad's arm. He cleared his throat. 'Well, now, Gavin, there's no need to snap at your mother. She has your best interests at heart.'

'Yes, I do, and I still say it's no place for a well-educated boy to work.' Mum folded her arms defensively.

I stepped in. 'Mum, I promise you, it's a legitimate company. It does seem to treat its staff well and the management programme is a good one.'

I felt a tug on my jacket. 'Mummy, is the shouting over? It's hurting my ears.'

I bent down and scooped Clara into my arms. She snuggled into my shoulder. Looking at Mum, I said, 'Yes, pet, the shouting's over now. We're all going to have a snack and talk about birds.'

'Sorry, sweetheart, Granny just got a bit of a shock.' Mum kissed Clara's cheek.

'I'll take my leave,' Dad said, standing up. 'Clara's taught me enough about birds for one day. The only birds I want to see are the ones who work in Hooters.' Roaring with laughter at his own joke, Dad left the apartment. Mum glugged the last of her wine, shot a glare at me and Gavin and followed him. Gavin gazed at me with something like despair. I shrugged. I'd done all I could. He sighed, then followed Mum and Dad to the car, with an evening of dramatics and lectures in front of him.

Clara sat in the bath, looking at her fingers. She was listing all the passerine birds found in Ireland that we had discovered listed on Wikipedia: '. . . larks, swallows and martins, wagtails and pipits, kinglets, waxwings, dippers, wrens, mockingbirds and thrashers, thrushes and allies, cisticolas and allies, buntings and New World sparrows, cardinals and allies, troupials and allies, finches and sparrows.'

I clapped. She truly was amazing. 'That's incredible, sweetheart, I can't believe you memorized all of them. You're a little genius.'

The doorbell rang. It would be Sophie, dropping off Jess. I was babysitting her for a couple of hours while Sophie went to a work event. I pulled the towel off the radiator and went over to take Clara out of the bath.

'NO!' she shouted. 'The clock doesn't say fifteen.'

I looked at the digital clock. She'd been in the bath thirteen minutes. I knew if I tried to take her out before it said fifteen she'd have a meltdown that would go on for ages. I rang Sophie.

'I'm outside with Jess,' she said.

'I'll be there in a minute.' I didn't want to explain that Clara had to be in the bath for exactly fifteen minutes: Sophie would think it was over the top and I didn't want to get into a whole discussion about it.

They'd have to wait. I was too afraid to leave Clara alone in the bath while I went to open the door. She'd slipped once when she was two. I'd gone to get a fresh towel and when I came back she was under the water, thrashing about. The memory still made me shiver. I was terrified of her drowning and never, ever let anyone else bathe her. Not even Christelle or my mother.

A minute later Sophie rang. 'What's going on? Can you open the door? I'm going to be late.'

'Coming,' I said, willing the clock to hurry up. It was fourteen minutes past.

Finally it was fifteen, I scooped Clara out of the bath, sat her on the floor with her bird book and ran to open the door.

'About time!' Sophie was hassled. She hated being late. She kissed Jess and rushed off.

Jess followed me in and plonked herself on the couch, where she proceeded to text on her phone.

I left her to it and went to get Clara ready for bed. She had a very specific routine that she liked to stick to. It kept her calm and happy. Clothes off, neatly folded and piled in order of removal. Pyjamas on, always the top first, then the bottoms. Then I brushed her hair twenty times, followed by her teeth – ten strokes on each side and fifteen on the front. Finally she would cuddle up in her bed and list the non-passerine birds of Ireland for me before falling quickly into a deep sleep.

I loved our little routine. I knew my sisters would think it was far too rigid, but it suited Clara. I liked her to be calm before bedtime and this way she was. I kissed her beautiful little face and fought back tears. Watching her sleeping, I felt a wave of emotion. I couldn't believe I had her. I couldn't believe I was a mother. I couldn't believe I had so nearly let this pass me by. I had never wanted children, but then when I got pregnant so suddenly and had Clara, my life had changed. I felt so lucky. Clara was everything to me.

I went back to Jess, who was playing some noisy game on her phone.

'Do you want a drink or something to eat?' I asked.

She barely looked up. 'No, thanks.'

'OK. Well, do you want to watch TV?' Anything would be better than that annoying game.

'No, I'm fine.'

Her phone rang. 'Dad?' she said.

It was obviously Jack. I went into the kitchen to make myself a herbal tea and let her chat to her father in private. But then I heard her scream. I ran back into the lounge.

'What's wrong?' I went over to her.

Jess kept saying, 'No way, no way,' but she was smiling. Seeing me, she said, 'Pippa's pregnant! Isn't that awesome?'

What? It was a disaster. This would kill Sophie. It was one thing that Jack had a much younger girlfriend, but now a baby? Sophie would die when she heard.

'I am so happy, Dad . . . Over five months

already? She doesn't even have a bump. It's brilliant news,' Jess said. 'OK, see you tomorrow. 'Bye.' Jess hung up, her cheeks flushed with excitement. 'I can't believe it! I'm going to have a little brother or sister!'

'It's very exciting.' I tried to be enthusiastic, but all I could think about was Sophie's reaction.

'If it's a girl and she looks like Pippa, she'll be so stunning.'

'You're pretty stunning yourself, just like your mum,' I reminded her. Jess was like a mini-Sophie – blonde hair, blue eyes, tall and lean. She was a very pretty girl. Her front teeth stuck out, which she was very conscious of, but braces would sort that out.

'Pippa's so beautiful – she's like a supermodel.'

'Your mum was even more stunning when she was Pippa's age,' I said, wanting to make Jess see how gorgeous her mum was. I knew Jess's Pippa-worship was hard for Sophie. 'Sophie was the top model of her day.'

Jess shrugged. 'That was ages ago. Mum's old now.'

Ouch! Thank God Sophie hadn't heard that cutting comment. It was sad because, as a little girl, Jess had adored Sophie. They'd been the best of friends. But lately I'd noticed a distance between them. Pippa's arrival had definitely caused problems.

Maybe it was just growing up. Maybe when girls hit nine, they no longer thought their mothers were so great. If I was honest, I'd never had my own mother on a pedestal. I'd never felt she understood me. I wondered if all kids were like that. Would Clara suddenly go from thinking I was wonderful to just being her 'old mum'?

While Jess rang all her friends to tell them the good news, I ran into my bedroom to call Julie.

'Hi.'

'Pippa's pregnant,' I blurted.

'What?' She sounded as shocked as I felt. 'Oh, God, poor Sophie.'

'She doesn't know yet.'

'Oh, Louise, this is a disaster. It'll destroy Sophie.'

'We'll have to support her. It's going to be really hard for her.'

'How did you find out before her?'

'Jess is here and Jack just called her. Sophie's at a work thing. She's on her way back now.'

'You have to tell her before Jess does. Call her now.'

'I don't want to tell her over the phone. I'll wait for her outside my front door and tell her then. It'll give her a few minutes to process it before she sees Jess.'

'Bring your makeup bag. She'll be upset.'

'Poor Sophie, she doesn't need this.'

'She certainly doesn't. Her confidence is already rock-bottom. Now, Louise, make sure you tell her gently. Don't blurt it out.'

'I won't.' I wished they'd all stop telling me I was blunt.

'Oh, God, poor, poor Sophie.'

'I'd better go.'

'Good luck. Don't forget the makeup, and go easy.'

'I will!'

'Call me later. I'll be waiting by the phone.'

'OK.'

I hung up, picked up my makeup bag and hovered by the front door until I heard Sophie's footsteps.

'Hi,' I said cheerily. I was determined not to get it wrong. I needed to be subtle. I'd already hurt Sophie with my bluntness. But the bottom line was that Pippa was pregnant and there weren't too many ways of saying it.

'Is everything OK? Is Jess all right?'

'Everything is totally fine. Jess is inside watching TV.'

'OK, so why are you standing outside your front door with a makeup bag, looking very suspicious?'

'I need to tell you something and it's not a good thing.'

Sophie frowned. 'What is it?'

'It's something that will affect your life for . . . well . . . kind of for ever, I guess.'

'Jesus, Louise, what is it?'

'It's to do with Pippa.'

'Just spit it out.' Sophie was getting angry.

I raised my hands in surrender. 'Pippa's pregnant.'

Sophie recoiled as if she'd been shot. 'What did you say?'

'I'm sorry, Sophie, but Pippa's pregnant.'

Her hand flew to her mouth. 'Oh, no . . . no . . . no . . . Oh, God, no.'

I went over to steady her. She pushed me away. 'How do you know?'

'Jack just called Jess.'

'How did she take it? Is she upset?'

I hesitated and decided not to tell her that Jess was over the moon about it. 'Not really. She seems OK about it. She's fine, honestly.'

Sophie sank into a ball on the floor. 'Why is Jack doing this? Why now? What's the rush? Why so soon? He's got it all now. A whole new life. And I've got . . . nothing . . .' She began to weep.

Sophie was falling apart and I needed her to keep it together for Jess. 'Sophie.' I grabbed her shoulders, pulled her up and shook her. 'You don't have nothing. You have Jess and your family, your job and lots of things. Now you need to pull yourself together. Don't let Jess see you like this. Sophie? Come on now.'

I shook her harder. 'Sophie, think about Jess. You can fall apart later when she's asleep. I'll call you, we can talk about it all night, but right now I need you to calm down and focus.'

Sophie took a few deep breaths and allowed me to put makeup on her blotchy face. I did my best, and when we went in to get Jess, she looked almost normal.

We needn't have worried. Jess barely glanced at

her mother. She was still busy calling her friends to tell them the 'great' news.

I squeezed Sophie's hand. 'Hang in there.'

She nodded, shoulders slumped, staring straight ahead. Shattered.

CHAPTER 9

Sophie

Jess stuffed her pink Stars and Stripes hoodie into her weekend bag. 'I'm so excited to see Pippa. I wonder if her tummy is bigger. Can you believe she's five and a half months pregnant and still only has a tiny little bump you can hardly see?'

'I'm sure it'll be huge by the end,' I replied.

'She has such an amazing figure. She looks incredible pregnant.'

I counted to ten. Since Louise had told me about Pippa's pregnancy, I had been trying not to snap at Jess. That night, when I'd picked her up from Louise's, I had only just managed to get home and get her to bed before I locked myself into the bathroom and cried for two hours. It had hit me like a steam train. Pregnant!

I knew how happy Jack would be. He'd always wanted more children but I had said no. I'd fallen apart after Jess was born and ended up on antidepressants. I was too frightened to go through that again. I knew it would be worse the second time. Jack would have put the same pressure on me when the new baby was born as he had after Jess's arrival. He hadn't liked coming home from work and finding me still in my pyjamas, breast-feeding. He'd wanted his wife back. He'd made it clear that I had to look and act like the old Sophie. So, I had lost weight, taken happy pills and forced myself to play the perfect wife. Jack was content and, eventually, so was I. But I'd known I couldn't do it again. The strain was too much.

And now here he was, with a younger model. I wondered if he'd make the same demands of Pippa that he had of me. After we'd lost everything, I'd told him about the anti-depressants and how terrible he'd made me feel as a new mother. He was full of remorse and said he'd had no idea, that he'd thought he was 'helping me to snap out of it'. He had never meant to hurt me, just wanted life to go back to 'normal'. He'd never tried to push me: he thought I needed some encourage-ment, that was all. Perhaps he'd go easy on Pippa. Maybe after hearing what I'd been through, he'd be more sensitive and kind. Pippa might get the new improved Jack.

But, regardless, I knew he'd be thrilled to become a father again. I'd bet my life that Pippa would give him the son he wanted. Of course she would: she was perfect Pippa. But the part that hurt most was that I knew Jack was gone now. He had a new life and a new family. I'd sent him a text to say congratulations: I couldn't face talking to him about it. He'd sent one back: *Tks, we are over the moon.*

Jack didn't use expressions like 'over the moon'. He was cynical and sarcastic . . . and yet . . . He sounded like a boy in love. *Over the moon.* It was such a happy expression. It made me feel old and tired and sad. I hadn't felt 'over the moon' about anything in years.

The other issue was Jess. She was so excited. She talked about it non-stop and told everyone she met about her new baby sister or brother. One of the mums in her school had congratulated me on my 'great news'. It was mortifying. I'd had to explain that it was Jess's dad's girlfriend. The poor woman went bright red, apologized and scurried off.

The baby would be in my life for ever because Jack was in my life for ever. Jess would come back and tell me how cute her sibling was, what an amazing mother Pippa was and how happy Jack was and . . . Oh, God, I couldn't bear it.

'Come on, Mum. I need to go now. I want to see Pippa and have some *fun.*'

I drove her to Jack's penthouse apartment. I let her go in by herself. I wasn't ready to face Jack and I definitely wasn't ready to face his happy pregnant girlfriend. The way I was feeling right now, I might just punch her in the face.

Jess ran into the lift without a backward glance. I longed for the days when she'd hugged me, telling me she loved me and that I was the 'bestest

114

mummy in the whole world'. They seemed very far away.

Louise and Julie had arranged to take me out for dinner to discuss 'the news' and cheer me up. I spent ages getting ready. I thought if I looked better I'd feel better. But no amount of makeup could conceal the black circles under my eyes or the crows' feet that were always much more pronounced after a few sleepless nights.

In the entrance to the Garden restaurant I bumped into Daniella. She was one of Victoria's best friends, someone I'd been friendly with and seen a lot of in the heydays of my past. She looked amazing.

'Hi,' I said, much more enthusiastically than I felt. Daniella had dumped me almost as quickly as Victoria had.

'Oh, my gosh, Sophie!' she said, looking me up and down. I knew she was taking in my high-street outfit, just like I was looking at (and lusting after) her Prada dress. I'd seen it in *Vogue*.

'You look great,' I said. And she really did. Her skin was smooth and line-free – clearly the work of a good dermatologist. But it was her boobs that caught my eye. They were up and proud. I couldn't take my eyes off them, they were so perky and round, like a twenty-year-old's.

She giggled. 'I can see you're looking at my birthday present from Ken. Aren't they fabulous?'

'They are,' I had to admit. It was the best boob job I'd seen. They were bigger, but not too big.

They made her waist look smaller and generally gave her whole figure a lift.

'Hodgson in the Manor Park Clinic did them. He's the best,' she said. 'Honestly, Sophie, they've given my whole life a lift, no pun intended.' She giggled again.

'Wow,' I said. 'He's certainly got the gift. You look fabulous.'

She tilted her head to one side. 'And how are you? I heard about Jack and Pippa's pregnancy. It must be hard. You look tired and stressed. Are you OK?'

Her fake concern made my blood boil. This was a woman who had sent me exactly one text after my life had fallen apart: *Sry to hear things bad. Thinking of you.* And that had been it. She had never phoned to ask how I was or invited me out for coffee or lunch, nothing. And now she was pretending she gave a damn about Pippa's pregnancy solely because she wanted to get my reaction so she'd have some gossip for Victoria and her other shallow friends.

I smiled brightly. 'It's wonderful news. Jess is thrilled about it. I'm not stressed at all. I'm just incredibly busy working, building up my business and being a single mum to Jess. I must dash.' With that I turned on my non-designer heels and went to join my sisters.

Julie handed me a glass of wine before I'd even sat down. I took a big sip.

'Thanks,' I said, putting my handbag on the floor. 'I needed that.'

'You've had a rotten few weeks.' Julie took my hand.

'How're you doing?' Louise patted my shoulder.

Tears sprang into my eyes. 'Stop! Seriously, don't be nice to me or I'll end up crying again. I don't want that wench Daniella to see me upset. Say something funny.'

'Mum thinks Gavin is working as a gigolo,' Louise said.

'WHAT?' I started laughing.

'Very effective.' Julie winked at Louise.

'Tell me everything,' I begged. I wanted all the lurid details.

Louise distracted me with the story of Mum calling into Gavin in the shop and dragging him out. We all fell about laughing. It was a tonic. Julie kept our glasses topped up and I felt the tension and upset begin to lift.

After our main course, I saw Daniella leaving the restaurant. She waved. 'Did you notice her boobs?' I asked my sisters.

'They look so fake,' Louise said.

'They're very obvious,' Julie agreed.

'I think they're great,' I said, glancing down at my own saggy ones.

'She has no movement in her face and her boobs are up around her neck. It's pathetic.' Louise was not a fan of plastic surgery.

'You look so much better than her,' Julie said. 'You're naturally gorgeous.'

'Thanks, Julie, but I look twenty years older than

her. I know you guys think she looks fake, but I don't.'

'Forget about her. She's a waste of space,' Louise said. 'Let's talk about you. How are you doing?'

Julie poured us another glass of wine. I took a sip. 'To be honest, I'm shocked at how difficult I'm finding it. I just completely fell apart when Jess told me. Not in front of her, thankfully. When I'm on my own I can't stop crying.'

Julie's eyes filled with tears. Whenever anyone was upset, Julie always cried too. 'Oh, Sophie!' She hugged me. I wept into her shoulder.

Louise handed me a tissue. I dried my eyes. 'Sorry, I'm a mess.'

'It's really hard on you.'

'I just can't get over how thrilled Jess is, and Jack sounds ecstatic. I just keep thinking my family is gone now. Even though we were separated, we were still united by Jess. Jack and I had got to a good place and we even had brunch together as a family some weekends. But then Pippa arrived on the scene and it all changed, and now Jack is going to be consumed with his new family and Jess is part of it but I'm not. It's completely separate from me. Jess is going to have this whole family life without me and it's killing me.' Being able to express the emotions that I had been feeling was such a relief. I could be completely honest with my sisters. They were my lifeline.

'But Jess will always be your daughter and she'll always love you,' Julie said.

'But it's different, Julie. Since Pippa arrived, Jess wants to be with them all the time. Pippa is so much "fun" and I'm boring. It really hurts.'

'And now she'll be even more wrapped up in Pippa and her new brother or sister,' Louise said.

'Exactly. I feel like I'm being dumped again. It's as if Jess is divorcing me too.'

'If it's any consolation,' Julie said, 'the triplets have no interest in being with me. I'm only useful for food or transport. I miss being needed. I miss being important in their lives.'

'But isn't it nice to have a break after all the years of non-stop chaos?' Louise wondered.

Julie fiddled with her napkin. 'I thought it would be, but I miss it. I feel kind of useless now.'

'Julie, you need to enjoy it. You've earned a break,' Louise said.

'I know what Julie means,' I said. 'I can see that part of this change is that Jess is nearly ten and children do become more independent and need you less. But it's her worship of Pippa that really bothers me, and I just know she's going to want to be with Jack and his family unit instead of alone with me.'

'You'll have to find common ground,' Louise said.

'What do you mean?'

'You need to find something that Jess likes to do and do it with her. Whether it's dance classes or cycling or ice-skating. Whatever it is, you need to have a link. It's like Clara and birds. I'm not particularly interested in birds – to be honest, I find them quite dull – but I'm reading up on them now so we can bond over it. Her interest is becoming my interest.'

'I'd better brush up on football statistics and fart jokes then.' Julie sighed.

'At the moment, all Jess wants to do is shop and talk to her friends,' I admitted.

'Well, she didn't lick that off a stone!' Louise laughed.

'I wasn't like that at *nine*,' I said.

'Come on, Sophie, you were exactly the same,' Julie said. 'We used to have to wrestle the telephone out of your hand, and when you weren't talking to your friends, all you ever wanted to do was shop and have fashion shows in your bedroom.'

I smiled. They were right. I had always been obsessed with clothes and fashion. 'I'd forgotten about that. Right! I need to do something about Jess before I lose her.'

'You'll never lose her. Look at me and Mum,' Louise said. 'We were never close. She didn't understand my need for independence and I just wanted to get away from home and live my own life. But when I had Clara, I began to lean on Mum and ask her for advice, and we've become much closer. We're still very different people, but I talk to her almost every day now. When I was in London, I only spoke to her once a month and even then reluctantly.'

'And look at Gavin,' Julie said. 'He's twenty-seven and he keeps moving back home between jobs. I don't think they'll ever get rid of him.'

'He needs to make this job work,' Louise noted. 'He has to stop messing around and get serious. I actually think this company suits him, and he seems very enthusiastic about it.'

'He's always enthusiastic at the beginning,' Julie reminded her.

'I know, but I really feel Stars and Stripes is the right fit for him.'

'If Mum hasn't got him fired!' I said.

Louise shook her head. 'I composed an email for him to send to his boss last week, explaining the whole thing, and he got a reply, saying, "Don't worry about it, we value you as an employee." So he's safe . . . for now anyway.'

'How's Jack's job going?' Julie asked me.

'Good. He's making bigger and bigger commissions. I must say, he's very fair about money. He went to his lawyer last month and increased his payments to me. I'm going to be able to start saving soon, which is such a relief because I really want the security of a rainy day fund.'

Julie took my hand in hers. 'Sophie, you know if you ever need any money, I'd be happy to give it to you.'

I smiled at her. Julie had insisted on giving me money when Harry's inheritance had come through. I had accepted a fraction of what she offered. I'd taken five thousand euros and put them into an account for Jess. Julie was so generous that she would have happily given me half of the amount they had come into. 'I know, Julie, thanks, but I'm actually doing well now. I'm out of debt and beginning to breathe again, which is lovely. I might even be able to afford Botox soon.'

'Sophie!' Louise snapped. 'Don't put that crap into your face.'

'You look lovely as you are – better without that stuff,' Julie agreed.

It was easy for them to say. Julie was happily married and Louise had a 'sex buddy'. She had an arrangement with a UK client, Oliver, who came over once every six weeks or so and they had good, uncomplicated, no-strings-attached sex. It suited them both perfectly. The fact that he was married didn't bother Louise. She said it was better for Oliver's wife that he was having sex with Louise, who wanted nothing from him, than some needy secretary who'd try to force him to leave his wife or one day ring her up and tell her.

Julie didn't approve and had told Louise exactly what she thought. I didn't either, but Louise had never been conventional and always did things her own way, including motherhood. But she was a brilliant sister and friend so I stayed out of her private life.

I was reaching for the wine bottle when I heard an all-too-familiar voice from my past.

'Hi, Sophie. Daniella told me you were at this table, right down the back. How are you? Long time no see.'

'I'm great,' I said, forcing my mouth into a huge smile. 'Never better. Busy running my company and raising Jess.'

'I'm running around all the time, too, trying to keep up with my committees and charities. I barely have time to eat.'

'I hardly think sitting on the board of a charity is the same as running your own company.' Louise snorted.

I hid a smile. Good old Louise. 'This is my sister, Louise. I believe you know Julie.'

Victoria wrinkled her nose. 'Oh, yes, hello there. How are your boys? Still causing trouble?'

'No, they're being really good, actually,' Julie said quietly.

'That's not what I heard. They really are making their mark at Castle Academy – everyone knows about them, both parents and staff. They're infamous.'

I looked at Julie, expecting her to pounce, but she just picked up her wine and took a large drink.

'I had to come over to say how thrilled I was to hear about Jack and Pippa's baby. Daniella said you're really happy about it. How sweet of you,' Victoria purred.

'Of course. Why wouldn't I be?' I beamed at her. Pretty soon my face was going to crack.

'Well, it must have been hard on you when Jack took up with someone *so* young and *so* stunning.'

'I hardly expected him to end up with an old hag.'

'Well, she certainly isn't that. Gerry and I bumped into them the other day. They were all over each other. It was almost embarrassing.'

'Is Gerry here with you?' I asked.

'Yes, he's over there.' She pointed to a table in the middle of the restaurant, where Gerry was talking into his phone.

'I see he's still attached to his mobile. It must be frustrating for you to be ignored when you're out for dinner.'

Victoria bristled. 'Gerry runs a very successful global business so he has to deal with all kinds of time-zones.'

'Are you sure he isn't playing Solitaire? Remember the time I caught him playing it at my dinner party.'

'That was a once-off. He was bored with the company. Gerry is an excellent businessman who would never invest in anything foolish, like Jack did.'

'Gerry Carter-Mills, right?' Louise asked.

'Yes, do you know my husband?'

'Not personally, but I read about his disastrous investment in Gregorby Oil. He took a big hit on that one.'

Victoria's face went red. She looked shocked. 'What? Well . . . no one is always right.'

'I guess everyone makes mistakes.' I smiled sweetly.

'Well, I'd better get back. He'll be wondering where I've got to.'

We all looked at Gerry, who was still talking on his phone. Victoria tottered over to him. He ignored her. Knowing she was being watched, she tugged at his sleeve. He swatted her away and went on with his conversation.

I turned to Louise. 'Looks like all is not so rosy in the Carter-Mills garden.'

'What a brainless idiot. How were you ever friendly with her?' Louise asked.

'I guess I was a brainless idiot too.'

'She's such a bitch,' Julie said.

'Why didn't you tell her to stuff it when she criticized the boys?' Louise asked.

Julie shrugged. 'She practically runs the school and she hates me already. I don't want to antagonize her even more. I'm worried she'll try to get the boys thrown out. Even though I'm not keen on Castle Academy, because I don't fit in, they're actually doing really well and they're happy.'

'Fine, but don't let her walk all over you. She's a complete fool who doesn't even know what her husband is investing in. How ridiculous is that?'

I caught Julie's eye and winked. I knew she had no idea about or interest in Harry's investments, just like I hadn't had a clue where Jack had put his money.

As we polished off our bottle of wine, laughing about Gavin's attempts at getting a six-pack, I saw Victoria and Gerry leaving. Victoria was shaking her head furiously and I'm pretty sure I heard her hiss 'oil shares'.

CHAPTER 10

Julie

I concentrated on what the instructor was doing and tried to copy her, but it was impossible. My body just wouldn't stay up. I flopped onto my new yoga mat and looked at the rest of the class, all posing perfectly.

I had joined this class at the very posh studio because I'd overheard one of the mums at school saying it had tightened up all the bits she hadn't been able to tone since having kids. I needed to tone up and I had lots of time on my hands, so I'd signed up for ten classes.

But when I'd arrived that morning for my first class, the other twelve women were fully made-up and wearing really cool yoga clothes. Until that moment I hadn't realized there was such a thing as yoga clothes. I thought you did it in your tracksuit bottoms and a T-shirt. I was wrong.

I always seemed to get it wrong. Even though I had nice clothes now that weren't covered with kids' vomit and food, I still never managed to match the right outfit to the occasion. I was either over- or underdressed. Now I'd have to go and find a yoga shop and spend money on the 'right gear'. Or, I thought, as I watched the women, in perfect harmony, twist their bodies to the left, I could just leg it.

I opted for the latter. Waiting until they were all upside-down in downward-facing dog pose – what dog ever stands like that, with its arse sticking up in the air? – I stood up and, puce with embarrassment, left the class muttering about a sick child. It was only when I got to my car that I remembered I'd left my new yoga mat in the studio. There was no way I was going back in there. Between the mat and the ten classes I had signed up for but was not going to attend, I had just wasted 180 euros. I sat back in the car and sighed. I missed my old chaotic life. I had far too much time to myself and it was overrated.

Maybe I'd keep Tom home from school tomorrow to hang out with me. He could come grocery shopping and I'd take him for a hot chocolate after. I'd have to lie to Harry and say Tom was running a temperature. He'd go mad if he thought I was keeping him home from school just to keep me company.

I drove home, and when I opened the door to the kitchen, Gloria, my cleaning lady, was lying on the couch watching TV.

'Hi, Gloria, is everything OK?' I asked.

She waved at me. 'I was reaching up to get the

rubber gloves and felt my back go, so I thought it best to have a little rest.'

'Are you OK? Do you need some Nurofen?'

'No, love, you're all right. I need ten minutes on the couch and I'll be grand then. I won't get much done today, mind. I'll just iron Harry's shirts and then I'll have to go.'

'Would you like a cup of tea?'

'Oh, Julie, you're an angel. I'd murder one, and a few of those nice chocolate fingers you have would go lovely with it.'

I busied myself making Gloria her tea and chuckled to myself. Sophie and Louise would have heart attacks if they saw my cleaning lady lying on my couch watching TV while I served her tea. They thought Gloria was the biggest chancer around. She'd been coming to us for years and claimed to suffer from arthritis so she rarely did much work. But when the triplets were younger, she was the only person who would babysit them. I could leave them with her and not expect fifteen phone calls to tell me what bedlam they had caused. Gloria was able to stop the boys messing with one of her killer stares.

In fact, Gloria was still the only person who ever babysat for us, except Christelle, who was also brilliant with her half-brothers. Christelle had that French way of being really scary without trying. Her piercings made her look tougher than she was. The boys adored her and were a little frightened of her.

Gloria wasn't just a cleaner and a babysitter, she was also someone I could talk to. Sometimes I thought she knew our family better than anyone else. So, even though Gloria came just once a week and did little or nothing, I loved her and would never dream of firing her. I handed her a cup of tea and some biscuits.

'Lovely. Well, how are you? Were you out exercising?'

I took a bite from a chocolate finger. 'Trying to, but it didn't go very well.'

'I reckon all that exercise is overrated.' Gloria patted my knee. 'Sure you've a lovely figure and Harry is mad about you, so you don't need to be out running around lifting big cow bells in the rain.'

'It was yoga this week and it didn't go much better than my boot-camp disaster.' I shoved the rest of the biscuit into my mouth.

'Are you missing the boys?' Gloria asked.

I nodded. 'Yes, a lot. And I never thought I'd say that. At least when they went to Montessori I still had Tom with me, but now it's so quiet.'

'It's hard on the mums when the kids are off in school. People don't say it, but it is. Don't worry, you'll get used to it. It takes a while to adjust. It'll be worse when they leave home. You'll be heart-broken. You'll wake up one day and it'll just be you and Harry.'

If it was just me and Harry, I'd be on my own all the time, I thought grumpily. Harry was never home. I sighed and picked up another biscuit.

'My mother always said to me, "Gloria, mind your man, because one day soon it'll just be the two of you again." But sure my Billy was in prison when the kids left home, so it was actually just me on my own.'

OK, prison was a lot worse than the golf club. At least Harry wasn't doing time behind bars. 'That must have been so hard for you,' I said.

Gloria's husband was in prison for armed robbery. He hadn't hurt anyone, but he was caught red-handed and sentenced to ten years. He was due out in two years' time. But I don't think Gloria wanted him to come out at all.

Gloria munched her fourth biscuit. 'To be honest, it wasn't hard when Billy was put away. It was much more peaceful without him there annoying me. And, anyway, by the time my youngest left home, my eldest, Sandra, had got herself knocked up, so I was only on my own for three weeks. Sandra moved back in with me and never moved out. But sure I'm mad about little Kylie. She's a dote.'

Good God! I certainly hoped that three weeks after Tom moved out one of the triplets wouldn't move back in with a pregnant one-night stand.

'So what are your plans for the rest of the day?' Gloria asked.

Clean the house you haven't cleaned, I thought. 'I'm meeting Marian for coffee. We're going to that new place everyone's talking about, the Green Kitchen. It's supposed to be really nice. Everything is organic.'

'Tell Marian I was asking for her. Is she still as mad as ever?'

I laughed. 'Yes.'

'She's a heart of gold that one. Underneath all the cursing and carrying on, she's a good person.'

'I agree.' Gloria was one of the few people who 'got' Marian, like I did. My family thought she was certifiable. Harry liked her in very small doses and he hated her cursing in front of the children. But Gloria saw the Marian I saw, the kind, caring and damaged friend that she was.

'Well, I'll go and get changed and leave you to it,' I said, in what I hoped was a nice but encouraging way. I needed Gloria to get off the couch and do something. Harry was beginning to talk about us having to let her go because she did nothing.

'I'll just catch the end of this and then I'll get those shirts done.' Gloria un-paused her TV show and poured herself another cup of tea.

Forty minutes later I was sitting at a corner table in the Green Kitchen sipping a cup of soy milk latte, which tasted awful, waiting for Marian. I heard her before I saw her. She came thundering in, dragging a screeching Ben.

'Sit there and shut your mouth. You're making a show of yourself. I'm not buying you a vegan muffin because you won't bloody eat it. It's full of that natural shite. Now, if you stop howling for a minute I'll give you some chocolate.'

Ben stopped crying. Marian pulled him onto a

chair and handed him a Milky Way. He ripped the paper off greedily. 'He's off school with a bad ear so I had to bring him.'

'It's fine.' I leant over to Ben. 'How are you, pet? Is your ear very sore?'

'Not really. I gotted the pink medicine and it's not super-sore now.' He polished off his Milky Way.

Marian handed him her phone. 'Now, play with that and do not ask for anything, moan, groan or interrupt me for twenty minutes, OK?'

He nodded. 'Mummy?'

'What?'

'Can I play Angry Birds?'

'Yes, but you have to put the earphones on. You know the noise of that game does my head in.'

Ben nodded, put in the earphones and started to play.

Marian took a sip of the cappuccino I'd ordered her and wrinkled her nose. 'What the hell is this? It tastes like river water.'

'It's an organic coffee from Africa with soy milk,' I explained.

'It's muck is what it is. I'm not drinking that.' She pulled a can of Diet Coke out of her bag and opened it.

'So, how are you? You look good,' I said, suddenly noticing her makeup and low-cut top. Marian was not one for making much of an effort with her clothes, especially during the school week, but she was quite dressed up today. 'Is this all for me?' I was doubtful.

133

She grinned. 'Not exactly.'

Her eyes were shining and she had that flush of happiness. Oh, my God! 'Have you just had cyber-sex with Greg?' I whispered.

'No, but I've had . . .' Marian checked Ben's earphones were on properly '. . . real-life sex with Lew.'

My coffee cup fell into the saucer. 'What?'

'It was mind-blowing.' Her face flushed and her eyes sparkled at the memory.

'Marian how . . . when . . . I mean, where? What are you doing?'

She leant back in her chair and crossed her arms. 'Having the time of my life.'

'But what about Greg?' I mouthed, not wanting Ben to hear.

'You don't need to whisper. He can't hear anything with those earphones in,' she assured me. 'As for Greg, I'm pretty sure he's up to no good. He hasn't called to speak to the kids in days. He's suddenly very busy in the evenings.'

'But you don't know?'

'I don't have proof, but I know. A wife knows. And, besides, I refuse to feel guilty about something that was so good.' She winked.

'How good?' I couldn't help it, I was curious to hear more about the mind-blowing sex.

Marian put her face close to mine; her back was now to Ben. 'Incredible. He took me to places I have never been.'

'Positions?'

'Put it this way, I'm a whole lot bendier than I ever thought I was.'

'How bendy are we talking?'

'Madonna at her bendiest.'

'How did it all start?'

'He came in two days ago for his lunch and I just happened to be wearing a very short skirt and a low-cut top, and when I bent down to give him a sandwich I saw him staring at my boobs and smiled at him. The next thing I knew, I was sitting on his knee and we were eating the face off each other. Then he had his hand up my skirt and suddenly I was lying on my kitchen table being banged like never before.'

I didn't know whether to laugh or cry. It sounded so sexy and fantastic, but she was married, and if Greg ever found out, he'd leave her.

'How many times have you . . . you know?' I was watching Ben, but he was completely immersed in Angry Birds.

'So far, four times. Each time was better. D'you know what the great thing about having sex with a younger guy is?'

'They have better bodies?'

'God, he's so toned – you should see his six-pack – but that's not the best part.'

'Really? The amazing body isn't the best part?'

'No, the brilliant thing is that they're all about you. Lew is very focused on me being satisfied. He's all about the foreplay. Greg just rolls on top of me, sticks it in, jiggles about, grunts and falls asleep.'

135

I burst out laughing. Marian certainly had a way with words. 'Come on, that's a bit harsh.'

'No, it's the truth. But with Lew,' Marian sighed happily, 'it's incredible.'

It sounded pretty fantastic. I was almost jealous. 'But, Marian, you have to stop. Greg's your husband. He's the father of your children – you need to concentrate on your marriage.'

'*He*'s not prioritizing it. He cancelled coming back from Dubai this month and he hasn't bothered to phone in the last few days. Why should I sit about waiting for him to deign to contact us? I'm sick of being on my own with the kids, managing everything, budgeting, dealing with all their needs and tantrums. They're all acting up at the moment because they miss Greg. But he's off in the sun in his nice apartment, having a great time, while I'm stuck here in the pissing rain, raising our kids and trying to earn some extra money. I'm sick of it. My life is a drudge. Every day it's the same old crap. I'm always on my own. The weekends are bloody endless. Sunday is the worst because the kids don't have activities so I have to come up with ways to keep them entertained that don't cost much money.' Marian took a long drink of her Coke. 'Being a single mother sucks.'

It was really difficult for her. I knew she was struggling, but I hadn't realized just how lonely she was. That was the thing about Marian: she rarely showed weakness. She just got on with things. I felt terrible. I hadn't been there for her enough lately. 'Marian, I'm—'

She put up a hand to stop me. 'Don't start telling me you're sorry for not inviting me over, Julie, you are a brilliant friend. Over the years you've helped me out way more than anyone else. You constantly listen to me moaning. I don't know what I'd do without you. I'm just blowing off steam.'

'I know, but I feel bad that I didn't realize how lonely you are.' I wondered if Louise and Sophie struggled, too. I knew Sophie found the weekends difficult when Jess was with Jack, but Louise seemed fine. Then again, she'd never had a husband to miss. But it would be hard on your own. Harry was out a lot in the evenings, these days, and I hated it. Imagine if he left me, or lived in a different country. I'd really struggle. I needed him to help with the boys – they were so boisterous. I couldn't shower or bathe them on my own. I had to wait for Harry to be there. When Harry was working late, they sometimes went for days without washing. Single motherhood was the hardest job there was.

'I'm fine, Julie,' Marian assured me. 'Especially now that I have a toy boy to distract me.'

'What are you going to do about Lew?'

'Shag him senseless,' she said, grinning at me.

'Seriously.'

'I am being serious. I've started so I'll finish. I've been unfaithful, so I might as well go for it. He's going to be working on the house for two or three more weeks. It's a finite period and I intend to enjoy it.'

'OK, but be careful and maybe you should call Greg for a chat, make contact.'

Marian crumpled her Coke can. 'He's due to ring tomorrow. I'll be as nice as I can. To be honest, all the sex is making me much calmer. I needed it. I was really beginning to struggle.'

'Maybe I could send Lew around to Sophie's apartment to "fix something" when he's finished working on your house. She needs some fun.'

Marian frowned. 'Oi, hands off my Lew. I'm not sharing him with your gorgeous sister. When I decide to end it, I'll give you his number. But for now, he's all mine.' Marian checked her watch. 'Shoot! I have to go – I'll call you.' Marian took the earphones from Ben and packed them away in her bag. She hugged me goodbye and headed for home, her arm around her five-year-old's shoulders. She bent down to hear something he was saying and laughed, kissing the top of his head. I hadn't seen her so relaxed in a long time. The sex was clearly doing her good.

I wondered if Harry and I should try to spice things up. Maybe we should try some new positions. We had got very stale in the sex department after the kids were born. Then, just when we were beginning to get some sleep and have more regular sex, Harry had taken up golf. He was always exhausted when he came home after playing eighteen holes.

It used to be me falling asleep the minute my head hit the pillow but now it was Harry. Maybe I should go back to yoga and try harder. If I was bendier, I might be able to dazzle him with some new moves.

My conversation with Marian had made me think about the sex I'd had in my past. As I drove home, I amused myself remembering those carefree days in college when I had no responsibilities and had sex at all times of the day or night. I suddenly wondered what had happened to the two serious boyfriends I'd had before Harry. I'd dated Kieran for a year and Dan for two. I decided to look them up on Facebook.

When I got home, I poured myself a glass of wine, took out the iPad and went searching. Harry had set up a Facebook page for me but I never used it. I didn't really understand how it worked. Besides, I had nothing interesting to put on it – married, four kids. That was my life . . . Dull.

I found Kieran. He was living in Australia with his wife and six kids. He had lost his hair and put on weight. He didn't look good at all.

I searched for Dan Williams. A few matches came up, but I recognized his photo straight away. He hadn't changed at all. I clicked onto his page. He was married with two kids and lived in New York. He looked great. Seeing his cheeky smile reminded me of all the great sex we'd had. Dan and I had never had a huge amount in common, but physically we were fantastic together. He was the opposite of me: ambitious, pushy and determined to succeed at all costs. That was why we'd broken up. He had gone to New York to find fame and fortune, and I had refused to go. I hated the idea of a big city full of shouty people pushing their way to the top. Besides, I knew Dan and I were never going to end up together so it was a good excuse to break up. I had gone to London where Louise was living and met Harry after only a few weeks.

I looked at Dan's wife, good-looking, big white teeth, shiny hair, tanned skin. She was a trophy wife, exactly what Dan would have wanted. His daughters were pretty and there were lots of photos of them skiing, sailing and doing sporty things. Emboldened by the wine, I decided to send him a message: *Hi Dan, a blast from your past here, Julie Devlin. How are you doing? I'm good. I'm married now with four boys and living in Dublin.*

I decided not to say I was a full-time mum – it sounded so lame. So I left it. I closed the iPad feeling a bit foolish. What was I doing? Memory Lane would be another cul-de-sac in a life now full of them.

CHAPTER 11

Louise

I sat in front of a weeping Wendy and tried to keep my face impassive.

'It's just so hard. Freddy's a terrible sleeper and I'm exhausted.'

'I understand, but the mistake you made has cost this department fifty thousand euros,' I reminded her.

'I know, and I feel terrible about it, but I was sure I'd printed out the updated contracts. I'm sorry, Louise. I know you're furious.'

Furious was an understatement. I was beside myself with rage. Her stupid mistake had cost us a lot of money, but it had also put a stain on my department's record. Dublin was a village and I didn't want James Kilbrian telling everyone about the incompetent job that Price Jackson and Louise Devlin had done for his Internet company. I prided myself on my skill and proficiency in the law, particularly in the area of securitization, and now Wendy had tarnished the department's reputation.

I'd had my CEO, John Gillinan, in that morning, wondering what had happened. I'd explained that one of my juniors had slipped up but that I was handling it. He reminded me – as if he needed to – that James Kilbrian was an important client and we needed to keep him happy. I could have killed Wendy: she'd made me look bad in front of the CEO.

Wendy continued to sob. I could see she was struggling, but if you worked for a dynamic and ambitious law firm, you had to do whatever it took to keep up.

'Wendy,' I said in a neutral voice, 'I can see that you're completely overwhelmed with your life at the moment. And I think—'

She jumped up and clutched the edge of the desk. 'Don't fire me. Please don't fire me. I need this job. I have to support Freddy.'

I got up and walked around to her. I eased her back into her chair and handed her a glass of water. 'I'm not going to fire you. You need to take a deep breath and listen to me. You cannot continue to do this job at this level. You're going to have to take a step back.'

'I can't take a pay cut. I bought this stupid house with a garden for Freddy and the mortgage is killing me.'

I remained very calm. Wendy was hysterical, but I needed to make her see that she was going to have to take a demotion and a pay cut. I didn't want her in my department making huge mistakes.

'Why don't you take a few days off and think about it? If you're in a less stressful role, it might come with a slightly smaller salary, but there are other ways of making it work. You'll be able to cut back on childcare costs because you won't be working late all the time.'

Wendy twisted a tissue in her hands. 'I have an au pair. I pay her a flat rate every week.'

'All right. Maybe you can cut back on something else. There are always ways to make savings. I really think a less demanding role will help you to get a better work–life balance.'

'But I've worked so hard to make junior partner. My parents were so disappointed when I got pregnant and my so-called partner left me and moved to Australia. I'm trying to prove to everyone that I can do it. I want my family to see that I'm not a failure – that I can be a successful lawyer and a good mum.'

This story was all too familiar to me. I tried to be understanding. 'Look, Wendy, I had to make changes when Clara was born. All women do. You either hire a full-time nanny and work sixteen hours a day or find a way to make your job less all-consuming. I wanted to spend more time with Clara so I gave up an amazing job I had worked for twenty years to get, and I moved back to Dublin and set up this department. I still work long hours, but nothing like what I was doing in London. Every decision you make has consequences. And one thing is very clear.

143

You can't continue like this or you'll have a nervous breakdown.'

'But look at Sheryl Sandberg. She's chief operating officer of Facebook and she has three kids.'

Oh, for goodness' sake! I was so sick of hearing about Sheryl Sandberg, not to mention her stupid book *Lean In*, which I hadn't been able to finish because it annoyed me so much. 'Sheryl Sandberg has a hands-on husband and a lot of staff who make it possible for her to do her job.'

'What am I going to do?' Wendy began to cry again.

Stop bloody crying and feeling sorry for yourself, I thought. 'You need to go home, look at your budget and find a way to make your life work on a slightly reduced salary. We can put your partnership on hold for a year until you get Freddy settled. Then, when your home life is calmer, we'll talk about reinstating you as a junior partner. How does that sound?'

'It sounds like a nice way of saying I'm useless and my career is going backwards.' Wendy's voice shook.

I was beginning to lose patience. An email popped up on my computer. Oliver had just checked into the Four Seasons and wanted me to meet him for dinner and 'dessert'. Yes! I needed some sex badly. I wrapped up the meeting by standing up and leading Wendy towards the door. 'Well, Wendy, it's been good to talk. Your career isn't going backwards, it's just being put on pause temporarily. Try to see this as an opportunity to re-evaluate your life and where you want to go in the firm.' I opened the door of my office and gently nudged her out.

'But I want to—'

'Any other questions, you'll need to talk to Hilary in HR.'

I closed the door and leant against it. Thank God that was over. I couldn't stand victims. She had made the decision to have the baby; she had made the decision to apply for a job in a top law firm. Stop bloody crying about it and find a way to manage work with raising a child. Millions of women did it; single motherhood wasn't unusual. She needed to stop feeling sorry for herself and focus on getting her life together.

I went straight to my desk and rang Christelle to ask her to babysit that evening, but she couldn't so I rang Gavin. He said he would, but he wanted to bring Shania because they were supposed to 'hang' together that evening. I wasn't thrilled about Shania coming too – Clara took a while to be comfortable with new people – but all I could think about was hot sex with Oliver, so I agreed.

When I got home, I gave Clara her bath, got her into her pyjamas and brushed her teeth. Then I settled her on the couch with her bird books and went to get ready. I lathered my body in scented lotion, put on my new sexy red lace underwear and a fitted red dress that clung to all the right places and showed off my toned arms. I hummed as I did my makeup. I was looking forward to seeing Oliver. He was the only man in my life. A relationship was out of the question: between work and Clara I didn't have time for dating and, from Sophie's horror stories of the dating scene, I was glad not to.

All I wanted was a few nice meals, some decent wine, great company and sex. Oliver ticked all those boxes. He was good-looking, smart and amazing in bed. He spent all of his spare time cycling, so his body was tightly toned. We were very compatible. And the best part was that he was married, so there was no drama or fighting or silly romance. The arrangement suited us.

Gavin and Shania arrived at seven. They were both dressed head to toe in Stars and Stripes. I ushered them in.

'Wow,' Shania said, looking around the lounge. 'Your place is so tidy. You wouldn't know there was a four-year-old living here.'

'Clara's inherited my tidy gene. I can't stand mess.'

Gavin threw himself down in a chair. 'Louise doesn't do clutter. Everything has to have a place and a use, or it gets chucked out.'

'God, I'm so the opposite. I, like, keep everything,' Shania said. Then, looking at me, she added, 'You look hot. You've got an awesome body for, like, an older woman. Very Courtney Cox.'

'I'll take that as a compliment.'

'So, hot date?' Gavin grinned.

'Kind of.' I wasn't about to get into my arrangement with Oliver with my little brother. I knew he'd disapprove, like Julie. I'd never mentioned Oliver's name in front of her since the night I'd told her about him and she'd given me a twenty-minute lecture on women like me destroying marriages. I'd pointed out that it was better for Oliver's wife that he was being unfaithful with me because I'd never want anything more. I didn't want an emotional connection. I wasn't hurting anyone and Oliver was a happier man, probably a better husband even, because he was able to blow off steam with me. Julie said I could sugar-coat it any way I wanted, but I was still sleeping with a married man and that was wrong.

'If Harry was sleeping with some woman in England, I wouldn't care how little emotional involvement she wanted, I'd still be heartbroken. It's immoral, so stop trying to justify it,' Julie had shouted.

Sophie was more relaxed about it. I thought she should try to find a similar arrangement, but she said she wanted love. Sophie had always been a romantic at heart. I couldn't remember her being on her own until she and Jack had split. She had always had men running after her, and it was hard for her now that things had changed so much. There weren't queues of men looking to date a forty-two-year-old single mother.

But I thought it had been good for Sophie to be on her own. She needed to stand on her own two feet and realize she was capable of earning her own money and providing for Jess. She'd been so dependent on Jack. Their life had been so flash and fake. They had lurched from party to charity ball to holiday and back again. I always suspected Jack wasn't as bright as everyone seemed to think he was. He had been adept at making money in the good times, but he had got cocky and made some incredibly risky decisions that had led to his ruin. He was a nice guy and a good dad to Jess and I was glad he was back on his feet, earning a good salary. It would take some of the pressure off Sophie.

But I was worried that Sophie might slip into her old ways. She was obsessed with looking younger. When she was with Jack, she was constantly having Botox and fillers and at times had overdone it. I understood that her whole life had been based around her looks, from her job as a model to dazzling Jack and marrying him, but it was time to let it go and move gracefully into her older years.

'What time does Clara go to bed?' Shania asked.

I looked at my watch. It was seven fifteen. 'Seven thirty. She likes to look at the clock to make sure it's exactly half seven, so you need to show her the time on one of the digital clocks.'

'She's so quirky, just like my little brother. He had all these rules and routines that my mum had to follow or he'd freak out.'

'Did he grow out of it?' Gavin asked.

'Uhm . . . no, not really.' Shania looked uncomfortable.

I nodded. 'Highly intelligent children often have their quirks. Wait until you see this.'

I went over to Clara on the couch and whispered, 'Will you stop reading for just two minutes while we show Uncle Gavin and Shania how clever you are at maths? Is that OK?'

She frowned, slowly looking up from her book. 'OK, Mummy, but then I need to finish the book before bed.'

'I know, pet. Don't worry, you'll have plenty of time.' Raising my voice, I said, 'Clara, what is twelve plus forty-five?'

'Fifty-seven,' she answered almost immediately.

'Fifteen plus thirty-eight?'

'Fifty-three.'

'Sixty-seven plus fourteen?'

She paused for just a few seconds. 'Eighty-one.'

I beamed at her.

'Dude, that's incredible.' Gavin came over to high-five her. 'I was still trying to work out the first answer when you finished the last one.' Looking up at me, he said, 'Seriously, Louise, she's like a little genius.'

'I'm speechless over here,' Shania said, applauding.

I felt so proud. 'I think she's going to be really clever.'

'Like her mother,' Gavin said. 'Why couldn't

God have shared the brains around more evenly in our family? He gave you way more than the rest of us.'

'Don't give me that sob story. I was the only person in our family who studied all the time. While Julie was reading novels and chatting to her friends, Sophie was shopping and you were running around chasing a ball, I was inside with my head stuck in a school book.'

'But he's right, you do have to be born clever, and obviously you, like, totally ran with it, which is cool. But there's no way, no matter how hard I studied, that I would ever have been super-bright.' Shania sat on the floor crossing her long legs.

I glanced at my watch: seven twenty-six. I was going to be late. I grabbed my coat and crouched in front of Clara. 'Sweetie, Mummy is going out, but I'll be back soon. Uncle Gavin is going to put you to bed in exactly four minutes, OK?'

'Is it seven twenty-six now, Mummy?'

'Yes, pet.'

'OK.'

'Can I have a hug?'

She put her arms up and held me tightly.

I was in the taxi when my mobile rang. It was Gavin. I could hear Clara shrieking in the background. 'Louise, she's freaking out because it was seven thirty-one on the clock in her bedroom when I went to put her down.'

'Jesus Christ, I told you to do it at exactly seven thirty.' I looked at the clock in the taxi: it was seven thirty-four. Damn. Clara's tantrums could go on for a while.

'What do I do? She's going mental here. I thought the triplets were hard to babysit!'

'Get Shania to distract her by reading out lists of birds. Go into the kitchen and the bathroom and reset the clocks so they say seven thirty, then bring her in and show her. Unplug the clock in her bedroom and tell her the battery must have gone dead, which is why it said the wrong time. Keep reassuring her that it is seven thirty, then bring her to bed and let her list the non-passerine birds of Ireland before she goes to sleep.'

I could hear Shania listing birds as Clara continued to shriek. My stomach knotted. I knew it would take her a while to calm down. Why the hell couldn't Gavin follow simple instructions? I'd never ask him to babysit again. Christelle was the only one I could trust to stick to the exact routine. 'Call me in ten minutes. If she hasn't calmed down, I'll come back.' I crossed my fingers that the clock trick would work. Otherwise it would be a very short date.

151

CHAPTER 12

Sophie

There was a knock on the door. I checked my makeup and applied some lip-gloss. I always made sure I looked my best when Jack brought Jess home. It was silly, but I wanted him to remember that I was an attractive woman and hadn't let myself go. I'd felt I had to make an extra effort since he'd met Pippa. I knew there was no competition: I'd seen Pippa's picture splashed all over magazines. She was younger, fitter and more beautiful than me – but I wanted to look my best so Jack wouldn't feel sorry for me.

Sometimes he'd come in for a quick chat, but lately he'd just dropped Jess off and dashed back home. I liked it when he came in. I missed male company and Jack and I had always got on well. We had the same sense of humour and Jess liked it when we chatted.

I put on my best smile and opened the door. 'Hi—'

My smile faded and my mouth dropped open.

Jess was standing beside Pippa, who was taller, blonder and even more stunning in the flesh. Her skin was like silky caramel – I almost wanted to reach out and touch it. I was wearing dark denim jeans and a simple pink top, but when I saw her I felt old and frumpy. Pippa had that really cool boho look. She was like a younger, taller, prettier Sienna Miller.

I felt sick. I had never imagined she'd be so gorgeous. No wonder Jess had her on a pedestal. She was dazzling. I felt crushed. It was so much worse seeing her face to face. I'd never get this image out of my mind. She was one of those women whom everyone turns to stare at. I looked like her mother. I wanted to cry – no, I wanted to scream.

I pulled my stomach in and put my shoulders back. I needed to take control of the situation. I was supposed to be in charge here.

Pippa smiled, revealing a set of gleaming white teeth. 'I'm Pippa.' She beamed, proffering a perfectly manicured hand.

I finally found my voice. 'Hi. Sophie.'

'Jack's stuck on some conference call so I said I'd drop Jess over.'

Damn Jack. Why the hell hadn't he warned me that his girlfriend was going to turn up on my doorstep? I felt completely ambushed. I wasn't ready for this. Meeting Pippa properly for the first time was a big deal and I'd wanted to do it on my terms, in my own way. I wasn't prepared. I would have worn different clothes, something edgier, cooler.

'I kind of wanted to meet you anyway,' Pippa said. 'I mean, we're almost going to be related now.'

I frowned. What on earth was she talking about?

'You know, when the baby arrives. Jess will be its sibling.'

I looked down at her almost imperceptible bump. How could she be so neat at almost seven months? 'Right, of course. Uhm . . . congratulations. How are you feeling?' Judging by her glowing skin and glossy hair, I'd say she felt pretty damn great.

Pippa smiled. 'Not bad, thanks. I felt a bit queasy the first few weeks. I was a bit snappy to poor Jack. I felt terrible about it, but then he told me you'd been a nightmare during your first trimester so I didn't feel so bad.'

I had not been a nightmare. How could Jack say that? I'd been a perfect wife. How dare he criticize me to *her*?

Oblivious to my fury, Pippa went on, 'Jack said you've been totally cool about the baby and everything, which is great. It's so much easier when the ex isn't a psycho.' She laughed. 'My friend Jasmine is seeing this guy and his ex keeps ringing him up and crying and begging him to go back to her and she's really rude to Jasmine.'

Was that supposed to be a compliment? 'Well, breaking up can be a very emotional time,' I said, trying to retain my composure. Boho Babe seemed completely unaware of anyone's feelings but her own . . . and her stupid friend Jasmine's. Was she incredibly shallow, incredibly stupid or just incredibly young? Whichever it was, it was incredibly irritating.

'But the woman should have some pride. I'd never let a guy see me crying over him. It's embarrassing.' Flicking her hair, she turned to Jess and said, 'Remember that. Don't ever let a man see you cry. They like strong, confident women.'

I pinched my hand to stop myself shouting at her. I did not want this airhead giving my daughter advice. 'Jess is nine. She really doesn't need to worry about that for a while,' I said.

Pippa shrugged. 'To be honest, Soph, kids grow up much faster now than in your day. I had my first boyfriend when I was ten.'

Soph? Was she seriously calling me *Soph?* Was she my best buddy now? And what the hell did she mean by in 'your day'. I was forty-two, not eighty-two.

'Yeah, Mum. Three of the girls in my class have already kissed boys,' Jess said.

'Tongues?' Pippa asked.

What?

'Yes,' Jess answered.

I put my hand up to halt the conversation. 'Hold on a minute. Are you telling me that three girls in your class have snogged boys? I'm sorry but I don't believe it. I bet they're lying.'

Pippa laughed, a sexy, throaty giggle that made me want to stab her. 'They don't call it snogging, Soph. It's called "meeting" now.' Looking at Jess, who was also laughing at me, she said, 'You need to give your mum some lessons in modern-day lingo.'

'She's, like, back in the dark ages.'

I knew I was going to say something rude very soon. My temper was at boiling point. I needed to get Pippa off my doorstep. 'Right, well, thanks for all that. Tell Jack I'll be in touch.'

'Mum, I want to show Pippa my bedroom,' Jess said.

'Not now, sweetheart.'

'Why not? Please. It'll only take a second.'

I really didn't want Pippa in my apartment. It was too much. I didn't want her in my personal space. Besides, it wasn't tidy enough. I hadn't been expecting anyone. But I knew Jess would freak if I said no and I didn't want to have an argument with her in front of Pippa. 'OK, just a quick look because we're heading out.'

Jess took Pippa's hand and led her through the open-plan kitchen and lounge into her bedroom.

I followed, feeling like the third wheel on a date. They were so in synch with each other and I was this out-of-date loser tagging along. Jess showed Pippa her posters of One Direction, her wardrobe, her bookshelf, her bed and her desk.

Pippa leant over to look at the photos on Jess's cork board. There was one of me and Jack on our wedding day and another of us on holidays with a newborn Jess. 'Wow, you look great,' Pippa said to me. 'You were good-looking back in the day.'

I pinned my hands to my sides so as not to hit her.

'Mum was a top model,' Jess said proudly. I could have kissed her.

'Really?' Pippa seemed very surprised. 'Jack never said.'

'She was gorgeous,' Jess said.

I smiled at Jess. She was being sweet. But they were both talking about my looks in the past tense. They were making me feel ancient . . . a has-been . . . past my sell-by date. Was I that bad now? Was it over for me? Had I lost all appeal?

Pippa's phone rang. 'Hey, baby,' she said. 'I'm here with Jess and Soph.' I could hear Jack's voice. 'She's been really nice, actually.' She winked at me. 'I'm coming home now . . . I miss you, too, baby.' She hung up.

Baby? I miss you, too? My God, it was like being in a really bad teenage sitcom. Did Jack call her 'baby' as well? Did he really say, 'I miss you,' after they'd spent half an hour apart? What had happened to my husband? Where was the cool, suave, independent man I'd married? Was this what happened when you met someone younger? Did you end up behaving like a teenager? It seemed so ridiculous and fake. But Pippa was radiant and Jack was 'over the moon', so maybe I was just jealous. Old farts like me got to sit in and watch movies alone with a face mask on in the desperate hope that it would slow down the ageing process.

Pippa left in a whirl of 'Later, *amigos*' and hugs for Jess. I closed the door and breathed a sigh of relief that she was gone. But her presence, like her overkill perfume, lingered on.

'Isn't she awesome?' Jess said. 'Don't you just love her?'

'She's very . . . friendly.' I tried to be positive.

'I'm so glad you like her. I was worried you mightn't. She's so much younger than you I wasn't sure you'd click.'

'She's not that much younger. I'm not ninety, Jess.' I was getting sick of being called old.

'Well, she's closer in age to me than she is to you,' Jess pointed out.

'I'd prefer not to think about that,' I said. 'Look, Jess, the important thing is that she's nice to you. That's all I care about.'

Jess beamed. 'She's super-nice to me. Wait until you see what she bought me.'

I can't bloody wait, I thought darkly. Jess ran into her bedroom and came out a minute later wearing a dress that was too short, too tight and too sparkly for a nine-year-old. It had Babelicious written in pink sequins across the chest.

Jess twirled. 'Isn't it *soooooo* cool?' she gushed. 'Pippa spotted it and said I had to try it on and it fitted me perfectly.'

She looked like a miniature hooker. I wasn't

being overly critical because Pippa had bought the dress: it was just plain awful. I wasn't one of those fuddy-duddy mothers who never allowed their daughters to wear cool clothes. I knew fashion. I worked in fashion. But this dress was totally unsuitable in every way.

'Jess, it's very tight and . . . well, it looks a bit cheap.'

Jess threw herself onto the sofa. 'I knew you'd say that. I said it to Pippa. I said, "My mum will say it's too short and too tight." Pippa said her mantra in life is, "If you've got it, flaunt it." And she says I have it, so there!'

I threw my hands into the air in utter exasperation. 'That's the most ridiculous thing I've ever heard. Doesn't she realize you're nine years of age?'

'I'm nearly ten!' Jess shouted. 'And Pippa thinks I look amazing in it.'

'Pippa is not your mother, OK?' All attempts at remaining calm were now gone. 'I am your mother and you will never leave this house wearing that. You are a beautiful young girl. You don't need to wear trash like that.'

'I hate you,' Jess screamed. 'You're just a stupid boring idiot who knows nothing about fashion.'

'Don't speak to your mother like that.'

Jess and I spun around. Julie was standing behind us, in her coat. 'Sorry, the door was open so I didn't knock.'

With all the drama, I had completely forgotten that I'd arranged to take Julie shopping.

'Julie,' Jess said, hands on hips, 'what do you think of this dress?'

Julie looked her up and down slowly. 'Honestly? I don't like the shape. I don't think it flatters you. I also think you should listen to your mum. She has great taste. In fact, I'm here because I need her to help me buy an outfit. Will you come too?'

Jess looked at me. 'Do I have to?'

'Yes.'

'OK, but I'm bringing my phone so I won't die of boredom.'

'Thanks for being so sweet, Jess,' I hissed.

I took Julie straight to House of Fraser. While Jess sat outside the changing room, texting and playing games on her phone, I helped Julie try on some different outfits.

'What exactly is this for?' I asked.

'It's the school concert. Apparently everyone gets quite dressed up, but not too dressed up.' Julie sighed. 'It's a bloody minefield. If you're over-dressed, you look like you're trying too hard. If you're underdressed, you look clueless.'

I smiled at her. 'Don't worry. We'll find something.'

'Thanks, Sophie. You know me, I haven't really got a clue about clothes. I've never been that interested in them.'

'I must have got your share of the fashion genes.'

I was obsessed with clothes. Less so since I'd had no money, but when Jack and I were rich, shopping was my favourite pastime. I'd had some incredible clothes back then. Although I'd sold most of them, I'd kept a few key pieces, which I used for important work meetings – my Armani suit, a Miu Miu coat, two pairs of Louboutin shoes and a Prada dress.

Julie tried on a raspberry Gerard Darel dress that skimmed her hips and fell just below her knees. It had little capped sleeves and a nice detail on the neckline.

'It's perfect on you,' I said. And it was. I had specifically chosen it because it had a peplum band that hid her stomach. Julie had definitely put on weight again. She really needed to keep away from the chocolate biscuits.

'Are you sure?' Julie asked.

'Positive. You look gorgeous.'

Julie tugged at the dress. 'I'm not sure. Is it a bit much?'

I placed my hand on her arm. 'Julie, are you OK? You seem very uptight about a school concert. Is it really that big a deal?'

Julie sat down on the changing-room bench. 'It's just that I want to fit in. Not with Victoria and those awful women, just with some normal mothers, if I can find any. I don't have any friends at the school and our neighbours are very cold and unwelcoming. I miss having Marian next door to chat to. It's a bit lonely, to be honest.

The boys are happy at Castle Academy and doing really well. They're not as wild now that they're in an all-boys' school playing sports half the day. They've slotted in so well and I want to try to do the same.'

Julie was genuinely upset. I tried to reassure her. She seemed intimidated by the school. I knew how overbearing Victoria and her gang could be and I knew Julie would never be, or want to be, friends with them. She needed to find some nice women to hang out with. The school gate could be a lonely place.

It had taken me a while to get to know the mums at Jess's school when she'd moved from her expensive playschool to the local national school. Because I was working, I was always dashing off and didn't have time to nurture friendships. It had been at least three months before I'd met a mum I'd felt comfortable with. Julie had more time than I did to focus on her friendships, because she didn't work, but she was shyer than I was. I was good at small-talk. I liked to keep things light. I didn't want a new best friend. I didn't want to get into heavy conversations. I didn't want to swap tales of woe. I just wanted to chit-chat and organize playdates. But Julie was the opposite. She was hopeless at small-talk. When Julie met someone new, she never talked about the weather or traffic, she'd jump right in with how difficult the triplets were to manage, or how Harry had discovered a daughter he never knew he had or how she secretly prayed that Tom would turn out to be gay so she'd have someone to hang out with.

'Look, Julie, it takes time to get used to a new school and new people. You have to sift through all the crazy mothers to find the nice ones. It took me a good few months to fit in at Jess's school.'

Julie pulled the dress over her head. 'I just didn't think it'd be this hard.'

I hung the dress back on its hanger while Julie got dressed. 'Anyway, enough about me,' she said, then whispered, 'How are things with Jess?'

'Not great,' I whispered back. 'Her adoration of Pippa is really beginning to bug me. I actually met the woman today.'

'WHAT?' Julie's eyes almost popped out of their sockets. 'How could you let me rattle on about stupid school-gate nonsense when you had this big news? What was she like?'

'Sssh,' I said, not wanting Jess to hear. In a very low voice, into Julie's ear, I said, 'She was more stunning, more annoying and more stupid than I'd imagined.'

'Wow!' Julie said. 'And are you OK?'

I shrugged. 'What can I do? She's part of my life now. This baby is Jess's sibling.'

'Let's go for a glass of wine. I need one too,' Julie suggested.

I looked at my watch. It was three o'clock. 'OK, just a small one.'

'Oh, live a little,' Julie said. 'You need a drink after that encounter. We'll order a bottle and see how we get on.' She linked my arm as we headed off to the Harvey Nichols bar with a grumpy Jess following.

While we were having a drink, Julie told me she'd been in touch with Dan, her ex-boyfriend. She blushed when she mentioned it.

'What kind of "in touch"?' I asked, intrigued by her red cheeks.

'It started with just a Facebook hello and now he texts or emails the odd time.'

'What does the "odd time" mean?'

Julie went even redder. 'A couple of times a week or more.'

'Is there any flirting?' I asked. I remember Dan as cocky, over-confident and really tight with money. I hated men who weren't generous – it was such a turn-off. He was so not Julie's type, but they'd always had amazing chemistry.

Julie looked away. 'No. Not really . . . Well, he is a little bit flirty sometimes, but I'm not.'

I watched as she fidgeted with her drink. 'Is it fun?'

She nodded. 'It is, actually. It's harmless, but it makes me feel young again. It reminds me of the old days.'

'Well, just be careful it doesn't get too flirty. You wouldn't like it if Harry was getting over-friendly with his old girlfriends.'

Julie sighed. 'Harry is so infatuated with his new social scene at the golf club that I don't think he'd notice if I was having Skype sex with Dan.'

I was taken aback. Julie seemed really angry with Harry. They'd always had a really nice relationship. Even with triplets, no sleep and no money, they had managed to muddle through. But Julie seemed restless at the moment, restless and unsure of herself. This new school was knocking her confidence. She needed a little boost. Hopefully her contact with Dan would be innocent enough and give her the lift she needed.

Jess pulled out her earphones. 'Can we please go now? This is so boring.'

I knew my time was up. I took my grumpy daughter home and left my sister finishing her wine alone.

CHAPTER 13

Julie

I put on my lipstick and came out of the bathroom to show Harry my new dress. I knew
Sophie had chosen it because the peplum hid
my stomach. I was trying to stay away from the
chocolate biscuits, but I always ate too much when
I was stressed. I'd have to watch it, though. I didn't
want to be chubby again. I was a size fourteen and
that was the highest I wanted to go.

'Ta-dah!' I twirled for Harry in front of the long
wall mirror in the walk-in wardrobe. I still couldn't
believe I had a walk-in wardrobe – me, Julie, who
had hardly any clothes with a whole room for
them. It still felt strange.

Harry was staring at Bloomberg on the big flat-
screen TV on our bedroom wall. He barely moved
his eyes.

'Mm, very nice.'

'Harry!' I was exasperated. 'Can you at least
look at me?'

His phone beeped. 'Just a second. I need to reply
to Donald.'

166

I resisted the urge to get the phone and crush it under my high heel. I took a deep breath and went over to him. I waited patiently until he'd finished texting.

'Sorry, you look lovely.'

'Can I have a kiss, please?' I asked, in what was supposed to sound like a playful voice but ended up needy and desperate.

'Of course.' Harry turned to me but his phone beeped again. He read the message.

I cursed under my breath, stood up and tried not to scream. Harry, sensing my fury, finally put his phone down, came over to me and kissed me lightly on the lips.

'*Groooooooooooooooooss.*'

I looked round as Liam made vomiting noises. 'You two are disgusting,' he said.

Harry stepped back and turned to the mirror to put on his tie. 'There is nothing disgusting about kissing a woman. You'll understand that in a couple of years' time.'

'I will never, ever, ever, ever kiss a girl. I'd rather die in shark-infested water.'

'Are you talking about kissing girls?' Luke came into the room in his boxer shorts and socks.

'Did Liam kiss a girl?' Leo trailed behind his brother.

'No, I did not.' Liam thumped his brother's arm. 'I said I'd rather be eaten by sharks than kiss a girl.'

'I'd rather be burnt in a scorching hot fire and die in agony,' Luke said.

'I'd prefer to be stabbed, like, a zillion times with a knife than kiss a girl,' Leo said.

'Why are they talking about kissing and dying?' Tom shuffled into the room in his Transformer pyjamas, followed by Christelle.

'I'd rather die from an infected tattoo that oozes pus and slime than kiss a boy,' Christelle said, outdoing her little brothers, who stared at her wide-eyed.

'That's gross,' Liam said.

'Not as gross as your stinky arse,' Christelle replied.

Liam squealed and jumped on top of her. They proceeded to wrestle. Then Leo and Luke joined in, but they were no match for Christelle. She did kickboxing. She flung one after the other onto our giant bed as they laughed hysterically.

'Tom,' she crouched down to him, 'do you want to fly too?'

He nodded. 'But not too high, please,' he said. Christelle picked him up and chucked him on the bed on top of his brothers. Tom's laughter was tinged with fear. He scrambled off quickly, out of the way of his older brothers' wrestling.

'OK now, boys, come on, I need you to get dressed and be downstairs in five minutes. Your uniforms are laid out on your beds, clean, ironed and ready to go.' I tried to drag them off the bed, but they just dived under the covers and kicked out when I tried to pull them.

Even with Harry and Christelle's help, as soon

as we got one out, the other two would crawl back under. After five minutes I was beginning to sweat and could feel wet patches forming under the armpits of my new dress. I tried to catch Luke's leg, but he kicked out with the other and connected with the side of my face.

'Ouch! Just get out of the bloody bed and put your uniforms on,' I snapped, rubbing my throbbing cheek. They all dived back under the covers.

'I'm going night-night, Mummy,' Tom said.

I bent down and gave him a sweaty kiss. 'You are the only sensible child in this family. You're my angel,' I said, kissing his sweet face.

'You're my angel too.' He gave me a toothy smile.

Harry stood at the end of the wriggling duvet. 'Come on, boys, that's enough. You can't be late for the concert. Out you get.'

They ignored him. Just as I was about to take my dress off, put on my tracksuit and start yanking them out again, Christelle came back into the room holding a Nintendo DS and a hammer. 'I'm going to count to five and then, if you are not out of here and in your bedrooms getting dressed, I'm going to smash this DS into little tiny pieces.'

'No, you won't, because it cost loads of money and Dad won't allow you to,' Leo said, peeping out from under the covers.

Christelle looked at Harry. 'Your dad's not going to stop me because, in case you forgot, he's my dad, too, and he knows I'm right. Don't you?'

Harry was slow to punish the kids, but there was no way he was going to disagree with Christelle. She was formidable when she was riled. He nodded.

'Go for it,' I urged her.

'One . . . two . . .'

'Dad! You can't let her do it,' Leo shouted.

'It's your choice, boys. Come out now and nothing will be broken,' Harry said.

'. . . three . . . four . . . five . . .' Christelle put the DS on the floor, raised the hammer and, just as she was about to smash the game into smithereens, the three boys came charging out from under the covers. Leo swooped down, grabbed the DS, and they scarpered into their bedrooms.

'Nice one,' I said, grinning at my step-daughter. 'I must use that next time.'

'Even I was a bit scared.' Harry laughed.

'Growing up in France with a tough American mother, I learnt all about discipline. You Irish are way too easy on your kids. You need to kick some arse around here.'

'Feel free to come and kick arse anytime you want,' I said.

Christelle smiled and reached for Tom's hand. 'Come on, Tommy. Let's read you a story.'

Tom looked up at her in awe. 'Would you really smash it all up?'

'Damn right I would,' she said.

'Do you smash Clara's toys when she's bold?' he asked.

'Clara's never bold. She's like you, a total sweetie.' Christelle picked Tom up and kissed him.

He snuggled into her shoulder. 'I like it when girls kiss me.' He sighed contentedly. Then his head snapped up. 'But don't tell the boys.'

'Don't worry, Tommy-boy, your secret is safe with me.' Christelle hugged him.

As we watched them walk out, I said to Harry, 'I think she got more of her mother's genes than yours.'

'I thought my father was strict,' Harry whispered, 'but Christelle would have given him a run for his money. Is it weird to be slightly afraid of your own daughter?'

I giggled. 'Probably. She's brilliant, though. She knows exactly how to talk to the triplets on their level and how to discipline them. Every time she comes over I learn a new trick. She should have her own show – *Chastise with Christelle* has a nice ring to it.'

'*Control Your Kids with Christelle*,' Harry suggested, and we laughed. It felt nice. We hadn't laughed together in ages.

'Right, let's get going. We cannot be late,' I said. 'The boys are performing in the first half of the concert.'

'What exactly are they doing?' Harry asked.

I grabbed my bag and headed for the stairs. 'They're singing a song, but they wouldn't tell me which one. They said they've been practising in music class.'

'It can't be too bad then . . . can it?' Harry wondered.

Fifteen minutes later, with a lot more chasing and shouting, and one quick glass of wine to calm my nerves, we were finally in the car on the way to the concert.

'What song are you singing, boys?' Harry asked.

'Not telling,' Luke shouted.

'It's supposed to be a surprise,' Leo explained.

'OK, well, are you all singing together or taking a verse each?' Harry seemed to think there was going to be some kind of structure. I was less optimistic.

'Luke's singing. Leo and me are the band,' Liam said.

'What do you mean?' I was puzzled. 'You don't play any instruments.'

'I play the drums and Leo plays guitar.'

'But you only took those up a few weeks ago,' I pointed out.

'The drums are easy, Mum. Any moron could play them,' Liam said.

'Yeah, even a loser like you.' Luke stuck his finger into his brother's ear.

I turned round in my seat. 'Can you play the guitar after only a few weeks?' I asked Leo.

He shrugged. 'Yeah, kind of.'

'Why did you choose Luke to be the singer?' Harry enquired.

'Because he's the only one who can remember

all the words. Me and Leo kept forgetting bits,' Liam answered.

'Probably a wise decision, then,' Harry said. He looked over at me and mouthed, 'Disaster!'

My heart sank. He was right. I just hoped it wouldn't be a total fiasco.

While the boys ran off backstage, we took our seats. I silently thanked Sophie. The dress she had chosen for me was perfect. Not too much, not too little.

Victoria swished up to us. 'I'm surprised to see you here. I didn't think your boys would be allowed to perform.'

'Why on earth not?' Harry was confused.

'Because they're wild and out of control and terrorized my son.' She moved past us and went to air-kiss one of her clones.

'What does she mean, terrorized her son? What did they do?' Harry asked.

I was furious. 'Nothing. Her son is an idiot who freaks out if anyone looks at him sideways. She's just being a bitch as usual.'

'OK. Good. I want the boys to get on well here. They mustn't rock the boat. I couldn't show my face in the golf club if they got expelled. Most of the members are ex-Castle Academy.'

Before I was able to tell Harry how little I cared about his stupid golf-club friends, Emily came over and we chatted about the concert. Her son, a quiet boy called Joshua, was doing a solo piece on the piano. 'Did you hear Sebastian's playing the violin?' she added. 'Apparently he's very talented.' She caught someone's eye and dashed off.

'Who's Sebastian?' Harry asked.

'Victoria's son.'

'The violin's a difficult instrument,' Harry noted. 'I hope he doesn't make a show of himself.'

'Oh, he won't. I'm sure he's had daily lessons from some Russian violin expert to make sure he's performance perfect.' I glared at Victoria, who was holding court, surrounded by twittering women, all of whom were mothers in the triplets' class. I glanced around and spotted her husband, Gerry, flirting with the very young Spanish teacher. I smiled to myself. Victoria might be the queen of the third form, but her husband was king of sleaze.

The lights went down and a hush came over the crowd. I tried to push my nerves aside and enjoy the first few performances. The triplets were scheduled to come on fifth.

The first boy, a second-form student, sang 'Ave Maria'. It was so beautiful that the hairs on the back of my neck stood up.

'They're setting the bar very high,' Harry muttered.

Next was a boy in fifth form who played a jazz piece on the piano that was incredible. His fingers whizzed up and down the keys like rockets. My stomach began to knot.

He was followed by four boys from third form

who were like a barber-shop quartet. They weren't as good as the first two acts, thank God. One of the boys was a bit off key. I began to relax.

Next was Sebastian and his violin. Victoria was standing up, holding a ridiculous camera with an enormous lens, completely blocking the parents behind her. Gerry was typing on his phone, not paying the least bit of attention to his son. I watched as Victoria poked him hard in the shoulder and he looked up.

Sebastian shakily introduced himself and announced that he was going to play Brahms' Lullaby.

Harry snorted. 'Sure any child with half a brain could learn that.'

I wasn't sure our 'geniuses' could even hold a violin correctly. Sebastian did well, and when the piece ended, Victoria, still standing, led the loud applause.

'Right, here come our lads,' Harry said. I squeezed his hand. Please, dear God, let them do OK.

The triplets came onto the stage in multi-coloured wigs and sunglasses. Liam attempted a cartwheel, which resulted in him falling off the stage into the orchestra pit, much to the annoyance of the eleven-year-old oboist he landed on. Leo tried to do the splits in mid-air while holding onto a guitar he had no idea how to play. Mid-leap we heard a rip as the back of his trousers split open. The boys in the orchestra and backstage began to point and laugh. Leo glared at me and shouted, 'I told you these trousers were too small for me.'

I pretended to laugh as the other parents strained to see who 'owned' these kids.

Luke pushed his brother out of the way and grabbed the microphone. As Liam limped over to the drums after his fall, Luke told the audience, 'We're the Three Dudes and we're going to perform a song we made up.'

Liam banged the drums and Leo made a twanging sound with the guitar. Luke began to . . . well, shout is the only way to describe it. It definitely wasn't singing.

We are the three dudes
We go to this school
We used to have no money
My mum didn't think it was funny
But then an old lady died
And left us loads of dosh
And my mum cried
Now we are rich and posh
We go to this cool school
And we triplets rule
We can go on holiday
Cos our dad can pay
With the money from the dead woman
Our life is way more fun.
Mum is so happy now she's got all this money
Cos we can finally go somewhere sunny

She hated being skint
But now she's got a mint
So she can be flash
And show off her cash
And when we go to the sun
We . . .

Luke forgot his words. He turned to Leo, who was plucking the guitar tunelessly. 'What's the next bit?'

'You dork, it's "We can buy a ton".'

Luke turned back to the audience:

We can buy a ton
Of sweets and gum
Being rich rocks!

Liam banged on the drums as Luke and Leo took a bow. But no one was clapping. There was a stunned silence. I looked at the exit. I wanted to make a run for it and deny they were my kids. I was humiliated and mortified.

Now everyone in the school knew our private business. The triplets had made complete fools of us. I wanted to die. Behind me I heard a man say, 'What kind of people are they letting into the school now?'

'I know,' his wife said. 'Families like that give the school a bad name. We'll have to talk to the headmaster.'

Harry, who had sat as still as a stone during

the performance while I'd dug my fingers into his arm in horror, raised his hands and began to clap. The boys looked over and smiled. 'Awesome, right?' They gave us the thumbs-up. Oh, to be a completely clueless, elephant-skinned nine-year-old, I thought, as I gave them a weak smile.

A few kind parents clapped feebly, the boys bowed and waved at their 'fans' and then the dean of the third form came out and ushered them off the stage. Coming back on, he said, 'Well, that was certainly original.' He then went on to introduce the next boy.

I looked up and saw Victoria pointing at me. She didn't even bother whispering. 'That's the mother,' she said loudly, to the woman beside her. 'There doesn't seem to be any discipline at all, utterly wild.'

'They're positively feral,' the other woman said. 'I don't want Patrick exposed to this kind of vulgarity.'

'They obviously get it from home,' Victoria said, looking innocently at me.

I could hear similar murmurs around the hall, and I knew that if I didn't leave, I'd start to cry. I grabbed Harry's arm. 'We need to go now.'

He leant in and said, 'Don't be ridiculous. We belong here as much as they do. We're staying.' His jaw was set. I knew that look. Harry was determined to stay and nothing was going to change his mind.

'Well, I need to pop to the Ladies, then,' I lied.

It was only when I stood up that I realized my legs were shaking. I stumbled out of the hall and made my way to the Ladies. On the way, I spotted the room where the after-show reception was being held. There were glasses of wine laid out. Checking no one was around, I snuck in, downed a glass, then hid another behind my bag.

I went to the cloakroom, locked myself into a cubicle and sat on the toilet seat, drinking the second glass. I could feel the alcohol working its magic as my heart rate began to slow.

I loved the boys, but why did they have to humiliate me? I know they didn't mean it, but they had made me sound like some money-grabbing wretch.

I heard the cloakroom door open. I froze. A group of women came in. 'Can you believe those triplets? I mean, what kind of parents do they have?'

'Did they win the lottery? I didn't really understand the song.'

Then I heard Victoria's unmistakable voice: 'Apparently some wealthy aunt left them money and they bought their way into Castle Academy. I heard the boys were expelled from several schools. They have utterly traumatized poor Sebastian. We really need to rally together and talk to the headmaster. Castle Academy does not want that kind of common element dragging the school down.'

'Where is the mother?' someone asked.

'Obviously she's out spending all her new money,' another mother said, and there was a cackle of laughter.

'She's actually very nice.' Emily's voice rose above the pack.

'Oh, Emily,' Victoria drawled, 'you really need to be more discerning. I knew the mother's sister, Sophie Devlin, and she was just the same – completely obsessed with money and social climbing.'

I dug my nails into my thigh to stop myself storming out of the cubicle and punching that bitch in the face. But my family had made enough of a show of itself for one night. I finished the wine and waited for the witches to leave. When I came out, the room was empty. I splashed water on my face, trying to wash away the humiliation.

CHAPTER 14

Louise

I glanced down at my BlackBerry: two missed calls from Clara's school. What was going on? Her teacher, Helen, seemed like a capable woman, so if she was calling something must be up. I'd made it clear at the beginning of the year that I didn't want to be disturbed at work for silly things, like if Clara was arguing with another child or if she seemed a bit introverted. I had explained to Helen that Clara was an only child and liked playing by herself. She was quiet and I was fine with that. I didn't need some over-zealous teacher telling me that my child needed to be more sociable. She was happy and that was all I cared about. Besides, I had liked my own company as a child too. I'd always found other kids really immature and juvenile.

I knew it wasn't an emergency because I had told Helen to call my secretary, Elaine, if ever there was one at school and she couldn't get hold of me. I could see Elaine through the conference-room glass door, typing away. Her phone hadn't rung.

181

Still, I wanted to wrap up this meeting, but Janice Whitney was in mid-flow, asking me to explain exactly how the Asset Covered Securities Amendment Act 2007 enhanced Ireland's position in the bond market.

'It's quite straightforward,' I replied. 'These amendments enhance Ireland's position in the highly competitive covered bond market. Asset-covered securities are backed by a defined pool of prescribed assets, like mortgages. They differ from mortgage-backed securities in that they are issued directly by the originator or a subsidiary rather than through a special-purpose vehicle, thereby retaining the mortgages on the originator's balance sheet.'

Janice leant forward, refilling her coffee cup for the third time. She was clearly settling in for the day. Damn. I wanted to call Clara's teacher. 'I just wonder if you could be more specific,' she said.

Specific? Was she joking? How could I possibly be more specific? I nodded and concentrated on being polite. Janice had inherited a fortune when her husband died and left her his publishing business. She was obviously lonely and she was currently spending all of her time tormenting me and my colleagues with requests for information and clarification. She was driving us all crazy. We didn't have time to sit around explaining our different sectors of the law. But she had deep pockets and the potential to bring us a lot of business, so I had to tread carefully.

'I thought I was being very specific, Janice. I'm not sure what further information I can give you on that point.'

Janice waved a wrinkled, bejewelled hand at me. 'I'm not entirely clear on the mortgage-backed securities part.' She picked up a biscuit and sat back in her chair, anticipating my response.

My BlackBerry lit up. It was Clara's school again. 'If you'll just excuse me for one minute, I need to pop out to take this call.'

'All right, but don't try to fob me off on one of your junior team members. It's you I want to deal with. I will only speak to the senior partners. I'm not going to be anyone's guinea pig. The juniors can practise on other clients.'

'Yes, of course.' I backed out of the room and cursed under my breath.

'Hi, is Clara OK?' I asked Helen.

'She's fine. Sorry to disturb you at work, but there has been an incident.'

'What do you mean?'

'Well, there was a tussle this morning between Clara and Angela.'

'Yes, and?'

'It resulted in a bit of unpleasantness.'

For the love of God would she ever get to the bloody point? I didn't have time for this. 'What exactly happened, Helen?'

'Clara, who is a lovely child and we're all so fond of her here—'

I cut across her. 'What did she do?'

'I'm sure she didn't mean it, but unfortunately she got a little annoyed when Angela took her Lego and she . . . Well, I'm afraid Clara let her temper get the better of her and she bit Angela, who is very upset.'

I rolled my eyes. Big deal. All kids bite. Gavin had been a terrible biter. He'd almost had to be muzzled. Whenever he lost his temper, which was quite often as he was constantly being taunted by his three older sisters, he'd go all red in the face and bite our arms.

'Well, I'm sure Angela is fine. I mean, Clara's not Jaws. Lots of kids bite – it must happen all the time in school.'

'Not really, and in this instance Clara bit poor Angela quite deeply. There are distinct tooth marks on her arm.'

'I'll talk to Clara tonight after work. I'll make sure it doesn't happen again.'

As I was about to hang up, Helen said, 'Actually, Louise, I was wondering if you could come to the school at pick-up time. Angela's mother would like a word with you.'

You have got to be kidding me. Now I had to go and listen to some over-protective mother who was freaking out about a bite. I had back-to-back meetings all day.

'I'm sorry, Helen, but I have a crazy day in work and I just don't have the time to come down to school for a chat. Give the woman my number and tell her to call me.'

There was silence on the phone, then Helen said, 'I suggested that because you mentioned how demanding your job is, but Angela's mother was most insistent. She mentioned lawyers and plastic surgeons.'

'Is this a wind-up?' I asked.

'No.'

'Come on, Helen, plastic surgery?'

'Well, yes . . . I know . . . but . . .'

'I'll see you at twelve thirty.' I hung up and had the very strong urge to go and bite someone myself. I opted instead for kicking the wall. Now I was going to have to reschedule my entire afternoon to meet this ridiculous woman and her whiny, pain-in-the-arse child.

At twelve thirty I jumped out of a taxi and went to meet Clara's 'victim'. As soon as she saw me, Clara ran outside. Her eyes were red from crying.

'Hey, pumpkin, are you OK?' I hugged her.

'Miss Helen is cross with me.'

'I know. Did you bite Angela?'

Clara pulled back from the hug and looked down. She nodded. 'I know it's bold to bite but she took my Lego.'

I crouched down. 'I understand that it's annoying when someone does that, but you mustn't bite them. Just tell the teacher.'

Clara's eyes welled. 'I was making a mockingbird and Angela just came over and took the tail. She just snapped it off. It took me ages to make it.'

I wiped a tear from her eye. I couldn't bear to see Clara so distressed. 'It's OK. I'm not cross with you. I think Angela's a very silly girl for making such a big deal about it.'

'I said sorry to her.'

'Good girl. Do you know who used to bite me all the time?'

'Who?'

'Uncle Gavin.'

Clara's eyes widened. 'Does he bite now? Does he bite Shania if she takes his Lego?'

'No, he doesn't. He stopped doing it because he knew it wasn't nice. Just like you're not going to bite again, right?'

'Yes, Mummy.'

Helen came over and tapped me on the shoulder. 'Louise, this is Caroline, Angela's mother.'

I looked up grumpily, expecting to see some hippie-dippy earth-mother with long, straggly hair wearing one of those stupid ponchos that have tiny little mirrors sewn into them. She was wearing a poncho but it was a cashmere one and her hair was blow-dried in long curls. She had one of those ridiculously oversized designer totes on her arm and six-inch spike-heel boots. She looked over-dressed and overdone.

I stood up, holding Clara's hand, and decided to take control of the situation. 'Hello.' I shook Caroline's hand firmly. 'I believe my daughter bit yours. I've spoken to Clara and it won't happen again. I really don't think we need to make a big deal of it. As you can see, Clara is upset and has apologized.'

Caroline smiled a tight, unfriendly smile. She pulled up her daughter's sleeve and thrust her arm in my face. 'As you can see, Angela's arm has tooth marks all over it.'

There were tooth marks, but only one set and the kid was clearly fine. I took a deep breath. 'Angela,' I said, addressing the child directly, 'Clara is very sorry for biting you and she will never do it again. Can you make up now?' I wanted to add, 'Because I really need to get back to work,' but restrained myself.

Angela nodded.

'Right, well, there we go. All sorted.' I pulled my bag over my shoulder.

Caroline held up a manicured hand. 'Hold on a minute. We're far from finished here. Your daughter has scarred my daughter's arm. You can't just brush this off.'

I looked at the tooth marks. 'They really aren't that bad. I'm sure by this time tomorrow they'll be invisible.'

Caroline stared down at Clara, who looked away. 'Clara, what you did was very naughty. Look at me when I'm talking to you. Clara?'

Clara never looked at people she didn't know very well. She was shy like that. This bloody woman was beginning to get up my nose. It was my turn to hold up my hand. 'Excuse me, do not speak to my daughter like that. Clara said she was

187

sorry, this little incident is over, and I'm now going back to work to a meeting that I postponed to come here for this mini-drama.'

'Don't you dare walk away from me,' Caroline hissed. 'I've not finished. I want you to pay for the GP appointment I'm taking Angela to now. I want them to check her injury. She may need a tetanus shot.'

That was it.

I took a step forward and eyeballed her. In a very calm voice, I said, 'My daughter is not a dog. I happen to be a lawyer, a very good lawyer, and I don't like or appreciate people insulting my child. So, if I was you, I would be very careful about what you say in front of me or my daughter because I will happily drag your sorry arse through every court in the land.'

She blanched. 'What? How dare you? Your daughter is aggressive and odd. She never plays with anyone and she's—'

'Let me stop you right there, Caroline, before you say something else that could be slanderous. Here's what we're going to do. I am going to give you sixty euros to pay for your doctor's appointment and you are never going to bother me or my child again.' I handed her the money, then, to Clara, I said, 'Clara, from now on you stay away from Angela and, Angela, I want you to stay away from Clara.'

Turning on my heels I marched down the road to my waiting taxi, Clara at my side. I could hear

188

Caroline shouting at Helen that Clara would have to be expelled and that I was a monster. I smiled. I doubted she'd bother me again.

In the taxi on the way home I asked Clara if she minded not playing with Angela.

'No, Mummy.'

'Do you play with any of the other kids sometimes?'

She shook her head. 'Not really. I did make a birdhouse with David one time but he wasn't very good. He was too slow.'

'Do you like the school? Because if you don't, we can try another one.' I wanted her to be happy.

She looked out of the window. 'I'd like to stay at home with my bird books. School is very noisy, Mummy.'

'I know, sweetheart, but you need to go to school to become even more clever than you already are.'

'OK, Mummy.' She sighed.

I leant over and hugged her. My little angel.

Two minutes later I dropped Clara home, where I had arranged for Christelle to be waiting, and headed back to work.

The next morning I decided to drop Clara at school in case Caroline would say something to her or try to harass Christelle. I saw her talking to a group of other mothers outside the school gate. When I arrived they stopped talking and stared at me. I waved. 'Morning, ladies.' Caroline turned her back on me.

I walked Clara to the door, where Helen was waiting. Clara went in, hung her coat on her peg and headed straight for the Lego. She looked so small and alone. I hoped she'd be all right and the other kids wouldn't be mean to her.

'Louise, could I have a word?' Helen asked.

I sighed. 'If this is about yesterday, I've dealt with it. I have nothing more to say.'

Helen nodded. 'It's not. Well, it is, but it's not just about yesterday. It's about a few things, really.'

I crossed my arms. 'Go on.'

Helen asked her assistant to keep an eye on the children while she ushered me into a small office. 'Please take a seat,' she said.

I remained standing. 'I'm fine. I really don't have much time. I've a meeting at nine thirty in town.'

Helen took out a folder, which she nervously began to fidget with. 'Louise, I wanted to talk to you about Clara.'

'I gathered that.'

She smiled. 'Clara is a wonderful child, so ahead of her peers in many ways. Her language skills and reading ability are astonishing.'

'I know. She's exceptionally bright.'

Helen nodded. 'Yes, she is. I'm a little concerned about her social skills. She is very much a loner, and although I've tried to get her to play with the other children, she refuses.'

'She prefers her own company. I think it's

because she's so bright and also because she's an only child – she spends a lot of time with grown-ups.'

Helen twisted her wedding ring around her finger. 'She seems very reluctant to make eye contact with others. Does she do this at home too?'

I glanced at the clock. I had five minutes left and then I had to go or I'd be late. 'She's shy. Shy kids don't like looking at people's faces. It's just the way they are.'

'Have you noticed her being a little clumsy? When we do our exercises she has trouble with her balance.'

I smiled. 'Look, I'm sporty, but my sister Julie is a disaster. She has two left feet. Poor Clara's just inherited it from her.'

'I see.' Helen's cheeks were red now. 'Clara also gets very fixated on things. It can be difficult to persuade her to sit at the table and engage with the class. She gets very lost in her own thoughts.'

'So what? She's ten times brighter than any of the other children.' I really needed to go. 'She's always been obsessed with birds. But so are lots of children. Now I'm afraid I have to go or I'll be late for my meeting.'

Helen stood up. 'Louise, I wondered if you'd ever considered having Clara evaluated.'

I put on my coat. 'Her IQ? Yes. I'm thinking about it.'

'No, for behavioural and developmental issues.'

I laughed. 'She bit someone, Helen. She's not insane!'

As I opened the door, Helen handed me an envelope. 'Please just read this.'

'Fine.' I dashed out of the door and headed for work.

CHAPTER 15

Sophie

The cocktails-and-canapés party was in full swing when I arrived. It was being thrown by Style Central department store to introduce everyone to its new management team in Ireland. I really wanted to sign them up as a client. They currently used several modelling agencies, but my aim was to secure exclusivity for the Beauty Spot.

I searched for Quentin. He caught my eye and waved. I crossed the room, which was full of industry people and models, all looking suitably stylish.

Quentin, in his favourite red velvet suit, greeted me warmly and introduced me to the man he was talking to. 'Darling, this is Andrew Longhurst. He's the new financial controller of Style Central.'

Andrew was extremely attractive.

'Great to meet you,' I said, giving him my best smile.

'Sophie is my partner in the Beauty Spot, but not in life.' Quentin chuckled at his own joke.

'I have a feeling your partner in life would be more of a Simon than a Sophie,' Andrew said, with a grin. Then, turning back to me, he added, 'Very nice to meet you. I've heard great things about the Beauty Spot. You have a reputation for hiring the best-looking models.'

I smiled. 'We aim to please.'

'That's music to my ears.' Andrew gave me a flirty wink.

'I must go and see about . . . something.' Quentin wandered off and gave me the thumbs-up behind Andrew's back. I tried not to laugh.

Andrew and I chatted about work and life. He was very charming and attentive and I could feel myself coming alive again. It was so nice to feel attractive for once. I had barely been out since my fiasco with Julian, and Andrew was good-looking, confident and funny. I smiled, flirted and laughed a lot. I was the old Sophie, the fun Sophie, the happy Sophie. I felt my confidence soaring. I could tell that Andrew was attracted to me. There was an electricity between us. But I was wary. I didn't want to make a fool of myself again. Yet it was hard to resist the chemistry.

I never normally drank at work events, but I allowed myself one glass of wine. I was having too much fun. It didn't feel like work. It felt very much like play.

When Andrew told me a funny story about his time at university, I laughed loudly. 'You're so funny,' I said, batting my eyelids at him.

'And you're a very beautiful woman,' he said.

Yes! He did like me. I wasn't imagining it or misreading the signs. I could feel my cheeks flushing and my eyes sparkling. I missed male attention so much. This was wonderful.

Andrew and I chatted on and after about an hour he asked me if I was attached. I flicked my hair back. 'No, I'm divorced, but I have a daughter, Jess. She's nine.' I wanted to be upfront and I never hid Jess. I was proud to be a mum and she would always come as part of my package.

'Me too,' he said. 'I'm separated with two daughters. Kate is fifteen and Amber is thirteen.'

'It looks like we have a lot in common.' I smiled up at him.

'It certainly does. I'd like to know exactly how much.' He smiled a slow, sexy smile and my stomach flipped. 'How about we get out of here and have a drink somewhere away from our colleagues?'

I wanted to jump up and down and whoop but, thankfully, I managed to control myself. 'I'd like that. Just let me grab my coat.' I floated to the cloakroom to pick it up.

As I was putting it on, Quentin pounced on me. 'Well?'

I grabbed his hands. 'Oh, Quentin, he's perfect. We really hit it off. He's taking me out for a drink now!'

Quentin hugged me. 'I'm so glad. You really

need cheering up. It's been rotten for you lately. Now go out and shag him senseless.'

We giggled like teenagers. 'I feel young again,' I admitted.

'You're glowing. Now go. Don't leave him waiting.'

Two drinks and a lot more flirting later, Andrew dropped me home in a taxi. He walked me to the door and bent to kiss me. I lifted my face to his and we kissed deeply and hungrily. I could feel all of my senses burning. I really wanted to have sex, but I couldn't bring him up to my apartment with Jess there.

'I would love to ask you up, but the apartment is small and my daughter is a light sleeper.'

He cupped my cheek with his hand. 'It's OK, I understand. We'll just have to do this again soon.'

'I'd really like that.'

'I'll call you.'

'Great.' As he turned to go, I pulled him back and kissed him again. It had been years since I had kissed a man passionately. I longed for the physical closeness.

'Wow, you're quite a tiger, I bet you're fantastic in bed.'

'If you play your cards right, you may just find out.' I winked at him and went into the lobby of my apartment. All the dating books would have said, 'Don't look back,' but I couldn't resist. I turned to see if he was still there. He was standing at the door watching me go. Yes!

When I walked into the apartment, Gavin and Shania were flaked out on the couch, watching a movie.

'Is Jess asleep?' I asked.

'Yep, she's been in bed since nine thirty, as instructed.' Gavin yawned.

'Thanks. Sorry I'm a bit late.'

'You're all glowy.' Shania was looking closely at my face. 'OMG, did you get laid?'

'Dude, that's my sister.' Gavin was appalled.

I blushed bright red.

'Oh, my God, did you?' Gavin asked.

'NO! Stop staring at me. You're making me really uncomfortable.' I pulled a cushion over my face like a child.

'I think someone's had a hot date,' Shania teased.

'Who were you with? I thought you said you were going to a work thing,' Gavin said.

'It was a work event, but I did meet someone very nice.'

'Go on,' Shania encouraged me.

'Well, he asked me out for a drink and we had a lovely time.'

'Did you arrange to meet up again?' she asked.

'He said he'd call.'

'That's, like, amazeballs. I love when you meet

someone and they give you butterflies in your tummy. It's so awesome.' Shania beamed at me.

'Did you feel like that when you met me?' Gavin asked.

'Totally, babe,' she said, planting a kiss on his cheek.

I kicked off my shoes and sank into the couch. 'How's work going?' I asked Gavin.

'Good, actually. I've been promoted to assistant manager.'

'He's being totally fast-tracked,' Shania said proudly. 'They love him in Stars and Stripes. I think he's going to end up being, like, the CEO or something.'

'That's great, Gavin. Well done.'

He shrugged modestly, but I could see he was thrilled. Gavin knew that we all thought he was a bit of a joke when it came to working. It was good to see him sticking to something and being successful at it.

'What about you?' I asked Shania. 'Do you like working in Stars and Stripes?'

She wrinkled her nose. 'I'm just there while I try to work out what I really want to do. Daddy wants me to do a Cordon Bleu cookery course in France, but I'm so not into cooking. It's boring. Besides, I'm, like, totally dyslexic so I struggle to read English. Trying to read French cookbooks would be torture.'

'Have you ever thought of modelling?' I asked.

'I did a bit when I first left school, but I got,

like, sick after doing a bikini shoot in January and ended up in hospital with a really bad chest infection. So my dad was, like, no way.'

'What did your mum think?'

'She died when I was ten, so . . .'

'Gosh, I'm sorry. That must have been awful.' I tried to picture Jess if I died and felt tearful.

'Yeah, it was, but I've had loads of therapy so I'm fine now,' Shania reassured me.

'Well, if you ever wanted to try modelling again, I promise I'd look after you and make sure you'd never have to do a bikini shoot in January.'

Shania looked at me. 'Really? Maybe I will try it again. I'm kind of over folding clothes and dealing with teenage girls stamping on my toes and pushing me out of the way to flirt with the guys in work.'

Gavin stood up and stretched. 'Actually, babe, that could be cool for you. Stars and Stripes is a waste of your talent. You could be the next Irish supermodel. You should be modelling our clothes, not selling them.'

I wasn't sure about Ireland's next top model. Shania had a very pretty face but it was more suited to catalogue work than high-end fashion. Mind you, she'd look good on a runway: her legs went on for ever.

'OK. Give me your digits and I'll call you.' Shania picked up her bag.

Gavin, sensing my confusion, explained, 'It means your phone number.'

'Oh, right.' I smiled. I might not feel it tonight after my date, but I was old. I'd have to try to keep up so I'd know what Jess was talking about. I didn't want to be one of those mothers who hadn't a clue what was going on. I bet Pippa knew what 'digits' meant. I'd have to work harder at keeping up so Pippa didn't totally take over my daughter's affections.

Shania typed my number into her phone, then she and Gavin left. I tidied up the living room and went in to check on Jess. She was sleeping peacefully. She looked so young and sweet. I tidied her clothes and put her books in a neat pile on her desk. When I glanced up, I saw it. In the middle of the cluster of photos on the cork board over her desk there was a big picture of Pippa and Jack. They were at some black-tie ball. Pippa was wearing a shimmering silver dress and Jack was gazing at her adoringly . . . the way he used to look at me.

It was obvious that Pippa had given Jess the photo to put up. Clearly she hadn't been happy to see all the photos of Jack with me and had wanted to stamp her mark. The sneaky cow. I was tempted to take the photo down and rip it into tiny pieces, but I knew Jess would go mad. So I left it . . . for now. It might just get vacuumed up 'by accident' during the week. It was bad enough that Pippa was living with my husband, having his baby and worshipped by my daughter. I didn't need her stupid face beaming at me in my own home as well. She must have been born without a single sensitive bone in her irritatingly perfect body.

The next day I hummed as I put on my makeup. I applied it carefully, smiling to myself as I thought about my great night. I looked younger and everything about me seemed shinier. It made me realize that I hadn't been happy in a long time. I decided to wear my Prada dress, the one I had kept from the good old days. I got dressed, stood in front of the mirror and, for the first time in ages, I liked what I saw. Instead of concentrating on my flaws I focused on the positives, and it wasn't half bad.

When I came into the kitchen, Jess was eating her cereal with her earplugs in, listening to music.

I leant down and pulled them out. She glared at me.

'You know it's rude,' I said. 'So, what's happening today in school? Anything interesting?'

Jess rolled her eyes. 'School is the same every day, *boooor*ing.'

'Well, I hope you're working hard. I want you to do well in school. Every woman needs to be able to work—'

Jess cut across me '—and earn her own money. God, Mum, you're always going on about it.'

'That's because it's important, Jess. After what happened to Dad's company, if I hadn't been able to work, we would have been homeless.'

'No, we wouldn't. Granny and Granddad would have let us stay with them.'

'The point is, you need to be able to earn money in case anything goes wrong. I learnt it the hard way. I want you to go to college and be brilliant, like your aunt Louise.'

'I want to be a TV presenter like Pippa. She didn't go to college.'

I took a deep breath. It was astonishing how quickly my good mood had vanished. 'I didn't go to college either and I wish I had. Louise doesn't need a man to look after her or Clara. She's completely self-sufficient. I really admire her for it.'

'Louise is kind of scary, Mum. She never laughs or has fun.'

'Yes, she does.'

'When?'

I paused. When did Louise have fun? She worked long hours and was very serious about her job and about raising Clara. The weekends were full of exercise and educational activities with Clara. Had I seen her laughing and having fun lately? Not really.

Then again, until last night, I hadn't had any fun for ages either. And Julie didn't seem to be having a barrel of laughs. Gosh, when had we all got so serious and stern? We did laugh together sometimes, but Jess was right: of we three sisters, Louise was probably the one who let go the least. She was very controlled and controlling.

I wondered if she had fun with the man she had sex with. I hoped so. But somehow I couldn't see Louise whooping with laughter during foreplay. I could more easily imagine her ordering him about – 'To the left . . . up a bit . . . Harder . . . Deeper.' I smiled to myself. I doubted Louise ever relinquished control, even in the bedroom.

I decided to change the subject. 'So, what do you fancy doing this weekend? I was thinking we could go and see that new *Glee* movie on Saturday.'

Jess played with her spoon. 'Actually, Mum, Pippa has tickets to the première on Thursday night, and she wants to take me. Dad's away working, so she wants me to be her date.'

Of course she had tickets to the première. Anything I could do, bloody Pippa could do better. 'It's a school night, Jess,' I reminded her.

'I know, but it's going to be amazing. Apparently the new guy, Brad Hooper, is flying into Dublin for the première and he is, like, so gorgeous. You have to let me go, Mum, you *have* to.'

'I don't actually have to let you do anything, Jess.'

She slammed her hand on the table. 'Don't say no. Do not ruin my life.'

I sighed. 'Can you please not be so dramatic? I just don't—'

My phone buzzed. I glanced down. It was Andrew: *Morning. I really enjoyed last night. U free Thurs for dinner?*

I looked up at Jess, who was waiting with bated breath for my answer. 'OK, you can go.'

She jumped up and hugged me. She hadn't done that in months. It felt so nice. I hugged her back. Andrew was already having a positive impact on my life.

CHAPTER 16

Julie

Harry droned on and on about investments, stocks rising, blue-chip companies, commodities . . . I sipped my wine and looked around the restaurant.

'Julie?'

'What?'

'Have you been listening to a word I've said?' Harry asked.

'Honestly? No. I'm sorry, Harry, but all you talk about is money. When we had none I hated talking about it, and now that we have a lot, I still don't want to talk about it. I feel that money has had a stranglehold on us for ever, whether we were poor or rich. Can we please talk about something else?'

'I just want to keep you in the loop about our investments, but if you really aren't interested, I won't bother.'

Harry was grumpy with me because I'd forced him to cancel a dinner with Donald to go for dinner with Sophie and Andrew. Sophie seemed really smitten and I wanted to be supportive. I was interested to meet Andrew, too. It had been just a few weeks, but Sophie talked about him constantly.

'Look, Harry, I trust you with our finances. I know you'll do the best for our family. I'm confident you'll be careful with the money. When we had none, I spent a lot of time budgeting and worrying, so I just want to enjoy not having to stress about it now. OK?'

Harry folded his napkin. 'Fair enough. I just don't want to end up like Sophie and Jack.'

'We won't, because you're not a risk-taker. I'm sure all your investments are very solid and secure.'

Harry looked affronted. 'I take risks sometimes.'

I snorted. 'When?'

'That time I went surfing.'

'Harry, it was ten years ago and you lasted five minutes. Come on, you're not someone who likes danger and I'm glad of that.'

'But you're saying I'm dull.'

'No, I'm not. I'm saying you're sensible, which is a good thing.'

'Would you prefer if I went out and bought a Lamborghini and a speed boat?'

'No. I'd prefer you not to play golf all weekend. I'm always on my own and I hate it. It's bad enough being alone all week – the weekends should be precious. You need to spend more time at home with me and the boys.'

'The golf pro said I need to play in weekend

tournaments to get my handicap down. Besides, I'm going to the boys' rugby with you tomorrow.'

'Big deal. You played golf all last weekend and you're playing all day Sunday. And you're always having dinner at the club with Donald or one of the other men you think are so great.'

'I'm enjoying it. I thought you'd be pleased that I've found a sport I like to play. You used to say I needed a hobby.'

'Yes, but not one that takes over your life. Why can't you play tennis for an hour instead of golf for a whole day?'

'Why don't you take it up too? We could play together.'

I sighed. I didn't want to join his stupid golf club. I didn't want to have to make a huge effort getting to know lots of new women, who probably wouldn't like me anyway. I could think of nothing worse than being stuck for four hours smacking a small ball into bushes while making conversation with strangers. It was bad enough having to go to Castle Academy every day and see all those mothers who avoided me. My confidence had been knocked badly since the concert. I was completely paranoid about all the parents thinking we were dragging down the school's name and trying to get the triplets kicked out.

After the concert Harry and I had had a huge argument. I wanted to take the triplets out immediately. I didn't want them to stay in a school where the parents were so snobby. But he had dug his heels in because, despite the rudeness of some of the parents, the triplets were happy and thriving. He refused even to consider moving them.

I'd felt better after we'd received their report cards. They were, for the first time ever, really good. The boys had never had good reports before. The teachers in Castle Academy, who were mostly young males, seemed to 'get' them. They understood boys. They knew how to channel their endless energy. Harry was probably right: there was no point moving them now that they were settled and doing well, no matter how awful some of the parents were. I'd just have to 'suck it up'.

Harry was particularly impressed with the comments from the rugby coach, who said he thought the triplets were 'extremely talented' and had 'high hopes' for their future in the sport. Harry was a huge rugby fan and, although he had never been good at it himself, he was very keen for the boys to play and was thrilled that they had impressed the coach already. I was just hoping they'd be good at rugby because I knew all the practice would tire them out.

Harry's phone rang. 'Sorry, I need to take this. It's Donald about our game on Sunday.' He stood up and walked outside to talk to his new best friend.

I sighed, sipped my wine, then took out my own phone and sent Dan a text: *How u?*

A message came straight back: *Was just thinking*

about you! Saw movie last night with a young Juliette Binoche. She reminds me of you. Very sexy!

I felt the blood rush to my cheeks and a thrill in my stomach. I bent my head and typed, *Not so sexy any more.*

He came straight back: *Bet u are!*

Well . . .

Harry came back to the table and sat down. 'Who are you texting?' he asked.

I quickly put my phone away. 'Just Sophie,' I lied. 'She said she's sorry she's late and she's only a minute away.'

'How's her romance going?' Harry asked.

'Really well. She's a new woman,' I told him. 'It's so lovely to see her happy again. It's very early days, but this guy has already given her confidence such a boost. I hope it works out. She's had a tough time.'

'Well, that's what you get for marrying a tosser.'

'Jack wasn't that bad.'

Harry raised an eyebrow. 'He was incredibly arrogant.'

He had never liked Jack. To be honest, none of us had. He was so flash with his money, always buying bigger cars and fancier holidays . . . There was nothing subtle about Jack. But Sophie had bought into the lifestyle. She loved it too. She had been hard to relate to then. Louise and I had definitely drifted away from her. All she ever talked about was shopping and fashion, jewellery and beauty treatments. She had become very caught up in her moneyed life and rather shallow. We all preferred the new Sophie. She was so much more open, honest and kind.

When we had come into money I had worried that I might end up losing the run of myself and turn into a superficial 'lady who lunches' too. But when I'd voiced my worries to Marian, she roared laughing, and said, 'Sorry, Julie, but you just wouldn't fit in. Those ladies wouldn't have you. You're not glamorous or phoney enough. They don't spend weeks making Death Eater costumes for Hallowe'en like you. They don't read the sports section of the paper like you do so that you can chat to the boys about football. You're never going to be one of them, so stop worrying about it.'

Marian, as usual, had been blunt but right. I would never fit in with Sophie's old crowd of socialites, as I had found out at Castle Academy, and didn't want to. They were not my type of people. Marian was my type and she was completely bonkers.

'*Hiiiii,*' Sophie trilled, rushing in and kissing me and Harry on the cheek. 'This is Andrew,' she said, introducing a tall, attractive man in his mid-forties.

Andrew reminded me a bit of Jack. He had the look of someone who spent just a little too much time getting dressed. His shirt was clearly tailor-made, his trousers were a perfect fit, his hair looked like he'd just stepped out of a salon. He had a big gold Rolex watch and veneered teeth. He was exactly Sophie's type. I couldn't help feeling a stab of disappointment. I had hoped the new Sophie would go for someone different.

They sat down and we ordered some food. Sophie kept touching Andrew's arm and laughing far too loudly at everything he said. He really wasn't that funny.

'So, Andrew, Sophie tells me you have two daughters,' I said.

'That's right. Kate is fifteen and Amber is thirteen. I can tell you, the teenage years are a nightmare.'

'Oh, God, don't say that. The boys are a handful as it is,' Harry said.

'Sophie told me you have triplets and then another boy.'

'Yes, we're a testosterone-fuelled household.' I smiled.

'I'd love a son. Girls are a bloody headache.'

'Well, they can certainly be tricky,' Sophie said.

'I sent my two to boarding-school this year. They need a firm hand. My ex has no sense. She just gives them whatever they want. They were turning into spoilt brats, so I put my foot down.'

'Do they like it?' I asked.

He grinned. 'They hate it, but they'll get used to it. I went to boarding-school. It makes you grow up and be independent.'

The waitress came back with our main courses. I noticed Andrew glancing at her legs a little too closely. He caught me watching him and, instead of being embarrassed, he winked at me. 'I'm a sucker for legs. Luckily, Sophie's got a great pair.' He reached down and rubbed Sophie's thigh. She giggled and leant in to kiss him.

I looked at Harry, who subtly raised an eyebrow.

'So, Harry, what do you do? Sophie told me you came into a pile of money recently.'

Harry's fork froze mid-air. He coughed. 'Well, my aunt kindly left us some. But I work in IT for the county council.'

'A civil servant!' Andrew snorted. 'So you're one of those guys who gets ten weeks' holidays a year and works three hours a day.'

Harry bristled. 'Not quite.'

'What do you do, Andrew?' I asked, changing the subject before Harry poked him in the eye with his fork.

He sat back in his chair and, in a very bad attempt at modesty, proclaimed, 'Oh, I'm just a cog in the Style Central wheel. Isn't that right, Sophie?'

Sophie punched his arm playfully. 'Andrew is the financial controller of Style Central.'

Andrew shrugged. 'Well, I do my bit.'

God, he was annoying.

Sophie babbled on: 'He's amazing with people as well as figures. Everyone in the company loves him.'

'Your sister is easily impressed.' Andrew chuckled.

'Yes, she is,' I said, irritated by him.

'No, I'm not.' Sophie frowned at me. 'I just know a great man when I meet one.'

'What about Sophie here?' Andrew said. 'Partner in her own business. Gorgeous and smart. Killer combination, don't you think, Harry?'

Harry, who had been checking his phone under the table, looked up. 'What? Oh, yes, Sophie's great.'

'And hot.' Andrew nuzzled her neck. When he came up for air, he turned back to me. 'What do you do, Julie? Are you one of those domestic goddesses?'

Harry snorted into his wine.

'I'm a full-time mum,' I said. I hated saying it. Even though it was true, even though I chose to be at home, even though I knew there was nothing wrong with it, I always cringed when I said it. It sounded so lame and utterly underachieving. When I'd worked for the newspaper I'd been able to say I was a columnist, which I'd loved. It had made me feel less insignificant, but now I had nothing to offer. 'I'm a full-time mum' translated socially as 'I do nothing, I'm boring and uninteresting. Run away from me now before my dullness rubs off on you.' Saying it made me feel useless and ashamed. I knew it didn't make sense, but that was how I felt.

'Good for you. We need more of those,' Andrew said, patting my arm. I thought briefly about stabbing his hand with my knife but managed to control the urge. 'Stay-at-home mums are unsung heroes. Looking after children is such a hard job. I really admire you, Julie. We guys don't appreciate all that you do. Am I right, Harry?'

'Uhm . . . yes, I suppose so,' Harry said, and tugged his earlobe. It was our secret SOS sign to each other. Harry wanted to get the bill and go. He wasn't alone.

He pretended to go to the Gents and discreetly paid so we could get the hell out of there.

Andrew's phone rang. It was the James Bond theme tune. I tried not to laugh. 'Hello?' he bellowed. 'Speaking . . . Oh, hello, John. Can you hold on just one minute?' Turning to Sophie and me, he said, 'Sorry, lovely ladies, I have to take this. It's the CEO of Style Central. He needs some advice. You know how it is, never off the clock.'

'You never stop,' Sophie told him.

'Back in a minute. Don't go anywhere, gorgeous. The night is young.' Andrew squeezed Sophie's thigh yet again, then got up and went to the foyer, where we could still hear him talking loudly into the phone.

'So?' Sophie looked at me excitedly. 'What do you think? Isn't he wonderful?'

'Yes . . . Well, he's very self-assured and he seems keen on you.'

'I know.' Sophie sighed, like a cartoon princess. 'I really think this is it, Julie. He's the one. I'd completely given up hope. I never thought I'd be lucky in love again, but he's perfect.'

'Just be careful, Sophie, it's very early in the relationship. Take it slowly.'

She smiled. 'Julie, when you know, you know. Andrew is the one.'

I didn't know what else to say. How could I protect her without hurting her? If I told her what I really thought of Andrew, she'd hate me.

'Sophie, all I want is for you to be happy, but please don't jump in feet first. Take your time with Andrew, there's no rush. Get to know him properly before deciding he's the one.'

Sophie squeezed my hand. 'You don't have to worry about me any more. I've found the perfect man. I'm really happy for the first time in years.'

'What a complete tosser,' Harry said, rinsing his toothbrush.

I sighed. 'I know, but she's in love.'

'She needs someone nice and decent. Why does she always go for these idiots?'

'She likes confident, flashy guys.'

'She's far too good for him.' Harry switched off the bathroom light and climbed into bed.

I lay down beside him. 'You're right, but I have to admit Sophie is happier than I've seen her in years. Maybe he's not as bad as he seems. Maybe he just gives a very bad first impression.' I was trying to convince myself more than anything.

Harry turned off his bedside lamp. 'I don't have much confidence that Andrew's going to grow on anyone. The man is obsessed with himself.'

'I just hope he's nice to her and doesn't break her heart,' I said, turning off my own light. 'And speaking of sisters, we're having Clara to stay next week. Louise has to go to Brussels and Christelle's away, so she's stuck.'

'We probably won't even notice she's here, the poor thing is so quiet. I hope she'll be all right with the noise in our house,' Harry said.

'Noise really seems to bother her. I'm looking forward to having her over and getting to know her better. She's always got her head stuck in a book or rushing off to some after-school activity. I'm happy that I'll get to spend some time with her.'

'I presume Louise will be sending you a detailed document pertaining to Clara's routine.'

I looked at him and smiled. 'I'd say it'll be a thesis. I'll have to stay up late and study it. Imagine if I get something wrong – she'll never speak to me again.'

We laughed.

Harry pulled up the duvet and rolled onto his side.

'Do you fancy some Friday-night sex?' I asked. 'It's been a while.'

He yawned. 'Sorry, Julie, I'm wiped out and we have to be up early for the boys' rugby. Can I take a rain check?'

'Fine.' I rolled away from him to the other side of our enormous bed. At least Sophie would be having sex tonight, unlike me.

Harry fell asleep straight away. Once I heard the snoring start up, I sent a text to Dan. I was feeling cross and restless.

Juliette B is saying goodnight.

What is JB wearing to bed?

Something French & frilly!

Stoooooop, now I really can't concentrate.

I giggled and typed, *Bonne nuit.*

I'm picturing u & getting hot under collar!

Concentrate!

I can't.

Try harder.

Ur killing me here. I'm horny as hell!

I squirmed with embarrassment and delight. It was like being a teenager again. I hadn't flirted with anyone in decades. I knew we were being a bit naughty, but it was fun. Besides, he lived on a different continent, what harm could it do? I sent a final text, *Easy, tiger! I'm signing off now before u get urself into trouble.*

Thanks a lot, JB! Get me all worked up and then go to sleep!

I decided to end the conversation. It was getting a bit too intimate. *Talk soon, love, JB. Xx*

I deleted the messages, lay back in bed beside my snoring husband and thought about sex with Dan.

CHAPTER 17

Louise

When I arrived at my parents' house for lunch, Gavin was already there, flaked out on the sofa watching football. 'Not working today, then?' I asked.

'Don't start. I've worked twelve days straight. Two of my staff have been out with the flu. I'm wrecked.'

'Welcome to the world of responsibility. So, how are things going?' I handed Clara her bird book and she sat on the floor beside Gavin.

'Apart from working my arse off, it's going pretty well, actually. My store's sales are up by six per cent, so I'm getting a lot of high-fives from the management.'

'Wow, that's impressive. How did you do it?'

He winked at me. 'I hired the hottest bird you've ever seen. I swear, Louise, she looks like Eva Mendez, but taller and with a bigger rack. I have her standing outside the shop in this little crop top and denim shorts. If it's, like, really freezing I let her wear a cardigan, but it has to be open.

Those knockers have got to be on view. No hetero-sexual dude can walk by without staring at her, and when she asks them to come into the shop and look around, they literally cannot say no. She tells them what they should buy and they just nod and obey.'

I rolled my eyes. Gavin was always going to be a man-child.

'What's a heterosexual?' Clara asked.

I looked at Gavin. 'Would you like to explain that to my four-and-a-half-year-old?'

He shrugged. 'It's when boys like girls and girls like boys.'

'I'm a girl and I don't really like boys, so what am I called?'

'Martina Navratilova.' He snorted.

I swiped the back of his head with my hand. 'Stop it.'

I leant down to Clara. 'Darling, you find boys a bit noisy and annoying now. I did, too, when I was little. But when you get older, you'll probably see that they can be fun.'

Clara shook her head. 'I don't think so, Mummy.'

Gavin interrupted. 'Clara, you like me, don't you?'

'Yes.'

'Well, when you're a big girl, if you're really, really lucky, you might meet a boy like me.'

'But you're not a boy, you're a man,' she pointed out.

'That's debatable.' I smirked.

'She's impossible to argue with – she's like a genius in a tiny body.'

I smiled. 'So what does Shania think of your hot new staff member?' I asked, presuming Shania wouldn't be as thrilled about her as Gavin was.

'She quit. She's working with Sophie now.'

'Did you break up?'

'No, we're totally together. Sophie offered her some modelling work. The money was better, and it's a lot more fun than folding T-shirts, so she left.'

I was glad: despite Shania's dodgy American accent, she was a sweet girl and for some reason she seemed to think Gavin was great. Also, if I'm being honest, the fact that her father was loaded was also a bonus. While Gavin seemed to be doing well and was enthusiastic about Stars and Stripes, he could change his mind easily and get bored. So if he did end up with a rich girl, it would take the pressure off us having to bankroll him.

Dad came in. 'Ah, there you are. How are things?'

'Good, thanks.'

'How's my little pet?' he said, bending down to say hello to Clara, who kept her head stuck in her book.

'Say hello, darling,' I urged her.

She kept reading.

'Never mind, she's just like you were. Once you had your head stuck in a book, you never looked up.'

Sophie and Jess arrived. Sophie was wearing a black fur coat.

Dad stared at her with disapproval. 'How many animals died for that?'

'It's *faux*-fur,' Sophie replied.

'It's a bit much for a Sunday afternoon,' Dad said.

'No offence, Dad, but I'm hardly going to take fashion advice from a man wearing a brown jumper with a golf ball on it.'

'What's wrong with it?'

'Everything,' Sophie and I said, at the same time.

'I've given him some cool stuff from the shop, but he won't wear it,' Gavin said.

'For God's sake, I'm not going around with a T-shirt that's sprayed onto me or some stupid sweatshirt with a surfboard on it.'

'To be fair, I don't think Dad would do your brand any favours,' Sophie said to Gavin.

'We're always looking to expand our market,' he drawled.

I laughed. 'Seventy-five-year-old men might be a little off the mark.'

Dad sat down beside Gavin to watch the football.

'How's Andrew?' I whispered, making sure Jess couldn't hear me. I needn't have worried. Jess was, as usual, sitting in the corner with her headphones plugged in. I thought kids became antisocial in their teenage years, not at nine. I hoped Clara wouldn't turn out like that in a few years' time. Julie had told me all about meeting Andrew, and he sounded awful. I was worried about Sophie.

'Brilliant.' Sophie's eyes sparkled at the mention of his name and she couldn't stop smiling. 'It's the first sex I've had since Jack. Can you believe it? It's been too long. God, it's great.'

'You certainly needed that!'

'I really did. Honestly, Louise, I was like a lunatic. I couldn't get enough. I hadn't realized how much I missed it. I'd kind of forgotten about it. Isn't that terrible?'

'It's like riding a bike, though – you never forget!' I winked at her.

'He's just so . . . well . . . perfect.'

Sophie was radiant. I hadn't seen her so happy in years. Maybe Andrew was just like Jack. None of us had liked Jack all that much, but he had made Sophie happy. Until he'd messed up.

I really hoped Andrew was keen on her – I could see she was besotted. If he wasn't, the rejection would be unbearable for her.

'It's amazing, Louise. I don't even care about Jack and Pippa and their baby any more. I'm just really happy for the first time in ages.'

I hugged her. 'You deserve it.' I meant it, but from Julie's awful description of him, I couldn't help wishing she was with someone who deserved her more.

There was the sound of shouting and thumping from outside. It was Julie, late as usual, with the boys. As she walked through the front door, Mum came in from the kitchen.

'Hello, everyone.' She kissed us all. She told me

I looked tired; she told Sophie she was wearing too much makeup; she told Gavin to get his feet off the couch; she told Julie to send the boys straight out into the garden, then asked where Harry was.

'Playing bloody golf,' Julie muttered.

'Again?' Sophie said. 'He's always playing these days.'

'He's obsessed with it,' Julie huffed.

'Ah, well, now, to be fair, it is an addictive game when you first take it up,' Dad pointed out.

Julie's phone beeped. She grabbed it from her jacket pocket and texted back. I was surprised as she usually ignored her phone or had it buried at the bottom of her bag.

'So we have no men at all today, then?' Mum said.

'Don't I count?' Gavin waved his hand.

'Sure you're only a boy,' Mum said.

'No, Granny. Gavin is a man. He's over eighteen, so he's a grown-up,' Clara corrected her.

'Thank you, Clara,' Gavin grinned. 'It's nice to have someone defend me in this house.'

Ignoring them, Mum complained, 'Three daughters and not a man in sight! You'd want to watch Harry,' she warned Julie, who was still texting.

'What?' Julie looked up.

'I said you'd need to be careful of Harry up in that golf club. He's very eligible now. They'll all know about his big windfall and, mark my words, the women will be all over him.'

'I think I'm safe enough. The only person he seems to be smitten with is Donald McGreegan. He's in awe of him. Honestly, it's like a teenage crush.'

'Donald is a good businessman, but he has a huge ego,' I said. I'd met him once at a business lunch and he was an insufferable bore. But he certainly knew how to make money. He was one of the only businessmen who hadn't been stung by the recession. He'd seen the property slump coming and sold everything.

'Well, Harry thinks he's God,' Julie said, with a hint of anger in her voice, which wasn't like her.

Julie's phone beeped again and she started texting.

Mum frowned. 'That's enough of that, Julie. Lunch is ready. Phones off.'

Julie finished her text, then put her phone on silent and placed it beside her on the table.

I sat Clara beside me and put her food on her plate the way she liked it. No food touching and the chicken cut up into very small pieces.

'No, Mummy, no chicken. It's too chewy.'

'Just a few very small bits,' I said. 'Look, I cut it up really small.'

'No, Mummy. I don't want it.'

'All right. Eat some peas and your mashed potato, then.'

Mum clicked her tongue. 'It's ridiculous, Louise. You indulge Clara too much. She only ever picks at her food. You need to stop pandering to her and let her get on with it. If you don't nip that in the bud now, you'll have trouble later.' Turning to Clara, she said, 'Come on now, eat up. Chicken is good for you.'

Clara shook her head. I could see she was clenching her fists under the table and I was worried that she might have a tantrum.

'Mum, drop it. She's getting upset,' I said firmly.

Mum raised her hands. 'Fine, she's your child, but I think you need to be a bit firmer with her.'

I needed to change the subject. 'Gavin said Shania is working with you now, Sophie. How is she getting on?'

'Really great. I must say, she's a very sweet girl, Gavin. You did well there. I'd hang onto her. She's a natural on the catwalk, too. We did a big show for Style Central last night and she really stood out. All of the Style Central team commented on how good she was.'

'I knew she'd rock it,' Gavin said, through a mouthful of food.

The triplets, followed by a frozen-looking Tom, tumbled into the room. Leo – well, actually, I'm not sure which of them it was: I can never tell them apart – complained to Julie, 'Mum, it's freezing out there. We've been out for ages. We're starving.'

'Sorry. Here, sit down and I'll get you some plates.'

Julie went into the kitchen and Mum called after her, 'Not my good ones, Julie. Anything chipped or old will do.'

The boys squashed in at the end of the table and noisily hoovered up the food Julie handed them.

'Slowly, boys, you'll give yourselves indigestion,' Mum said.

Ignoring her, they continued to shovel large fork-fuls of food into their mouths. Julie glanced at her phone and smiled. She texted back under the table so Mum couldn't see her.

'How's school, Jess?' Dad asked.

'Boring as usual,' she replied.

'Jess!' Sophie frowned at her.

'"Boring" is a silly word,' Mum said. 'You need to participate more and then you'll enjoy school.'

'I love school,' one of the triplets said.

'Me too. It's deadly. We get to play rugby every day,' another added.

'I like school too,' Tom said. 'And when I'm a big boy, I'm going to school with my brothers and I'm gonna play rugby too.'

'No, you won't. You're a midget,' his brother said.

'Yeah, no one's going to pick you for their team. You're too small and skinny,' said another.

Julie put her phone down. 'Leave Tom alone. He's a perfect size.'

The triplets laughed.

'Poor Tom,' Sophie said, patting his head. 'Ignore your mean brothers.'

Gavin put his fork down with a bang. 'Well, now you see what it was like for me with you three witches picking on me all the time. I was the Tom in our family.'

'No, you weren't,' I said. 'You're always coming out with this rubbish. The truth is you were spoilt rotten.'

'I was tormented by you. Remember when you all told me I was adopted, and that if I looked closely at the milkman, I'd see he was my dad? Or the time you babysat me, put the clock forward three hours and made me go to bed at five o'clock? You also told me that when the microwave pinged we had ten seconds to get out of the house before it exploded. You told me I was lazy—'

'Poor Gavin,' I interrupted. 'Having the run of the house when we all left home. Having your choice of bedroom, the TV all to yourself, the fridge full of your favourite food. You had Mum fussing over you, washing, ironing and cooking for you. Dad giving you pocket money even when you were finished college and should have been working. Poor you.'

'Not to mention the money I gave you in the good times,' Sophie said.

'And all the times you cried on my shoulder and I comforted you when your mad ventures didn't work out,' Julie reminded him.

'And all the jobs I helped you get,' I added.

'OK, OK!' He put his hands up. 'Maybe it wasn't quite so bad. But you three were no picnic.'

'I want money from Granddad and Sophie,' a triplet said.

'I want a TV all to myself,' said another.

'I want a fridge full of my favourite food,' the third added.

'I wish I was Uncle Gavin,' Tom said.

Sophie, Julie and I smirked at Gavin. He shrugged. 'I guess there were times when it was worse than others.'

The lunch went well until one of the triplets pushed another off his chair. He fell against the sideboard and smashed Dad's golf trophy.

Dad was livid, so we all left shortly after. Julie promised to replace it, but Dad told her it was irreplaceable and that her children were like wild animals. Julie was in tears leaving.

I followed her outside to her car. 'Don't mind Dad. He's just upset.'

'I'm sick of people saying my kids are animals.' She wiped away a tear. 'They're my children, for God's sake. How would you like it if they said Clara was a nightmare all the time? I know they're a handful, I live with them every day, but I love them and I'm fed up with people giving out about them.'

I felt bad. I thought the triplets were a nightmare too, but Julie was right: they were her kids and she adored them. It wasn't fair that everyone gave out about them. I hated anyone criticizing Clara in any way. I'd have to have a word with Mum and Dad about their attitude to the boys. They were tough going and they had broken a lot of things in Mum and Dad's house so I did understand their frustration, but I felt bad for Julie.

Later that evening, when I was putting Clara to bed, she asked me, 'Mummy, if cutting onions makes you cry, are there any vegetables that make you happy when you cut them?'

I bent down and kissed her nose. 'No, but you're very clever to think of that. Honestly, you amaze me.'

She smiled and rolled over, falling asleep almost immediately.

I went into the lounge and sat at the table to catch up on some work. I opened my briefcase to take out some files and caught sight of the envelope Clara's teacher had given me. I'd forgotten about it. Christelle had been taking Clara to school and collecting her all week, so I hadn't seen Helen.

I pulled out a sheet of paper from the brown envelope. It was headed, *Children with Asperger's Syndrome: symptoms and the importance of early diagnosis.*

What the hell?

CHAPTER 18

Sophie

Andrew handed me a box. It had a big red bow on it. I wanted to cry. It had been so long since a man had given me anything. I opened it and inside was a black lace bra, thong, suspender belt and fishnet stockings. I giggled.

'I want you to put those on when we get back to your place,' Andrew said.

'My pleasure.' I kissed him. Jess was with Jack, so we had the apartment to ourselves. Andrew was so wonderful. He made me laugh and he treated me like a princess. I felt absolutely like the old Sophie, the one before everything went wrong. 'Actually,' I said, leaning over and whispering into his ear, 'I'm not that hungry. Let's get out of here and try these out.

'God, you are so hot.'

We laughed all the way home. I never got to wear the new lingerie. We ended up having sex on the hall floor. Later that night, when we were lying in bed and Andrew was asleep, I cuddled into him and told him I loved him. I knew it was too soon to say it to his face, but I did love him. I really, truly did.

I floated into my morning meeting with Quentin.

'Wow, someone looks happy,' he said. 'I take it things are going well with Andrew?'

I nodded. 'Wonderful, actually.'

'Good. Long may it last.'

'It will. He's the one, Quentin, I'm sure of it. He's my second chance.'

Quentin turned his silver letter-opener around in his hand. 'OK, Sophie. As your friend I'm going to tell you to take it slowly, and as your partner in the firm I'm going to tell you that, whatever happens between you guys, we need the Style Central account. Losing the Harmann account was a big blow.'

He was right, it had been terrible. Harmann had accounted for a tenth of our annual revenue. 'Don't worry, Quentin, we've got the Style Central account in the bag. They were really happy with the fashion show we did last week. Andrew said he's running it by head office and hopes to have the go-ahead to sign us exclusively next week.'

Quentin looked relieved. 'Thank God for that. Well, whatever happens, don't break up with him until the contract is signed.'

I leant over the desk and patted his hand. 'I'm not letting this one go. He's a keeper. I know it sounds ridiculous after only five weeks but I'm forty-two and I know this is the guy for me.'

'Darling, you've never looked better. He's the tonic you needed. I just don't want you to rush into anything. You've got all the time in the world.'

I smiled. I knew Quentin was just looking out for me. Louise had called me during the week to say the same thing. But I wasn't some innocent, naïve twenty-year-old. I'd been around the block. I had a broken marriage, for God's sake. I knew what I was doing.

I got home before Jess came back from dinner with Jack so I had time to call Andrew for a quick chat. He was going to the UK for a week, so we wouldn't see each other. He got a bit saucy on the phone and told me how much he was looking forward to sex next Friday night after work. Style Central was hosting a charity fashion show for which we were providing the models, and we had arranged to go for dinner afterwards.

'Wear that lingerie I bought you,' Andrew said, 'and really high heels.'

The doorbell rang.

'Sorry!' I said. 'That's Jess. I have to go. But I promise I'll be so hot you won't know what hit you.'

I was still giggling as I answered the door. Jack was with Jess. 'Hi, Jack, great to see you.' I leant over to kiss his cheek.

He was startled: he wasn't used to me being so enthusiastic. I was usually so tired after work that I could barely hold a conversation.

'Do you want to come in for a glass of wine?' I asked him.

'Uhm, yeah, OK,' he said, staring at me with curiosity.

Jess turned to him, hands on hips. 'She has a boyfriend. That's why she's acting all hyper.'

I hadn't told Jess anything about Andrew. 'How do you know?' I asked her.

She rolled her eyes. 'Please, Mum, it's so obvious. You've gone from grumpy to all happy and bouncy. And you keep going into your room and whispering into your phone. It's so lame.'

'Don't speak to your mother like that. You're being rude.' Jess was clearly surprised that Jack had scolded her – I was a bit surprised myself. She slunk off to her room and slammed the door.

I poured Jack a glass of wine. He sank into the couch and sipped it. 'So,' he grinned at me, 'who's this guy?'

'Someone I met through work.' I grinned back.

Jack studied my face. 'You look great, Sophie. Really happy and . . . well, like the old Sophie.'

'Thanks. I feel about ten years younger. I hadn't realized how lonely I was until I met Andrew. It's not easy being a single mother.'

'I know.' Jack nodded. 'I'm glad you've met someone. You deserve it. I just hope he's a good guy and that he looks after you.'

'He's amazing.' I noticed Jack flinch slightly. Ha! Now he knew how I felt when he went on about Pippa. It wasn't easy to hear your ex waxing lyrical about their new love. I knew it was mean, but I decided to elaborate. 'He's really successful and treats me so well.'

'Great,' Jack said unenthusiastically.

I decided to stop being mean. I was happy so I should be nice. 'Anyway, how are you? How's Pippa's pregnancy?'

'Pippa's fantastic. She literally hasn't skipped a beat. She hasn't that long to go but she's still working and looking fantastic and she never complains.'

Normally a comment like that would have put me into a rage, but now I didn't care about Pippa, her fabulous body and her joyful pregnancy. 'Long may that last,' I said, and had a glug of wine.

'So, how long have you been seeing this guy?' Jack asked.

'A while.' I was deliberately vague.

'Is it serious?'

'Yes.'

'Well, you look great.'

'Thanks.' Jack had always wanted me to be thin and beautiful when we were married, which was why I'd spent so much time at the gym, the beauty salon and the dermatologist's surgery. It felt nice to have him look at me and see the old Sophie.

His phone rang. He answered immediately. 'Hey, baby.'

I tried not to throw up.

I could hear Pippa's loud voice. 'Hi, baby. Can

you pick up some rocket and hummus on your way home? Hurry up, I miss you.'

'Me too. I'm on my way.' Jack jumped to his feet.

Pippa really had him wrapped around her skinny little finger. If I had asked Jack to buy groceries, he would have hung up on me. Keeping the house running smoothly had been my job. He had had no interest in hearing about it or being asked to get involved. He had given me an unlimited budget and expected me to get on with it. Clearly things with Pippa were different.

'So, you do the shopping now, do you?' I couldn't help myself.

He frowned. 'Not a lot, but I help out when I can. Pippa works very hard.'

'Maybe I should have got a job when we were married and you would have helped out more.'

'You didn't want to work, Sophie. You liked hanging out with your friends, shopping and going to the gym.' He was getting annoyed.

'And you liked having me at home running a perfect house, being the perfect wife,' I retorted.

'Well, I guess we've both changed.' Jack picked up his coat and headed for the door.

Jess came out to say goodbye and hugged him. She barely ever hugged me. Jack kissed the top of her head. ''Bye, Jess. See you next Friday. I'll be home a bit late, I'm flying in from London, but Pippa will be there. And she's got a surprise for you.'

'OMG – what?' Jess looked ecstatic.

'I can't say. She'll kill me.'

'Give me a clue. I can't wait that long.' Jess hung onto her father's arm.

I hadn't seen Jess so animated in a while. Jack obviously got the sweet Jess. I got the bolshie one.

Jack smiled. 'OK, but don't let her know I told you. It's small and it's furry and it woofs.'

Jess screamed. 'A puppy? Seriously? I've wanted one for ever and Mum kept saying no. This is the best news ever! I love you, guys.' Jess threw her arms around her father.

Despite all of my loved-up happiness, I still wanted to stick a knife in Pippa's head – and, if I'm being honest, in Jack's, too.

CHAPTER 19

Julie

As I'd predicted, Louise came over the night before she went to Brussels with a file of instructions for me.

'I *have* raised four children, Louise. I do know what I'm doing.'

Louise looked up as Leo came sliding down the stairs on a tray, smashing into the wall opposite him. Thankfully, he was wearing his bicycle helmet, so he wasn't concussed or brain-damaged. Louise gave me one of her tight smiles. 'I think our approaches to parenting are a little different.'

I sighed. 'You don't have boys. Believe me, if you did, you'd understand why I have to let some things go. They need to burn off energy and it's been raining all afternoon, so I said they could play that game as long as they wore helmets.'

We watched as Harry came zooming down with Tom in his lap. He put his feet out to stop them crashing into the wall.

'Hi, Harry. Interesting game,' Louise said.

'It's good fun – you should try it.' Harry grinned

and took off his helmet. 'Right. I'm off to the club.'

My head snapped up. 'What? I thought you were staying in tonight. I told the boys we'd watch *Harry Potter* together.'

Harry shook his head. 'Sorry, Julie. Donald wants to introduce me to a top German banker he thinks I should meet. It's an honour to be included in the meal.'

I bit my tongue. I didn't want to have an argument in front of Louise. 'Fine, go.'

'I won't be late.'

I ignored him and turned back to Louise. Harry left the room.

She raised an eyebrow. 'I see what you mean about his interest in Donald.'

'It's as if he's having an affair, and it's doubly insulting because it's with an old man.'

'I suppose now that he has all this money, it's important to talk to people and decide carefully how to invest it.'

'But it's taken over his life. He obsesses about it, and he's so impressed by successful people it makes me sick. The old Harry didn't give a damn about any of that. The new Harry thinks wealthy businessmen are all wonderful.'

Louise tucked her legs under her on the couch. 'Well, it's probably the first time he's been exposed to top-level people and it can be a bit dazzling at first. I'm sure the novelty will wear off soon, when he sees how dull and pompous some of them are.'

'I hope so. I miss the old Harry, the one who didn't care what anyone did and wasn't trying to be part of some inner circle of businessmen. He's not much fun now. I kind of wish he'd never inherited the money.'

'Julie!'

I put my hands up. 'Our life is much easier and we have a lovely house and all that, but I feel I've lost Harry in the process.'

Louise smiled sympathetically. 'He'll come back down to earth. He's just getting used to it. I've seen it happen with clients who suddenly come into money. It puts them off balance for a while, but then they settle down.'

'I hope you're right. Anyway, let's not talk about it any more. I'm sick of it.'

Louise opened her colour-coordinated file. 'The main thing you need to know about Clara is that she's very specific about routine, and if things aren't done the way she's used to, she can have meltdowns.'

I waved a hand. 'Sure all kids are like that. I promise I'll follow the routine exactly as it is. We'll be fine. Now go off to Brussels and enjoy yourself.'

'Julie, you can't be casual about this,' Louise stressed. 'Clara needs everything to be exactly the way she's used to.'

'Louise, it's OK. I promise I'll do things exactly by the book. Harry is going to look after the boys and I'm going to devote myself to Clara. I'll read the instructions very carefully.'

Louise bit her lip. 'I just wish Christelle didn't have to keep visiting her mum in Paris. She knows Clara's routine.'

'Louise, relax, it'll be fine. I'll send you regular photos and updates, OK?'

Louise talked me through the routine. It was, as I'd imagined, completely over the top. She told me I had to have a stopwatch for Clara's bath! If I left Clara in for less than, or more than, fifteen minutes, she'd freak. I had to make sure she listed all kinds of birds before she went to sleep: if I didn't, she wouldn't drop off. She had to put her tights on inside out because she hated the feel of the seam at the end of the toes. Loud noise really upset her, so I had to try to keep the boys calm around her – fat chance! She had to get dressed in a very specific order: pants, vest, tights (inside out), top, skirt. If the skirt went on before the top, I'd be in trouble. She hated the smell of tuna and she had to have her food cut into small, bite-size pieces. She didn't like anything chewy, so meat and chicken were out, and she liked her food to be very salty . . .

I listened, I nodded, and I realized that my sister was mad. This was ridiculous. The child was being completely pandered to. That must be what happened when people had only one child. They treated them like precious jewels and overindulged them. It would do Clara the world of good to stay with us and muck in with the boys. She was far too quiet and shy. She needed to be brought out of herself. But I wanted Louise to stop fretting, so I promised to obey the rules.

'Clara doesn't really like to be touched by other people. She only hugs me, Christelle, Mum and Gavin. Don't take it personally. She's just reserved.'

'Louise, seriously, relax. I won't do anything she doesn't like. You know you can trust me.'

Louise clenched her fists. 'Sorry, it's just that because Clara is so clever and shy, people think she's odd but she isn't. She's just like I was.'

Louise kept saying that, but I remembered her differently. There was only sixteen months between us so we were very close growing up. Although Louise was like Clara in some ways – she was incredibly bright and was reading at four, too – I don't remember her being anywhere near as quiet as Clara. Louise was born opinionated and was always arguing with Mum and Dad. She was also very sporty and competitive. When we were small she was brilliant at climbing trees, running and gymnastics. She could do the splits at four while I could barely do a forward roll.

When Louise started at playschool, she took over the place. She bossed all the other kids around – even the older ones – and made everyone play her games, where she was always the star. Louise had been very outgoing and quite domineering while Clara was like a little mouse.

Louise stood up and paced around the living room. 'It just drives me insane when people try to put labels on my kid because they're too stupid to realize she's a genius.'

She was really wound up. Someone must have said something to her. Whoever it was, I bet they regretted it. I wouldn't want to be on the wrong side of Louise. She was pretty scary when she was angry. 'Is everything OK? Did someone upset you?' I asked gently.

Louise ran her hands through her hair. 'Oh, it's nothing. It's just . . . Clara's moron of a teacher is trying to psychoanalyse her. God, I hate these stupid women who think they know your child better than you do. They are IDIOTS.'

I hadn't seen Louise so angry in years. She was shaking with rage. I stood up and went over to her. I put my hand on her shoulder. 'Hey, don't let some silly teacher upset you. We all know how special Clara is and how brilliant her mind is – just like her mother's.' I could feel Louise's tension ease.

'Thanks, Julie. I'm sorry. I'm totally wound up because I hate leaving her and I'm overreacting to everything. I'll be fine.'

'How about a nice glass of wine?'

'That would be great, but only a small one – I'm driving.'

I went into the kitchen, dodging the boys on their whizzing trays. I poured Louise a small glass and myself a large one. I checked my phone. A message from Dan! *Q: What did the hurricane say to the coconut palm tree? A: Hold onto your nuts, this is no ordinary blow job!*

I giggled. He was always sending funny jokes,

photos and comments. Some were a bit cheesy, but it was fun. My life was so boring, and I loved having this contact with Dan: it was something to look forward to and it made me feel young again. I drank some wine and quickly texted back. *What's a blow job?!*

He came straight back with *U shld know, u used to give great ones.*

I gasped. Luke walked in. 'Mum, why is your face all red?'

'I'm just hot,' I lied, drinking more wine to settle my stomach. I always felt giddy after Dan's texts, but this was a whole new level.

I held the glasses up to my cheeks to cool down, then went back to Louise. I handed her a drink.

'Thanks, Julie, and thanks for taking Clara. I know you all think I'm over-protective, but she's so young and sensitive, I have to mind her.'

Liam came in naked, wearing my sunflower shower cap on his head. He was covered with talcum powder and had 'I am incredibel' written across his chest in my red lipstick.

'That's not how you spell "incredible",' I pointed out.

'What? Oh, crap.' He charged back up the stairs, leaving clouds of white powder in his wake.

I turned to my sister. 'As you can see, I'm in no position to judge anyone on their parenting.'

Louise laughed. We drank our wine, and she left me to study my notes on Clara.

* * *

The next afternoon, Louise dropped Clara at the house. We brought her upstairs to show her the bedroom she'd be sleeping in. I'd bought some toys for her – intelligent things that I thought she'd like – and some bird books.

Louise put Clara's favourite well-thumbed bird books on the bedside locker and unpacked her clothes, which were all in plastic bags with labels on them. Each pile was organized in the order Clara liked to get dressed. She gave me some last-minute instructions and then she knelt down, facing her little girl. 'Now, sweetie, I have to go, but I'll be back after two sleeps, OK?'

Clara nodded. 'Forty-two hours.'

'Yes, pet, forty-two hours until I come and get you.' Louise hugged Clara tight. The little girl clung to her mother. Then Louise stood up abruptly so Clara wouldn't see her crying.

While Clara sat down with her bird books, I walked an emotional Louise to the front door and hugged her. I'd never seen her like that. She was always so in control and together. It was actually really sweet and I felt emotional myself. I tried to reassure her. 'Everything will be fine. Now, go and don't worry about a thing. See you on Sunday.' She nodded, unable to speak, and drove away.

After Louise had gone I went to find Tom, who was absorbed in his Lego in the playroom. I asked him to come upstairs with me to say hello to Clara and to see if she was hungry. She was sitting on the floor, reading her bird book.

'Hello, Clara,' Tom said.

She didn't look up. He went over and crouched in front of her. '*Hellooooo.*'

'Hello, Tom,' she said, still not looking up.

'Would you like a snack?' I asked her.

She shook her head. Louise's notes had said that Clara didn't often feel hungry and it was important to encourage her to eat. She was allowed healthy snacks – raisins, rice cakes or popcorn.

'Would you like some popcorn? I could make some for you.'

She shook her head again.

'Would you like to come and play Lego with Tom?' I suggested.

She didn't seem to want to do that either.

Louise's notes had said that Clara preferred to play alone and that I wasn't to worry if she didn't want to play with Tom. She also said that the triplets would be far too boisterous for her and could I please keep them away. This poor child spent far too much time alone. She needed to be around other kids. Her stay with us would do her the world of good, once she relaxed and got used to things.

I went downstairs with Tom, made him a sandwich and poured myself a glass of wine. It was going to be a long weekend.

At five o'clock, I had to go and collect the triplets from rugby training, so I went up and explained to Clara that we had to go in the car now. Louise said to give her lots of notice and explain things very clearly and precisely.

'How many minutes will it take to get to the school?' she asked.

'Uhm, five or ten.'

'Exactly how many?'

I tried to be more precise but had to guess. 'Well, I'd say exactly ten.'

'That's six hundred seconds.'

She really was a genius. Tom could barely count to twenty. Then again, Tom didn't require this crazy routine, went everywhere without any fore-warning and never complained. He might not be a whiz at maths, but he was the easiest kid in the world.

I opened the car door and told Clara and Tom to climb in. Tom clambered into his seat and strapped himself in, but Clara froze.

'Come on, pet, in you go.'

She shook her head, clearly horrified, and pointed to the seat. I peered over her head. The seat was covered with crumbs. I leant over her and swept them onto the floor. 'Now, all clean. Sit down.'

'It's dirty.'

'No, it's not. I've just cleaned it.'

'I can see bits of food there.'

I took a deep breath and brushed the few tiny remaining crumbs onto the floor. She still refused to sit down.

'Clara,' I said firmly, 'if we don't leave now, I'll be late. So I need you to sit down.'

She shook her head again. I cursed under my breath and looked around. There was an old rain jacket in the back. I opened it up and put it, lining side up, on the seat. 'Now, lovely clean seat.'

Clara touched the material, finally seemed satisfied and sat down. I put on her seatbelt, then drove like a maniac to pick up the boys. On the way, my phone beeped. Dan. *How's my Juliette today? I had another dream about you last night, X rated.* The car swerved as I reddened.

'You're not allowed to use your phone in the car.' Clara sounded shocked. 'It's dangerous. If you lose concentration, you could crash and kill someone.'

'What?' Tom said, in surprise. 'Mummy's always on her phone in the car.'

'No, I'm not,' I lied.

'Yes, you are.' Tom landed me in it.

'I just had to check that message. It was important.'

Clara wasn't letting me get away with it. 'You could be arrested. Mummy says that no message is important enough to make you use your phone in the car.'

Bloody Louise and her bloody law-abiding ways.

'I won't be using it again.' I was itching to reply to Dan's message, but I'd have to wait. I was being dictated to by a four-year-old – she was her mother's daughter!

When we got to Castle Academy, the triplets were standing in the car park covered with mud.

'It took thirteen minutes and twelve seconds to get here,' Clara announced. 'You said it would take ten.'

'I suppose there must have been more traffic than I thought.'

Before Clara could continue with her stopwatch routine, the triplets clambered into the car, shouting and pushing each other. I watched Clara's face. She became very quiet and retreated into her shell. Then, as Liam roared at Luke for kicking him in the head when he was climbing over him, she put her hands over her ears.

'Liam,' I said, 'I told you we need to be quiet for Clara. She doesn't like noise. She's not used to rowdy boys.'

'She's staying with us so she has to get on with it,' Leo said. 'You always say when we go to someone's house we have to live by their rules.'

'Yes, and for this weekend the rule in our house is not to shout.'

'What are we supposed to do? Go around whispering?' Luke snorted.

'That would be absolutely wonderful.' I smiled. 'I can think of nothing nicer than a quiet house.'

'You always say you'll miss us when we leave home and the house will be too quiet,' Liam reminded me.

'I probably will at first, but I'll get over it.'

'I'll live with you for ever, Mummy,' Tom said.

'Lick.'

'Sucker-upper.'

'Loser.'

I put my hand up to silence the triplets. 'Leave your little brother alone.'

'What do you mean, lick? Lick what?' Clara asked Leo.

'Lick-arse.'

'Leo! It's a silly expression. Ignore him, Clara,' I urged.

'Do you mean that Tom should lick someone's bottom?'

Oh, God, would she just drop it? 'Forget it, pet,' I said.

'Yes, I mean Tom is a lick-arse, as in he licks Mum's bum.' Leo warmed to his subject.

'Do you, Tom?' Clara asked.

'No, I do not. Leo's a liar!' Tom roared.

'Why would you lick your mummy's bottom? Only animals do that and we are humans.'

'Clara, it's just a silly expression. Pay no attention to Leo.'

'I licked Luke's bum for a dare.' Liam chuckled.

'*Groooooss!*' Leo squealed.

'It was all hairy, like a gorilla's.'

'Shut up! It is not.' Luke punched his brother, they began to fight and Clara ended up getting an elbow in the face.

Expecting her to cry or shout, I turned to her, but she just flinched slightly. A red mark was clearly visible on her cheek. 'Are you all right, pet? Did Luke hurt you?'

'It hurts a little, but I'm not in a lot of pain.'

She sounded like a fifty-year-old woman. I leant over and touched her cheek gently. She moved away from me. 'Julie, your breath smells really bad.'

What? 'Really?'

'Yes.'

'Oh, OK.'

'I think you need to brush your teeth.'

'That's rude,' Liam said.

'She didn't mean it.'

'But, Mum, you—'

I cut across Liam: 'How about some nice calming music?' I turned on Lyric FM.

'Boring.'

'Crap.'

'Rubbish music.'

'It's Chopin, he's my favourite,' Clara announced.

By the time I crawled into bed that night, I was exhausted. Harry had watched a movie with the boys while I put Clara to bed. After eating five tiny pieces of mashed potato and three carrot sticks, she'd said she was full. Louise's file had said not to push her when it came to food, so I left her.

We went up to the bathroom and I set the timer on the clock to fifteen minutes. Clara got undressed and folded her clothes into a neat pile. Then she tested the water with her hand. It was too hot. Then it was too cold. Eventually when the bath was almost overflowing, she said it was the correct temperature.

I was texting Dan when the clock turned to fifteen minutes.

'Julie,' Clara stood up, 'I have to get out now.'

I finished my text and drained my glass of wine.

'Now, Julie, quick. Now!'

'OK, OK, keep your hair on.' I went over and wrapped her in the towel Louise had packed. It was an old towel, not fluffy at all, which surprised me. Louise always had the best of everything, yet she had said I had to use this old towel to dry Clara.

'My hair is on,' Clara said.

'What?' I gently dried her with the baldy towel.

'You said, keep your hair on. How could I take it off?'

God, this kid was literal. 'It's just another of those silly expressions.'

'Why does everyone in your family use silly expressions?'

I looked at her serious little face. She never seemed to smile. She was such a solemn little thing. I wanted to kiss her cheeks and tickle her to make her roar with laughter, but Louise had said she didn't like a lot of physical contact. I had hugged her earlier, after the triplets had shouted at each other during dinner and she had looked upset. But she had frozen in my arms. Louise had been a bit like that, though. She wasn't a big hugger. I wanted to bring out the child in Clara. I wanted her to have fun and be carefree, but when I'd suggested giving her a piggy-back up to the bathroom earlier, she had refused.

She was a very pretty child. She had long blonde curls and big blue eyes. She looked nothing like Louise, with her dark hair and brown eyes.

'Clara, we use silly expressions because sometimes it's fun to be silly,' I said. 'You should try it.' She really needed to lighten up and have some fun. She was four going on forty.

'How can it be fun to be silly?'

'Make a silly face, look.' I pulled my mouth open and stuck my tongue out.

'You look ugly when you do that.'

I gave up. We went into the bedroom where she put on her pyjamas and got into bed. I sat on the edge while she recited a very long list of birds to me. I almost nodded off, but thankfully managed to stay awake until she finished.

I leant down and gave her a very gentle kiss on the cheek. That seemed to be OK. 'You're a wonderful little girl. No wonder your mummy is so proud of you.'

'Thank you, Julie. Mummy says you are the kindest sister. She says you are always really nice to everyone.'

I felt a bit teary. 'That's lovely to hear. Your mummy's very special too.'

'I know that.' Clara looked at the clock. 'Mummy will be back in thirty-five hours.'

How the hell did she do that? She was four and a half! I turned out the bedside lamp but left the door open, with the corridor light on. Just as instructed. 'Sleep tight and don't let the bed bugs bite.'

'What bed bugs?'

Damn! 'Just one of those silly expressions,' I muttered, as I went downstairs to pour myself a large glass of wine and put my feet up.

The next day Harry took the triplets to rugby and Tom went with them to cheer his brothers on. Gavin and Shania were calling in for coffee. I was glad of the company and they were both really good with Clara.

When they arrived, I put the kettle on while Shania got down on the floor with Clara to talk about birds.

'So, how are things?' I asked Gavin.

'Good. Working really hard, but it's going well.'

'Do you think you'll stick it out?' I asked. Gavin was always honest with me about his jobs, probably because I was the only sister who didn't work. He was a bit afraid of Louise and her incredible work ethic, and now that Sophie had got back on her feet and turned her life around, he felt he couldn't complain to her either.

He poured some milk into his coffee. 'Well . . . I like it and I'm pretty awesome at it, but does it set my world on fire? No.'

'Gavin, let me give you a little inside info. Ninety-nine per cent of the population do jobs that don't set them on fire, OK? Even Bono probably has days when he just doesn't feel like singing.

This is the real world. If you've found something you're good at, and that you like, stick with it. You're twenty-seven. You can't keep job-hopping. And, believe me, having nothing at all is far worse. Being stuck at home all day is pretty soul-destroying, I can tell you.'

He opened the cupboard and took out a packet of chocolate fingers. 'Twenty-seven is not old and I don't job-hop. I just have a low boredom threshold. I like to be challenged.'

I threw my head back and laughed. 'Come on! You don't have a low boredom threshold. You have the attention span of a goldfish. Look, all I'm saying is that I think you should stick at this for at least a year.'

He shrugged. 'I'll try.' Then, looking at Shania, he said, 'Isn't she hot?'

She was. Very hot. The kind of hot that made a forty-four-year-old woman like me feel flabby and over-the-hill. She was wearing a short, skin-tight black dress with opaque tights and biker boots – cool, effortless and very sexy.

Sensing someone staring at her, she glanced up. 'What?'

'Just admiring the view.' Gavin winked at her.

She beamed at him. 'I like what I'm seeing too.'

He walked over and kissed her – a full-on snog. I turned away. Clearly, all they wanted was to have sex with each other. I remembered the days when Harry and I were like that. God, it was so long since I'd snogged Harry. When did you stop

254

kissing your husband? When kids came along, I supposed.

'Get a room!' I said. They were making me feel uncomfortable and Clara was sitting beside them – granted her head was in her book, but still . . .

'Sorry.' Shania giggled.

'How are you getting on with Sophie and the modelling?'

'Good. Sophie's so great – she's, like, super-professional. We're doing a big fashion show tonight in Style Central.'

'Great. Well, good luck. Now, Clara, pet, would you like some juice and a biccie?' I asked.

Without looking up, she said, 'No, thank you. Juice is bad for your teeth and so are biscuits. But I would like a rice cake, please.'

'Go on, have a chocolate finger,' Gavin urged.

Clara looked up. 'Chocolate finger?'

'It's not really a finger. It's a biscuit that looks like a finger.' I held it up.

'That doesn't look like a finger,' Clara pointed out.

'How about fangs?' I put two chocolate fingers into my mouth.

'You look really silly.'

I took the biscuits out of my mouth and ate them.

Shania came over to have some coffee.

'Clara's very serious,' I whispered. 'I'm trying to draw her out and make her laugh, but it's hard going.'

Shania looked at Gavin. He dropped his eyes. I sensed something. 'What?'

'Can I say it?' Shania asked Gavin.

'Yeah, go on, you can say it to Julie.'

Jeepers, what was going on?

'Clara's like my little brother,' Shania said.

'In what way?' I asked. I felt a cold chill running up my spine. I had a bad feeling.

Shania looked at Gavin, then back at me. 'He has Asperger's.'

My hand flew to my mouth.

Gavin looked upset. 'Shania clocked it the first time she met Clara. She kept trying to say it to me, but I kept telling her to be quiet. Then I googled it and I've been watching Clara. I think she's right.'

Suddenly everything made sense. I knew they were right. Oh, Louise!

CHAPTER 20

Louise

I worried about Clara all weekend. I was concerned about the noise in Julie's house – her boys were wild. But with Christelle away, Mum and Dad on a golf weekend and Sophie working all day Saturday, I'd had no choice.

I knew Julie would be loving and caring. I was just afraid she'd get distracted and Clara would fall or the boys would push her down the stairs on a tray with no helmet on. That particular image almost made me get the next flight home.

But Julie had been brilliant. She'd sent photos and regular text updates, which had really helped, and I had called Clara each evening to say goodnight. She sounded so young on the phone – her sweet little voice just melted my heart.

Oliver had been at the conference and was a welcome distraction. We'd had dinner together on Saturday night and then he came back to my room and we'd had sex. But not our usual steamy, energetic sex. For the first time ever, it was flat, quick and functional.

I thought it might have been because I was preoccupied with Clara, but Oliver definitely wasn't performing well either.

'What was that?' I turned to him, propping my head on my hand.

'Terrible sex.' Oliver leant over and took a glass of water from the bedside table.

'I know what my excuse is. I'm worried about my daughter. What's yours?' I asked.

Oliver took a sip of water and then said, 'My mother's dying.'

'Oh, Oliver, I'm sorry.'

'My wife has been, well, incredibly supportive and I just don't think I can . . . do this, as in cheat on her, any more. It suddenly feels wrong. I'm sorry, Louise.'

'Hey, we had a nice thing going, but there were never any strings attached. We said that whenever one of us needed to end it, there would be no drama.'

Oliver reached over and kissed me. 'You truly are amazing.' He looked very relieved.

I stood up and put on a towelling robe. I was disappointed. It had been lovely to know I could have regular (and usually great) sex with a man I liked. But Oliver wasn't my first no-strings-attached lover and he certainly wouldn't be the last.

'Drink?' I asked, opening the mini-bar.

'Open the champagne. Let's toast a great couple of years and some really steamy nights.'

I smiled. 'Champagne it is.'

★   ★   ★

I drove like a maniac from the airport so I would get to Julie's in the forty-second hour. I knew Clara would fret if I was late and I didn't want her to worry or have a meltdown. When I turned into the gravelled driveway, I saw her face at the window.

I jumped out of the car and ran to the door. My heart was pounding. I was dying to see my little angel. Julie opened the door and stood back while Clara rushed out and held up her arms for a hug.

'Forty-two hours and fifty-four minutes,' she said.

'I know. I've missed you so much.' I clasped her tightly as she clung to me.

'I want to go home, Mummy. It's too noisy here.'

'Sssh, pet. I just need to talk to Julie and thank her.'

I stood up and walked in. Clara's bag was packed and sitting at the hall door.

'She insisted on packing this morning.' Julie smiled.

I hugged my sister. 'Thank you so much. I really appreciate it. All the photos and texts were so reassuring. Was everything all right?'

'Yes, great.' Something about her voice made me feel unsure. She sounded a bit nervous.

'Are you sure? Did she have a meltdown?' I whispered. Julie wasn't telling me something.

'No, she was really sweet. I did everything by the book. She certainly likes a routine.'

I nodded. 'Just like me. I always like to know what's going to happen. I hate surprises.'

Julie fidgeted with her necklace. 'Louise, remember you said Clara's teacher was trying to psychoanalyse her?'

'Hold on.' I turned to Clara and said quietly, 'Will you get into the car, sweetie? I just want to talk to Julie for two minutes. OK?'

'OK, Mummy. Two minutes.' Clara walked down the steps and climbed into the car.

I looked at Julie. 'The teacher is an idiot. I'm thinking of moving Clara. They don't understand or appreciate her intellect in that school.'

Julie was almost strangling herself with her necklace. 'But what was it that she said about Clara?'

I waved my hand dismissively. 'Some nonsense about Asperger's tendencies or something. Geniuses are always being mislabelled. Don't you remember when my maths teacher accused me of cheating in my test?'

'Yes, I do, but you were different from Clara in many ways. You were more outgoing and less . . . well, insular.'

'Clara's an only child with one parent. Of course she's quiet. I had three siblings so I had to fight my corner.'

'I know, but have you considered the possibility of taking Clara to a psychologist to be assessed?'

'Assessed for what?'

'Well, I just thought that maybe she could get

help in learning to play with other kids and being less obsessive about time and stuff.'

I didn't like being told what to do with my child by my sister, whose children were out of control and had been asked to leave their playschool. 'Julie, you said to me that I didn't know boys. Well, I'm telling you that you don't know girls. She's a happy, well-adjusted child and, no offence, I don't need parenting lessons from you.'

I heard a loud bang and the sound of breaking glass. 'You'd better go. It sounds like the boys have broken a window. Again.' I headed down the steps towards my car.

'Louise!' Julie called after me, but I didn't want to talk to her. I wanted to go home, be with my perfect child and block out all the people who kept telling me she was different. To Hell with them all. I knew my child.

I spent a lovely evening with Clara, the two of us chatting and reading books. Just before she fell asleep she said, 'I'm glad to be home. I much prefer this apartment to Julie's big house.'

'I'm glad to be home, too. I missed you, my little pet.' I kissed her cheek and turned out the light.

I was making myself a cup of green tea when I heard a knock on my door. I looked through the peephole. It was Sophie. She looked weird. I opened the door.

'Oh, my God. Sophie, what's wrong?'

Her face was puffy and red from crying. Her eyes were like two slits in her head. She looked like hell. Unable to speak, she fell against me and began to sob.

For ten minutes she cried like a baby on my shoulder. I tried to get some sense out of her, but she was incoherent with grief.

'Is Jess OK?'

She nodded.

'Is it Jack?'

She shook her head.

'Pippa?'

She shook her head again.

'Mum, Dad, Gavin?' I was really worried – she was in such a state.

She shook her head a third time.

I led her to the sofa. 'Sophie, I need you to take a deep breath and tell me what's going on.'

'A-A-Andrew.'

Oh, no! 'What happened?'

She shook her head. 'I'm – such an – uh – uh – idiot.'

Oh, God. She had fallen far too quickly and far too deeply for him. She had made herself so vulnerable. I hoped it was a lovers' tiff and could be patched up. Otherwise she'd be devastated.

I went into the kitchen and poured her a vodka and orange juice. 'Have a drink. It'll help calm you.'

Sophie exhaled and drank deeply from the glass.

She put it down on the table and wiped her eyes. 'How could I have been so stupid?' she said, quiet tears running down her face now. 'Why on earth would a successful man in his early forties go for me? I'm past it. I am officially over the hill.'

I hated to hear her talking like this. It was so defeatist and so belittling to herself. 'Don't be ridiculous, Sophie. You're gorgeous and any man, no matter what age, would be lucky to have you.'

'Really, Louise?' Her sorrow was turning to anger now. 'No successful middle-aged man wants to date a woman his own age when he can have someone younger.'

'That's not true! Look at Sarkozy – he married Carla Bruni and she's not young.'

Sophie snorted. 'He's fifty-nine and she's forty-six! There's thirteen years between them, for God's sake.'

Damn. I'd thought they were about the same age. Sophie put her head into her hands and began crying again. 'It's no use, Louise. It's just no bloody use.'

'Tell me what happened.'

Sophie took a deep breath and launched into the story. 'We were doing a big fashion show with Style Central last night so I went early with the models to set up and do a run-through before the show. I was really excited because I hadn't seen Andrew in eight days. We'd been on the phone a lot and he was going to take me out for dinner after the show and then back to his apartment. He suggested I wear the sexy lingerie he'd bought me, which I did . . .' Sophie's lip wobbled. 'I was so happy the night he gave it to me.'

She bent her head and continued, 'He arrived looking all gorgeous. I was so happy to see him. He seemed pleased to see me too. When no one was looking he pinched my bum, and when I flashed my lacy bra strap at him, he said he couldn't wait to get me into bed. Then Shania came out—'

Sophie's voice tapered off. She gulped her drink and gathered herself.

'She was wearing black leather hot pants and a sequined vest top that had a plunging front. It was one of the outfits for the show. Shania said one of the girls needed help because the zip was broken on her dress. I introduced her to Andrew as my brother's girlfriend and I went to help the other model. I never even thought . . .'

Oh, God, not Shania! Seriously? She didn't seem the type to go for an older guy. Maybe she was sick of Gavin and his lack of money or real ambition. Maybe she wanted a man with money to wine and dine her.

Sophie continued, 'So I sorted out the problem, got the zip down and freed the model from the dress. As I rushed back out to spend more time with Andrew, I saw it.'

'What?'

'He was groping Shania and she was trying to get away from him. He had his hand on her bum and he was pulling her towards him. I heard her say, "I have a boyfriend, stop," but he just laughed and said, "You need a real man," and then she said, "But you're with Sophie," and he said – he said—' Sophie began to cry again.

'Oh, Sophie, what did the bastard say?'

'He said, "Sophie? She's way too needy. She's practically stalking me. I don't need a desperate forty-two-year-old. I've been married already. I'm looking for someone young and hot, not old and clingy."'

'How dare he?' I raged. 'How bloody dare he say that? What a complete arsehole!'

Sophie was sobbing again. 'That's exactly what Shania called him. She said, "Sophie's great. You're an arsehole." She's a decent girl, but it doesn't change anything. Andrew's right, I am desperate. I've spent almost five years trying to get myself together, be independent, work hard, be self-supporting. I've tried to be strong and show Jess that a woman shouldn't depend on a man or wait around to be "minded" or "looked-after", but underneath it all, I just want to be married again. I *want* a man to mind me. I *want* a man to look after me. I hate it, Louise. I absolutely hate being on my own.' She broke down.

I rubbed my sister's back and waited for her sobs to subside. I knew she found it hard being single – and that she was insecure about her looks – but I hadn't realized how much she hated being alone. I'd always been on my own so I was used to it. I liked it. I deplored the idea of someone minding me. My independence was very precious, but Sophie and I had always been very different.

As if sensing what I was thinking, Sophie said, 'I know you must think I'm pathetic – you're so strong and brilliant. But I'm not. I've really tried, Louise, but I just can't bear it. I'm so lonely. I never wanted this life. I want to be half of a couple. I want to be loved and cherished. I miss my old life so much. I know it's silly and immature and all those things, but I can't help how I feel.'

'Now you listen to me. No one is judging you. You have done an incredible job getting back on your feet, working and looking after Jess. You should be really proud of yourself. And as for how you feel, that's just who you are, Sophie. You've always loved being in a relationship. I can't remember a time before you were married when you didn't have a boyfriend, so it's totally under-standable that you feel lonely.'

Sophie finished her drink and banged the glass on the coffee-table. 'I hate Jack! I hate him and his happiness. It's not fair! He ruined everything yet he gets to be happy and have a new life and family. And I get walked all over and dumped.'

'What did you do about Andrew, after you saw him with Shania?' I asked.

Sophie shrugged. 'I ran to the Ladies to throw up. When I came out, I met Quentin. He knew by my face something was up, so I told him. He said I had to pretend nothing was wrong because we so badly need the account. He's right, we do. So I somehow pulled myself together and got through the show. It's all a complete blur, to be honest.'

'Did you speak to Andrew at all?' I asked.

'I managed to avoid him for most of the night and Quentin was great – he never left my side. But when the show was over and Andrew had obviously been rejected by Shania and God knows who else he propositioned, he decided I'd do for dinner and a shag. He came over to me and asked if I was ready to go. Quentin was squeezing my hand to give me strength, so I very calmly said I was too tired and that I needed to go home and get a good night's sleep.'

'Was he surprised?'

'Shocked. He'd presumed, of course, I'd be my usual lap-dog self. But at least I held it together and didn't ruin my business as well as my private life. Quentin is going to take over the account, so hopefully I won't ever have to see him again.'

My little sister's face was red and blotchy – she was so sad and forlorn. I reached over and hugged her. 'I know it's not much consolation now, but I'll always be here for you and so will Julie.'

Sophie clung to me, like a little child, and muttered, 'Thank you,' into my shoulder.

Five minutes later we were in my bathroom and I was applying a thick layer of makeup to her face. Jess was being dropped home in twenty minutes and Sophie didn't want her daughter to see that she'd been crying.

'The last thing I need is Jack dropping Jess off and both of them seeing my red eyes. I need to be strong for Jess and I couldn't bear Jack's sympathy – it would literally push me over the edge. I don't want his pity. More mascara, please. My hands are still shaking too much to do it.' She smiled sadly. 'We seem to be making a habit of this.'

'Of what?'

'Me crying myself stupid and you patching me up with makeup.'

'You're just having a rough few months. It'll pass. You'll see.'

I put on another layer of mascara and walked my sister to the door. 'Good luck, and call me later. Let's have dinner with Julie this week – you need a night out.'

'Thanks for everything.' Sophie kissed me and walked towards the lift, shoulders hunched, a broken woman.

CHAPTER 21

Sophie

I don't know how I got through the next few days. They were a complete haze of work, home, looking after Jess and crawling into bed. I obviously wasn't doing a very good job of pretending everything was OK because on Thursday morning Jess looked up from her porridge and shouted, 'Mum!'

'What?'

'I've asked you three times for money for my school trip.'

'What money?'

She groaned. 'I told you last night. We're going to some boring concert and I need ten euros for the coach.'

'Oh, right. Where did I leave my wallet?' I fumbled around for my bag, to no avail.

'For God's sake, it's right there on the counter.'

I unzipped my wallet and asked, 'How much did you say?'

'Ten euros!'

I pulled out a fiver and some coins.

Jess counted them. 'There's eight here. Come on, Mum, it's not hard.'

I thrust the wallet into her hand. 'Here, you do it.'

She counted it out, zipped my wallet up and put it carefully back into my bag. She stood up and put the money into the pocket of her backpack.

With her back to me she asked quietly, 'Did you break up with that man?'

I was going to lie, but I was too tired and weary to bother. 'Yes, I did.'

'I thought so. You've been weird all week.'

'Have I? Sorry.'

'Are you sad?'

'Sad' didn't come close. I was devastated, humiliated, mortified, heartbroken . . . but my nine-and-a-half-year-old didn't need to hear that. 'I'm OK, just a bit tired, that's all,' I croaked, trying to hold it together.

She turned. 'There's no point crying over spilt milk,' she said.

I smiled for the first time in days. 'Where on earth did you hear that expression?'

'Granny said it to me all the time when I was sad about you and Dad breaking up. She used to sit me on her knee and tell me not to cry over spilt milk.'

Good old Mum, with her sage advice. I stood up and went to give Jess a hug. She allowed me to put my arms around her, but didn't hug me back. Oh, well, it was better than nothing.

She pulled away from me gently. 'So, you know I've got Pippa's baby shower this Friday night, right?'

I'd completely forgotten. What a ridiculous notion, having a party before your baby was born. I just didn't get it. To me, it felt like tempting Fate. I'd been so nervous throughout my pregnancy with Jess, convinced something would go wrong. There was no way I would have allowed anyone to buy me presents before I held the baby in my arms.

Jess had been talking about it for weeks, but it had kind of gone over my head because I had been so distracted and happy. Now I'd have to listen to it.

'Are you sure you should go, Jess? It's probably just for Pippa's friends.'

Jess's face darkened. 'I am her friend.'

'You're her partner's daughter, Jess.'

Jess glared at me. 'Pippa said I'm the most important guest because I'm the baby's sister.'

I didn't have the energy to argue. 'Fine.'

'I want to take out a hundred euros from my bank to buy a present.'

Was she insane? There was no way she was spending that kind of money on a present. She had three hundred euros saved in her account from her first communion last year. I wanted her to keep it safe. 'That's far too much. I'll help you choose something after school today. It's late-night shopping on Thursday – we can go to Mothercare or Next and find something cute. I'll pay for it and you can say it's from both of us.'

'No way. I'm not buying some outfit that someone else might get her too. I want to buy her something really nice. Pippa's so cool, I have to give her something that totally rocks.'

I looked at the clock. If I didn't leave now, I was going to be late. I'd been late every day this week and Quentin had been very understanding, but we had a meeting at nine thirty to go over the monthly figures and I had to be on time.

I grabbed my coat and rushed Jess out of the door. 'We'll talk about it later,' I said, postponing the inevitable battle that would take place that evening.

I arrived at the office at exactly nine thirty, out of breath and sweating. I plonked myself down opposite Quentin and caught my breath.

'Coffee, darling?' he asked.

'Yes, please.'

'Drop of brandy in it?'

'I'd love it, but I'm going to say no. I'm afraid if I start to drink, I may never stop.'

He handed me a cup of coffee and kissed the top of my head. 'My poor Sophie.'

'I have no one to blame but myself. I behaved like a silly teenager, thinking it was love after such a short time. It was nothing but a casual fling, if it was even that. God, Quentin, when did I become this needy person? I used to be quite cool, remember, in the old days when I first started modelling and men actually did fancy me.'

'You were the toast of the town. Every eligible man in Dublin was chasing you around.'

'I ended up with Jack and look how that turned out,' I said, bitterness creeping into my voice.

'You and Jack were very happy for a long time and you have Jess. I know it ended badly, but he did adore you, Sophie.'

I put my coffee cup down. 'I know, and I was mad about him too. But now he adores someone else, someone younger and prettier than me. And to be honest, Quentin, I think he's more in love with her than he was with me. He absolutely worships her.'

'It's early days. They're still in the honeymoon period. Wait until the baby arrives and he has to get up in the middle of the night. He won't be so smug then, and Miss Pippa won't be looking so good with leaky breasts and no sleep.'

I loved Quentin. He always made me feel better. I savoured the image of Pippa with unkempt hair, milk-stained clothes and black shadows under her eyes.

'I met Andrew last night for a drink. He wants to know why you're off the account,' Quentin said.

My stomach turned at the mention of Andrew's name. 'What did you say?'

'I told him you had some personal matters to attend to and that you were taking a step back for a little bit. I had to say something that sounded

273

viable because we need the account, darling, you know that.'

'That's fine, very nicely put. What did he say?'

Quentin pushed his coffee cup to the side. 'He said he was sorry to hear that because you were excellent at your job.'

I was hurt that he hadn't even asked how I was. 'He hasn't bothered to call, or even text. He obviously never gave a damn about me. Why was I such a fool?'

'Lonely people are vulnerable. I know it myself. The last young man I had back to the house robbed my watch on his way out. It's not easy to find nice partners.'

'Quentin, that's awful.'

'I know, darling, but a lonely old queen like me is an easy target. If only we could marry each other.'

'Do you think I'll ever meet someone? Be honest,' I urged.

'Honestly? I think you will because you're gorgeous and lovely, but it's hard out there.'

'The problem is that unless I go for much older men, I'm competing with women half my age. I don't find sixty-year-olds attractive. I like men my own age, but they like much younger women. Look at Jack, for God's sake. No single man in his forties wants to be with a woman in her forties. It's just not fair – it's a man's world!'

'No, it's a heterosexual man's world,' Quentin corrected me. 'The only reason a younger man

274

would go for me is for money. It's dog-eat-dog for us older gay men too.'

I patted his hand. 'I think you're a great catch.'

'Ditto. Now, what else is new?'

'Jess wants to spend a hundred euros on a baby-shower present for Pippa.'

Quentin raised a perfectly trimmed eyebrow. 'I presume you said no.'

'Obviously, but she went mad, so I said we'd talk about it later. She's so enamoured of Pippa it's . . . well, frankly, really irritating. She wouldn't spend even ten euros on a present for me and yet she wants to take out a huge chunk of her savings for Pippa. It just pisses me off. I know I should be mature and understanding and not take it personally, but I'm feeling very raw and I am taking it personally.'

Quentin poured us both more coffee. 'Darling, the novelty will wear off. Pippa is like a big sister or a cool aunt to Jess. But, I guarantee, the minute that baby is born, Jess will find herself pushed aside and you'll need to be there for her when it happens.'

In a horrible way, I hoped Quentin was right. I was shocked that I was wishing for Jess to be hurt, but I wanted her to see through Pippa. I wanted her to come back to me, to appreciate me, to want to be with me. I missed my little girl. She never wanted to spend time with me. She just counted the days until she could be with Pippa and Jack and it really hurt. Between my daughter and Andrew, I felt I wasn't good enough for anyone.

I sipped my coffee and tried not to feel sorry for myself. Life had not turned out the way I had planned. What would happen to me? Would I end up alone for the rest of my days? The thought terrified me. 'I have to do something, Quentin. I cannot spend the next forty years on my own.'

'Andrew was just a bad experience. Don't panic,' Quentin said. 'There are plenty more fish in the sea.'

I narrowed my eyes. 'Don't lie.'

'OK. There are some other fish.'

'Would you date someone your own age?'

Quentin flinched. 'It depends what he looked like. I usually go for younger men, but if the guy was very fit and had a nice face, then maybe.'

'Liar! There is no way you'd go out with a sixty-year-old and you know it.'

He shrugged. 'It's unlikely, unless he looked like George Clooney.'

I twisted my bracelet around my wrist. 'This whole Andrew thing has made me really look at myself. I know I want to meet someone – under fifty. I don't want to be on my own any more. Meeting Andrew made me see how lonely I am. So I've decided to be proactive and do something to make myself more attractive. I'm going to get my boobs done.'

Quentin wasn't remotely shocked, as I'd known he wouldn't be. He'd seen it all during his years in the modelling industry. I knew I could trust him. 'It's a serious procedure, Sophie. You have to be sure.'

'I am.' I was. I'd seen good and bad boob jobs and I knew what a difference the good ones made to a woman's body. Especially after having children and getting older, when your boobs were sagging. I hated my breasts.

'Sweetie, you've only just broken up with Andrew. Give yourself a few weeks before you rush into anything.'

I shook my head. 'This isn't because of Andrew. I've been thinking about it for ages. I really want to get my boobs done. I don't want big page-three breasts. I just want them to look perky, not small and droopy, like they are now. I just know it will make a huge difference to my body and my confidence.'

Quentin nodded. 'Make sure you go to someone reputable. No cutting costs.'

'Can you ask around and find out who the best surgeon is? I can't say it to anyone. My sisters would kill me if they knew I was even contemplating it.'

'Your secret is safe with me,' Quentin assured me. 'I'll find out who the best surgeon is and get back to you. But in return I want you to think about it for a few more weeks before you go rushing under the knife.'

'Thanks. Will you come with me when I get it done? Will you be my in-case-of-emergency person?'

'Of course I will, darling. I'll hold your hand the whole way through. You never know, I may meet a nice young intern.'

'Young!' I wagged my finger at him.

He chuckled. 'Oops, sorry.'

So that was it. Now I'd said it out loud, I knew for certain I'd go ahead and do it. The surgery would change everything for the better. I was excited now at the prospect. Obviously my sisters would notice when they were done, but I wasn't going to breathe a word about it until then. I'd deal with their reaction when the time came. I knew they'd go mad. I knew they'd tell me how stupid and shallow I was and how it made no difference blah-blah-blah. But they were wrong. They weren't looking for a husband. I was, and I had to make myself more attractive to compete with the younger women I was up against.

It felt good to have a new plan. I pictured myself in six months' time, with new boobs and a new man. I had to look to the future because the present was so awful.

CHAPTER 22

Julie

The doorbell rang. I quickly replied to Dan's text and went to let Marian in. I was nervous about her seeing the house. I'd kept putting her off calling in by saying we were having work done and that it wasn't finished yet. But today she had insisted on calling over and I had run out of excuses.

I was embarrassed because it was so big, shiny and new. Marian and I had bonded over budgeting, saving and scrimping. But now I was in a mansion and her life was still a struggle financially. Although now Greg was in Dubai earning a decent wage, they would hopefully start paying off their debts and things might get easier.

I opened the door.

Marian pushed past me. 'Is this a joke? You do realize that your house is bigger than Buckingham shagging Palace? I knew it was going to be big, but this is ridiculous.'

'Come on in.'

'Should I park my car around the back? You

don't want a piece of shit like that in your driveway.'

I rolled my eyes. 'Stop it! Come into the kitchen and we'll have a drink.'

'Jesus, check you out. Lady of the manor drinking at ten. I'm usually the one pushing the booze.'

'Coffee with a splash of brandy?' I asked.

'Don't mind if I do.' Marian looked around my vast kitchen. 'Seriously, Julie, it's incredible. Did you do it all up yourself?'

I shook my head. 'Not really. Sophie helped with most of it. She has great taste and I hadn't a clue what to do with all the space.'

I handed Marian her brandy coffee and sat down. She took a sip. '*Whoooo!* That's strong. You'd better lash on some toast. I need food to soak this up or I'll be arrested for drunk driving.'

I popped some bread into the toaster. 'So, how are you?'

Marian grinned. 'Pretty fucking great, actually.'

'I take it you're still having sex with Lew?'

'I certainly am.'

'What about Greg?'

'Greg has checked out of our lives. He Skypes to talk to the kids every second day, but has nothing to say to me or them. It's as if he's completely disengaged from us. He's living in "Greg world" over there in Dubai. I can see that he has no interest in his family. Calling us is a chore for him.'

'Come on, Greg loves you and he adores the kids.'

Marian shrugged. 'I was listening to this show on the radio last week. Women whose husbands work abroad for months on end were calling in and saying things that I could relate to. They all said if your husband is away for longer than a month they begin to detach, and that the longer they're away, the worse it gets. One woman said when her husband comes back after two months away working on oil rigs, it takes him a month to get back to normal and then he goes off back to work and the whole bloody cycle starts again.'

'What's the solution?' I asked, as I handed her a plate of buttered toast.

'He needs to come home and reintegrate into the family. But that's not an option because he can't get a job here. So there is no solution. We're screwed.'

'Hold on. If he came home once a month, like he used to, it would work.'

Marian shook her head. 'We got through the first year because we thought it was just a year and we really worked on staying in touch. Greg missed us and came home as much as he could. But now he's less bothered about it and I'm used to him not being around. Even the kids are getting used to it. When he came home regularly, the children were all over him, which he found claustrophobic. And when he left, they were devastated and I had to pick up the pieces. But now that they see him even less, they just accept that he's never really around. To be honest, it's easier when he doesn't come back, for all of us.'

'It's such a tough situation. But Greg's a good guy. Don't write off your marriage yet.'

'I'm not. Well . . . not completely. Anyway, enough about the crap stuff, let's talk about Lew!'

'OK, go on. I can see you're dying to tell me about the great sex.'

'It's sensational. It keeps getting better. These younger guys are where it's at. He even brings props with him.'

What? I was almost afraid to ask. I took a large sip of my brandy coffee. 'What props?'

'Sex props. Handcuffs and silk scarves to blindfold me with. He turned up with a whip the other day and asked me to walk on his back and whip him.'

'And did you?' I was shocked. I thought that only happened in X-rated movies.

'Hell, yes! I was a bit worried about walking on his back. I was afraid I might break it or rupture his kidney or something. Anyway, once I got going, I was well into it. Whipping a man is very therapeutic. I was walloping him, but he loved it.'

I tried to get the image of Marian, naked, whipping a beefy young Polish guy out of my head. 'Does he whip you?'

'Yes, but not hard, and it's actually very erotic. I swear it's like *Fifty Shades of* bloody *Grey* in my house, these days. I haven't felt this alive in years. I always hated my body, but Lew loves my curves

282

and my big boobs. He can't get enough of me. I sometimes wonder if he's mentally challenged. Why the hell is he with me when he could be whipping hot young Polish girls?'

'Stop that. You're lovely.'

Marian raised an eyebrow at me. 'I'm a forty-six-year-old woman with four kids and saggy bits. But Lew says he's always loved older women.'

'They should clone him and send him around to all bored housewives of a certain age.'

'Well, when I finish with him, you should definitely have a go.'

'Marian!'

'What? Don't pretend you wouldn't like a bit of steamy action.'

'I have Harry.'

Marian threw her head back and roared laughing. 'Harry . . . with a . . . *whiiiip*! Ha-ha-ha-ha-ha.'

I began to laugh too.

Marian wiped her eyes. 'Sorry, but the idea that Harry would be adventurous in the bedroom is too funny.'

'It's not just Harry, it's me too. I've never tried anything . . . you know, *different*.'

'Neither had I. But that's the whole point. Why was *Fifty Shades of Grey* such a hit with women? Because secretly women in their forties, fifties and beyond are bored sexually. Men watch porn – I know some women don't believe that their husbands ever watch porn, but they do. What do we watch? We watch our children running around all bloody day long and we go to coffee mornings where we talk about our kids. It's so boring. No wonder so many housewives are on Prozac.'

'Are they?'

'Come on, Julie! Do you live with your head permanently in the sand? Every second woman is on happy pills because she's so unfulfilled in her life, mentally, sexually and emotionally.'

Were they? Was I completely naïve and clueless? If I was to be honest with myself, didn't I feel that way too? Wasn't that why I'd loved reconnecting with Dan? It was a buzz and a high that I hadn't had in so long.

I decided not to tell Marian about Dan. I was worried she'd make it into a big thing and it wasn't. It was just a little harmless fun.

'Earth to Julie?' Marian waved a hand in front of me.

'Sorry, I was just thinking about what you said. I suppose you're right. A lot of women are restless and fed up.'

'That's why I went back to work. Well, obviously I went back because we needed the money too, but I wanted something else in my life. My kids bore me. What the hell is interesting about home-work and sport? Nothing. I've spent hours on the side of pitches, freezing my arse off, watching Brian and Oscar running around after a football, or bored out of my mind watching Molly thundering about in some church hall in a pink leotard thinking she's Darcey flaming Bussell.'

'Come on, it's lovely to see them playing. I feel really proud when I see the triplets playing rugby.'

Marian chewed her last piece of toast. 'That's because they're good and they score goals or whatever you score in rugby. My lot are brutal at sports, but I still have to go and cheer them on. Last Saturday Oscar, who plays for the worst team in the club, lost his football match nine–nil and he was the bloody goalie. I had other parents giving me filthy looks because Oscar let in all the goals, even though their kids were shite too. And then I had to deal with him crying the whole way home. I ended up pulling into a garage and buying him half a ton of sweets to shut him up. Then Molly said she wanted sweets but I told her ballerinas never eat sweets, only vegetables. So now all she'll eat is bloody carrots because they are the only vegetable she likes. I actually think her skin is turning orange. She'll be the first ever tangerine ballerina.'

'Poor Molly!'

'Poor me!' Marian said. 'I'm always on my own. I have to deal with all their dramas and their moods, their teachers and after-school activities. I'm sick of it. When Greg comes home next month I'm going to run away for a few days just to get away from the kids. I am so sick of them. Yes, I love them, ya-di-ya, but I need space from them. It's too much. If it wasn't for the great sex with Lew, I'd be wallowing in a vat of wine or Prozac – or maybe both.'

I felt for her. Even though Harry had been a lot more absent lately, he still took the boys to rugby and helped them with their maths homework and bath time. I would hate to be doing it all on my own.

Marian insisted on having a full tour of the house, and seeing it through her eyes made it seem even bigger and fancier. I felt awkward and wanted it to be over. I hated the fact that coming into money had made me 'different' from her. I wanted our relationship to be the same. I didn't want her to think I'd changed because I really didn't feel that I had.

Marian lay back on my huge bed. 'Comfy!' She spread her arms wide. 'So, is Harry still spending all his spare time in the golf club?'

I nodded. Marian knew the old Harry, the lovely Harry. She crinkled her nose. 'Now that I've seen the house and how nice your lifestyle is, I kind of get why Harry's changed.'

'What do you mean?'

'I can see how all of this could go to your head.'

'It hasn't gone to my head. I'm still the same.'

Marian looked up at me and smiled. 'Yes, you are. Harry will come round. He just needs to get used to being loaded. God, I'd love to have a millionaire aunt. A big injection of cash would sort out all my problems.'

'You know I'd be happy to—'

Marian put up her hand. 'Stop. I know what you're going to say and I really appreciate the offer, but I never mix money and friendship. If you gave me money, I'd owe you.'

'But I don't care about money. I'd never think about it again.'

Marian sat up. 'But I would. Every time I saw you, I'd remember you'd given me money and I'd feel obliged to be nice to you.'

'But you are nice to me.'

'Yeah, but if I felt I had to be, I mightn't want to be. You know what a contrary cow I am.'

I fiddled with the curtain ropes. 'I'd love to help, so if you change your mind . . .'

Marian stood up and hitched up her jeans. 'I won't, but thanks. Besides, I've thought of a way to make millions.'

'I'm all ears.'

'Sex lines.'

I stared at her in disbelief. I could see she was relishing my reaction. 'Are you serious?'

'Deadly.'

I threw my arms up in the air. 'Marian!'

She wagged a finger at me. 'Don't knock it. I saw this programme a few weeks ago about sex lines and how half the women do the sex talk while they're ironing, cooking or doing laundry. Basically you can do it while your kids are in school and you're doing the housework. It's so easy, it's a joke. All you have to do is a bit of panting and some dirty talk. It's the easiest money ever. I talked to Lew about it and he says he could put me in touch with some Polish girls, and

Lithuanians and Russians, who'd love to earn some extra cash. So I'm thinking of setting up an international sex line.'

'Are you actually being serious?'

'Absolutely. I've been researching it and it's really not that hard to start one. And it's a lot more lucrative than selling bloody insurance. But first of all I need to get some practice, so I've signed up with a sex line for a few weeks to see if it's as easy as it seems. I'm "going live" tomorrow.'

I was worried. 'Marian, are you sure? It sounds really dodgy.'

She patted my shoulder. 'It isn't. It's totally anonymous. It's the easiest money I'll ever make. Sexy Cats is the company I signed up with and they put me in touch with this woman, Shelly, who does it all the time. She's got five kids, and she said that if you're good, you can earn up to fifty euros an hour. Happy days!'

'Are you sure they can't track your number?'

'Positive. I'm getting a separate mobile phone. They prefer you to use a landline, but I said I wanted to use a pay-as-you-go phone, which you don't have to give any details to get. So I'll be completely anonymous and untraceable. Shelly said the older men tend to want to chat for longer while the younger ones just want quick relief, if you get my drift.'

I put my hands up to my face. 'God, Marian, do you really want to get involved in that? It sounds kind of seedy.'

'I think it'll be fun. Shelly said that, if I want, I can get into the webcam stuff too.'

'Have you lost your mind?' I shouted. 'They'll be able to see your face on the webcam.'

'No! I'd be wearing a wig and glasses. Shelly says they pay more to see her ironing in a G-string or cooking with just a frilly apron. Either way, I get to do my housework and get paid at the same time.'

Now I was really worried. I grabbed her shoulders and shook her. 'You cannot have your face online. OK? You'll be putting yourself and your family at risk. For God's sake, Marian, there are nutters out there. If you want to try the phone thing, fine. But under no circumstances are you to go on any webcam. Promise me?'

She raised her hands. 'OK! Chill out. I won't do the webcam.'

'Swear?'

She nodded, in what I hoped was a genuine way.

I had to admire her, though. She was always looking for ways to make money and improve her situation. She never sat around feeling sorry for herself. I wanted to be more like her. I'd decided to stop moping and get a part-time job to fill my days, but when I'd tried to update my CV, I had a ten-year gap of nothing. Ten years of being a mum. Ten years of absolutely nothing useful, except writing my little column about parenting, which wasn't going to impress anyone. I could still barely use a computer and it made me realize how hopeless I was. Who the hell would ever hire me? I was good at nothing. I wasn't even a particularly good mother. I was literally unemployable.

I wished I had Marian's confidence. She was so sure of herself. I knew Louise was probably the best person to talk to about jobs, but I couldn't bear her to see how completely useless I was. She was so efficient and clever, she'd be shocked to find out I couldn't even use PowerPoint or Excel. I knew I'd have to do a computer course, but even that terrified me. The thought of walking into a room full of young people who were quick learners made me feel sick. I knew I'd be the dunce. I just couldn't face it.

As Marian was leaving, Mum arrived. When she saw Marian, she stiffened. She thought Marian was a bad influence on me because she cursed so much and was, as Mum put it, 'uncouth'.

'Good morning, Marian,' she said. 'How are you?'

'Knackered. I've just had a tour of the mansion and my legs are killing me from all the walking and climbing of stairs.'

I laughed. Mum didn't.

'How are the children?' Mum asked.

'Driving me shagging mental as usual, to be honest.'

Mum flinched and pursed her lips. 'I always thought children were a blessing.'

'Did you?' Marian seemed surprised. 'Maybe

they get more interesting and less needy as they get older. I bloody hope so.'

I stepped in. 'OK, I'll be in touch,' I said, leading Marian to her car.

I waved her off and went back in to talk to Mum.

'I don't know why you're friendly with that woman. She's so coarse.'

I held up my hand. 'I know that Marian can be a bit foul-mouthed, but she's a really good and genuine friend. She's been so kind to me over the years.'

Mum sniffed and put her handbag on the marble kitchen counter. 'I'll take your word for it. Now, what's so urgent that you had to see me in person?'

I sat up beside her on a stool and took a deep breath. 'I wanted to talk to you about Clara.'

Mum's eyes narrowed. 'Go on.'

'I think she might have some . . .' I paused and fidgeted with my earring, trying to find the right words.

'Get to the point,' Mum urged me.

'I think she has Asperger's,' I blurted out.

Mum stared at me. Her eyes slowly filled with tears and she began to nod. 'I think so too,' she croaked.

Soon both of us were in need of tissues. As she dabbed her eyes, Mum said, 'I've been worried about Clara for ages. I raised four children and I know a child that's not quite right. About a month ago I was watching some programme on the BBC and it was all about these children with Asperger's and Clara had a lot of the same symptoms.'

'Did you say anything?'

Mum looked at me as if I was mad. 'To Louise? She'd eat me alive for suggesting it. I was hoping she'd realize it herself soon.'

She had a point. Louise would have snapped her head off. We were all a bit afraid of her, even Mum and Dad.

'Do you think she knows?' Mum asked.

'No. I tried to broach it last week when she came to collect Clara, but she completely dismissed it. She thinks Clara is a genius and that there's nothing unusual about her behaviour.'

'I think, deep down, she knows something is wrong but she doesn't want to admit it. I don't blame her.' Mum dabbed her eyes with a tissue. 'No one wants their child to be different. Life is difficult enough without having extra burdens. Poor little pet, she's such a sweet child.'

'I know, she's a dote, but she is hard work. She's so specific and particular. When Louise gave me her schedule I thought it was just her usual over-parenting. But if I was even ten seconds late with something, or did something out of Clara's routine, she began to panic. It was really sad, Mum. She's going to struggle in primary school and the "real" world. She needs professional help.'

Mum nodded. 'All the websites I looked at say early intervention is vital. I have to talk to Louise.

I was just trying to pluck up the courage and pick the right time.'

I smiled wanly. 'There is no right time. Maybe if we talk to her together, we can persuade her to get Clara seen.'

'I suppose we have to try. I just think if it was one of your boys or young Jess, you or Sophie would handle it better. Louise is so hard on herself. She's spent her whole life pushing herself to achieve great goals. She always wanted to be top of the class, then she wanted to be the best lawyer and now she wants to be the perfect mother.'

Mum was right. Louise always strove for excellence in everything she did. She had a very competitive streak that had completely passed me by. Sophie had a little bit of it, and Gavin, like me, had none.

Louise would not take kindly to having a child who was different. I could see that she thought Clara was like her, incredibly bright and a high achiever, but Clara's path would probably not be the same as Louise's, she was going to need help negotiating life.

We agreed to take Louise out to dinner the following week and talk about Clara. Mum hugged me tight before she climbed into her car. 'And to think I always thought it would be your wild boys who were going to need professional help.'

She drove off before I could tell her exactly what I thought of *that*.

CHAPTER 23

Louise

When Clara's teacher, Helen, asked me if I'd read her note, I told her that I had and that I thought it was nonsense. She seemed disappointed and upset, which irritated me. I couldn't stand looking at her annoying face, and it was clear that she didn't understand or appreciate Clara's genius, so I decided to move my daughter to another school.

I found one that was a bit further away and twice as expensive, but the headmistress seemed a very intelligent woman. I explained about Clara being very bright and she said she'd be honoured to have her in the school.

Christelle was a bit put out when I told her on Friday evening after I'd got back from work. 'But it's going to take us at least twenty minutes to walk there and you know how much Clara hates walking.'

'Well, you'll just have to put her on the back of your bicycle. I'll get you one of those child seats.'

'What about all the rainy days?' Christelle said.

I exhaled, keeping calm. 'I'll get you both rain ponchos.'

'But Clara likes the school she's in. Why are you moving her? You know how much she hates change.'

I didn't want to be questioned about my decision. I knew better than anyone how much Clara loathed change, but it was for her own good. 'Look, Christelle, Clara's teacher was young and foolish and she completely overstepped her mark. I want Clara to be taught by someone intelligent and experienced.'

Christelle seemed surprised. 'Really? I thought Helen was nice and smart. Clara seemed happy there.'

I tapped my foot impatiently. 'Well, it wasn't good enough. She needs more stimulation.'

Christelle put her hands up. 'OK, she's your kid. I'm just saying she's not going to react well to a new school.'

'She'll be fine. I'll bring her in the first few mornings and settle her. But I need you to collect her. OK?'

Christelle shrugged in that very nonchalant French way. 'Sure. I'll bring her to the pet store to look at the parrots after her first day. That always makes her happy.'

I felt myself relaxing. 'Good idea. I'll see you here on Monday, then, when I get home from work.'

Christelle went in to kiss a sleeping Clara

goodbye. She had become really attached to her and it was wonderful to have someone I trusted with Clara while I was at work. Christelle understood Clara and her funny little ways.

As Christelle was leaving, I asked her what her plans were for the weekend.

'I'm going to see the triplets play in a rugby match at their posh school tomorrow and then Julie invited me back for lunch. I'll probably go to a gig tomorrow night. What about you?'

I pointed to my briefcase. 'I've got tons of work to do and I'll just hang out with Clara.'

'Do you ever get lonely?' Christelle asked.

'Honestly, no. I've spent most of my life living alone. I've never shared a flat with anyone. I like my own company.'

'I'm a bit like that, but I always thought it was because I was brought up as an only child. I don't know how Julie stands the noise and the chaos.'

I smiled. 'She's a saint.'

'She really is. Harry's been such a pain lately. He's always playing golf or talking about money. He keeps buying me things. I told him to stop. I want him to be my father, not a cash machine.'

'He's just excited about it, that's all. He'll calm down after a while. Maybe you should take the gifts and the money – you never know when you may need them. Look at Sophie. It was only by selling all of her possessions that she was able to get through those first few months when they lost everything.'

Christelle shook her head. 'No. I'm going to be like my mother and you, Louise – completely independent.'

'Good for you. It's a great way to live.'

I spent a lovely weekend with Clara. I decided to wait until Sunday morning to broach the new-school topic with her.

Clara was busy drawing birds when I said, 'So, sweetie, you know your school?'

She nodded, not looking up.

'Well, it's a bit too babyish for you because you're so clever. I've found another one that's especially for super-bright children like you and they really want you to go there.'

Her hand froze in mid-air.

Damn. I kept talking, trying to reassure her. 'You'll be getting up at the same time, you'll have the same breakfast and wear the same clothes. We might have to leave fifteen minutes earlier if we want to walk, or else Mummy can drive you there or Christelle can cycle you. You can sit on a special seat on the back of her bike. Wouldn't that be fun?'

Without looking up, she asked, 'Will Helen be my teacher?'

'Well, no. You'll have a new teacher, called Alice. She's really nice and she can't wait to meet you. There are only eight children in the class, so it'll be smaller and less noisy.'

Clara continued to draw. 'Is it the same classroom?'

'No, Clara, it's a different school, but it's lovely.'

'NO!' she shouted. 'I will not go there. I want to stay in my school.'

I had to get her to stay calm. I kept my voice even. 'Clara, look.' I placed my iPad under her eyes. 'I took pictures of your new school and your new teacher and your new classroom. See?'

She examined the photos closely, flicking back and forth.

'You'll make new friends. It'll be fine.'

'I don't make friends, Mummy.' Clara's blue eyes looked up at me.

'Of course you will.'

'No. I don't like playing with other people. I want to play by myself. I don't like it when other children try to play games with me. It makes me cross.'

'Well, Clara pet, you must try to make more of an effort with the children in your class. It's good to have friends. It makes school more fun.'

Clara slammed my iPad on the table. 'I'm not going to the new school,' she shouted.

'Yes, darling, you are,' I said firmly.

'NONONONONONONONONONONO!' She thumped the table with her fist and then began throwing her markers and paper all over the floor.

'Pick them up,' I ordered.

Ignoring me, she flung her bird book across the room.

'Clara,' I scolded her, without raising my voice.

She stood up and kicked me. I grabbed her arms

and tried to calm her down, but she was lashing out. I held her in a tight hug and kept talking, trying to soothe her.

'It's OK. Don't get upset, sweetie. Mummy will be with you. It's going to be great. Everything else will be the same. It's only one tiny change. I'll come in and sit with you . . .'

Clara's meltdown lasted more than half an hour. By the end of it, we were both exhausted. I had a piercing headache and, for once, was having second thoughts about my decision. But I couldn't leave her in that school with Helen telling me she needed to see a psychologist. I had to protect Clara from people like her. I wanted to surround her with people who understood her. She was reading books that the average eight-year-old would struggle with. I had been that child. I had been bored at school. I knew how important it was to be stimulated and valued.

No. I had made the right decision. She'd see that. Clara would come round once she started at her new school, where they prized clever children and didn't try to force them to play with other children if they didn't want to.

I snuggled up with a worn-out Clara on the couch, and while she watched her favourite birds-of-prey DVD, I read through some files.

Clara clung to my leg. I bent down. 'Clara sweetie, you must let go now. Mummy has to go to work.'

She tightened her grip. Alice, her new teacher,

crouched beside her. 'Clara, would you like to see the bird books we have? Your mummy told me you love birds so I took all the books with birds in them and put them on a table for you.'

Clara buried her face in my skirt. I glanced at my watch. Damn. I'd been here for twenty minutes. I had to go or I'd be late. I peeled Clara from my leg and held her by her shoulders. 'Mummy has to go now. OK?'

'Don't leave me,' she pleaded. 'I don't like it here. I want my old school.'

'We talked about this, Clara. This is your school now and I know you're going to like it.'

'I want to go home with you, Mummy.'

'But I have to go to work, you know that.'

'Take me to your work. I'll be quiet. I'll read my books and you can do your work, like at home.'

I felt a wave of emotion creeping up my chest. Fighting it back, I said, 'I have a lot of meetings today that children can't come to. You need to stay at school and learn lots of new things. Now I really have to go.'

Alice leant down and took Clara's hand. Clara tried to pull away. She reached out and grabbed the corner of my coat. 'Don't leave me, Mummy.'

I pulled my coat free and ran out of the door before the tears came. I cried all the way to work, almost crashing the car several times because I was blinded by tears.

Head down, I rushed into the cloakroom and locked myself in a cubicle to compose myself. I felt sick. Had I done the right thing? Clara had been distraught.

I never questioned my decisions at work, but with Clara it was so much harder. I only wanted the best for my little girl, but she was so sensitive and needed lots of care and support.

I gathered my things and went into my office, where Wendy was waiting for me. I really didn't want to deal with her right now.

'Is it important?' I asked briskly. 'I've got a crazy schedule today.'

Wendy paced up and down, refusing to meet my eye. Despite my urgings, she had refused to step down and had continued as junior partner. In the last few weeks she hadn't been late or made any mistakes, so I presumed she had sorted out her life. I didn't want the details, I just wanted professional behaviour in the office.

'Wendy!' I barked. 'What is it?'

She wrung her hands. 'It's not my fault. I was just so tired. I didn't mean to do it. It was just a small mistake, but it's kind of a big deal, but I think I can fix it so—'

I held my hand up to interrupt her babbling. 'Wendy,' I said. 'Tell me what happened. Get to the point.'

She bit her lip. 'Don't freak out, but I sent an email meant for a colleague to our client, Jay Goring.'

Judging by the state she was in, the email hadn't been flattering. 'What did it say?'

Wendy's eyes welled up. 'Well, it was kind of jokey and a bit . . . uhm . . . unprofessional.'

I really was not in the mood for Wendy and her bullshit. Clenching my jaw, I hissed, 'Go and print out the email and bring it to me.'

She looked as if she might throw up. 'There's no need. I can sort it out. I just wanted to give you a heads-up in case Jay called you.'

Leaning across my desk, I roared, 'Get me that bloody email NOW.'

Wendy scuttled out. I collapsed back into my chair. I really didn't need this. My morning had been bad enough. I wanted to kill Wendy. I felt incredible rage towards the stupid, useless cow.

She came shuffling back in, holding a piece of paper in her trembling hands. I snatched it from her.

Holding it up, I read it out loud: ' "Hey Suzie, I heard you got stuck with the admin on the Goring file. Can you believe what a moron Jay *Boring* is? He honestly thinks he's God's gift to business – and women! Don't these people get it? The only reason we give him the time of day is because he's stinking rich and we can bill him zillions of hours. He never questions the invoices, by the way, so a word from the wise – feel free to add in extra hours when you're billing him." '

I gasped and dropped the piece of paper onto my desk. I was in shock. Then I looked up at Wendy, who was now sobbing. 'Do you have any idea what you've done? Are you mentally unstable?

302

Because I see no other excuse for this than complete insanity.'

This was beyond bad. This was the most appalling breach of trust and professionalism I'd ever experienced. It reflected horrendously on us as a firm and appallingly on me as head of the department. My blood was boiling. The headache I already had from the stress of leaving Clara so upset was now threatening to split my head open.

'I'm sorry, Louise. He was never meant to see it.'

In a voice shaking with rage, I said, 'Go to your desk, pack up your things and leave. Go home and do not contact anyone at this firm. I will have Human Resources contact you to discuss terminating your contract.'

It was Wendy's turn to look shocked, but her remorse turned very quickly into defensive anger. 'You can't chuck me out. I have rights.'

How dare she? I took a step towards her. 'Your mistake will probably lose us one of our top clients. Your lack of professionalism and respect, your carelessness and your complete disregard for time-keeping and the reputation of this firm are completely and utterly unacceptable. I don't want you in my department, and I guarantee that, after this, no one else will either. You have sabotaged your own career with this piece of stupidity, so don't try to blame anyone else.'

Wendy poked me in the chest. 'You're a bitch,' she shouted. 'You have no feelings or empathy for anyone. Do you know what we call you? The Ice Queen. You're always so perfect and so in control. You're like a fucking robot.'

I turned my back to her and went to sit down at my desk. 'Get out, Wendy, before you make an even bigger fool of yourself.'

She leant across my desk and shoved her finger in my face. 'I feel sorry for you. You're a cold-hearted cow. I pity your kid. I'd hate to have a mother like you. I bet you make her feel like crap all the time because she's not good enough. I bet you're a bitch to her, too. I bet you never hug her or praise her. I hope she's got her father's genes and isn't a freak like you—'

It happened so quickly that I didn't even have time to register the action. I flung my coffee cup across the office. It smashed against the wall, shattering into a thousand pieces.

'Well, well, well, not such an Ice Queen after all,' she sneered. 'I've obviously hit a nerve, haven't I?'

My heart was pounding. I never lost control. But now I saw red. The only reason I'd thrown the cup was to stop myself hitting Wendy. I so badly wanted to wallop her nasty face. 'Go and crawl back under the rock you came from,' I said, in a voice that sounded a lot calmer than I felt.

Wendy stormed out, slamming the door hard behind her. I sank back into my chair.

Could this day get any worse?

I glanced down at my mobile phone. Three missed calls, all from Clara's new school.

As I picked up the phone to call her teacher, my secretary burst into the room. 'I'm so sorry to interrupt, Louise, but Jay Goring is on the phone. He said it's urgent.'

I took a deep breath, picked up the receiver and went into crisis-management overdrive. Not letting Jay speak first, I said, 'I've just seen it. I'm appalled. She's been fired. Wendy will never darken our door again. She was a black sheep and I should have got rid of her ages ago. You can check your billing hours, Jay. They are completely above board. You know me. You know you can trust me. I have never let you down, nor will I . . .' I talked and talked, reassuring him constantly until he eventually interrupted me.

'That's all very well, but I'll still be taking my business elsewhere. I respect you, Louise, and you have an excellent reputation, but that girl worked for you, in your department. If you could employ someone as appalling as her and allow her to sully your name, then you're not as clever as I thought.'

'Jay, wait. Don't be hasty. Let me take you out to lunch and we can talk about it. Wendy's an anomaly. She had a child and hasn't been able to cope. I've been wanting to get rid of her for ages, but you can't just fire someone. You know how it is, these things take time.'

'I would never have someone like that working with me. I would have found a way to move her.

As head of the department, the buck stops with you, Louise. You are ultimately responsible. I won't be changing my mind. I'm taking my business away from you.'

I squeezed my eyes shut. 'Is there anything I can say to dissuade you?'

'Nothing. Good day.' He hung up.

I destroyed a second item in my office that day when my phone hit the wall and shattered.

CHAPTER 24

Sophie

Jess came back from the baby shower on a high. She went on and on about it until I wanted to scream. But I bit my lip and tried to look interested.

'OMG, Mum, Pippa's friends are, like, *soooo* cool.'

'Really? Were there many there?'

'Well, no, because Pippa says when you work in TV people get really jealous of you, so she just had three friends and me. But one of her friends is an actress, one is a beautician and one is a fitness instructor. They're all so glamorous.'

'Well, I suppose they're all young.' Young with no children and no financial worries or husbands who left them, I thought grimly.

'I dunno. I think one of them was, like, nearly thirty, but they all look amazing. Their clothes rock.'

'What has the actress been in?'

Jess swung her legs. 'She said she's doing loads of auditions, but nothing's come up yet. She'll definitely make it to Hollywood, though, because she's so beautiful. She looks like Kim Kardashian.'

How the hell did Jess know what Kim Kardashian looked like? I never let her watch any of that reality-TV rubbish. 'How do you know who—'

Jess rolled her eyes and cut across me: 'Don't start freaking out. Pippa lets me watch *The Kardashians*.'

'You know you're not allowed.'

She shrugged. 'In this house, but in their house I can pretty much do what I want. It's so much more fun over there. They don't treat me like a child.'

'You're nine years old, Jess.'

'Nearly ten, Mum.' She flicked her hair, an annoying new habit she'd picked up from Pippa. 'Anyway, Pippa loved my present. She said it was her favourite by far.'

'Well, that's nice.' Jess and I had compromised on a fifty-euro limit to her spending on the baby-shower gift. She had decided to buy a pale yellow nappy cake, which contained booties and blankets, muslin cloths, bottles and mittens.

'So, is she big now? Her due date's not far off.' I hoped she was a whale.

'No, she's still tiny with just a bump. She said she's only put on eighteen pounds. Her friend Heather said Pippa will be back in her skinny jeans the day after the baby is born!'

I tried not to think evil thoughts, but it was difficult.

'Was your dad there for any of it?'

'Mum, I forgot to tell you the best bit. Dad arrived at the end of the shower and gave Pippa a Tiffany necklace with a big diamond P on it. It's so amazing.'

My stomach twisted. Jack had bought me one of those necklaces, with a big diamond S on it, back in the good old days. I'd sold it to pay a couple of months' rent when everything had fallen apart.

'Wow! Well, Pippa certainly seems to have been spoilt.'

'She so deserves it, though. She always says, "Good things happen to good people." She also says a positive attitude is, like, super important. When I told her you'd been dumped, she said you needed to work harder on being full of sunshine, like her.'

I decided to leave the room before I told my nine-year-old daughter exactly what Pippa could do with her sunshine.

I rang Jack at work.

'Hi. How are you?'

I wasn't in the mood for niceties. 'Pippa is letting Jess watch *The Kardashians*. You know how I feel about her watching those reality-TV shows. She's too young and impressionable, Jack.'

'Are you sure?'

'Yes.'

'OK, I'll have a word with Pippa. But I have to

say, Sophie, Pippa has been amazing with Jess. They get on like a house on fire. She's really stepped up to the plate as a stepmother. She's so welcoming to Jess.'

I couldn't face another bloody Pippa love-in. 'Fine. But we both agree that Jess is too young for that trashy TV. So make sure she doesn't let her watch it again.'

'OK. No need to bite my head off. I heard you broke up with the guy. I'm sorry, Sophie. Jess said you've been in terrible form.'

'No, I haven't. I'm just tired from working and being a single parent,' I snapped.

'You're not a single parent. I see Jess as much as I can,' Jack replied.

'I'm with her eighty per cent of the time Jack, OK?'

'Your choice, Sophie. If you want, I'm happy to take her more. Pippa would like it too.'

To Hell with Pippa! I wanted to scream. 'It's fine, Jack, just sort out the reality TV. I have to go.' I hung up before I took out all of my anger with Andrew, Pippa and life in general on my ex-husband.

On Wednesday evening, I sat in the restaurant, drumming my fingers on the table. I was cross that Mum and Julie were late. I was worried Louise would arrive first because I still had no idea why we were having this dinner. Mum and Julie had promised to be on time. We'd arranged to meet fifteen minutes early so we'd all be there before

Louise arrived and they could fill me in on what was going on.

I had a really important breakfast meeting with a prospective new client at eight thirty the following morning, so I wanted to get to bed as early as possible. It was already eight forty-five and I was getting cross. I badly needed a good night's sleep.

Julie had called me two days ago to tell me I had to come to this dinner because it was vital that we were all there. She said we had to confront Louise about something. But then she hung up because one of the boys smashed the TV with a football.

I'd tried to call Mum to find out what on earth was going on, but she hadn't rung back. She'd just sent a text saying she was tied up, but would explain all when she saw me.

Finally Mum and Julie arrived and plonked themselves down at the table. Julie poured herself a large glass of wine and glugged it back.

'Steady on,' Mum said. 'You need your wits about you tonight.'

'Can someone please tell me what this is all about?'

Mum looked around, checking Louise wasn't coming, then leant in and said, in a low voice, 'We think Clara has Asperger's and we want to confront Louise about it because she's putting her head in the sand when early treatment is vital.'

What? It took me a moment to process all that – it was the last thing I'd expected to hear. Clara?

Could she be? I thought about it, and suddenly it made sense. All of her quirks could be explained by Asperger's. But this was certainly not the right way to go about talking to Louise. I had to stop them. 'Are you mad?' I said. 'Louise is going to see this as a sabotage or weird intervention. You should talk to her one to one.'

Julie put down her glass. 'I tried Sophie, but she brushed me off. We need to make her see that Clara needs help.'

Before I could say anything else, Louise arrived, cross and fed up. She threw her handbag down, poured herself some wine and gulped it. 'Christ, what a bloody week this has turned out to be,' she said. It was unlike Louise to complain, or to drink quickly. The fact that she was already in a bad mood did not bode well.

'What's up?' I asked.

She ran her hands wearily through her hair. 'Work, Clara, everything. Anyway, what was so urgent that we had to meet for dinner mid-week?' she demanded. 'I'm having the week from Hell and I really don't have time for this.'

Julie and Mum looked at each other. Mum leant over and squeezed Louise's hand. 'I'm sorry to hear that, pet.'

Louise pulled her hand away. 'Can we order? I'm starving and I can't stay long,' she said.

'Neither can I,' I said. Then, staring hard at Mum and Julie, I added, 'I think we should all just have a nice relaxing meal.'

Mum shook her head at me. There was no stopping her: she was on a mission.

We concentrated on our menus, then ordered our food.

'So, what's going on?' Louise asked, glancing at her BlackBerry.

Julie looked at Mum. 'Go on.'

Mum smiled in a fake way. 'We're here because we want to talk to you, Louise.'

'About what? Did you hear about the Jay Goring palaver? It hasn't reached the press, has it? I think I made sure of that. Christ, I hope Jay isn't telling everyone about it. I asked him not to out of respect for me and he said he wouldn't, but you know what gossips people are. I hope—'

Julie interrupted her: 'Louise, we want to talk to you about Clara,' she said.

'What about her?' Louise snapped.

I sat back in my chair, powerless to stop Mum and Julie now, waiting for the inevitable explosion from Louise. This was madness. Mum and Julie should have known better.

'Well, it's just that we feel that it might be a good idea to have Clara seen by a psychologist, to help her integrate better and come out of herself.' Julie had another swig of her wine.

Louise's eyes narrowed. I could feel her whole body tensing beside me. 'Julie, I told you already that Clara doesn't need any testing. She's fine. Why are you bringing this up again?'

I felt sick. This was not a good idea.

'What is this? Some kind of intervention? Are you seriously telling me I don't know my own child?' Louise's voice was getting louder as her anger grew. 'I am sick of people telling me that Clara's different. She isn't different, she's a genius. Why can't you get that into your thick heads?' Louise slammed her hand on the table.

'Calm down, Louise,' Mum begged. 'We all love Clara, sure she's the sweetest child in the world, but I'm worried about her. She's very introverted.'

'So what? So was I. I always had my head in a book too.'

Mum shook her head. 'No, Louise, you were not an introvert. You were the opposite. You had an opinion on everything, you bossed everyone else around, you organized games, you were competitive and ambitious, you loved a challenge . . . You were not shy or quiet.'

Now that Mum had reminded me of Louise as a child, I realized she was right. I had always thought Clara was like Louise, but she wasn't. Louise had been a bossy cow when we were kids. I had been terrified of her. My heart sank. Julie and Mum were right about Clara.

Gavin arrived. He threw himself into a chair and picked up a bread roll. 'Jesus, you could cut the air in here with a knife. I take it you've already told Louise that we think Clara has Asperger's.'

'What?' Louise glared at him.

'Shit,' Gavin said.

'How dare you say that about Clara? What would

you know about anything? You can't even hold down a job. Don't you ever say anything about my Clara again. She's more intelligent at four than you'll ever be.' Louise's face was bright red and she was spitting fire.

Gavin chewed his bread. 'You can be as much of a bitch as you want, Louise, but I know I'm right. I love that kid. She's the most amazing little girl in the world, but she's different. And before you tell me I'm a stupid, ignorant fool, hear me out. I think she has Asperger's and I've looked into it. It's not a bad thing, it just needs to be picked up early. Once she's diagnosed, she can get all the extra help she needs to deal with the world.'

Louise stood up. She was shaking. 'My child does not have Asperger's. She's just really, really bright and someone as thick as you will never understand that. I'm leaving before I hit you.'

I put out my hand to stop her. I could see she felt put upon and was reacting like a cornered cat. She felt we were insulting her baby. Gavin had been far too abrupt. 'Louise, we all adore Clara. Please sit down and let's just talk.'

She yanked her arm away from me. 'I'm not staying another second to listen to you all insulting my daughter.' I could see tears in her eyes.

Julie stood up and went over to her. She took Louise firmly by the shoulders. 'Louise, you know all I want is the absolute best for you and Clara. You know I love her. You know I would do anything for you both. Please listen to what we have to say. We only want the very best for Clara. We want her to have the most amazing life possible. Sometimes when you're very close to someone you don't see things. I'm begging you to sit down. If, after you've listened to us, you want to tell us all to shag off and storm out, I won't try to stop you. But we're your family and we love you and we want to help.'

Louise very reluctantly sat down. 'You've got exactly five minutes,' she said, tapping her watch.

Mum cleared her throat. 'I've always thought Clara was an extraordinary child. She's incredible, but I did notice that she always avoids eye contact. She never plays with other children and gets very fixated on things.'

'So what? So do loads of so-called normal kids,' Louise snapped.

'Let her finish,' I said quietly.

'Then I began to notice her obsession with time, how she likes to get dressed a certain way and how she can't stand the various foods on a plate to touch. All things that individually are no big deal, but together began to make me worry. I've raised four children and I knew Clara was different, but I couldn't put my finger on it. Then one night I saw a programme about children with Asperger's syndrome and everything began to make sense.'

Louise said nothing. She looked thunderous.

Julie added gently, 'I only realized how intense her quirks are when she stayed with me. Then I

316

knew something was up. Louise, she'll have a brilliant life. She just needs help in some areas and you're the best person in the world at fixing problems.'

I put my hand on Louise's rigid shoulder. 'You really are. You're the person we all go to with our issues. Clara's lucky to have you as her mum. Whatever she needs, you'll get it for her. She's still your little girl, still your precious Clara. She just needs some assistance.'

Louise picked up her BlackBerry and her bag. Standing up slowly, she said, in an icy tone, 'None of you has any right to put disgusting labels on my daughter. Clara is the most incredible human being on this planet. She is streets ahead of your pathetic children. I am shocked, appalled and disgusted by your behaviour. You make me sick.'

She stalked out of the restaurant and we all stared at each other. I could tell Julie was thinking the same thing as me – pathetic children?

'That went well,' Gavin said.

'You shouldn't have come blustering in like that,' Julie snapped. 'It's an incredibly sensitive issue. She was completely thrown. You're an idiot.' She was fighting back tears. 'It was a disaster.'

'It didn't go well,' Mum said, 'but Louise would always have reacted badly. She's a very proud woman and she's devoted to Clara. It's hard to hear things about your child that you don't want to hear. She'll come round. She needs time to process it. She's a very intelligent woman and she'll see we're right. These things take time. We must be gentle with her.'

I felt sick. Louise only had Clara, just like I only had Jess. We lived alone and our daughters were our lives. Louise had been incredible to me when I'd lost everything. I wanted to be there for her. I decided to run out and see if I could catch her before she drove off.

When I got to the car park I saw her car, parked in the corner. The headlights were on, but she was still there. I ran over, and as I was about to knock on the window, I stopped. Louise was bent double, with her face in her hands, crying as if her heart would break.

I had never seen Louise cry. She was the strongest person I knew. She was the most capable, determined, talented, intelligent woman I had ever met. Yet here she was, crushed and heartbroken.

I hesitated, then opened the car door, leant in, put my arms around my older sister and held her tight.

CHAPTER 25

Julie

I was very shaken after the dinner with Louise. I felt we had handled the situation badly, and when Sophie had sent me a text from the car park saying she had to drive a hysterical Louise home, I'd felt physically sick.

I began to think we'd done the wrong thing, but Mum kept saying that no matter how or when we'd broached the subject Louise would have been angry and upset. These were completely normal reactions. When she had had time to reflect and take it all in, she'd see we meant only the best, that we loved Clara and were looking out for her best interests.

I had tried calling Louise and texting her, but so far she hadn't responded. Sophie said we needed to give her some space.

In the days following the dinner I didn't feel like meeting anyone, so I'd been staying at home reading books and texting Dan, who was in Germany on some business trip and kept sending me hilarious messages about his German colleagues

319

and saucy ones about big German sausages. His messages were the only thing that brightened my day. I felt very flat. Besides the Louise fiasco, I'd applied for two jobs as a receptionist. I didn't tell anyone about it. I saw so little of Harry now that it hadn't occurred to me to share it with him. Anyway, I figured receptionists wouldn't need that many skills and certainly wouldn't need to know stuff like PowerPoint or Excel. I'd had a 'no thank you' from one and the other hadn't bothered replying. When I called to follow up, they said I'd been out of the workplace too long and they needed someone with specific receptionist experience. I was mortified. I was officially useless. Thank God for Dan, with his ability to distract me and make me laugh.

On Friday morning, after texting back and forth, Dan said he had to go to a conference. The morning loomed long and lonely ahead so I decided to call Marian for a chat.

She answered the phone and whispered, 'Hold on one second.' Then I heard her talking to someone else.

'Yes, John, you do have a beautiful dick . . . Yes, it is big, so big, the biggest ever . . . Oh, you naughty boy . . . Where do you want to put it? . . . John, you are so bad . . . Oh, yes, I'm loving this . . . Oh, John, don't stop now . . . Keep going . . . Concentrate . . .'

Marian was back with me. 'Sorry, Julie, I'm nearly finished here.'

'I'll call you back.'

'No, it's grand. He's nearly done.'

Going back to John, she shouted encouragement at him: 'Go on, John . . . go on . . . Yes . . . yes . . . yes . . . Are you done? . . . Ah, come on, John, focus . . . You're inside me now, in and out, in and out, oh, yes, John, this is fantastic, I'm whipping you, I'm slapping you . . . Oh, yes, I'm in ecstasy . . . Go, go, go! . . . Are you finished? For the love of God, man, will you get on with it? I'm beating you, I'm flogging you, I'm thrashing you . . . Ah, good man. Finally. Well done. Brilliant. That's the best phone sex I've ever had. You're a beast, John, an animal, a tiger. I'll talk to you next week, same time. 'Bye, big boy.'

I stifled my giggles. Marian came back on the line. 'So, how are you?'

'I think the question here is, how are you after all that sex?'

Marian laughed. 'It's the easiest money I've ever made. Honestly, men are mad. Imagine paying money to some stranger at the end of a phone to pretend you're having sex with them.'

'I know! Have you had any creepy guys?'

'Not yet. To be honest, a lot of them are lonely. Half the time they just want to chat. Yesterday I spent an hour on the phone to a farmer in Laois talking about harvesting. I actually learnt quite a lot.'

'Well, old John there didn't sound like he wanted to chit-chat.' I laughed.

Marian chuckled. 'Sometimes they don't concentrate and you need to get them back on track. Otherwise you'd be on the phone for hours waiting for them to climax. I know it's more money for me, but it's hard to keep up the momentum, even on the phone. I'd never be able for Tantric sex. I don't have the patience.'

I squirmed. 'I cannot believe we're talking about strange men climaxing at ten in the morning. How do you do it so early?'

'Well, I can hardly be huffing and puffing when the kids get home from school, so it's mornings and late nights only.'

'How's your real sex partner, Lew?' I asked.

'To be honest, he's gone a bit cool on me, the bastard.'

'Oh, no.'

'I think he's found another housewife. He's working on a new job and he keeps telling me he's too busy to see me. I'm pretty sure he's moved on.'

'Are you OK?'

'I'm grand. Sure I knew it was only a fling. He was hardly going to move in with me. Mind you, it was nice while it lasted. To be honest, with all the phone sex I'm having, I wouldn't have time for the real stuff.'

'Any word from Greg?'

'He's coming home for Molly's birthday, so we'll see how we get on. I'm not looking forward to seeing him at all. But it'll be nice for the kids.'

'I bet when you see him you'll be happy.'

Marian paused. 'I'm not sure. We need to sit down and have a very frank conversation.'

I sat up on the couch. 'You're not going to tell him about Lew, are you?'

'Actually, I think I will. I know Greg's been up to no good too. We need to be honest with each other and see if we can salvage our marriage or if it's over. I don't know how I feel about him any more. I need to see him and spend some time with him, then decide what to do. I'm used to being on my own, so that doesn't frighten me. I put the bins out, I pay the bills, I deal with the kids. I do everything.'

I was on my own a lot, too. Harry was often out, and when he was at home, he wasn't present. He was always on the phone or messing around on his laptop. He only really engaged with us all when the boys were playing rugby. It was as if he lived in the house but was mentally elsewhere. That was why I was texting Dan so much these days. At least he was interested in what I had to say. At least he thought I was sexy and funny.

'I think you and Greg just need to spend some time together and reconnect. All marriages go through ups and downs. It's normal – it doesn't mean it's over. Talk to him when he comes home and see. I'll take your kids for a night so you can be alone to chat.'

Marian whooped with laughter. 'Julie, you're really sweet, but I wouldn't inflict my kids on you.'

'I'd be happy to have them. My house is chaotic anyway and, besides, I've nothing else to do.'

'Thanks, it's a really nice offer. If I need to take it up, I'll get back to you. To be honest, having the kids around is a good buffer for me and Greg. They're all we have left in common.'

'Well, the offer's there. Think about it.'

'I will. Listen, I gotta run. My sex line's ringing. It's Damian – he likes the dominatrix stuff.' She answered her other phone. 'Damian, hold on a second, you low-life prick. I'll be there in a minute to beat you senseless.'

Back to me she whispered, 'Talk soon, Julie.'

I hung up quickly before I caught any more of her sex talk.

That Saturday, the triplets were invited to a fancy-dress party by one of the boys in their class. Apparently this kid was obsessed with bats, spiders and ghosts, so his mother had decorated their ballroom – yes, they had a ballroom! – like a haunted house. There was going to be a magician doing 'gross magic' and a zookeeper was coming with spiders and snakes for the boys to hold.

The triplets were beside themselves with excitement. Leo was going dressed as a mummy, Luke as Dracula and Liam as a vampire. Although Tom wasn't going, he wanted to join in and dress up as a pirate.

'You're such a dork,' Luke said to Liam. 'Dracula

is a vampire so you're just copying me. Go as something else.'

'No way. I'm going as a vampire and I'm going to be way scarier than you, you big fat moron.'

'Stop being so rude to each other,' I snapped. 'You can both be vampires but different.'

'Duh, Mum, vampires have a black cape, sticky-out teeth and fake blood. He's totally copying me and it's not fair.' Luke was not giving in.

I turned to Liam. 'Perhaps you could go as something else. How about a pirate?'

Liam looked at me as if I was completely insane. 'Pirates are lame.'

'I'm wearing a pirate costume,' Tom piped up.

'Exactly. Lame.'

'Don't be mean to Tom just because you're in a grump,' I scolded him. To Tom, I added, 'You'll be a brilliant pirate.' He gave me a grin.

'Why don't you just go as a monster or something?' I suggested to Liam.

'I want to be a vampire. Luke can't just force me to be something else. It's not fair.'

'You're just a copycat. Come up with your own idea,' Luke shouted.

Liam's face went red. 'Shut up, you idiot.'

As Liam rushed over to hit his brother, I stepped in and stopped him. 'Right, that's enough. You're both going as vampires and I'll do different makeup on you so you don't look the same.'

'I want to have more blood because it was my idea,' Luke huffed.

'Fine,' I said.

'*Nooooooo*,' Liam shouted. 'That's not fair. I don't want to look like a crap vampire. I want to look really gross. I want loads of blood.'

I put my hand up. 'I promise to make you both look really awful.'

Tom tugged at my sleeve. I bent down. 'Mummy, I don't want any blood,' he whispered.

I hugged him. 'Don't worry, pet. I'm only putting it on the triplets and it's not real, just red water. OK? And you do know that you're not actually going to the party, don't you?'

He nodded. 'Yes, but I want to dress up like the boys.'

'I know and that's fine.' I kissed his eager little face. Tom was going to have a lifetime of trying to keep up with his brothers.

Half an hour later, as I was sending Harry a very grumpy message for being late back from golf – again – he was supposed to be dropping the boys to the party – I heard an almighty thump. I ran out to see Leo prostrate at the bottom of the stairs, wrapped from head to toe in toilet paper.

'Mmmmmm,' he muttered.

I rushed over to him. He was staring at me, wide-eyed. His mouth was stuffed with toilet paper. I pulled it out. 'Are you all right?'

'I hate them!' he shouted. 'They wrapped me up and then when I couldn't move because my arms and legs were all tied up, they put toilet

paper in my mouth. I was trying to find you to
get it out, but I fell on the stairs.'

'Are you hurt?'

'MUM! I just fell down the stairs! Of course I'm
hurt, but I don't think anything is broken.'

'Let's get this off you.' I began pulling at the
toilet paper.

'What are you doing?' he roared. 'You're ruining
my costume.'

'But I want to see if you're all right.'

Wriggling about, Leo somehow managed to
stand up. 'I'm fine. I just didn't want to die of
suffocation before the party.'

He hopped back up the stairs. I followed him
to see how the others were getting on. The bathroom door was locked and I could hear squealing.

'What's going on? Open this door,' I said.

I heard giggling.

'Boys? Open up.'

'Hold on, Mum, we just need to finish something,' Luke said.

I could hear squirting noises and raucous
laughter. Oh, Jesus, the fake blood. I ran to my
bedroom where I had hidden it in what I thought
was a safe place – in a shoebox under a pile of
blankets at the back of my wardrobe. It was gone.
Nowhere was safe from these guys.

I rushed back and thumped on the door. 'Open
this door or I swear I'll break it down.'

'Go away.'

'Open it now!' I shouted.

'NO! You're just going to freak out,' Liam said.

'If you do not open this door, I'll kick it down.' I was panicking now.

I could hear urgent whispering.

'We'll only let you in if you promise not to go mad.'

'I promise,' I lied.

'No way, Mum.' Luke knew me too well. 'You have to swear on the Bible.'

'OK.'

'No, you have to swear on our lives,' Liam said.

'OK.'

'So you swear that you will not go crazy and start shouting at us and telling us we're brats and that we're ruining your life and—'

Luke was interrupted by Liam: 'And saying we're not normal and we're always wrecking everything and we don't have respect for stuff and—'

Luke cut back in: 'And that we're spoilt and we have too much stuff now that we're rich and that we don't appreciate things and the kids in Syria have nothing.'

Liam added, 'And that you wish we were like other kids who are really good and sit in restaurants for, like, six hours, and don't fight, and eat slimy, squirmy fish and disgusting vegetables and never say rude words or shout—'

Liam was once again interrupted by Luke: 'And that we've given you another headache and you want to go somewhere quiet and lie down for a really long time?'

Did I really say all those things to them? Some of them sounded pretty mean when they were said back to me. I'd have to learn to hold my tongue. I'd be nicer and use kinder words and not lose my temper with them. After all, they were only nine and they were really good kids. I would remain calm, no matter what.

'I solemnly promise not to go mad.'

'OK.' The door opened. The bathroom looked like a violent crime scene. The walls, floor, toilet, sink and bath were covered with fake blood. 'You horrible little monsters,' I screamed. 'Get out of my sight before I kill you.'

They scarpered.

Harry didn't make it home in time to bring them to the party, so I had to drive them there, with Tom in the car. When we arrived, Tom had a complete meltdown – I'd known he would – as the boys ran into the party and he was left with me. Harry was putting his family second all the time. I was sick and tired of his absence and his obsession with money and investments. I wished his aunt had left him nothing. His inheritance was turning him into someone I didn't like or recognize.

I took Tom to the park, then for some juice and a big chocolate muffin, which calmed him down, and went back eventually to collect the triplets. They clambered into the car, comparing their party bags, which were filled with Lindt chocolate truffles, Ferrero Rochers and solid silver key-rings.

'Mum, it was the most amazing party *ever*. The magician was brilliant!' Leo squealed.

'Guess what? Ralph's dad has a helicopter!' Luke said.

'What?'

'We saw it! It's parked in the back garden, which is ginormous,' Liam told me.

'Ralph gets twenty euros a week pocket money and he's allowed to spend it on sweets and he has a whole room just for his Wii and Xbox, and he has forty football shirts.'

I winced. Was this really what I wanted for my kids? To grow up thinking a helicopter in the back garden was normal? 'Well, Ralph is very unusual. I mean, very few people would have what he has. I don't want you thinking you're ever going to have forty football shirts in your cupboard.'

'We know that, Mum. We get one on our birthday and one at Christmas from Santa,' Leo said.

'Anyway, who wants forty shirts? You'd never get to wear them all. Loads of Ralph's still had their tags on,' Luke said.

'Ralph's crap at football. It doesn't matter what shirt he wears, he still can't score a goal,' Liam added.

They all began to laugh at poor Ralph's lack of football skills.

'I want to go in a helicopter,' Tom piped up.

'Only his dad goes in the helicopter, you dork. Ralph said he's never even been in it,' Leo said.

'Yeah. He had to buy it because he can only be in Ireland for one hundred days a year or something,' Luke said.

Aha! So Ralph's dad didn't pay taxes here.

'He says his dad basically lives on an island that's, like, near Ireland,' Luke added.

'That sucks,' Liam said. 'I'd rather have no money and my dad live in Ireland than zillions of money and no dad.'

Good for you, I thought, although we currently had money and an absentee dad.

When we got home, Luke stuffed one of the sweets into his mouth, then made a choking noise. 'Gross!' he said, spitting one of the truffles from the party bag into his hand.

'I don't like nuts,' Liam wailed, as he tried to eat a Ferrero Rocher.

'Posh sweets suck!' Leo grumbled.

'Here you go,' I said, feeling sorry for them. I handed them a bag of jelly snakes I had in the cupboard.

'Thanks, Mum!' They dived on the bag, ripping it open and fighting each other for ownership.

My phone beeped. I glanced down: a text from Dan. *URGENT. Am coming to Dublin next week for one night 2 c u b4 flying back to US. Booked room in 4 Seasons.*

My hand began to shake. Could I? Should I? Would I?

CHAPTER 26

Louise

I sat in the waiting room, fidgeting, and tried to distract Clara. It wasn't difficult because it was full of Lego, games, books and posters, all aimed at keeping children occupied while they waited.

While Clara built a bird out of Lego, I sat back and tried to do my yoga breathing. This last week had been, without a shadow of doubt, the worst week of my life.

After the awful dinner with my family, which I was still furious about, I had cried for hours. Sophie had driven me home and tried to come in to sit with me, but I begged her to go. I needed to be on my own. I needed to calm down and think.

I don't cry. I've never been a crier. I'd always thought it was a sign of weakness, unless it was related to grieving the death of someone. Julie's a big crier. If Julie hears a sad story she cries. It's really annoying. Sophie has more control, like me, but she still cries. I've just never seen the point. If something is upsetting you, fix it or move on.

That was until Clara came into my life. The first time I cried was when I went to Paris with my sisters and Clara was only about six months old. I woke up early on the Sunday morning and I just had to get back to her. It was a physical craving. I'd never felt anything like it before. We sisters were supposed to spend our last day in Paris together, but I went straight to the airport and got a morning flight home. I was back at my apartment in London by ten thirty.

When I saw Clara and held her to me, I burst into tears. It came from nowhere. I was completely taken by surprise, but I couldn't stop. It came over me quite suddenly because when Clara was born I'd felt nothing. I was completely underwhelmed by her. In fact, I found motherhood very difficult. It wasn't until that moment when I rushed back from Paris that I realized I was head over heels in love with my little girl. I'd never imagined I could love someone with such passion. I adored her, worshipped her, I just had to be with her. Since that day we'd only been apart once, when I went to Brussels and Julie had minded her.

Every time I looked at Clara, my heart skipped a beat. She had literally taken over all of my affections and made me discover a capacity for love that I honestly hadn't thought I possessed. I was still very unemotional about every other part of my life, but when it came to her, I just melted.

I still didn't believe there was anything wrong

with her. I was quite convinced that she was a genius, although I did accept that she had trouble communicating with other children. But I had decided to see a child psychologist to shut my family up and stop them interfering in my life. I was also hoping he would give Clara some tools to help her feel more comfortable in social situations, so people wouldn't mark her out as 'different'.

Julie had been stalking me since the dinner. She kept calling and leaving tearful messages about how much she loved Clara and how she only wanted to help. Mum was the same, but she wasn't emotional, just practical. She kept saying Clara was a wonderful child but she needed expert help in dealing with the world. Gavin sent a text only Gavin could send: *Dude I now ur angry but C has Aspies so axept it & get her help. I luv d kid, Ill help u out.*

I ignored them all. The only person I would communicate with was Sophie. I was too angry to deal with the others. I hadn't been sleeping. After that awful dinner, I'd gone home and googled Asperger's syndrome, but I had to stop because it was upsetting me. Clara did have some of the symptoms, but so would any intelligent, shy child.

The next morning I hunted down the name of the best child psychologist in the country and now here we were, in his rooms. His secretary had tried to give me an appointment in a month's time. She didn't know who she was dealing with. I got an appointment five days after I'd called.

'Clara Devlin,' the receptionist called.

I stood up. 'Yes, here.'

'Mr Fitzgerald will see you now.'

I led Clara, who was clutching her Lego bird, into the psychologist's office.

He stood up and came to greet us. He was younger than I'd been expecting, which was good. I didn't want some old fuddy-duddy who'd studied forty years ago. I wanted someone who was up to date and current in his practices. Experienced, but not out of touch.

He crouched down to say hello to Clara, who kept her eyes lowered. He asked her a few questions: her name, her age and what she liked. She answered them all, and when he asked her why she liked birds so much, she launched into a five-minute monologue. I smiled as I could see how impressed he was with her vocabulary and how articulate she was for such a young age.

He sat with her on a couch and got her to talk about school and the children in her class for a while. After about ten minutes he asked Clara if she could go outside and make him an eagle using Lego pieces. She marched out and set to her task happily.

With Clara peacefully occupied, Mr Fitzgerald turned to me and said he thought Clara was a wonderful child.

'Before you say anything else, I just want to be clear here,' I interrupted him. 'I know how amazing Clara is. She is a genius. I'm a high-achiever and was always ahead of my class as a child. I believe she's like me. However, my family and her teacher seem to think she has Asperger's, which is why I'm here. I know they're wrong, but I need to get them off my back so I'm having Clara seen by a specialist.'

'Mrs Devlin,' he tried to butt in, but I was having none of it.

'I know what you're going to say. Clara does have problems with eye contact and she can be shy with other children, but she's an only child and lots of only children are like that. She has no father – it's not a sad story, he's just not in the picture and never has been. To be frank, I'm annoyed with having had to take time off work to come here today. I'm in the middle of a huge case and this really is not the right time to be faffing about with psychologists when I know my daughter is perfect. In fact, she's more than perfect, she's unique.'

'Mrs Devlin.'

I put my bag over my shoulder and went to stand up. 'It's Miss – remember the part about there being no dad in the picture? So, anyway, I'm going to give your details to my sister Julie because her triplets are the ones who need to see a psychologist – they're absolutely feral. Honestly, you should see them. In fact, you could probably write a paper on them.'

'Miss Devlin—'

'Oh, for goodness' sake, call me Louise.'

'Fine, and you can call me Colin.'

I glanced at my watch. 'Damn. I've only got ten more minutes, so can we get on with this?'

He threw his head back and laughed.

I was a bit taken aback: what on earth was so hilarious? 'Have I missed something? Did something amusing happen?'

He looked at me, smiling widely. 'I'm sorry, but you came into my office, talked *at* me for ten minutes, then asked *me* to hurry up.'

'Well, you should have interrupted me.'

'I did try.'

I shrugged. 'Try harder. Are you a man or a mouse?' What an idiot.

He watched me for a moment, then took a deep breath. 'My initial impression is that Clara is a lovely child and, as you said, she is extremely bright and advanced for her age in many ways. I also think she may have some difficulties adapting to social life and all the challenges that it entails, particularly when it comes to integrating with others.'

What a ridiculous waste of time. 'Are you seriously going to charge me a hundred and twenty euros to tell me what I already know? You're just repeating what I said when I came in.'

'Louise, I would appreciate it if you did not interrupt,' he said. 'Now, if we are to move forward with this assessment, I will need to talk to Clara's teacher, her GP and any child-minder she may have. I will also need to talk to you in detail about Clara's family history and the history of her development from birth to date.'

'If there's anything wrong with her it's because of her bloody father's genes, not mine,' I grumbled.

Colin ignored me. 'During Clara's visits here I would like to observe and assess some specific skills and activities – we call this focused observation. I'd be looking specifically at language, behaviour, cognitive ability, et cetera. We would also need to arrange a detailed physical examination, along with testing Clara's blood for genetic conditions that are known to cause ASD.'

'What's ASD?'

My head was spinning. It would take months to get all this done just to prove what I already knew – that there was nothing to find out.

'Autistic spectrum disorder.'

I jumped up. 'What the hell are you talking about? *Autism?* My child isn't sitting in some room bashing her head off a wall. How dare you even use that word? You're obviously one of those students who went to some dodgy university in Azerbaijan to get your degree.'

He grinned at me. It was infuriating. 'I received my degree from Harvard Medical School.'

'You could be lying,' I muttered.

'Feel free to call Harvard then, to check up on my credentials.' He leant forward. 'I understand your fear, Louise. Every parent who comes into my office is worried about their child. That's why they're here. ASD is a general term that includes serious and also very mild forms of the disorder. Asperger's syndrome comes under the banner of ASD. Clara may prove not to have Asperger's, but I do think it's advisable to have her tested. And,' he said, holding up a finger to stop my interruption, 'you are going to have to become more informed on this yourself. You have a warped view of these conditions – talking about children sitting in corners hitting their heads off walls is unhelpful and totally inaccurate. You'll need to tackle your own fears so that they don't erupt as prejudice. I'll give you a reading list so that you can start learning all you'll need to know to help Clara.'

I tried to control my breathing. I could feel myself panicking. 'In your experience, what are the main symptoms of Asperger's? I don't want a lecture, just a really brief summary.'

He nodded. 'There are three main areas of difficulty: social interaction, social communication and imagination, and cognitive flexibility. Each of these diagnostic features can be present in different forms and to varying degrees.'

Clara walked in and handed Colin the most beautifully made eagle – even the beak was perfect. He crouched down. 'Well, you are clever. This is the most wonderful eagle I ever saw.'

She didn't look up. She just went to the chair, picked up her book and began to read.

Colin handed me a tissue. I hadn't even realized I was crying. My baby, my sweetheart, my pride and joy. She needed help, I knew it. I think I'd always known it, deep down. I just hadn't wanted to see it. I'd ignored it. I'd pushed back against it. I'd fought it. I'd refused to believe that she wasn't perfect in every way. But as I looked at her now, frowning in concentration, I knew we were going on a journey together that was going to be very different from the life I'd had mapped out for her.

CHAPTER 27

Sophie

Jess's screams woke me up. I looked at the clock: it was five a.m. I jumped out of bed and across to her room. She was leaping up and down shrieking.

'What's wrong?' I asked.

'Pippa had a baby boy!' she cried.

'Oh, great,' I managed.

'Dad just sent me a text.' Jess proceeded to read it to me: ' "Jess, you have a new baby brother, Robert Jack Wells. He was born at four o'clock this morning. He's magnificent. Pippa was incredible. All doing well. Can't wait for you to meet him." ' Jess looked up at me, eyes shining. 'I've got a brother!'

The news made me feel sick. I felt selfish, too, because Jack sounded so deliriously happy and Jess was so ecstatic, but their joy was incredibly isolating because I wasn't part of it. I was on the outside. I felt completely sidelined by this new family unit – Jess, Jack, Pippa and Robert.

I tried really hard to look happy, for Jess's sake.

I went over and hugged her. She gave me half a hug, but was too busy texting back to notice me. I could see lines of smiley faces and heart kisses being sent to Jack.

'Why don't you go back to bed, love?' I suggested. 'You'll be exhausted in school.'

'School?' Jess looked at me as if I was crazy. 'I'm not going to school! I'm going to the hospital to see my brother.' She began to rifle through her wardrobe.

I grabbed her shoulder. 'Jess, it's five in the morning. You're going nowhere but bed.'

She shrugged me away. 'Get off me, Mum. I need to see Robert.'

'Jess,' I said. 'Pippa has just given birth. She doesn't want to see anyone. She needs rest. Leave it until after school. I'll drive you over to see them then.'

'Pippa loves me,' Jess shouted, her face flushed with excitement and emotion. 'I know she'd want to see me immediately.'

'OK. Call your dad and ask him.'

Jess sighed dramatically and rang Jack. 'Dad! I'm so excited . . . Wow . . . Really? . . . Was she? She's so brave . . . I knew she'd be amazing . . . Is he? . . . Gorgeous? Wow . . . Can I come and see you now? . . . Oh. OK . . . Well, in an hour or two? . . . Oh . . . OK . . . Really? . . . Oh . . .' Her face fell. 'Mum said she'd drive me over after school . . . OK, I'll call and check first . . . 'Bye.' Jess hung up, deflated.

'Is Pippa tired?'

She nodded. 'Dad said she told him not to let anyone in. She's too wrecked.'

'It's understandable, pet. She's just given birth. It's very draining, physically and emotionally.'

'I know, but I'm family. I really want to see my brother.'

'Don't worry. You'll see him later today, and for the rest of your life.'

She climbed back into bed.

I went over and kissed her head.

'Dad says Robert's the most beautiful baby he's ever seen.' She yawned.

'Apart from you!' I added.

Jess rolled her eyes. 'He says he looks like Pippa, absolutely gorgeous.'

I decided not to say that it was a pity he didn't look like Jack. I tucked Jess's duvet around her and turned out the light.

When I got back to my bedroom, I sent Jack a text. I wanted to pretend to be happy for him and a text was easy: *Congratulations. A son & heir!*

He wrote straight back: *Tks. He's incredible. So happy. It doesn't get better than this.*

His joy leapt off the phone and made my loneliness so much more acute. I remembered how happy we'd been when Jess was born. Life had been so easy back then, so full of happiness and comfort and optimism. Now . . . I looked around my small bedroom, my empty bed, my solitary life and felt sad and alone.

★   ★   ★

343

Three hours later, Jess was up and ready for school before I had come out of the shower. Instead of me rushing her out of the door, she was giving out to me for taking too long to get ready.

I hadn't been able to sleep properly after the five o'clock announcement. As a result I looked exhausted and needed extra concealer around my eyes. I did not like what I saw in the mirror: I was getting older by the second.

I drove Jess to school, and as she climbed out of the car, she said, 'Don't be late picking me up. I want to go straight to the hospital.'

I sighed. 'For the fiftieth time, I won't. I told you I'll leave work early and bring you over there.'

Jess ran over to tell her friends about her new baby brother. I saw them all squealing and hugging her. Apparently it was big news.

When I got to work, I went to sit at my desk in the corner, away from the other bookers and the models who were in for morning jobs, and kept my head down. I didn't feel like talking to anyone.

I glanced idly through the newspapers, trying to motivate myself to work. A photo in the social column of the *Evening Herald* caught my eye. There was Andrew, his arm draped around last year's Miss Ireland. She was half my age with a figure to die for and a cleavage that would give Kim Kardashian a run for her money. I clenched my jaw. I couldn't cry, not here at work.

'Tut-tut,' a voice behind me said. It was Quentin. He removed the newspaper from my hands. 'I was going to tell you about them, but he's only recently started dating her. It won't last long.'

I blinked back tears. Quentin took me by the hand and brought me into his office, where he closed the door as I dissolved. 'He's not worth it, darling.' He rubbed my back.

'It's not Andrew,' I sobbed. 'Well, it's not only that. Jack had a baby boy this morning and he's ecstatic and I'm miserable. I know I have Jess and my job and my sisters and all that but I – I'm scared.'

'Of being alone for the rest of your life?'

I nodded.

'Yes, darling. I know exactly how that feels.'

I took a deep breath. 'Sorry, I'm a mess. I was doing really well and I was being so strong until recently. I don't know what's wrong with me.'

Quentin poured me a cup of coffee. 'You've had two big slaps in the face, Andrew being a bastard and Jack falling in love and having a baby. It's perfectly understandable that you feel fragile.'

'That's exactly the word,' I exclaimed. 'Fragile. I feel like a thin glass that could shatter at any minute. Even my skin hurts, like it's bruised or something.'

'It's very difficult for you at the moment, but you'll bounce back because you're very resilient.' Quentin handed me a cup. 'You've been through worse.'

'Have I? I honestly think I feel weaker and less able to deal with things now. Maybe I'm getting the menopause early or something. I feel so weepy and frail.'

'You're forty-two. You're not getting the menopause. Believe me, honey, you'd know if you were. You'd be sitting there in a puddle of perspiration. You're just lonely and frightened of the future because you don't know what it holds.'

I gave him a watery smile. 'You're right. Thanks for listening to me rambling on. I promise to stop weeping in work and be more professional.'

'Sophie, if it wasn't for you, I would have been out of business three years ago. You have revitalized this company. Remember that and be proud.'

I went over and kissed his cheek. 'Thank you.' Sitting down again, I looked at the wall of framed magazine covers of our models, all of them so young and beautiful and perfect. I'd never look young again, but I was damned if I was going down without a fight. I had to peel myself off the floor, make myself look really good, then get out there and meet someone. I deserved to be happy, but sitting around moaning wasn't going to get me anywhere.

'All of these recent events have made me even more determined to go ahead with my boob job. I'm going to do it. I need to boost my confidence. And I need to look hot.'

Quentin frowned. 'Are you sure?'

'Positive,' I said. 'Nothing's going to stop me. I need to feel good about myself again. I'm sick of being jealous of Pippa and every other young woman out there. I need to get on with my life and make changes to improve it. I'm starting with my breasts.'

I spent the morning doing a dress rehearsal for a big charity fashion show that was taking place on Friday. I helped the stylist dress the models from our agency so that the clothes looked fantastic. We were using our six top girls, who were all stunning. Sometimes I wondered if working with beautiful young women was part of my problem: being constantly surrounded by perfection wasn't good for anyone's ego.

I left work early to pick Jess up from school and bring her to the hospital. She was standing at the gate, hopping from one foot to the other impatiently. When she saw me, she rushed over and jumped into the car.

'Quick, Mum. Don't drive like a granny, drive fast.'

'I don't drive like a granny, thank you.'

Jess was holding a huge card in her hand. It was covered with hearts, sparkles and a very good drawing of a baby boy.

'Did you do that in school?' I asked.

'Yes. I asked Mrs O'Brien if I could do a special card during break time for my new baby brother and she helped me.'

'It's lovely, Jess. You're talented.'

'I'm just OK,' she said. Clearly she'd inherited my crummy ego. I wished she'd got some of Jack's.

347

She needed to be more confident. I wanted Jess to believe in herself, to feel she could do anything, be anyone, get any job and not be afraid to be on her own. I wanted her to be different from me.

'You're not just OK, you're really good at art.'

She rolled her eyes. 'God, Mum, you're always going on about how great I am at everything. It's embarrassing. I'm just average, OK?'

I patted her knee. 'Get used to it, love. I'll be telling you how wonderful you are for the rest of my life.'

She ignored me and leant over to change the radio station.

We got to the hospital about twenty minutes later and Jess leapt out of the car. I said I'd find a parking space and meet her in the lobby in half an hour. She was gone before I could finish my sentence. I watched her sprinting towards Reception, so eager to be with her new family.

I went to park the car, and while I sat and waited, my phone beeped. It was a long, convoluted text message from Julie, saying she was spending the night with me on Friday but that she wasn't actually going to see me on Friday and not to say anything to Louise or Harry, that she'd explain later and it wasn't anything bad: she just needed a little night out and she'd owe me one.

I frowned. She sounded drunk. I'd call her later to see what on earth the message meant. It had struck me recently that Julie was drinking too much wine. Every time I was with her, she was pouring big glasses and downing them. I'd been so distracted with my own life and also keeping an eye on Louise and Clara that I hadn't had time for Julie. I'd phone her when Jess was in bed and we could have a proper chat.

I threw my phone onto the passenger seat and bent down to pull a file from my briefcase. It was full of photos of models and celebrities. I narrowed the pile down to two photos. They were the shape and size of breasts I wanted – Victoria Beckham and Kelly Rowland. In my view, they were the nicest and least fake-looking.

I heard a tap on the window. I slammed the file shut as photos slid all over the car floor and looked up to see Jack grinning in at me.

I got out of the car. We kissed awkwardly on the cheek.

'Why don't you come up?' he suggested.

I smiled at him. 'I very much doubt Pippa wants to see your ex-wife just after giving birth.'

He grinned. 'I meant come up and see the baby. Pippa's having a manicure so Robert's in the nursery. I left Jess holding him – he's asleep in her arms. It's very sweet.'

I hesitated. Jack took my hand. 'Come on, he's a little cracker. Let me show him off. You know what my family's like – they won't be interested in him.' The buoyancy in Jack's voice had disappeared. His family had always considered him the black sheep. They were the most appalling intellectual snobs and they always put him down. 'Don't let them dampen your happiness,' I said.

'The only response I got from the messages I left was a two-word text from Mum, "Good news". I haven't heard anything from Dad or Roger.'

'Jack, they'll never change. You have to stop looking for their approval. It just brings you down. They live in their world of medicine. You'll never be good enough. Forget about them and enjoy this moment.'

Jack turned and hugged me. 'Thanks. You're the only one who knows how bad they are. Pippa doesn't seem to notice that they belittle her and me.'

Seriously? How dense was she? Jack's family were awful. 'I wish I hadn't wasted so much time trying to get them to like me and be nicer to you.'

Jack held the lift door for me. 'I'm glad you tried.'

'Enough about them. Let's focus on your son,' I said, as brightly as I could.

His face lit up. 'He's perfect. I can't believe I have a son. I never thought I'd have any more kids.'

'Well, it helps when you trade in your wife for a younger model.'

'Sophie, I tried to make it work.'

I was a bitch. I felt bad. 'Sorry, I know you did. We both did. Look, I'm really happy for you.'

'Thanks. I hope you can find someone wonderful

too. It's a pity things didn't work out with that guy you were seeing.'

I winced. I didn't want Jack's sympathy. It made me feel stupid and ridiculous and a total loser. 'It's no big deal. We weren't together that long. Plenty more fish in the sea,' I said, feigning cheeriness.

Thankfully, before Jack could say anything kind or patronizing, the lift doors opened and I followed him into the nursery. There was Jess, holding her tiny newborn brother, looking so proud.

'You're really great with him, Jess,' Jack said. 'Can I show him to Mum?' He lifted the baby from Jess's arms and held him up to me. He looked red and scrunchy, like all babies. I had adored Jess from the minute she was born, but I had never had any interest in other people's children.

I could feel Jess watching me, so I held out my hands enthusiastically and tucked Robert into the crook of my arm, where he promptly fell back to sleep. 'He's a handsome little fellow,' I said, to a beaming Jack and Jess. We huddled together, looking at the newborn.

'What the hell is going on?'

We turned to see Pippa standing behind us, her hands on her hips. Hair perfect, makeup on, nails done and a black silk kimono-style dressing-gown hiding her post-baby bump, which looked very small to me. Stupid cow. Couldn't she have the decency to look awful after giving birth?

351

'I was just – Jack just . . . He's beautiful,' I said, thrusting the baby into Jack's arms.

'Why is she holding Robert?' Pippa glared at Jack.

'I just thought it would be nice for her to meet him.'

Pippa didn't look as if she thought it was a nice idea at all.

Jess rushed over and hugged her. 'Oh, Pippa, you're amazing, he's gorgeous. I love him.'

Pippa pushed her away. 'You're hurting me, Jess. I'm sore.'

'Sorry.' Jess stepped back.

I picked up my bag. 'I brought Jess to see the baby and I popped in. Sorry if it seems—'

'Inappropriate,' she snarled. Turning to Jack, she hissed, 'He's one day old. I really don't need to come down and find your ex holding my new baby.'

Jack shrugged. 'I'm sorry. I was excited and wanted to show him off. Maybe it was a bit too soon.'

'You think?' Pippa barked.

I wanted to get out of there. 'I'll leave you to it. I'll see you later, Jess.'

'Hold on!' Pippa stopped me in my tracks. 'You're not leaving Jess here.'

I looked at Jack. 'Well, she's keen to spend time with the baby. Jack said he'd like her to.'

Pippa exhaled deeply and held up her hand. 'Jack is not in charge here. Jack has not just given birth. I need time to recover. I can't deal with another child right now.'

'But I've only been here ten minutes,' Jess said, blinking back tears. 'I won't bother you. I'll just sit here with Dad and Robert while you rest.'

At the same moment, Jack and I moved to stand by Jess. Pippa narrowed her eyes. 'I need to be alone with Jack and my baby. OK? Don't make a drama out of it. I just need space.'

I caught Jack's eye. He bent down and said to Jess, 'Why don't you come back tomorrow, when things are calmer?'

'Call first,' Pippa said pointedly.

I glared at her. 'Oh, don't you worry, I will. I won't let Jess walk in on this again.'

I took Jess's hand and, as we headed for the nursery door, we heard Pippa shriek. I turned around to see Robert vomiting all over his mother's kimono. I tried not to laugh as, covered with milky sick, Pippa shoved Robert into Jack's arms and stormed out of the nursery, cursing as she went.

Jack handed the baby back to me and rushed after her. Why was I the one left holding the baby? A nurse helped me change Robert into clean clothes and I placed him in his cot. I told Jess to say goodbye to her brother and we left.

Jess was very quiet on the drive home. I knew she was hurt by Pippa's reaction to her.

'Pippa's just tired and emotional. She'll be back to her old self soon. Don't worry.'

'I'm not worried, Mum. She thinks I rock,' Jess said unconvincingly.

I had a feeling the love-in was over. Pippa liked having Jess around when it suited her. Jess was a plaything, someone she could dress up and take shopping, someone who worshipped her and constantly told her how wonderful she was. And getting on with Jess made her look good in Jack's eyes. But now that Pippa had a baby, who puked and pooed and would be awake half the night, it seemed Jess would not be so welcome any more.

CHAPTER 28

Julie

I stood outside the building, trembling from head to toe. It probably hadn't been such a good idea to arrive so early. I'd killed time by downing three coffees and was completely over-caffeinated.

I glanced down at my grey dress and jacket. I had spent more money on them than I had ever spent on clothes before. The lady in the boutique said the outfit was smart and stylish. That was exactly what I wanted to convey. Well, that and capable.

When I walked into the interview, I wanted them to think I was a competent and able person. I really needed this job. I had to do something with my life. Dan kept texting me about meeting up, but I couldn't decide what to do. I needed a job to keep my mind occupied and stop me flirting with ex-boyfriends. A busy Julie would be a lot safer than a bored one. Since the boys were born I had barely had time to shower. But now I had too much time on my hands, far too much.

I smoothed down my dress, took a deep breath and walked into the reception area of the office building.

'Hello, I'm Julie Hayes. I'm here for an interview.'

'Hi.' The receptionist smiled. 'You're here for my job.' She pointed to her bump. 'I'm off on maternity leave.'

'Congratulations,' I said. 'Is it a nice place to work?'

'Lovely,' she answered. 'Very busy, but I like that. It makes the days fly by.'

Before I could ask her any more, the phone rang and she answered it, then typed furiously into a computer. Another phone rang. I retreated to the waiting area and began to sweat.

Why was there a computer there? Was it just for email and maybe a company directory? I could manage that. But did she have to do anything else? I wanted to ask her if she ever had to use Excel. I'd been too intimidated to join a course so I'd bought a book on Excel and PowerPoint and tried to teach myself, but I kept getting confused.

It had been really frightening. It was the final realization that, after ten years' lack of use, my brain was officially dead. I wanted to ask Harry for help, he was a whiz on computers, but I didn't want him to know about the interview. He wouldn't understand. He wanted me to have a nice, relaxing life. He told me I deserved it after almost ten years with the triplets.

But lounging around wasn't for me. I knew that now. I was a doer. I needed to be occupied, physically and mentally. I picked up the newspaper and flicked to the business section in case they were watching me. I wanted them to think I read it every day. I might only be going as maternity cover for the receptionist, but I was determined to impress them.

My name was called by a younger man, about thirty-five or so, who introduced himself as Kevin, assistant to the head of Human Resources. Kevin led me into a conference room where a woman of my own age was waiting for us.

She proffered a hand. 'Hello, Julie. I'm Rose Dean, head of HR.'

I shook her hand and sat down. My heart was pounding. I saw that they both had a copy of my CV in front of them on the table.

'I see from your CV that you've had a career break while you had children,' Rose said.

'That's right,' I croaked. I cleared my throat. 'I only intended to give up work for a short while, but the triplets required more time and energy than I'd anticipated.'

Kevin smiled. 'Triplet boys, I can only imagine.'

I nodded. 'Yes, it's been busy.'

'Why are you keen to get back into the workplace now?' Rose asked.

My palms were sweaty. 'The boys are all in school and I want to get back to work and use my brain again.'

Damn. I shouldn't have said that. It had sounded as if my brain had been switched off. 'I meant that I want to use my brain in a different way, as in fine-tune it. It's not like I switched off when I was at home or anything. I read the paper every day and do the crossword and Sukodo,' I lied.

I'd tried Sukodo once and my brain had almost exploded with the strain. I'd had no idea what the hell was going on. As for the crossword, I was lucky if I got two clues right.

'Do you mean Sudoku?' Kevin asked.

'Sorry, yes, absolutely,' I said, as my face burnt with shame. I wanted to die.

I saw a glance pass between Kevin and Rose. 'It says here that you are proficient on computers,' Rose continued.

Why had I said proficient? I could barely use email. But I nodded in what I thought was a convincing way.

'Are you a Mac or PC lady?' Kevin asked.

What? I began to panic. Did he mean politically correct? He must do. After all, it was a law firm. If PC was politically correct, what the hell was MAC? It must be management assessment competence or something. I'd have to wing it.

'I'm both,' I fudged.

'We're very PC-based here,' Rose explained.

I nodded furiously. 'Absolutely, I understand. I'm definitely very PC, too. I'd never let you down on that score. I'm very careful about what I say. I'm very discreet and I'm not racist in any way. I never give out about the Nigerian taxi drivers. I think they're actually very nice. I'm all for equality.'

Rose seemed perplexed. Kevin, on the other hand, had some kind of a coughing fit into his water glass. Rose had to thump him on the back. His face was all red.

'Do you know much about Kennedy, Lawson and Townsend?' Rose asked.

I had prepared this bit. 'Oh, yes. You're the seventh biggest law firm in Dublin. You do a lot of corporate work and your motto is *carpe diem*, which is from my favourite movie, *Dead Poets Society*. How good was Robin Williams in that?'

Kevin smiled, which I thought was a good sign.

But poker-faced Rose said, 'Actually, the original source for *carpe diem* is the lyric poet Horace. The term was first found in *Odes, Book I*.'

How could I be so stupid? Of course it wasn't an original phrase used by Robin Williams. Of course it was some olde-worlde term made up by some ancient guy from back in the day. Sweaty patches began to form under my arms. I prayed they couldn't see them through the jacket.

Rose continued to plough through my very short CV. 'Our receptionists do some typing for us, just straightforward documents and letters. How many words can you type a minute?'

'How many words do I type a minute?' I repeated, trying to buy time.

'Yes.'

'I – I don't actually know. I've never counted.'

'Would you mind doing a quick test for me here?' she asked.

'Now?' Sweat was dripping down my back.

'Sure. You can use this laptop.' Rose pushed it towards me and handed me a sheet of paper with a paragraph of text on it.

I bit my lip to stop myself crying. I knew this was going to be a disaster, but what could I do? I could get up and run out of there or suffer in silence.

I typed as fast as I could for a minute. The words were a blur because my eyes were full of tears.

When my time was up, Rose turned the laptop back towards her and printed out the page. Kevin leant over to study it while I died inside.

Kevin had another coughing fit, except this time I could see he was laughing. In fact, he couldn't control himself. Rose suggested he leave the room and come back when he was feeling better. She looked cross. Kevin excused himself. He backed out of the room unable to speak. I wanted the ground to split apart and swallow me.

Rose looked up. 'I'm afraid you only managed twenty-two words, and there are twenty mistakes.'

I was mortified. My dress was stuck to me. I was hot, sweaty and humiliated. I couldn't stand it any longer. I stood up and picked up my bag. 'Thank you for seeing me. We both know this has been a disaster. I'm an absolute joke. I'll see myself out. Don't bother sending me a rejection letter. I know I'm the last person on earth you'd hire. Sorry for wasting your time.'

Before Rose could say anything, I ran out of the building and just made it through the main door onto the street before I burst into tears. I stumbled down the road and saw a bar on the corner. I ran towards it, threw the door open, rushed up to the counter and ordered a large glass of wine.

'Are you all right, love?' the barman asked.

I nodded, wiping my tears with the back of my hand. 'Fine. I just need a drink.'

'Julie?'

I spun around. Louise was standing behind me, looking confused. 'I was getting out of my taxi and I saw you running in here. What on earth is going on? Are you all right? What are you doing in a bar at eleven in the morning?'

The barman handed me my wine and asked Louise if she wanted a drink. She said no and sat down opposite me.

I raised my glass. 'I'm drinking to my pathetic life.'

'What do you mean? What happened? Is it the kids? Harry?'

I shook my head. 'No, it's just me – stupid, foolish, brain-dead Julie.'

'Julie, talk to me, what is it?'

I shook my head and knocked back half of my wine, sobbing.

Louise rested a hand on my arm. 'Look, my office is around the corner. Why don't you come with me? We can close the door and talk privately. It's a lot nicer than here.'

'I like this dingy bar. It suits my mood. I want to stay here. I belong here, not in some fancy office.'

Louise was gripping my arm tightly now. 'Julie, what the hell is going on? Are you OK?'

'I'm fine. I've just made a complete fool of myself in an interview.' I knocked back more wine.

Louise crinkled her brow. 'Interview for what?'

'Receptionist.'

Louise looked shocked. 'What? Where?'

'Kennedy, Lawson and Townsend.'

'But, Julie, I know the managing partner. I could have put in a word for you. Why didn't you tell me you were going for a job there?'

I looked up at her, my eyes full of tears. 'Because I was ashamed – ashamed of my hopeless CV, ashamed of my lack of knowledge, ashamed of my uselessness.'

'Stop that.' Louise pulled the wine glass away from me. 'You're being maudlin. You are a very capable and smart woman. I wish you'd told me you wanted to go back to work. I had no idea you were even thinking about it. I can help you find something.'

'Really? Who wants to hire someone who hasn't worked in ten years and can barely switch on a computer?'

'There are lots of different jobs you can do. Now, come on, you're a great person with lots of potential.'

'No, I'm not. I'm just a stupid, middle-aged mother.'

Louise pulled me up from the stool and handed me my bag. She shook me by the shoulders. 'Stop it, Julie. Look, I'm really sorry, but I have to go to a meeting now. Why don't you come with me? You can wait in my office until I've finished and we can talk then.'

'I have to go. I have to pick Tom up in an hour.'

'All right. We'll discuss this later. I'll call you at home tonight and we can talk it through. I'll help you get a job. But for now, go home and pull yourself together. And have a coffee before you pick Tom up. OK?'

Louise led me outside and put me into a taxi, giving the driver my address.

'Julie? Will you be all right?' she asked. 'Text me when you get home so I know you're back safe and sound. I'll phone you tonight.'

While my successful, confident sister hurried off to her meeting, I sat in the back of the taxi feeling two feet tall. The world had moved on while I'd been having babies, and it had left me far behind. Useless loser.

CHAPTER 29

Louise

Clara was having another meltdown about going to school. I was late for work and was completely exhausted from the stress of the past week. I just wanted to lie down and for all of this awfulness to go away. I wanted to turn the clock back and for it to be me and Clara, happy, content in our little bubble.

Now all of those awful words were spinning around my head – Asperger's, autism spectrum, cognitive flexibility, modulating tone of voice and gestures . . . My head felt as if it was going to explode. I wanted everyone to see Clara as I did – perfect. And now my baby was going to have to go through all these tests and therapies and I hated it. I bloody hated it. I was furious with the world for doing this to her. Furious that people saw her as different when they should have seen her as exceptional.

'*Noooooooo*, Mummy, not school. I want to stay here with my books,' Clara shrieked.

'Come on, darling, the school is lovely and they

have lots of books there too. You can bring your bird books with you, if you like.'

'*Nonononononononono.*' She ran into her bedroom and locked the door.

'Clara! Sweetheart, you must come out. Mummy's going to be late for work and you'll be late for school.'

No reply.

The doorbell rang. I'd told Christelle not to come this morning, but maybe she'd forgotten. I opened it. Gavin was standing there, holding a plastic bag.

'What do you want?' I snapped. 'I really don't have anything to say to you.'

'Seriously, dude, build a bridge and get over it.' He pushed past me.

'Now is really not a good time. I'm trying to get Clara to school.'

'Judging by all the screaming I just heard, she's not too happy about it.'

I crossed my arms. 'Well, it's a new school and she doesn't like change.'

'What little kid does? Where is she?'

I pointed to her bedroom. 'She's locked herself in.'

Gavin walked over to the locked bedroom door. 'Hey, Clara, it's Uncle Gavin.'

'I'm not coming out.'

'Fine by me. I just came over because I got you this cool bird book. It's all about really unusual birds. I bet you've never even heard or seen pictures of these birds.'

'I know all the birds in the whole world.'

'Oh, yeah?' Gavin opened the book. 'Do you know the Tufty Puffin?'

'It's Tufted Puffin and, yes, I do. They can fly underwater with their wings.'

'OK, Miss Smartypants. What about comor-pants?' Gavin winked at me.

'They're called cormorants. They are also known as Phalacrocoracidae.'

'Well, look who swallowed a dictionary.'

'No, I didn't! You can't swallow a dictionary. You would choke and die.'

'Well, if you don't come out, I'm going to eat this bird book.'

'*Noooooo.*' The door opened and Clara tried to grab it from him.

'Hold on a minute. You can have this book if you get dressed and go to school on time. I want you to continue to be the cleverest kid I know. You have to go to school to get cleverer. I'll pick you up later and we can read the book together. I promise I won't eat it if you go to school. Deal?'

Clara nodded. 'OK.'

Gavin put out his hand. 'That's my girl. Give me a high-five.'

Clara high-fived him weakly and went back into her room to put on the clothes I had carefully laid out for her.

'Thanks,' I said to Gavin.

'No worries. How are you doing after that "fun" family dinner? Sorry I put my foot in it. I didn't mean to blurt it out like that. I'd been trying to say it to you for ages. I just couldn't find the right time and I knew you'd freak out.'

I threw my hands up in the air. 'She's my little girl! Do you think it was easy for me to hear that?'

'No, of course not. But we're all just trying to help you. We love the little dude.'

'I know. I've just had a really hard time accepting it.'

He punched me gently on the arm. 'Hey, she's still our little Clara. The same quirky, Einsteiny kid we're all crazy about. That's never going to change.'

I nodded. I was afraid of getting emotional again.

'So, I've been doing some research and I made up this folder for you because I know you're all into files and information.'

Gavin handed me a thick folder. I opened it. Inside was all the information I could ever have wanted about Asperger's. He had written a cover page on why he suspected Clara had it and how we could best help and support her. Then, in colour-coded chapters, he had divided up suggestions for her care with useful approaches and programmes he had found out about to help her. He had sections on interventions aimed at helping her to develop social skills, strategies to teach her to develop more appropriate forms of behaviour with other kids, how to develop insight into social situations, how to make sure she was never bullied or socially isolated, how her family understanding her condition was vital in supporting her and helping her along the way . . .

I felt my throat closing. 'Wow. This is incredible. Thanks.'

'It took me and Shania ages, but I think it'll help. I've made copies for everyone in the family. We're in this together, Louise. We're her family. Clara's the coolest kid I know. She rocks.'

I was afraid to speak. The lump in my throat was now the size of a golf ball. I squeezed his arm and mouthed, 'Thanks,' again.

'I know you hated us for saying it to you, but it's said now, so let's just get on with it. And if there's anything I can do to help, or Shania, just call on us, OK?'

I glanced at my watch. 'Are you free now, by any chance?' I asked.

'Yeah, I'm not in work until ten.'

'Could you take Clara to school? You may have to sit with her until she calms down. I have a really important meeting, and if I don't leave now, I'll be late.'

'Go and kick some corporate arse. Clara will be fine with me.'

I went to tell Clara that Uncle Gavin was taking her to school with her new bird book. She smiled. 'Oh, good,' she said.

As I was rushing out of the door, I stopped to kiss my brother's cheek. 'You never cease to amaze me,' I said.

He grinned. 'At least this time it's "amaze" in

the good sense and not in the what-the-hell-is-
he-doing-now sense.'

I laughed as I closed the door behind me, safe
in the knowledge that my precious child was in
caring and loving hands.

I was reading through a file when there was a
knock on my door. It was Wendy. I hadn't seen
her since the day of the disastrous email. HR had
dealt with her after that and I had just given
written proof of her tardiness, mistakes and
general lack of professionalism. She'd been on
leave since then.

'I've come to say goodbye. You won, Louise.
I'm being let go.'

I put down the file and took off my reading
glasses. 'I didn't win anything, Wendy, and I wish
you the best in the future.'

'God, you're cold. I'm jobless with a kid to look
after because of you.'

I could feel myself getting annoyed. 'No, Wendy,
you're jobless because of your own incompetence.
Take responsibility for your actions.'

'I pity your child. Her life will be hell with a
mother like you. She'll never be good enough. If
she's not perfect, you'll probably get rid of her.'

I gripped the side of my chair. 'How dare you
speak to me like that? You know nothing about
my child because, unlike you, I don't drag my
problems into work with me and whinge all the
time. You're never going to get anywhere in life,

Wendy, until you stop feeling sorry for yourself and blaming everyone else for your problems.'

'You don't know anything about problems. You and your perfect life make me sick. Normal people have shit to deal with and I really hope some day you get to see that first hand. It might just make you more human,' Wendy shouted.

I threw my head back and laughed. If only she knew the lifelong problems I was facing. She had no idea of the mountains I was going to have to climb.

'You're a psycho!' Wendy yelled, as she stormed out.

I laughed and laughed, to the point of hysteria.

By Friday morning Clara was less reluctant to go to school and I had to sit with her for just ten minutes before I could go to work.

I had been up every night until the wee hours of the morning reading Gavin's file and doing my own research into Asperger's syndrome. The information was overwhelming, but I knew that knowledge would take away the fear I felt about it. As I read through the typical symptoms of Asperger's, I realized that, regardless of how much I wished Clara didn't have it, it was very likely that she did. In fact, if I was being honest, I knew she did. She had all the signs. Now it was just a matter of finding out how severe it was.

We were due to go back to see the psychologist, Colin Fitzgerald, the following Wednesday, but I had too many questions that just couldn't wait. I needed answers now. I wanted to see Colin without Clara so that I could go through the list before our Wednesday session.

I called his secretary, Harriet, for an appointment, but she absolutely refused to be bullied or cajoled or even bribed – I was so desperate to see him that I had even offered to do any legal work she wanted for free.

'Mizzzz Devlin,' she almost spat down the phone, 'I've had quite enough of your tactics. Mr Fitzgerald is a very busy man. You are not the only mother who is eager to speak to him. You will have to wait until your next appointment. Now, please refrain from calling this number again or the only legal help I will require is with getting a barring order.'

I hadn't got to where I was in my career without being tenacious and bloody-minded. I was not to be deterred by someone's secretary. I got a taxi over to Colin's office at lunchtime and lurked about across the road in a coffee shop until I saw his old bat of a secretary coming out for her lunch break. I raced inside the building and went to burst into his office, but the outside door was locked. I couldn't see him, but I knew he was in there because I could hear him on the phone. So I knocked . . . and knocked . . . and beat on the door with my fists until he came out of his office, looking annoyed.

'What on earth?' He stormed across the reception area and unlocked the door.

'Coffee?' I said, smiling, as I swept past him and marched straight through to his office.

His desk was covered with open files. He hurried in after me. 'I'm in—'

'The middle of something. Yes, I can see that, but this won't take a minute.' I handed him a coffee and sat down.

He sat down opposite me and took a sip.

'Two shot, skinny, extra hot latte. Is it OK?'

He smiled. 'It's very nice, actually. So, may I ask why you are trying to break into my office while my secretary is on her lunch break?'

'It's called desperation,' I said. 'I'm new to the emotion. I have never been desperate in my life, and yet here I am, unable to sleep, unable to concentrate in work and apparently unable to see that my little girl needed help.' Christ, I was getting emotional again – what was wrong with me?

Colin rested his elbows on his desk. 'Louise,' he said gently, 'the emotions you're experiencing are all completely normal.'

I held up my hand. 'They're not normal to me. In fact, they're completely alien. I hate feeling this way. I despise being out of control in a situation. I'm appalled by my lack of judgement regarding Clara's behaviour, and I detest having to depend on other people for help and guidance. I've always done things on my own and never needed anyone. I cannot stand having to wait for appointments to have my child assessed. I want her fixed. I want

372

you to fix her.' My hands were shaking and spilling coffee on my trousers. I put the cup on the floor.

'Louise, this is not your fault. This is nobody's fault. But you need to understand that if Clara proves to have Asperger's syndrome it isn't something you fix. It's something you learn to live with.'

'But what kind of life will she have?' I asked, needing re-assurance. 'Will it get worse? The Internet says so many different things.'

'The key is prompt diagnosis, which is exactly what we're going to do. Clara is only four so we've caught it very early and I believe we can help her significantly moving forward.'

'But how bad is it? How bad will it get? Will she end up in a . . . in a home?' I bit my lip to stop myself falling apart. My biggest fear was no longer that Clara wouldn't be incredibly successful and happy. My biggest fear now was that when I died Clara would end up dumped in some awful home, which smelt of cabbage, where the minders were really mean to you and never stimulated you or were kind and affectionate to you.

Colin came around to sit beside me. He handed me a tissue.

I twisted it in my hand. 'I never bloody cry. I'm the strongest person I know and the most resilient. Everyone comes to *me* with their problems and I fix them. But I can't fix this and it's freaking me out. Is it my fault? Did I not love her enough? Did I push her too hard? Did I make her do too many activities? Did I mollycoddle her? Did I over-stimulate her? Does she need a dad? Would that help? Because if it would, I'll bloody well find one for her. Just tell me what to do!'

Colin sat back and smiled at me. 'Going out and grabbing a random man to be a father figure to your daughter is probably not the best place to start.'

Despite myself, I began to laugh, albeit with a manic edge.

'None of this is your fault. It's quite clear that you love your daughter and have done everything to stimulate her clever little mind and to make her life as comfortable and stress-free as possible. Clara is a lovely child and I can see that she has been cherished. But you will have to be patient.'

I raised an eyebrow. 'Not a strong point.'

'Having seen you almost break into my office unannounced, I didn't think it would be. But I'm afraid you're going to need to work on that. There is a long road ahead.'

I sat back in my chair and exhaled. 'It's funny. I have no patience whatsoever with anything except Clara. All of her little quirks, her obsessions with time, birds, routine and all that, never bothered me. For some reason I do actually have great patience with her, but not with anything else. Can I hire you to work with her full-time? I don't care how much it costs, I just want her to get the best help and apparently you're the best.'

Colin placed his coffee on the table. 'I'm very

flattered, but I have many patients in my care and I like helping as many families as I can.'

'To hell with them. Come on, Colin, put me out of my misery. Just say yes.'

He shook his head. 'Sorry, Louise. But I would like to work with Clara on a weekly basis and, when her diagnosis has been confirmed, I'd be happy to help you come up with a way to help her going forward.'

I put my head in my hands and groaned. 'This is not how I planned her future.'

'Life is never how we plan it,' Colin said gently.

I looked up at him. 'Be straight with me. Do you think she's bad? Do you think she'll have an OK life, a normal life . . . well, not completely normal, but a good life? A full life?'

'I think that, with you as her mother, she'll have the best life possible.' He regarded me for a moment. 'I'm not a religious person, Louise, but did you ever hear the saying that we're given only what we're able for? If you've been given a special child, it's because you already have all the qualities necessary to do this.'

'Jesus, don't be nice to me or I'll start blubbing again.' My hands were shaking. I stood up. 'Thank you for your time.'

'I didn't really have a choice. I think you'd call this breaking and entering.'

'I didn't technically break the door down.'

'You sounded as if you were going to.'

'I was.' I smiled.

'Try to stay calm and just enjoy Clara. I'll see you on Wednesday.'

As I was leaving, I did something completely out of character. I hugged him. He patted me on the back.

I pulled away. 'Sorry, I'm behaving like a complete lunatic. You've just been so nice and I've been so worried.'

'No problem.'

'Tom Ford, Extreme, right?'

He frowned and then, smiling, touched his neck. 'Yes.'

'My ex used to wear that aftershave.'

'I hope that's not why he's your ex.'

'No, it was one of the things I liked about him.'

I left the office to the sound of Colin chuckling.

I was in the taxi on my way back to work when I received a text from Sophie: *Get babysitter. Need 2 c u 2nite. Urgent. It's Julie.*

CHAPTER 30

Julie

I changed my mind every five minutes. I was going, I wasn't, I was going, I wasn't, I was going, I wasn't . . .

I got my legs, bikini and underarms waxed, just in case. I had a manicure and pedicure, on the off-chance I might go. I had my hair blow-dried on Friday morning because I wanted to. I got my makeup done afterwards because I had time on my hands. No other reason. None.

When I collected the boys from school, Emily whistled. 'You look lovely. Hot date with your husband?'

I blushed ten shades of red. 'Just dinner, nothing special,' I mumbled.

Victoria came up behind us. Ignoring me, she said hello to Emily.

'Wow, Victoria, those boots are amazing,' Emily fawned.

'Thank you, sweetie, they're the new YSL ones. I bought them for dinner tomorrow.'

'Where are you going?'

'Gerry's taking me to Le Gourmand.'

When Emily didn't react appropriately, Victoria added, 'It's the new Michelin-starred restaurant.'

'Oh, sorry, I'm hopeless. I'm so uncool. That's so exciting,' Emily said.

'It's impossible to get in, but Gerry knows *every*one,' Victoria said loudly. 'He always manages to get us a table. I'll wear my new Balmain dress to complement the boots.'

'It sounds fabulous.'

One of Victoria's clones arrived. 'Hi, are you going to the Tranders' party tonight?' she asked Victoria. 'I'm really looking forward to it.'

Victoria flicked her hand dismissively. 'I don't think so. Gerry's tied up with work and it'll probably be really dull. Their parties usually are.'

'Oh.' The clone looked crestfallen.

'Where are you going for dinner, Julie?' Emily asked me.

'What? Oh, uhm, just a local Italian place, nothing fancy,' I said. I'd never been a good liar.

'Sounds lovely,' Emily said.

'Pizza and bad red wine is hardly lovely,' Victoria sneered.

'I was going to go to Le Gourmand, but I heard the food was rubbish,' I snapped.

Victoria eyeballed me, and I eyeballed her right back. Emily watched anxiously. If Victoria wanted to dish it out, I was going to dish it right back. I'd had enough of her rudeness.

Thankfully, the boys came tumbling out before the argument escalated.

When I saw the triplets' innocent little faces, I decided I was definitely not going to meet Dan. No way. As they buckled themselves into their seats, I had an idea. 'OK, guys, let's do something fun tonight.' If I committed to doing something with them, I wouldn't be able to go.

'Like what?' Liam asked suspiciously.

'Watch a movie together?' I suggested.

'You never watch movies with us. You always say TV is the third parent,' Leo reminded me.

God, that kid had a memory like an elephant.

'Yeah, and you say we're a pain because we jump around all the time during movies, even in the cinema,' Luke added.

'Well, the last time I took you to the cinema you behaved like wild animals and we were asked to leave.' It had been a terrible afternoon. I'd never been kicked out of a cinema before. 'Anyway, I thought it would be nice for us to watch a movie.'

'What movie?' Leo asked.

'I don't know – *ET*?' I suggested.

'That is so *laaaaaaame*.' Luke groaned.

'Yeah, Mum, it's a dorky movie about a kid and his stupid alien friend,' Liam said.

'I like *ET*,' Tom said.

'That's because you're a dork who likes dorky movies,' Leo told him.

'Leave Tom alone,' I snapped. 'Why don't we watch *The Sound of Music*?'

The triplets began to complain loudly.

'All they do is sing. It's the worst movie ever made,' Luke said.

'Yeah, it's just stupid kids running around, and nuns and kissing and stuff. It's the worst movie in the universe,' Leo added.

'You have the baddest taste in movies, Mum. You're such a dweeb,' Liam said.

'What film do you lot want to watch then?' I asked, gripping the steering-wheel to stop myself shouting at them.

'*The Hunger Games*,' they bellowed.

'Don't be ridiculous. It's far too violent.'

'We like violence!' Luke shrieked.

'Yeah, blood and guns and knives!' Liam whooped.

'And big fights with everyone kicking and punching.' Leo punched his arms as a demonstration, catching me on the side of the head. Ouch.

'Let me be clear. We are not watching *The Hunger Games*. We'll watch *Madagascar 3*.'

'Yeah!' said Tom. 'I love that one. It's funny.'

'NO WAY,' Liam roared. 'It's for babies.'

'I don't want to watch some stupid film with you anyway, Mum,' Luke said.

'Yeah, me neither,' Leo agreed.

I really needed them to spend time with me. I was teetering on the edge and I wanted them to be with me so that I wouldn't fall off. 'Well, we could play games on the Wii instead. How about that?'

'Oh, Mum, we don't want to play with you,' Luke said. 'You're our mother, not our friend.'

It felt like a knife through my stomach.

'Only dorks play with their mums.' Liam drove it in further.

'Seriously, Mum, go and play with your own friends.' Leo twisted it.

'Let's play war,' Luke suggested, and the other two enthusiastically agreed.

'We can have three base camps in the house and . . .' The triplets chatted excitedly about the war games they were going to play as an exhausted and excluded Tom fell asleep in his car seat.

I tried not to take it personally. I knew that nine-year-old boys did not, generally speaking, want to play with their mothers, but I was feeling really sensitive today and it was upsetting me. When we got home, the triplets scrambled out of the car, leaving me to haul in their school bags and sports kits.

I caught my reflection in the huge hall mirror. I was a slave, a skivvy, a person whose only purpose was to run around after children who didn't notice I was there.

It wasn't their fault. I hadn't appreciated my parents when I was young either. But it didn't make it any easier to accept. I felt invisible. I sat down heavily on the couch in the hall and plonked the bags beside me.

My phone beeped. I took it out of my pocket, presuming it was Dan confirming our meeting time. It was Harry. *Sry but won't be able to take the kids to rugby tomorrow. Donald asked me to play in a four ball with some big US investment bankers. It's a fantastic opportunity to make contacts. I'm going to the driving range after work to practise. I'll be home about nine or ten.*

My blood boiled. Fuck you, Harry. Fuck you and your stupid bloody money. Now you're letting the boys down, too. The only bloody thing you still did around here was take them to rugby and now even they're getting dumped for Donald. To hell with you and your stupid bloody fake friends and bullshit golf.

That was it. I was going to see Dan. Nobody in this house gave a damn about me anyway. They wouldn't even notice if I was gone for the night. Harry wouldn't care: he barely registered my presence these days. To Hell with them all. I was going.

I texted Dan: *C u at 8, get the champagne on ice!*

He came straight back: *I'll be waiting!*

Dan cared about me. My stomach flipped with excitement. I blushed as I imagined ripping his clothes off and climbing on top of him . . .

But then, foolishly, I looked out of the window and saw Tom sleeping peacefully in the car. My resolve wavered. Was I a bad mother? Would my kids get sick and die because I was going to have sex with another man? Would God punish me for indulging myself with my ex-boyfriend? I needed advice. I called the only person I knew I could be totally straight with.

'Marian, I need to ask you something.'

'Hold on one second,' she said.

I heard her talking into the other phone: 'So you're saying I should try the Lidl pork chops? . . . OK, I will so . . . Right, I'll talk to you next week. Do you want to do the asphyxiation again or just the masturbation while I shout at you? . . . Asphyxiation? OK . . . And you want me to sound like I'm really dying? No problem, I can do that . . . Talk to you then.'

Marian was back with me. 'Sorry, how are you?'

'Don't ask any questions, just listen. If you had the chance to have a one-night stand with an ex-boyfriend who you knew was great in bed, no strings attached and no one ever finding out about it, would you do it?'

'Hell, yes! But we're not talking about me, are we?'

'No.'

'What about Harry?'

'Harry is an absent husband and father. I don't even know him any more.'

'He's a good man.'

'These days he's a man who ignores me and puts me last on his list of priorities.'

'Is the ex-boyfriend hot?'

'Yes.'

'And you're sure you won't get caught?'

'Positive. Unless one of my sisters happens to be in the Four Seasons lobby tonight, which is highly unlikely.'

'Well, then, my child, you have my blessing!'

I hung up before she could say anything else and ran upstairs to put on the new Elle Macpherson lingerie I'd bought yesterday. Then I remembered Tom. I rushed back down, lifted him out of the car and laid him, still asleep, on the couch in the lounge, covering him with a blanket.

I hurried back upstairs as I heard something crash in the kitchen. I didn't care what they broke, smashed or destroyed. I was going to have some fun for once.

As I was clipping on my suspenders – it was the first time I'd worn them in years and I'd forgotten how uncomfortable they were – I suddenly realized I had no babysitter. I'd told Harry I was going out with Sophie and he'd promised to be home by seven, but he'd obviously forgotten and now he was going to the bloody driving range. Shit, shit, shit.

I rang Gloria, told her it was an emergency and that I only needed her for a couple of hours until Harry got home. She hesitated, saying her back was killing her and she had pains in her shoulder. I offered to pay her double and she said she was on her way.

At seven forty I walked out of my house, leaving Gloria ordering the boys around. I sat in the back of a taxi, smelling, looking and feeling better than I had in years. I'd had two glasses of wine to take the edge off and I was ready for some hot, steamy sex. By God, was I ready!

★　　★　　★

When I arrived at the hotel, my legs began to shake. Dan had texted that he was on the first floor, Room 135. I was to go straight up. I went to the Ladies in the lobby to have a final check in the mirror. I examined myself. I looked about as good as I could. The black dress showed off my cleavage and camouflaged my stomach. Mind you, with all the nerves about tonight, I'd barely eaten in days and had definitely lost weight. My makeup was perfect. If only I could do such a good job myself.

As I was applying lip gloss, I heard a woman in a cubicle crying. She seemed to be talking to someone on the phone. There was something familiar about her voice.

'I knew he was up to something. I followed him. He's here, with some young tart. He had his hand halfway up her skirt when I saw him. He's such a bastard. I knew he wasn't completely faithful, but I thought he was discreet. He's flaunting this bitch all over town . . . Leave him? But what would I do? For God's sake, Mum, he made me sign a pre-nup, remember? I get four hundred thousand if I leave him and that's it. I like my life . . . I'm Mrs Gerry Carter-Mills. I'm someone in this town. I'm a socialite – people look up to me. Women want to *be* me.'

It was Victoria! I held my breath, straining my ears to hear her.

Her voice was breaking with emotion. 'I'm nothing without Gerry. I don't mind the affairs as long as he doesn't make a fool of me in public . . . You should see this girl, she's so young . . . It's mortifying. I'm going to go in there and sit down with them. I'm going to tell her I'm his wife and ask her to leave, and then I'm going to tell Gerry that he has to be more discreet. I don't want to cause a scene and I have to be nice to Gerry or he might leave me . . . I have to make sure he doesn't do that. I can't be on my own, I can't . . . I'm not, Mum, I'm not going back to my old shitty life. I don't care if he cheats. I'm not giving all this up. No way.'

The cubicle lock clicked back. I grabbed my bag to make a quick exit, but the toilet door swung open and Victoria was suddenly standing right in front of me. She blinked, then recognized me. I nodded and made to leave, but she clamped her hand on my arm.

'Did you hear my conversation?' she hissed.

I looked directly at her. Her eyes were red and she looked exhausted. I almost felt sorry for her. 'Yes, I did. But I won't tell anyone because I'm a nice person. If you'd bothered to get to know me, you'd have realized that. You're lucky it was me who heard you and not one of those ridiculous women who follow you around like puppies, waiting to stab you in the back.'

She narrowed her eyes. 'I can handle those women.' Then, catching her reflection in the mirror, she gasped. 'Can I borrow your makeup? I left mine in the car and I can hardly face my husband and his teenage lover looking like this.'

I was taken aback by this about-turn, but I handed her my little makeup bag. 'Sure, help yourself.' Louise and Sophie were not going to believe this – me and Vicky sharing makeup!

Within five minutes Victoria looked a whole lot better.

'Good job,' I said.

'Thanks.' She handed me back my bag, then looked me up and down. 'You look nice. But you should lose the necklace – it's too much.'

'Really?'

'Less is more.'

'OK.' I took it off.

As she pulled the Ladies' door open, Victoria turned back to me. 'I'll be polite to you when I see you, but we're never going to be friends. You understand that, right?'

I laughed. 'No offence, but I'd hate to be your friend. Polite is fine by me. But if you ever criticize my boys again, I'll tell all those bitches what I just heard.'

We had another eyeballing moment – we seemed to be making a habit of it. She nodded quickly and left to confront her philandering husband while I headed for the lift, trying to forget that I had a husband.

Dan opened the door and pulled me into the room. He held my hand and twirled me around. 'Let me look at you, you sexy thing.' His eyes took in every part of my body, lingering on my cleavage. 'You always had a great rack.'

He looked good, although a little plastic. His tan seemed a bit orange and his shirt was just a smidge too tight. He hugged me, and fondled my bum. I needed a drink. It was a bit too soon for bum-fondling.

'Where's that champagne?' I asked.

He frowned. 'The champagne was ridiculously expensive. I got the house white.'

'Of course. Great.' I suddenly remembered that he was tight. He'd always been really scabby with money, always the last man to the bar. How could I have forgotten that?

He poured me a glass and I literally downed it in one. I felt lightheaded. I'd now had three glasses of wine on an empty stomach.

'Someone wants to party!' Dan leant in and kissed me, nudging me backwards onto the bed.

His breath tasted of cigarettes and garlic. It wasn't particularly nice. Harry always brushed his teeth before kissing me or having sex with me. I thought it was silly and took away from any spontaneity, but now I appreciated it. Colgate tasted a lot nicer than second-hand garlic mixed with nicotine.

I tried to relax and let myself go. Dan seemed to get very excited very quickly. His hand was up my dress in seconds. His fingers slipped inside my underwear and I froze.

'Hold on.' I sat up, panting. 'Let's catch up a bit before having sex, shall we?'

Dan sighed. Then he placed his hand on the back of my neck and began to massage it. 'Honey, we've been texting for months. I know all about your life – housewife, four kids, blah-blah-blah. Come on, babe, you're so hot I can't help myself. Let's have sex first. We can talk after.'

'But—' I stopped talking because his tongue was back in my mouth and his right hand was forcefully massaging my left breast.

Despite his frantic approach to foreplay, I began to feel aroused. He was too fast and too aggressive, but it was still new and exciting and my body responded to his touch. It wasn't long before we were both naked. He reached his hand up. I thought he was getting a condom, but then he began to push my head down. I resisted, but he pushed harder.

'What are—'

'Come on, Julie, blow me.'

A blow job? Christ, I hadn't given one of those in years, possibly decades. Harry always used to say I'd married him under false pretences. Pre-marriage I gave blow jobs. After marriage I admitted I hated them and stopped.

Dan's hand upped the pressure on my head. I found myself sliding down his chest. Suddenly I found myself face to face with his red throbbing penis.

Oh, God, I'd have to close my eyes for this. I shut my eyelids and took a deep breath. I opened my mouth and Dan, seizing his moment, shoved it in. I began to gag and splutter. I jumped back, falling off the bed as I did. 'Jesus Christ, you almost choked me.'

Dan glowered at me. 'OK, fine, forget the blow job. Let's just have sex. Come on, up you get.' He reached over and pulled me back onto the bed.

But as I watched him fumbling to put on a condom, I knew it was over. This stupid little flirtation was finished. I didn't want Dan. I didn't even find him attractive. On text, he was very sexy. In real life, he wasn't. He was too aggressive and pushy. He had a fake American accent, a fake tan and it wasn't me he wanted, just sex.

I was frantic to get out of there, go home and have a shower. I was such an idiot. Who did I think I was? I was a desperate housewife – bored, lonely, delusional and pathetic.

I stood up and began to get dressed.

'What the hell?' Dan leapt up and grabbed my shoulders. 'What are you doing?'

'I'm really sorry, Dan,' I said, zipping up my dress and throwing my suspenders and stockings into the wastepaper basket. 'This just isn't going to work. You're a very nice guy, we used to have amazing chemistry, but it's just not there any more.'

His face went red and he shook his finger accusingly in my face. 'What the hell? You contacted me on Facebook. You sent me all those flirty texts. You totally led me on. Do you have any idea how much this room is costing me? I would never have stayed here if I hadn't thought I was going to get some action. I've got two kids in private school – I can't afford this.'

'I'm sorry,' I said, feeling a huge well of emotion bubbling inside me. I had to get out of there.

'You should be. You led me up the garden path, you bitch.'

I grabbed my bag and shoes and hurried to the door. 'Sorry,' I sobbed, and ran down the corridor to shouts of 'Prick-tease.'

I found a storage cupboard, went in, shut the door and sat down on a pile of linen, crying as if my heart would break. I cried for my old marriage, my old life, my old Harry. I cried because I had been an absent mother. I hadn't been nice to the kids recently. I'd been too interested in texting Dan and, between texts, staring at my phone wishing for more contact with him.

I hated my life. I hated what we had become as a family. We weren't a unit: we were like strangers all living separate lives. I hated myself. What kind of person behaves like a ridiculous teenager and runs to a hotel to have sex with a married ex-boyfriend? What kind of a mother would do that? Who was I?

After weeping into the clean hotel linen for what felt like hours, I dragged myself up. I opened my bag to take out my phone. I couldn't go home: I'd have to call Sophie and see if I could stay in her house.

There were fifteen missed calls from Louise and

Sophie. Plus lots of texts from both of them saying: *Where are you? What's going on? Are you OK? We're here for you. Call us. We're worried . . .*

Their concern made me start crying again. It was a full ten minutes before I could speak. I called Sophie.

'Jesus, Julie, are you OK?'

'Yes, I . . . *Nooooooo.*' I began to cry again.

'Where are you?'

'Hotel.'

'Which hotel?'

'F-Four – S-S-Seasons.'

'Are you with Dan?' Sophie asked.

'Ye-ye-yes.'

'What happened?'

'I'm such an idiot,' I cried.

'Are you hurt?' Sophie sounded really worried.

'No, I just feel s-s-so ash-ash-ashamed.'

'To Hell with shame,' Louise shouted into the phone. 'It's a waste of energy. Stay there, I'm on my way.'

'Stay on the phone with me while you're waiting for Louise,' Sophie said. 'I'm here, I'm listening. Talk to me.'

I sighed and massaged my aching forehead. I didn't know where to begin . . .

CHAPTER 31

Sophie

Louise brought Julie back to the apartment. Thankfully, Jess was asleep, so we were able to talk freely. Poor Julie looked a wreck. Her face was streaked with mascara and she was shaking uncontrollably. I opened a bottle of wine and we all had a large glass.

Julie told us everything. She admitted she had encouraged Dan and led him on.

'But I thought it was just a bit of fun – "Some harmless flirting," you said,' I reminded her. 'So when I got your text saying you wanted to pretend you were staying in my house, I was really worried. I knew it must be something to do with Dan. But you wouldn't return my calls or texts so I phoned Louise, she came round and we were about to call all the hotels in Dublin to find you. We figured the room would be under Dan's name. But then you got in touch, thank God.'

Julie buried her head in her hands. 'I'm such a fool. I just loved the attention. It started off with innocent flirting, but then it got quite sexy and I loved it. His texts kept me going. When he didn't text I'd be in terrible form and then I'd get one and I'd be happy again. It was so ridiculous – I thought I was falling for him. I'm just so lonely.' Julie began to cry. 'I'm on my own all day in my massive house with nothing to do. Everyone's so busy all the time and I'm just waiting for the time to pass until I pick up Tom. Sometimes I keep him home from school so that I have company.'

I leant over and put my arm around her. I'd had no idea she felt so isolated. Her life seemed so noisy and hectic with all those boys that I'd presumed she would relish the quiet when they were in school.

I had loved having money and Jess being in school. I'd had my Pilates classes and my sessions with my personal trainer, I'd gone shopping and met friends for coffee. I'd just assumed Julie would do all that too.

She was married with four kids, for goodness' sake. Loneliness was never something I'd thought she could suffer from. It was amazing to think you could be surrounded by people and still feel very alone.

'You should have told us how you were feeling,' Louise said, refilling our glasses.

'Come on, guys, you both have enough on your plates. You're dealing with real problems. How could I come along and start moaning about being bored and lonely? It would have sounded pathetic. It *is* pathetic. My boys are right. I *am* a loser.'

'Stop that,' Louise snapped. 'You're not a loser. Harry is behaving like a total moron, which has to stop, by the way. You need to talk to him properly about his absenteeism. Your life has gone from being constantly surrounded by children and chaos to being quiet and alone. You need to adjust to it and find a way to fill your mornings so that you don't feel useless. I told you I'd help you find something and I will.'

Useless! Sometimes Louise was too harsh. I decided to jump in. 'What you need to do is find something you enjoy doing. Something that makes you feel fulfilled.'

'You need to be busy,' Louise said. 'If you were busy, you wouldn't have time to be texting Dan and you wouldn't have ended up in a hotel room with his penis in your face.'

We all began to laugh.

Julie wiped laughter tears from her eyes. 'Thank you, guys. Honestly, what would I do without you?'

'Have bad sex with random men from your past.' I winked at her.

Julie smiled. 'That's enough about Dan bloody Williams and all that stuff. Now I want to forget it. Tell me, how are you doing? How's Clara?'

Louise's laughing face fell. She twirled her wine around in her glass. 'She's OK. It looks like she has Asperger's.' Her voice faltered. I went to squeeze her hand, but she pulled it away. Looking down, she said, 'Don't be nice to me. I'm doing my best to stay strong, but it's hard. It's the hardest thing I've ever had to go through.'

I looked at Julie. Silent tears of empathy were running down her face. I fought back my own. I'd never seen Louise so vulnerable. Her emotions were so raw. You could see she was hurting really deeply.

'Anyway,' she coughed, 'I've found this psychologist and he's agreed to see Clara, diagnose her properly and come up with a plan to help her.'

'She's an amazing little girl with an incredible mother,' I said.

'How can we help?' Julie asked. 'Please let me help.'

Louise gave us a crooked smile. 'Thanks. I'll let you know what you can do when I know more. Actually, Gavin's been great. He did up this whole folder for me with detailed research and a list of the books I should read. Apparently, Shania's brother has Asperger's and she helped him compile the information.'

'Wow! Maybe he's finally growing up,' Julie said.

Louise shook her head. 'I'll believe that when I see it.'

Julie smiled, then turned to me. 'How's Jack's baby and all that going for you?'

I pushed my hair back from my face. 'It's a bit strange, to be honest. It's hard for Jess. I think she's feeling a bit left out. Did I tell you Jack dragged me in to see the baby and Pippa arrived as I was holding her brand new son?'

'*No!*' Julie's eyes were wide.

'What did she say?' Louise asked.

'She snapped Jack's head off and stormed out.'

'I bet she won't like the leaky boobs and the fat waistline,' Julie said.

If only, I thought. 'She looked fabulous only twelve hours after giving birth.'

'I hate her even more,' Julie muttered.

'Don't focus on her. Concentrate on yourself and your own life,' Louise advised.

'I am, don't worry,' I assured her. And I was. I had booked my breast enhancement procedure and I couldn't wait. The new me was going to get out there, find a fabulous man and start a new chapter.

The next morning, Julie was up and gone at eight to get home, changed and take the boys to rugby. I hugged her goodbye and told her to talk to Harry.

'Julie, one of the reasons my marriage fell apart is because Jack and I weren't honest enough with each other. You have to tell Harry how you're feeling.'

She blinked back tears. 'I know, and I will.'

I closed the door and turned to find Jess behind me. I was surprised to see her up so early on a Saturday. 'Why did Julie stay the night here and why are her eyes all red and puffy?' she asked.

I decided to try to be honest. Jess had experienced a lot of upheaval and change in her short life so, in some ways, she was wise beyond her years. 'She kind of a had a fight with Harry so she decided to come here, have a chat and stay over.'

'Are they going to get separated?' Jess asked.

I winced. I hated her knowing about separation aged only nine. 'No, not at all. It's just a silly argument. She's going home to talk to him and sort it out.'

'I always think Julie and Harry seem really happy. Even with all the craziness in their house, they're never grumpy.'

It was true. Despite having four sons and no money for a long time, they were rarely in a bad mood. In fact, it was only in the last six months that I'd seen Julie upset and fed up. I never saw Harry now so I didn't know how he was.

'I hope they don't break up. It'd be awful for the boys.'

'Was it terrible for you when Dad and I split up?'

'The worst.'

'Oh, Jess, I never wanted you to have to go through that. I really wanted it to work out. We tried, but sometimes things don't go the way you hope.'

'It's OK, Mum. It's a long time ago. I used to wish you and Dad would get back together and we could be a family again, but then he met Pippa and everything was great.'

'Well, I'm glad you're not upset any more.'

Jess stretched and yawned. 'I just wish you could meet someone and be happy, like Dad and Pippa. I hate it when you're sad.'

I managed to say, 'Don't worry about me. I'm fine. I have you, work and my sisters – I'm happy.'

'No, you're not, not really. Not like Dad.'

'Well, there are different kinds of happiness,' I said. I was sad that Jess was worried about me. I had wanted her to have a carefree childhood and yet in her short life she'd seen her dad and me lose everything, fight, drift apart, separate, her dad have a new partner and baby, and her mother lonely. 'Jess, I promise you I'm fine. You are my sunshine. You are the love of my life. I don't need anyone else.'

'OK, Mum. Don't get all soppy on me.'

I kissed her head. 'I won't. Now, don't worry about Harry and Julie. They'll sort it out – they're like peas in a pod.'

'Like Dad and Pippa,' Jess said.

I decided to change the subject. 'Are you going to see baby Robert today?'

Her face lit up. 'Yes! Dad's going to pick me up at ten and bring me in. I can't wait to hold him again – he's so cute. And I'll get to see Pippa properly.'

I hoped Pippa was going to be nicer to her today. I was worried that Jess might get snapped at again if Pippa had been up all night with Robert.

'Jess, Pippa will probably still be exhausted, so don't stay too long. She'll need her rest. Babies are very tiring in the beginning. I remember you so well – you were always hungry.'

'Was I cute like Robert?' she asked.

'You were the most beautiful baby in the world. I used to spend hours just gazing at you. You were perfect and so sweet.' I felt myself getting emotional as the memories flooded back. Jess had been a wonderful baby and I had adored her. But what she didn't know was that I had suffered from post-natal depression and had really struggled to keep everything going that first year. I had covered it up so well that no one had noticed, not even Jack.

She rolled her eyes. 'Don't start crying.'

I smiled. 'I can't help it. I thought you were incredible then and I still do.' I tried to give her a hug but she ducked under my arm and went to get dressed.

I sat down at the kitchen table to have breakfast alone.

CHAPTER 32

Louise

I sat on the park bench and observed her. While all the other children played on the slide, see-saw, swings and in the sand pit, Clara stood apart. She was staring up at the sky, pointing at the different birds and muttering the names to herself under her breath.

I bit down hard on my lip. She looked so beautiful and angelic, her blonde curls framing her delicate face, her big blue eyes creased in concentration. I loved her so much it physically hurt. I wanted to protect her, to wrap my arms around her and make it all go away.

I had taken pride in the fact that she was so intelligent. I had been thrilled that she took after me and was going to have a life full of books, studying and a career that she loved. But I was wrong. She wasn't like me. She was her own little person with her own unique mind and her own view of the world.

I could see now that she would follow a different life path from mine. She wouldn't be a leader, she wouldn't smash glass ceilings in cut-throat London law firms. She'd never be an independent, self-sufficient person like me. She was different. I had to accept it. I had to understand that my precious little girl saw the world differently from me and 'normal' children.

I had grabbed life with both hands and thrown myself in head first. Clara shied away from the world and wanted to be alone or with very close loved ones. But being different didn't necessarily mean being worse off. Clara could still achieve great things and I would help her do that. We were a team, Louise and Clara. She had come into my life so unexpectedly and had not been at all welcome. But then . . . I had fallen in love with her.

I had never been fazed by anything, but I had been knocked sideways by Clara's issues. I lay awake every night worrying about her. How would she cope when I was gone? What was her life going to be like? Would she be happy? What did the future hold for my precious angel?

Clara had Asperger's. I didn't really need some psychologist and a bunch of other people telling me because I knew it. I'd read Gavin's notes, I'd trawled the Internet, I'd watched the programmes. Clara had Asperger's, and I needed to learn every-thing there was to know about it.

I decided to look at it as a project. I was always the most prepared lawyer, more informed, more up to date and smarter than the people I dealt with. I'd just have to be the same about this. 'It's a condition not a life sentence,' I kept repeating to myself. I thought if I said it enough it would sink in.

I had to become an expert on the subject. Understanding it would ease my fear and take away the panic I felt every time I looked at her. With my help, Clara would carve out her own niche. She'd be incredible in her own way. I would help her shine. I would make sure she was happy.

Clara came over to point out a bird sitting in the tree above me. 'Look, Mummy, it's a robin, *Erithacus rubecula.* They're five inches long and the male and female are similar in colour, with an orange breast, face lined with grey, brown upper parts and a white belly. The bill is dark and pointed and the legs black. They can appear very plump and rounded, especially in cold weather when the bird fluffs out its feathers . . .' Clara went on and on, quoting verbatim long passages from her bird books.

When she paused for breath, I pulled her close to me and hugged her. 'I love you, Clara. You're the most important thing in my life, you know that, don't you?'

She squeezed me tightly back. 'I love you, Mummy. I know I'm important. You're important to me too.'

I kissed her cheek.

'Ooooh, Mummy, it's wet. I need to wipe it off. It doesn't feel nice.'

Laughing through tears, I handed her a tissue. She carefully wiped my kiss away. I held her face in my hands. 'Clara, you're wonderful and clever and amazing.'

'You're clever too, Mummy. You know lots of things.'

I paused. 'Clara, when you're in school and other children want to play with you, why do you find it so hard to play with them?'

Her little forehead creased. 'Well, sometimes I don't really understand the games they play. Yesterday the girls in the class wanted to play princesses but they kept changing the game. First of all we were sisters and we were at a dance, but then Kayla said she wanted to be the queen and Freya said she was the bad guy trying to capture us and then Bella said she and me would be horses and I didn't really understand what was happening. They were all shouting and telling me to run faster and I got really confused. I didn't understand what I was supposed to do and I'm not a fast runner anyway, so I shouted back at them and then I went to play by myself. Sometimes I just prefer to be by myself. I like my own games with my own rules. I don't really like playing their games but I tried to because you told me to, Mummy.'

'Oh, Clara, I'm sorry. You don't have to play with them if you don't want to. I just want you to be happy in school and it's nice to have friends, or even one person that you can have fun with.'

Clara shrugged her shoulders. 'But I have you, Mummy. I don't need anyone else.'

'I'll always be here for you,' I assured her.

'I know.'

'Clara, what's the hardest thing for you about school?'

'The noise at break time when all the children from all the classes are outside. The talking and shouting makes me want to go home and curl up in my bed under my covers. Big noise makes me feel scared and my heart beats really fast. That's why I play by myself. If I can look at birds, I feel OK. Can I go and look at birds now or do you want to ask me more questions?'

I stroked her cheek. 'You can go.'

She turned to go back to her bird-watching. Would she ever find friends or people her own age she could relate to? The research suggested that children with Asperger's tended to be drawn towards other 'quirky' people and would befriend them.

Clara needed to find friends. She would have no siblings to rely on when I was too old to look after her. What was I going to do about her future? I shivered with dread and fear. What would happen to my little girl? As I pulled my coat around me and I reached into my bag for my scarf, I heard Clara's voice: 'Mummy, it's Granny!'

I looked up and saw my mother coming towards me, carrying a heavy bag. Clara rushed over to her. Mum dropped the bag and threw her arms around Clara.

'Tighter, Granny, tighter,' Clara said.

Mum hugged her tighter. I saw her blinking furiously, trying not to cry as she held her granddaughter in her arms. I had to look away or I thought I might cry too.

When Clara wandered off to spot more birds, Mum came to sit beside me. 'It would have been nice of you to respond to my calls, Louise,' she grumbled.

'I've been kind of busy dealing with this crisis,' I said.

'I know that, pet, but you mustn't block out those who care most about Clara. We are the ones who are going to help and support you through this. I love that child almost as much as you do. She's a gift from Heaven. I never knew such a lovely child. We're all here to do whatever we can to make her life and yours easier.'

My whole life I'd never relied on or needed my mother. I couldn't wait to leave home aged eighteen and move to England and I'd never looked back. When Clara was born and I came home to Dublin, Mum had been great. She was devoted to Clara and had babysat for me when she was younger and easier to manage. But when Clara had started being obsessive about time and order, I had pulled back. I realized now that I had done that on purpose. I didn't want anyone to be alone with her for long because I knew they'd notice how odd some of her behaviour was. I hadn't wanted to leave her with Julie when I went to Brussels, but Julie's kids were so crazy that I'd figured she wouldn't really notice.

'But now I needed help. I needed Clara to be surrounded by people who understood her – people who would appreciate her differences and embrace them, and would help her adapt to life. Clara adored Mum and Dad, Julie, Sophie and Gavin. They were her 'safe' people. They were the people I needed to explain her quirks to, the ones who could and would help her.

Mum reached down and pulled a heavy bag onto the bench. 'I brought you some books. I've been to every bookshop in town and I've got you a good selection. I'm worn out dragging them around. I went to your apartment, but you weren't there. I met your neighbour, who said she thought you'd come down here to the park. Anyway, here you go. There's enough information to do you a lifetime. I've been reading up on it myself. Clara will be fine. It was very important that we caught it early and got her help. Sophie tells me you've found a good psychologist.'

'Yes, he's excellent. He hasn't diagnosed her yet – he said it'll take time – but he's going to see her once a week and help me to make the right decisions for her.'

'That's very good news.'

I looked at Clara, who was crouched to watch a small brown bird. 'I just wish I could . . . I just wish she wasn't . . . that this hadn't . . . Well, I suppose I just want to make her better.'

Mum took my hand and held it between hers. 'Louise, there are some things even you can't fix. Let the people who love you and Clara help. I will move mountains for that child. Together we can all help to give her the best life.'

I looked at Clara. 'You know what the psychologist said? He told me we get only what we can deal with. That Clara is a gift given particularly to me because I can deal with it.'

Mum smiled at me. 'He sounds like a wise man. That's the best way to approach this, Louise.'

Then, for the first time in my life, I leant on my mother's shoulder and sobbed into it. I was a child again. I needed my mother now, just as Clara needed me. And she was there for me, just as I would be for Clara.

CHAPTER 33

Julie

I sat opposite Marian at her kitchen table. We watched her children running around the garden. It began to rain lightly. They raced up to the door. It was locked.

'I want to come in – it's raining,' Molly shouted through the glass.

'You're fine. You've got your raincoat on – it's only drizzle,' Marian shouted back.

'I'm bored,' Molly complained.

'Go and dance in the rain. Think of all the poor people in Africa who have no rain and no food. They'd be dancing if they were you,' Marian told her. 'Stay out for fifteen minutes more and I'll give you a chocolate bar.'

'I'm sick of hearing about the kids in Africa,' Molly whined. 'I wish they'd all come here and I could go there and be in the sun.'

'That's lovely, Molly, very charitable. Those poor children are dying of starvation and I've just offered you chocolate for fifteen minutes of peace.'

'I bet you the mothers in Africa don't lock their kids outside.'

'You're right, they don't, because mud huts don't have doors.'

'Daddy never locks us out,' Molly howled.

'Daddy's not bloody here!' Marian snapped back.

'I hate you.'

'Right now, I'm not too crazy about you either. Now stop being a brat and go and play football with your brothers, who are not moaning.'

Molly stomped off in a huff.

'She's been really difficult since Greg went back to Dubai.' She sighed. She picked up a bottle of wine to pour me a glass but I shook my head.

'No, thanks. Part of the mess with Dan was that I was drinking too much. I'm trying to cut back and clear my mind.' I was surprised to hear that Greg had gone back to Dubai already. He'd only been home for four days. 'Has he really gone back already?'

'He arrived the day before Molly's birthday and left two days later.'

'How did it go?' I asked, feeling terrible that I'd just blabbered on about my awful night with Dan and was only now asking about Greg.

Marian smiled sadly. 'You know how badly your non-one-night stand went with Dan?'

I nodded, blushing.

'It went about as well as that.'

Oh, God, that was not good. I was hoping she'd

410

sort everything out with him. 'What happened? Did he find out about Lew?'

Marian drank deeply from her wine. 'He breezed into the house, looking all tanned and relaxed and very confident. He'd bought Molly stupidly expensive presents, spent most of his time on the phone and slept on the couch.'

'Oh, no. Did you talk to him?'

'I knew the minute I saw him that he was definitely seeing someone. He was so cocky. So I just said it straight out and he didn't even bother denying it. He said he'd met an English girl in Dubai called Sally, and he's in love.'

My jaw dropped. 'What?' I whispered.

Marian nodded. 'The kids don't know yet, but they know something's up. They were devastated that he didn't stay longer. He just couldn't wait to get back to his mistress.'

'But it's probably just a phase, a little dalliance, like you and Lew. I mean, did you talk it out? He's not in love, he just thinks he is. I bet you it won't last.'

'Julie, the man is not so much in love with Sally as with himself. I swear he was almost having an orgasm gazing at himself in the mirror. He's never been so fit or looked so well. I wanted to stab him in the face. And it's not the affair – I'm no one to point the finger at him for that. It's the total lack of interest in my feelings or, worse, the kids. He just doesn't give a damn about anyone but himself.'

'But Greg's a good dad – he loves those kids.'

'Bollox.' Marian slammed her hand on the table. 'Greg was always all about Greg. It's just worse now. I've basically raised those kids single-handedly since they were born, which is why I'm such a nut-job. Greg dipped in when it suited him, but he was always off on business trips, taking naps because he was tired and sitting on his arse reading the Sunday papers while I took them out for walks and picnics.'

It was true. When I thought about it, Marian had often been on her own with the children. While Harry used to be full-on with our kids at the weekends, Greg was always looking for excuses to get out of spending too much time with his. But what on earth would happen to Marian and the kids now?

'So, did you tell him about Lew? Tit for tat and let's move on?'

She shook her head. 'No, and I'm not going to. Now that the prick is earning decent money, I'm going to make sure he pays up. I'm not giving him any ammunition to screw me with. He wants to get legally separated, then divorced.'

'Already?'

She narrowed her eyes. 'Oh, you should have seen him, Julie. He was as cold as ice. He told me he was happier now than he had ever been in his life. Sally is the perfect woman for him and the opposite of me. She's calm, never curses, nags or tells him he's an arsehole.'

'I can't believe he said that! How dare he?' Why was Greg being so cruel?

'I called his bluff. I said, "Well, Greg, why don't you fuck off back to Dubai to Calm Sally because I think you're the biggest arsehole in the universe? And, by the way, you're taking the kids too. I need a break from them."'

Good old Marian. 'What did he say?'

'Well, that stopped him in his tracks. He looked shocked and then said, "Don't be ridiculous. I'm not taking the kids." I told him I'd already booked their flights and it was all sorted.'

Despite the awfulness of the situation, we were both grinning. 'Did he freak?'

'He said I was being ridiculous and unreasonable. So I said, "Sorry, Greg, you can walk away from me, I couldn't give a damn, but you're not walking away from your children. You're going to be a man and raise them. You're going to come home once a month and spend the full weekend with them and be their father. If Sally is as laid back as you say, she won't care. I'm not having my kids being totally messed up because you're a prick. You are going to honour your duty to them and show up for them. You can be a dickhead to me, but not to them. If you miss one weekend, I will come out there to Dubai with them and I'll leave them with you and Sally, and let's see how relaxed she is when she's left with four kids she's never met before. And, furthermore, you will continue paying me proper maintenance. You don't get to waltz in here, shatter our lives and stroll out as if nothing's happened. You are going to explain to the kids why you're not moving home next year. You are going to tell them that we're separating because you met someone. I was prepared to work on this marriage but obviously it's no use now. While you're chilling out with chilled-out Sally, I'll be picking up the pieces of your children's broken hearts. Just remember that, you wanker."'

I reached over to her and held her hands. I tried not to cry, but I felt sick for my friend. 'Well said. You're brilliant. But I'm so sorry you have to go through this. What a horrible thing for him to do. It's so ruthless.'

She shrugged. 'I'm OK about it. I knew the marriage was over. But the kids are going to take it badly. I feel so awful for them. They're really great kids and they love their dad. It's not what I wanted for them. My own father walked out on us and I can still remember the pain. It was horrendous. I wanted my kids never to feel anything like that.' Marian bit her lip in an effort to control her emotions.

I hugged her. 'Now, you listen to me. Your kids are going to be OK because you are an amazing mother. You are not your mother. You'll be there for your kids. You'll get them through this because you love them and are devoted to them.'

It was true. Marian was an amazing mother. Aside from the cursing, she adored her kids and did everything for them. She spent her life driving them to after-school activities and she was constantly telling them how great they were and how proud she was of them. Her own mother had never got over her husband leaving and had suffered from terrible depression. Marian had had a very difficult childhood and had always been determined that her children would have a happy one.

She clenched her fists. 'I'll manage and the kids will get over it. I'll keep a close eye on them, and if they need counselling, I'll get it for them. I'll make sure this doesn't ruin their lives. I want them to be happy and well balanced. Having an absentee father isn't going to stop that. I'll make sure of it.'

'I know you will and I'm here for you. No one can be strong all the time, so please lean on me. Call over anytime, or I can take your kids if you need a night off. You're not alone. I'll do everything I can to help you.'

'Thanks. You're a real pal.' Marian smiled at me. 'You know, all this has really made me think about marriage and relationships. Julie, you need to sort things out with Harry. You guys aren't like me and Greg. Harry is a good man and you have a good marriage. Your problems are just a bump in the road. My road had a bloody crater in it, but yours is salvageable. Harry hasn't met anyone. He's just let the cash go to his head. You haven't met anyone either. Dan was just a stupid distraction because you were bored and lonely. Go home and sort it out, Julie. Don't let it go. Fight for it.

Stop dithering and talk to Harry. Be honest, brutally honest, and make him see that he's being a tosser. Work at it, Julie. You can save your marriage.'

She was right. I did need to be honest and I did need to stop dithering. I had arranged to go out to dinner with Harry on Saturday. I'd told him it was important but he hadn't been listening to me: he was on his computer. But when we were face to face in the restaurant, I was going to set him straight. I was going to make him see. I had to. I had to try.

The Dan fiasco had made me see what a total idiot I'd become, sitting around feeling sorry for myself and not doing something constructive to alleviate my boredom. God, I was pathetic. I despised myself for being so weak.

I told Marian, 'I'm going to talk to Harry at dinner on Saturday. He's tied up all week and, besides, I want to do it on a weekend night when I'm not chasing the boys around, trying to get their homework done. I need to be calm and clear-headed when I talk to Harry. I've booked the cheap and cheerful little Italian restaurant that we used to go to before we had money. I've always loved it there. I'm going to pin Harry to his chair and force him to see that we need to make a lot of changes in our life.'

'Good.'

'What are you going to do?' I asked her.

'What can I do? Keep on keeping on.' She put

her chin up and her shoulders back. 'On a more positive note, I'm doing really well with the sex line. It's generating a nice little income. So that, along with the fact that Greg is making decent money in Dubai, means I'll be able to do some work on the house. I'm planning an extension to the kitchen.'

'And who are you going to get to help you with that?' I asked, raising an eyebrow.

She smirked. 'Well, it just so happens that Lew is available. He'll be coming over next week to talk about the plans I have.'

I hugged her again. 'Good for you.'

'The great sex will keep me fit, and take my mind off things. Besides, I need to try out some of the moves the sex-line guys ask me to talk about on the phone so that I sound more realistic. Julie, it's important to research these things . . .'

'That's my girl,' I said, and kissed her cheek.

'You know me, Julie, down but never out. I'll bounce back. Besides, I'm going to be really busy for the next while. I'm definitely going to set up my own sex line. I know how it all works now. By February, I'll be in business. I'm calling it, Voulez Vous Sex.'

I laughed. 'Well, that certainly says it all.'

'I reckon in two years' time I could be living beside you in a big mansion. I'm convinced I'll make a fortune.'

'If anyone can do it, you can,' I told her, with absolute certainty.

'I need the distraction. Otherwise, I'm afraid I might sink under the strain of this.'

Once more, my arms went round her. 'Marian, I'm so sorry. You don't deserve this and neither do your kids.'

Marian went limp and cried into my shoulder. I patted her back and tried to soothe her. But there were no words. Her life had been turned upside-down. But if anyone could survive it, Marian could. I'd make sure to do everything I could to help her.

There was a loud thump on the back door. I turned to see a very cross Molly. 'Will you let me in now?'

Marian pulled away from me and, with her back to her daughter, brushed the tears from her eyes. 'Those are the last I'll shed over that bastard,' she said. Then she walked over to the door, opened it and pulled her daughter into a bear-hug. 'Come here to me, you grumpy little sod. Sit down there and I'll make you a nice cup of hot chocolate to go with your bar. You'll need it to give you energy before your trampoline class later.'

I left them to it, praying that everything would work out as they adapted to their new life and hoping I'd be able to save my family from breaking up.

CHAPTER 34

Sophie

Jess ran past me into her bedroom and slammed the door. I turned to Jack. 'What happened?'

He shuffled about uncomfortably. 'Pippa might have been a bit short with her.'

I frowned. 'That's the third day in a row she's come home upset.' I didn't add that his stupid girlfriend needed to stop being a bitch to my daughter or I'd go over there and slap her.

Jack threw his hands into the air. 'I know. Look, Sophie, I'm doing my best, but Pippa's tired. You remember how it is with a newborn.'

'Yes, I do. And I also remember I never snapped at anyone even though I was totally overwhelmed by it all.'

Jack sighed. 'You were great. Pippa just needs a good night's sleep. I'm going to do all the feeds tonight.'

'Is she not breastfeeding?' I asked.

'No. She said she doesn't want to because it ruins your boobs or something.'

I had breastfed Jess and my boobs had been ruined. But not for long, I thought.

'Anyway, I said I'd give the baby his bottles so she can sleep through.'

Jack getting up at night to feed the baby! She really did have him wrapped around her little finger. He'd never once fed Jess a night bottle when I'd weaned her at four months.

'Well, just tell her to go easy on Jess. And make sure you include Jess. I think she's feeling left out. I'm going to check on her.'

Jack nodded. 'OK, thanks. I'll call her later.'

When I reached the door to Jess's bedroom, I could hear sobbing. Jess rarely cried. Life had made her quite tough. She must really be hurting. I opened the door.

Jess was sprawled face down in the middle of her bed with her head in her pillow. I sat beside her and gently stroked her long fair hair. 'Are you OK?'

She shook her head.

'Jess, I'm sure Pippa didn't mean to snap at you. All new mums are a bit grumpy. Dad said he's going to do all the feeds tonight so Pippa can sleep. I'm sure she'll be in better form tomorrow. Maybe you could pop in for a quick visit then.'

Jess flipped over, her face blotchy from crying. 'I'm not going over there ever!' she said.

'Come on, Jess, it's not that bad.'

'Oh, really?' she snapped. 'You don't know what she said to me.'

I was beginning to get worried. 'What did she say?'

Jess's lower lip wobbled as she spoke: 'She said that she needed to focus on Robert and that I wasn't to call over without checking it was OK with her first. She said not to call Dad, because he'd just say yes. She said I had to text her to make sure it was a good time. She said to stay away for a while so she could get her head together. She said she needed time to be alone with Dad and Robert as a family. When I coughed, she freaked out and told me to go. She said she didn't want me coming in from school with germs and coughs because I'd make Robert sick.'

Jesus Christ, the stupid cow. How dare she speak to my daughter like that? I tried to speak in a calm voice: 'That was unkind of Pippa. I'm sure she didn't mean to upset you but she should be more careful with what she says. I'll talk to Dad about it. But in the meantime maybe you should give her a little space. She'll get back to normal soon. She needs time to get used to Robert. The first few months can be frightening for new mums. Don't take it personally. Pippa's just exhausted and emotional and over-protective.'

Jess blew her nose. 'She was really cross, Mum. Her face was all red and angry and she was shouting at me.'

'What did your dad say?'

'He wasn't there. He'd gone out to get her some special juice to help her lose weight. When he got back I was sitting outside the front door pretending to do my homework.'

'Did you tell him what happened?'

'No. He looked really tired and fed up. I didn't want to make him angry. I knew he'd give out to Pippa and I don't want them to fight about me.'

'Oh, Jess! You poor old thing.' I put my arms out and, for the first time in ages, Jess snuggled into me.

While I comforted my child, I smiled secretly. The selfish part of me was delighted that Pippa was showing her true colours. Jess was finally going to discover that Pippa wasn't Miss Perfect, that Pippa wasn't her 'best friend': Pippa wanted Jack all to herself and was not the wonderful human being Jess thought she was.

Mind you, I was going to call Jack later, tell him exactly what had happened and make sure he told Pippa never to speak to our child like that again.

'Mum, can we make pancakes for dinner, just this once?'

Nothing was going to make me break this happy moment. 'Of course we can, sweetie.'

We stood up and walked arm in arm towards the kitchen. I knew it wouldn't last, that Pippa would be back in vogue soon, but for now it was bliss.

My breast-enhancement appointment was for the Friday. Jess was due to stay with Jack and I really needed him to make sure that Pippa would behave.

I didn't want to worry about Jess while I was having an operation. I rang him on Thursday to confirm everything was all right. Jess hadn't heard from him or Pippa since Monday and she was as upset as I was annoyed.

'Sorry. Pippa's been a bit tetchy, so I thought it best that Jess stay away,' he said.

'She's upset, Jack, she feels really left out. Tell Pippa to get over herself.'

Jack laughed. 'Yeah, right. The way she is at the moment, if I did that, I'd end up with a black eye.'

Grow some balls, I thought darkly. 'Well, I need you to take Jess for the weekend as arranged. You cannot back out on me, Jack. I told you I'm going out of town for work,' I lied.

'I know, I know. I'll sort it out.'

'OK. And be extra nice to Jess.' I could hear Pippa roaring, '*Jaaaaaack!*' in the background. She had a fine pair of lungs on her for someone who was so exhausted.

'Yeah, sure. I've got to go.' Jack hung up, sounding hassled.

The next morning I hugged Jess at the school gate. She wriggled out of my arms. 'Mum, stop. All my friends are looking.'

'It's just a quick hug, I'm not making a show of you. I'll see you on Sunday. If you have any problems and my mobile is switched off because I'm in a meeting or something, call Louise. OK?' I'd told Louise I was going away for work and that Jess would call her if things with Pippa got bad.

She rolled her eyes. 'Yes, Mum. You've told me a zillion times.'

'Well, I hope you have a nice time with your dad. I told him to spoil you.'

'Did you?' Jess looked up at me.

I nodded. She gave me a smile that would have melted chocolate. 'Thanks, Mum.'

I watched as she skipped off to greet her friends, looking happier than she had all week.

Quentin held my hand as the nurse ran through some final details before I signed the consent form.

'So, you understand all aspects of the surgery and agree to proceed with the operation?'

I smiled. 'I've never been more ready in my life.' I signed the form and handed back the pen.

'How long will the procedure take?' Quentin asked.

'The operation lasts between one and two hours, but we'll monitor Ms Devlin overnight. She'll be able to go home tomorrow.'

As the nurse left us, Quentin squeezed my hand. 'So, this time tomorrow, you'll be a D cup, right?'

I grinned. 'Yes, a lovely round perky D. No more saggy fried-egg boobs for me.'

'How do they get the silicone in?' he asked.

'They insert it under the pectoral muscle. The incision is made in the fold of the skin under your breast, so the scar is hidden.'

Quentin raised his eyebrow. 'Look who swallowed the manual.'

I laughed. 'I've been researching this for a long time. I know everything there is to know. At first my new breasts will feel firm and swollen and they'll be sitting up quite high on my chest, but as the swelling goes down, they'll drop to a more natural position and I'll have the best boobs in town.'

'How long do they last?'

'At least ten years, sometimes twenty.'

'Are you nervous? It sounds painful.'

I shook my head. 'Not even the tiniest bit. I've never been so sure I'm doing the right thing. I need this, Quentin. I've felt so bad about myself lately. I hate what age is doing to my body and I need to look my best if I have any hope of meeting someone who doesn't have a bus pass.'

Half an hour later I was lying on the operating table, looking up at the anaesthetist, counting backwards. I drifted away, dreaming of myself in a flowing wedding dress with a handsome man by my side . . .

CHAPTER 35

Louise

C hristelle had the decency to be really upset when she told me she was going back to Paris and leaving me with no child-minder for Clara at the worst possible time.

I glared at her. 'You can't be serious,' I snapped. 'You can't leave now. You know how much Clara depends on you, as do I. You can't just bloody well dump this on me with no notice. You know what's going on, how important it is for Clara to be surrounded by people she trusts. What am I going to do?'

She held up her hands. 'Louise!' she shouted over me. 'Calm down. Of course I know that this is not good timing. I love Clara, too. I didn't see that she had problems, and I'd never even heard of Asperger's, but it makes no difference to me what labels they want to put on her. To me she will always be my Clarabelle. But I have to go! I have no choice. My mother needs me. She can't manage with two broken legs.'

She had bloody well landed me in it. I didn't

care about her mother's legs. All I cared about was Clara. 'I'll pay for a nurse to look after your mother. You can't leave.'

'Louise,' Christelle said firmly, 'my mother needs me. I'm going back to Paris.'

'How long will you be gone?'

She gave me one of those infuriating French shrugs. 'A month, maybe two.'

'WHAT?'

'Before your head spins off, I have already organized a replacement for me.'

'That's no bloody use. You know how long it takes Clara to get used to someone new.' I felt as if I was going to have a heart attack. I couldn't take any more stress.

Christelle smiled. What could she possibly find amusing about this? 'My replacement knows Clara very well and she adores him.'

I frowned. 'What?'

'It's Gavin,' she said. 'He's resigned from Stars and Stripes. He's not into retail any more, he says, so he's totally free. He didn't want to tell you and his other sisters about it because he knew you wouldn't approve. But when he told me, I knew it was the answer. He said he'd love to look after Clara while I'm gone. So, you see, I've arranged everything so your life won't be messed up.'

For once, I was very glad Gavin had no staying power when it came to jobs. He was perfect. Clara adored him and he totally understood her. Thank God. My knees buckled with relief and I had to put out a hand to steady myself. Clara was going to be fine. She wouldn't freak out with this change. It wouldn't affect her adversely. I was weak with relief.

I was in a meeting when my secretary burst in to tell me someone was on the phone and talking about an emergency. Thinking something had happened to Clara, I rushed out of the room and snatched up the receiver.

'What's wrong?' I barked.

'Louise?' said a man's voice I didn't recognize.

'Who's that?'

'It's Quentin Gill. I work with Sophie.' His voice was breaking. My heart began to thump.

'What's wrong?'

'She's – she's very—'

'Jesus, Quentin, spit it out,' I snapped.

'She's very sick. The operation went wrong and she's in intensive care.'

What was he talking about? What operation? 'I don't understand. She said she was at a work event.'

There was a pause on the line. 'She lied. She was having her breasts enlarged and it's all gone horribly wrong. They said she's allergic to penicillin and she reacted really badly to the anaesthetic or something like that. I was so freaked out I couldn't really understand what they were saying, but she's in trouble, Louise.'

Oh, my God. 'Is she going to be all right?'

'I don't know.'

'Where are you?'

'In St Anthony's Hospital.'

'I'm on my way.'

In the taxi I rang Julie. She started crying. Typical Julie. 'Jesus, Julie, stop that and get down to the hospital now.'

'I'm coming. Poor Sophie. I can't believe she didn't tell us.'

'Of course she didn't. She knew fine well we'd never have allowed her to go through with it. I can't believe she's so bloody stupid. A boob job? Christ, when will she ever grow up and stop obsessing about her looks?' I was so angry and worried that I wanted to punch someone.

'Louise, she's lonely. She's upset and miserable being on her own. She wants to meet someone and she's really insecure about getting older. Sophie's looks have always been her thing. Your brains are your thing. I haven't got a thing. Well, maybe my fertility.'

'Julie!' I said sharply. 'Stop rambling and get into the bloody car.'

I rushed through the hospital lobby and found the intensive-care unit. Quentin was pacing up and down, muttering to himself.

'What the hell is going on?' I demanded.

He looked awful. 'I don't know. They haven't told me anything. There was a lot of shouting and rushing about. They told me to wait here for news.'

'Why didn't you stop her?'

He wrung his hands. 'I tried to talk her out of it, but she was absolutely determined to do it.'

'You should have called me. I would have stopped it.'

'She made me swear not to breathe a word to anyone.'

'Idiot!'

Quentin's head snapped up. 'Don't come in here and shout at me. If you were a good sister, you'd have seen how unhappy she was and could have talked to her. Sophie didn't feel she could talk to you about this because you just boss her around all the time.'

'I do not!' How dare this stupid man accuse me of bossing Sophie about? I didn't boss her. I helped and guided her.

Before he could insult me any further, Julie charged in, her face smeared with tears. 'Is she OK?'

'We don't know yet,' I said impatiently. 'I'm not waiting around here for news. I'm going to find someone.' I stormed away and grabbed a passing nurse. 'I need information on Sophie Devlin.'

'Are you family?' she asked.

'I'm her sister.'

'I'll get the surgeon to come and talk to you as soon as she's free.'

'I need information now!'

She eyeballed me. 'I understand you're worried. I'll do my very best to find out how your sister is. Please go to the waiting room and I'll be back to you as soon as possible.'

'Please hurry. We're very concerned,' I said, my voice cracking.

She patted my arm. 'I will.'

I composed myself before I went back to Julie and Quentin, who were hugging and crying.

'Thank God you were with her. At least she had a good friend by her side,' Julie said.

'I told her it was a bad idea,' Quentin wailed. 'I told her she was beautiful as she is.'

'That's the thing with Sophie,' Julie sobbed. 'She has no idea how gorgeous she is. It's terrible, she has no confidence. Jack meeting Pippa was the final straw.'

Quentin nodded. 'And when Andrew turned out to be a creep, her ego took another battering. I think that was when she decided to get her breasts done.'

'Do you think she'll be OK?' Julie asked me, her chin quivering.

'Yes. If it was a reaction to penicillin, they can fix it. She'll be fine.' I tried to sound confident but really I had no idea. While Julie and Quentin talked, I googled 'reaction to penicillin in anaesthesia'. Christ! It said that a patient could go into full cardiac arrest if they failed to respond to initial treatment.

I turned to Quentin. 'Did they react immediately to her allergy?'

'Yes – well, I think so. It all happened very quickly.'

'Should we call Mum?' Julie asked.

I shook my head. 'Not yet. Let's not panic until we know more.' I tried to sound calm. I felt as if my heart was going to burst through my jacket. Was Sophie going to die? Was my little sister's life going to end over a stupid bloody boob job?

I couldn't stand it. I went back out to see if I could find a doctor. Julie followed me. 'What are we going to do if she dies, Louise?'

'She won't.'

'But what if she does? I'll take Jess.'

'Jack will take Jess.'

Julie started crying again. 'Sophie'd hate Jess to be brought up by Pippa. We'll have to share custody. One of us could take her every second weekend, me, you, Mum and Dad. That way we could talk to Jess about Sophie all the time and show her photos and stuff. You know, keep . . . her, uh – memory *aliiiiive*.' Julie was bawling.

'Stop it this minute, Julie! She's not dead. She's not going to die. Stop talking like that. Why did she have to be so stupid?'

'She's not stupid, she's insecure!' Julie shouted. 'You don't know what that feels like because you've always been incredibly confident. But for us mere mortals insecurity is a fact of life. Sophie's insecure about ageing and her looks. I'm insecure about my intellect, my marriage, motherhood and pretty much everything.'

My worry turned into rage. 'Going under the knife, putting your life at risk and possibly leaving your daughter motherless is not a very intelligent way to deal with insecurity!' I bellowed. 'What's wrong with a push-up bra?'

'You just don't get it. She's miserable. She's trying to fix her life. She's trying to make it better.'

'With stupid fake boobs?' I roared.

'YES!' Julie screamed. 'For Sophie, that's a solution. It might not be your choice or mine, but it's hers.'

'It could have killed her!'

'I'm aware of that!'

'Well, stop defending her decision,' I yelled.

'And you can stop damning her.' Julie's face was bright red.

'How do you think Jess is going to react if her mother dies having a boob job? What kind of example is she setting for her daughter? What kind of life lesson is that?' I was quivering with rage. How could Sophie have risked her life for something so ridiculous?

A nurse came over to us. 'Ladies, please, keep it down. We have sick patients.'

Julie shuffled to the corner and sank into a chair beside a vending machine. 'I don't know. But you have to stop judging everyone, Louise. We can't all live up to your standards.'

I sat down beside her. 'What standards? I'm just about getting through the day at the moment. I'm so sick with worry about Clara, I can barely focus in work.'

'Louise, she'll be OK – you're a brilliant mother.'

'Am I?' I asked. 'Don't you think a brilliant mother would have spotted it earlier and got help quicker?' My voice shook.

Julie clasped my hand. 'You're a wonderful mother. But none of us is perfect – we're all just doing our best.'

'I wish Sophie had talked to me.'

Julie smiled. 'She knew you'd go mad if she did. Sophie didn't tell us because she knew we'd judge her.'

I shook my head. 'It's not about judging, it's about making good decisions.'

'But for Sophie this *was* a good decision. She thought it would help her find a man and therefore happiness. Sophie's a romantic – she always has been. She loved being married, she loves being with a man. Being alone terrifies her. We have to understand that. It's the fear of being on her own that drove her to do this.'

'There are other ways to find a man than by mutilating your body.'

'I think we should call Mum and Dad. If she doesn't make it, they'll never forgive us.' Julie began to sob again.

'Not yet.' I got up, determined to find the surgeon. As I marched down the corridor and turned the corner, I walked smack into a woman in scrubs.

'Are you a relative of Sophie Devlin?' she asked.

I nodded, not trusting myself to speak. She looked very serious. It must be bad news.

'I'm her sister. Now just tell me,' I whispered. 'Is she going to be all right?'

She nodded. 'We believe so. Reactions like this are extremely rare. Everyone acted quickly and thankfully your sister responded well, but we'll need to monitor her carefully in the ICU for the next twenty-four hours. However, she is out of serious danger. Her surgery has had to be deferred to a later date.'

My legs buckled and I fell to the floor. Thank God, she was going to be OK. Lovely Sophie, fragile, stupid, foolish, beautiful Sophie was going to be fine.

The surgeon helped me up.

'I have to tell my sister.' I ran back to Julie and Quentin. 'Sophie's going to be OK!'

CHAPTER 36

Julie

I didn't bother getting changed. I had bought a new dress for my important dinner with Harry, but I didn't put it on. When I got home from the hospital, Gloria, who had come at a moment's notice to look after the kids while I rushed to St Anthony's Hospital, was sitting, fast asleep, on the couch while the four boys watched *Rocky*. Tom had a cushion covering his face as Rocky was getting his head smashed in by the other boxer. The triplets were shouting, 'Hit him back! Kill him! Punch his lights out!'

I woke Gloria and told her I didn't need her to babysit tonight because there had been a change of plan. I paid her double and thanked her again for helping me out that afternoon at such short notice.

Then I went into the kitchen, found the secret stash of sweets I kept and poured them all into a big bowl. I went back to the boys and paused the movie.

'*Muuuuuum!*' Liam groaned.

'I have treats for you,' I said, pointing to the bowl. 'But first I want to say something. I know I've been a bit distracted lately. I know I've been grumpy and short with you, and I'm sorry. Really, really sorry. You four boys are the loves of my life and I'm so proud to be your mum.'

Silence. They were thunderstruck.

'Seriously?' Leo said.

'Yes,' I said.

'For real?' Luke asked.

'Absolutely,' I assured him.

'Even when we're bold?' Liam didn't believe me. I nodded.

'I'm proud to be your boy, Mummy,' Tom said. I hugged him.

'Lick.'

'Suck-up.'

'Faker.'

I held up my hand. 'That's enough. Boys, I know I get angry and sometimes I have to because you break things and go a bit crazy. But the day you three were born and the day Tom was born were the two best days of my life. I cried with happiness.' I began to choke up.

'Are you crying now?' Leo asked.

'Yes, but only because I'm so happy to have four amazing kids.'

'You're weird, Mum.'

'Totally freaky.'

'Why would you cry about having kids?'

I put my arms out. 'Be quiet and give me a hug.'

'Do we have to?' Luke asked.

'Yes!' I said.

'Hugging is lame,' Luke grumbled.

'Hug me, and I'll give you the sweets,' I bribed them. They all threw their arms around me.

'Can we put the movie back on now?' Leo begged.

I nodded. 'Yes, and you can eat all of these sweets too.'

I snuggled up beside my four beautiful, hyper, infuriating, adorable, wonderful children and felt very lucky.

When Harry got home at seven thirty, he found us all in the kitchen. The boys were cheering me on as I flipped pancakes. The cream marble counter was covered with Nutella, as were the boys. We were having a ball. I didn't care about the mess. I was alive. They were alive. They were healthy. They were full of zest and life. I needed to be around my children. I needed to feel close to them.

Every time I thought of Sophie lying in the hospital bed, I became even more determined to fix my life. I fed off the boys' energy and we whooped as I flipped another pancake.

Harry smiled at the scene. 'Wow! You haven't made pancakes in ages. Can I have one?'

'Sure.'

'What time are we eating? Eight?'

I slid the pancake onto Leo's plate and turned

to make another. 'I've cancelled the reservation. We're going to stay at home. I'm going to cook dinner for us here.'

Harry took off his jacket and hung it on the back of a kitchen chair. 'That suits me, actually. I've a few emails to send, so I'll—'

'HARRY!' I roared. Everyone froze. 'You will sit down with us and eat pancakes. If you so much as look at your phone or laptop, I'll get a hammer and smash them into teeny tiny pieces. Is that clear?'

'OK. No need to be so aggressive,' Harry huffed.

'Smash the phone! Smash the phone!' the boys chanted.

'I won't have to because he's going to turn it off, aren't you, Harry?'

'Fine, OK. Relax.'

The boys were so high from all the sugar in the sweets and the Nutella that they went to bed late so Harry and I didn't get to sit down until half past ten.

Harry picked up his jacket. 'Actually, Julie, I'm not all that hungry. I think I'll just head for bed. I'm playing in a competition tomorrow so—'

I went over and closed the kitchen door. Turning to Harry, I said, 'If you so much as mention golf one more time, I will put my fist through your mouth. Now, sit down and shut up. I have something to say and you need to listen.'

'You've been watching too much of *The Sopranos*, Julie,' Harry said tiredly, sitting down.

I sat opposite him. There was no point beating around the bush so I dived straight in. 'How do you think our marriage is, Harry? Healthy?'

'What?' He hadn't been expecting that.

'You heard me.'

'Well, I – I don't know. Fine – normal.'

'Really? Because I think it's falling apart.'

He looked shocked. 'Julie!'

'I'm serious. Our marriage is in tatters, Harry, and if you can't see that, then we're in serious trouble.'

Harry shuffled about uncomfortably. 'It's not that bad. We're just adjusting to our new life, that's all.'

I thumped the table. 'I HATE our new life. I'm miserable – really unhappy. Did you know that? Do you even give a damn? Do you actually notice my existence any more?'

'Come on, Julie, there's no need to be dramatic.'

'Dramatic! Harry, I'm not sure if this marriage is going to make it to next week. I hate what we've become. I don't even know who you are any more. You're not the man I married. You're this awful person who's obsessed with money and impressed by every pompous businessman he meets. You spend all your time crawling up Donald's arse instead of being with your family. I married a family man. I married a man who adored his kids. I married a man who was devoted to his family. But since you inherited that bloody money you've become someone I don't even like. I wish we'd never got the money.'

440

Harry slammed his beer on the table. 'Really, Julie? You seemed pretty happy when we moved into a nice house. You certainly appeared to be very happy when you got your new car. The triplets are thriving in their new school. I don't think it's all that bad. As for my crawling up Donald's arse, as you so nicely put it, I actually like and respect him, and he's taught me a lot about business. I hadn't a clue about investments and bonds and derivatives until I met Donald. He's been like a father figure to me. The investments I've made because of his advice have been very sound. I'm doing everything I can to secure our future. I'm breaking my back to learn as much as I can about business so that we will never have to worry about money again. So shoot me.'

I waved a finger in his face. 'If you just put the bloody money in the bank, we could live off the interest and be loaded for the rest of our lives. You're making a big song and dance about nothing. You don't need to spend months analysing spread sheets. Just open a bloody savings account!'

'I'm trying to educate myself, Julie! What the hell is wrong with that?'

'What's wrong with it is that you're never here! Do you think the kids give a damn about your stupid golf-bonding games? They just want their father to be around. You never spend time with them now. You're missing out on their lives. Stop bloody fixating on the money. Come back to us.'

'I'm not . . . Well, maybe I have been a bit

preoccupied, but I'm doing this *for* the kids. It's for their future.'

I threw my hands into the air. 'Jesus, Harry, don't you see? By focusing so much on the bloody future, you're missing the present.'

'I'm here. I take them to most of their matches.'

'Not lately, not with all your bloody weekend golf competitions. And even when you do take them, you spend half your time on the phone. It's as if you're running away from us. Are you?'

He avoided my eyes. 'No.'

Oh, God, was he? 'Harry?'

He sighed. 'I'm not. I'm just trying to adjust. I'm a boy who grew up with very little and I never really made a success of my life. I had an average job and earned very little money. I always felt bad about that. I wanted more for you and the kids.'

'But we don't care about money. We were happy.'

Harry looked at me. 'Come on, Julie. It wasn't easy. We were constantly budgeting and it was hard for you. We barely put the heating on, we never went anywhere on holidays and our car broke down all the time. I know it was hard on you and I felt terrible about it. I felt like a failure. And when Christelle came into my life, I wanted to be able to help her financially but I couldn't, so I felt even worse.'

'She didn't want your money. She just wanted to get to know her father!'

'Julie, you're not listening to me. I'm telling you

how I felt. A man who cannot provide properly for his family is not a man.'

I reached out for his hand. 'I never thought of you as a failure. You were a great husband and you did your best. It wasn't your fault your salary kept getting cut.'

'That doesn't matter. I still felt responsible. So when this money came into our lives, I was thrilled because it made your life better and the kids', and I was able to pay for Christelle's college fees and rent. It felt so good to be able to make things better for everyone, but part of me felt like a complete fraud.'

'Why?'

'Because I didn't earn it. It was given to me.'

'But that's just good luck and you deserved it.'

He rubbed his eyes. 'It didn't feel right. I would have much preferred to earn the money. A real man would have gone out and made a fortune. I was given it. So in my spare time, I decided to learn everything I could about business so that I could turn my aunt's money into more money and prove that I could actually provide for my family.'

'But that's ridiculous.'

'Is it? Why?'

'Because no one cares.'

'I do.'

'But it's . . . I mean, we don't need any more money.'

Harry groaned with frustration. 'It's not about the money. It's about me being able to look after my family without depending on hand-outs from relatives.'

I tried to see his point of view. 'OK. So what you're saying is that you'll only feel like a real man when you make money on clever investments and therefore prove that you're a good businessman and can provide for your family?'

He nodded. 'More or less.'

'But what you're not getting is that while you've been doing your crash course in finance, your family has been left behind. We miss you, Harry. I miss you. I don't care where the money comes from. All I want is my husband back. I'm lonely, Harry, really, really lonely.' I began to choke up. 'I spent this afternoon in intensive care with Sophie – she had a boob job that went wrong and—'

'What?' Harry's eyes were wide with shock.

'You're not supposed to know, so never breathe a word to anyone. Anyway, the point is, she did it because she's lonely. She went in to have surgery to change her body because she's so desperate to meet a man.'

'Is she all right?'

'Yes, she's fine – well, obviously not fine, but she will be. It was a total nightmare. When I saw her through the window, lying there, so vulnerable and alone, it made me realize how lucky I am. I have a husband I love but never see, and I'm struggling, Harry. I know it's stupid. I have nothing to worry about yet I've never been so unhappy. I don't know who I am. I just sit around here all day waiting to pick up the boys. I'm so bored and I know it's my fault. I know I should do something, but I don't know what. I've spent the last three months trying to find a job. I only managed to get one interview and it was humiliating beyond belief. It crushed me. No one will hire me. I haven't worked in a decade. I loved my newspaper column and it really upset me when that dried up. I feel so useless and pointless. I'm not qualified to do anything. I can barely use a computer and I just feel, well . . . lost.' I began to cry.

Harry came over and sat beside me. He put his arms around my shoulders and I sobbed into his chest.

'What a pair we are. One of us running around like a headless chicken trying to be a big-shot businessman and the other at home feeling bored and lonely. I'd better be careful – you know what they say about bored housewives!'

Thankfully, we were still hugging so he didn't see my face go bright red. God, if only he knew that I'd had another man's willy inches from my face.

'I miss you, Harry.'

'I miss you too. I'm sorry I've been so distracted.'

'Come back to us. Forget about being the next Richard Branson – just be the old Harry. We love that guy.'

Harry pulled back and put his hand up to my cheek. 'I don't think Richard Branson has anything to worry about.' He grinned. 'Now, what are we going to do about you?'

'I don't know. I've got to find something.'

'Well, why don't we go to that little Italian restaurant tomorrow night and brainstorm? We'll think of something. Now don't freak out, but I need to get my phone so I can cancel my golf tomorrow. We'll go and watch the triplets play their rugby match and spend the day together. How does that sound?'

I kissed his cheek. 'Perfect.'

CHAPTER 37

Sophie

I was lying back, hooked up to drips and monitors, feeling utterly wretched, when they came in. Julie came and took my right hand. Louise went to the other side and held the left.

'Oh, Sophie.' Julie began to cry.

I closed my eyes as a tear rolled down my face.

'You're going to be fine,' Louise said, brushing a strand of hair from my forehead.

'We were so worried.' Julie sniffed. 'We love you so much, Sophie.'

'I spoke to the surgeon. You're going to make a full recovery and that's all that matters. We'll help out with Jess, and Quentin will run the office. You just need to rest and get better,' Louise said.

The thought of Jess made me want to howl. How could I have been so stupid?

Julie kissed my hand. 'I'm sorry you didn't feel you could tell us. We wouldn't have judged you. You're so beautiful, Sophie – you don't need any of this. You're perfect. God, if I had your body, I'd spend all day long in a bikini.'

I opened my eyes and looked at the ceiling. My head ached. 'I'm such a fool.'

'No, you're not,' Julie assured me.

Louise didn't say anything. I knew she agreed with me. I knew she thought I was a huge fool. I'd almost died trying to have bigger boobs. I looked at her.

She shrugged. 'Honestly? Not your best idea, but I understand why you did it. I know you'd been feeling bad about things lately. I guess I didn't realize how badly.'

'I wish I'd noticed how low you were. I'm so sorry, Sophie.' Julie dabbed her eyes with a tissue. 'I'm the fool in this family. I've been so distracted trying to have sex with someone I don't even like that I didn't see my sister needed help.'

I shook my head from side to side. 'You're the best sisters ever. I knew you'd stop me because it was a bad idea. I just wanted to look better so I'd meet someone.' Tears flowed down my cheeks. I had barely stopped crying since I regained consciousness.

Julie sobbed beside me and wiped my tears with a handkerchief, but her own tears were falling all over my face so it was futile.

'Sophie,' Louise said, 'listen to me. You've had a really difficult time and I know Pippa's been a bitter pill to swallow. And the Andrew fiasco didn't help. But you're so much more than your looks. You're smart and strong and successful.'

Julie joined in: 'And a great mum, a brilliant

sister and drop-dead gorgeous. Sophie, if you could only see what everyone else sees. I feel like a big fat frump beside you. You don't need to change anything. You'll meet someone who adores you just as you are. Any man would be lucky to have you on his arm.'

I blinked back tears. 'It's just so hard out there and I'm so lonely.'

'But you've got work, Jess and us,' Louise said.

'I'm not like you, Louise. I wish I was, but I'm not. It's not enough. I hate being on my own. I know it's weak and pathetic, but I do.' I was getting really upset now. I tried to slow my breathing. I needed to stay calm.

'It's not weak. We're all different. I promise you that from today I will make it my mission to find you a nice, successful man. I'm going to trawl every law firm in the city for you,' Louise promised.

'And I'll find all the divorced dads in the school and introduce you to them. You can come to the boys' rugby on Saturday mornings – all the dads are there,' Julie added.

I smiled weakly. 'Thanks.'

'You could always shag Gerry just to get up Victoria's nose!' Julie grinned.

'Brilliant idea,' Louise said.

I laughed. It hurt. 'If I didn't find him so repulsive, I'd think about it.'

'It would be worth it to see that snotty cow's face,' Louise said. 'Now what do you want to do about Jess?'

449

My face crumpled. 'Please don't let her find out. Can one of you look after her until I get out? The surgeon said I should be home in three days.'

Louise laid a reassuring hand on my shoulder. 'Don't worry, Jess can stay with me. Gavin's looking after Clara for the moment so Jess can come and hang out with them. Gavin will pick her up from school and all that.'

'I don't want her to know her mother is a shallow, pathetic fool. I've tried so hard to set a good example for her. This will ruin everything. She'll see how stupid and superficial I really am.'

'Stop it!' Louise snapped. 'You're not superficial. When Jack lost everything, you went out, got a job and supported your family. You're a strong woman. Don't forget that.'

'You really are amazing, Sophie. Everything you've achieved in the last four years is incredible. I'm so proud of you,' Julie gushed.

'We'll just tell Jess that you felt sick in work, went to hospital and had a big cyst removed.' Louise, as always, had a solution.

'Thank you,' I whispered. I could feel the exhaustion pressing down on my head, but I had to stay awake a little longer to get everything sorted.

'Just concentrate on getting better. I'm going to talk to your surgeon. I'd like some more information on your post-op treatment.'

'I'll call Mum and tell her about the cyst,' Julie said.

'Only us sisters and Quentin will know the truth. Your secret is safe with us. Now get some rest.' Louise bent and kissed my cheek.

That evening, when I woke up from a painkiller-induced sleep, Jack was sitting beside my bed holding a bunch of white hydrangeas.

I smiled at him. 'My favourite.'

'I had to go to three different florists to find them.'

'Is Jess with you?'

'No. Louise said she'd bring her in to see you later. How are you feeling?'

'As rotten as I look,' I said.

'Louise said it was a huge cyst. It sounds painful.'

I looked at my ex-husband. I wanted to tell him the truth. I knew he'd understand. He knew me – he 'got' me. I took a deep breath. 'It wasn't a cyst. I was supposed to be having a boob job but it went horribly wrong. It turns out I'm allergic to penicillin so I went into shock and my heart almost shut down. But I'm fine now. They've done lots of tests and everything seems OK. I'm getting out of here in two days, thank God. I just want to go home and be with Jess.'

Jack stared at me, open-mouthed. 'Jesus, Sophie, I had no idea. That's terrible.'

'Terribly stupid.' I fiddled with the petals on the flowers. 'I don't want Jess to find out. You can never breathe a word of this to Pippa. Swear?'

Jack made a cross sign over his heart. 'I promise.

451

You know you can trust me. But why did you do it? Your boobs are fine. You look really good for your age.'

'Jack, you know how it is. You didn't end up with a forty-two-year-old woman, you ended up with a twenty-five-year-old. It's hard out there. I want to meet a nice guy who doesn't take his teeth out at night. All the men my age want young hotties like Pippa.'

Jack took my hand. 'Sophie, men will fall in love with you because you're an amazing woman. You're gorgeous, and you're kind, thoughtful, considerate, smart and resilient – and good fun too. I was very proud to be your husband.'

I looked at the flowers and tried not to cry. 'Thanks. The feeling was mutual.'

'On top of all that, you're also great in the sack.' Jack grinned and I slapped his hand playfully.

'Seriously, though, you should have more confidence in yourself. Any guy would be lucky to have you. You're really great, Sophie.'

'Stop it. You're going to make me cry.'

'I mean it.' He picked up my hand and kissed it. 'You're the best.'

Well, why hadn't I met anyone? If I was such a great catch, why was I still alone? 'Let's talk about something else. How's Robert?'

Jack sank back in the chair. 'Exhausting.'

He looked tired. The shadows under his eyes were almost as bad as mine. 'Is he up all night?'

'Pretty much. Pippa's finding it hard going so

452

I'm trying to help but it's affecting my work. I made a mistake yesterday, an expensive one. I can't do that. I'm still relatively new to the company and I need to impress the boss. It's a great job, but I have to be really sharp. There are younger, brighter, more ambitious kids snapping at my heels.'

'Be careful, Jack. You have to tell Pippa you need your sleep.'

'I tried to, but she just freaked out and said I was implying she was less important than me.'

Stupid, selfish cow, I thought. 'Isn't she on maternity leave?'

'Yes.'

'Well, tell her to get someone in to help in the daytime so she can go for a nap.'

'She has someone.'

What? Well, she was just being a prima donna. Jack was working, he needed sleep. It wasn't a question of who was more important. It was a question of who was working and who was at home with the baby.

'You'll have to be firm, Jack,' I urged him. 'You can't lose that job.'

He rubbed his eyes. 'I know. But I'm trying to help her because of what happened with you. I never knew you had post-natal depression and I still feel terrible about it. I'm trying to be there more for Pippa so she doesn't get it.'

Bloody Pippa. I'd been left alone every night with Jess, while Jack snored peacefully in the other room, but Pippa got to sleep while Jack fed the baby. That was crazy. If Jack lost his job, I'd be back to supporting Jess alone and I really didn't want that. It was nice to have extra money and not be worrying about bills. It was wonderful to have spare cash at the end of each month.

'Jack, Pippa will be fine. You need to get some sleep or you'll end up with no job and I don't see Pippa sticking around if you're homeless.'

He gave me a crooked smile. 'Are you implying she's shallow?'

I shrugged. 'She's young. She's a Celtic Tiger cub. They expect more from life. Just be careful, Jack. Focus on work.'

'You're right, as always. We had good times, didn't we, Sophie?'

'The best,' I said.

'We really lived it up.'

'It was great. We were lucky to have all those carefree years with no money worries and non-stop parties.'

'I miss it sometimes,' he said.

'You're starting to make good money again and you've got a beautiful young girlfriend to party with. You'll probably get to do it all over again while I'm at home alone with saggy boobs.'

He laughed. 'Right now, I'm so knackered that the idea of going out past nine o'clock terrifies me. I'm too old to have a baby.'

'No, you're not. You're just suffering from lack of sleep. You'll be fine.'

He looked at me intently. 'And so will you, Sophie. I know you will.'

'Thanks. How's Jess getting on with Pippa?'

'I spoke to Pippa and told her she needed to be careful around Jess, so she's making an effort. I'm trying to bridge the gap. I took Jess to the cinema last night and fell asleep. Is that bad parenting?'

I laughed. 'No, it was a nice thing to do.'

The door opened and Gavin's head popped in. 'Hey, sis, do you want me to come back later?'

Jack stood up. 'No, come in. I have to go now anyway. Good to see you, Gavin.' They shook hands.

'You too. Man, you look like shit. Have you, like, not slept since the nineties?'

Jack laughed. Then, before he kissed me goodbye, he whispered in my ear, 'Sophie Devlin, you're stunning. Believe me, you're a real catch.'

Gavin sat down and began to eat the chocolates Mum had brought me earlier. It had been awful lying to her about my 'cyst', but I couldn't tell her the truth. I was too ashamed.

'So, are you OK?' Gavin asked.

'I'm fine.'

'Did they get the cyst thing out?'

I nodded. I hated lying to Gavin, too, but I had to. The fewer people who knew, the safer my secret was.

I decided to change the subject. 'How are things

455

with you? I hear you have a new job looking after Clara.'

Gavin's face lit up. 'She's such a brilliant kid. I just totally get where Clara's coming from. I understand the way her mind works.'

'Louise said you've been amazing.'

'Well, I owe her. She's set me up with loads of jobs, given me money to start companies that failed and always gives me cash when I need it. And don't tell her, but when Christelle told me she had to go, I handed in my notice immediately so I could take care of Clara and help her out. But she can never know that,' he warned me.

I made a solemn cross over my heart. Good old Gavin, coming through in the end.

'But you know what? I've really enjoyed the research and finding out about Asperger's. Shania spotted it first because of her little bro, and when I started looking into it, I knew that was what Clara had. So I started finding out all I could because I knew Louise would be into charts and graphs, bullet points and statistics and all that stuff, so that's what I did. I made this, like, reference folder for her, which she uses all the time.'

It was nice to see Gavin so enthusiastic. And Louise said he was amazing with Clara, incredibly patient and encouraging, brilliant at drawing her out and making her laugh. Maybe he was finally growing up.

'Good for you. Clara's lucky to have you.'

'I'm kind of hoping that, by the time Christelle

456

comes back, Louise will want to keep me as Clara's minder. Christelle doesn't need the job – she told me that Harry pays her rent and gives her an allowance.'

'Keep doing what you're doing and you'll definitely get to keep the job.'

Gavin popped another chocolate into his mouth. 'Well, I've gotta go and mind her now so Louise can come and visit. I'll see you, sis.'

'Thanks for coming and eating all my food.'

'You never eat sweets. Your body is a temple, right?'

'Not any more,' I said, and stuffed one into my mouth.

'Good. You need to eat something. You're way too thin. Men like chicks with meat on their bones.'

With those wise words, Gavin left me and my box of half-eaten Cadbury's.

Jess came in later with Louise, who tactfully left us alone, muttering something about getting coffee.

As soon as the door closed, Jess threw herself on top of me and started bawling.

'Hey, it's OK, sweetheart.'

'I was so – sc-sc-scared, Mum. Louise collected me from school and her face was all white and freaked out and she said you were in hospital and I knew it was serious. She kept telling me it was fine and you were OK, but I really wanted to see you. She wouldn't let me. She said you needed sleep.'

'Oh, honey, I'm sorry.'

'After I spoke to you on the phone I felt a bit better, but you sounded really tired and kind of sad, and I wanted to see you. But Louise said I had to wait until now because you had to have tests all day yesterday. She's so bossy.'

'I'm sorry you were worried. I rang you so you'd know I was OK and you wouldn't worry.'

'But talking isn't the same as seeing. This morning I heard Louise talking to Julie on the phone and she was saying that they need to mind you because you're really sad.' Jess's lip began to wobble. 'Are you sad, Mum? Is it because of Pippa and the baby?'

I hugged Jess and kissed her head. 'Jess, I'm not sad, just silly.'

She tightened her arms around me and buried her face in my shoulder. 'No, you're not. You're brilliant.'

'Listen to me, Jess. I'm not sad, because I have you. I'm so proud of you. I love being your mum and you honestly make me so happy.'

'But you have been sad, Mum. I've heard you crying in your bedroom.'

I really should have been more careful. After Andrew dumped me, I'd gone on a bit of a pity-party rampage. Poor Jess was far too young to be worrying about me. I needed to be honest but reassuring. 'I felt a bit sorry for myself when I broke up with that man I was dating. But he wasn't very nice, so I'm glad it's over. If I'm being honest, I did find it hard when Dad met Pippa and when Robert was born. I suppose I was afraid of losing you to them. I thought you'd want to be with them all the time. And it's OK, I understand if you do. Please don't feel bad about it. It's normal that you'd want to be with your little brother. I want you to spend time with him and get to know him. He's lucky to have a wonderful older sister like you.'

Jess looked up at me, her face stained with tears. 'But, Mum, I never want to leave you. I never want to live with Dad and Pippa. Anyway, Pippa's been really narky. She's really grumpy to Dad too. And Robert's cute, but he cries a lot.'

'Well, that's normal. All babies do.'

'Did I?'

I stroked her cheek. 'Actually, no. You were the sweetest baby in the world.'

'I love you, Mum. Don't ever leave me.' Jess hugged me again.

'I won't, pet. I'll always be here for you. We're a team.'

And we were. If I ever met a man, he'd have to accept that Jess was my priority. I'd never let a man be mean to her or make her feel left out. I'd never let a man take over my life. He'd have to fit into it. I was a mother and that was my main job. If I did meet someone amazing, great. If not, well, I'd have to embrace all the other facets of my life – my daughter, my work and my family. I'd find a hobby, too, so that on the weekends when Jess was with Jack, I wouldn't feel so lost. Maybe I'd take up tennis again, join a running club or play golf. Yes, I'd take up golf. A game took ages so it would fill my day and there were lots of men in golf clubs. Who knew? Maybe I'd meet a nice, handsome, not-ancient golfer who'd be delighted to take on a nine-year-old and a woman with small, droopy breasts.

And if I didn't? To Hell with it! I'd be fine.

CHAPTER 38

Louise

I hugged Clara goodnight. 'Bye-bye, Mummy,
see you later,' she said.

'I won't be late,' I said to Gavin.

'Whatever, it's cool.'

'Uncle Gavin, it's your turn,' Clara said.

They went back to their game of cards. Gavin
had found a deck with birds on them and was
teaching Clara to play poker. She loved it and
was turning into quite the card shark.

Who would have thought that my little brother
would turn out to be the person who understood
her best? In the three weeks Gavin had been
looking after her, Clara had thrived. Between his
care, Colin's guidance and my absolute determination to help her navigate life, she was already
making progress.

I still woke at night panicking about her future. I
still worried about how she would cope as she got
older and her differences became more apparent
to other people. I worried about how she would
manage in school. Would she make any friends?

461

Would she be bullied? Would she ever be able to 'fit in'?

But the pain in my chest was easing and I didn't feel so emotional. I was back in control. In the last two sessions with Colin I hadn't cried. I'd been more like myself, which was a relief. I didn't want him thinking I was an emotional wreck.

When I arrived at the restaurant, Julie and Sophie were already there. I was glad to see Sophie looking so much better. The washed-out look was gone and she had some colour in her cheeks. She'd cut her hair into a short bob with a heavy fringe. It looked fantastic. 'I love your hair,' I said.

She ruffled it with her fingers. 'Thanks. I decided I wanted a whole new me. I've had long WAG-like hair for too many years.'

'You look ten years younger. It's gorgeous.' Julie beamed at her.

'Thanks. I feel like a new woman.' Sophie smiled. It was good to see.

I sat down and picked up a menu. 'Can we order? I had to take Clara to see Colin this morning so I skipped lunch and I'm starving.'

We ordered our food and some wine. 'How was your session today?' Sophie asked.

'Good, actually. He's really wonderful with her. He's got a gift.'

'He's very good-looking. I googled him,' Julie said.

'Really?' Sophie raised an eyebrow.

'Come on, guys, he's my daughter's psychologist.'

'So what?' Sophie said.

'Don't be ridiculous,' I said, feeling uncomfortable with the conversation because, in truth, I found Colin very attractive.

'Is he single?' Julie asked.

'That doesn't matter to Louise,' Sophie said, with a grin.

'He's separated, actually,' I informed them. '*Touché*, Sophie.'

'How do you know that?' Sophie asked.

'It came up in conversation.'

'Really?' Julie winked at Sophie.

'Stop it.'

'I think someone fancies the doctor.' Sophie giggled.

'I don't.'

'Well, how come you're wearing that sexy article? It was hardly for your clients.'

She had me there. I had chosen a dress that I never normally wore to work because it was a bit too sexy. I had matched it with a conservative jacket for the office, but had ditched the jacket when I got to Colin's office. I found myself looking forward to our appointments with him more and more. It was such a cliché to fancy your child's doctor. Besides, he was very professional and never flirted with me, although I had caught him looking at my legs today . . . 'Can we please change the subject?' I begged.

'OK, but we know we're right,' Julie said.

'If he has a hot brother, let me know.' Sophie laughed.

'How's your golf going?' I asked.

'I'm pretty awful at it, but it's fun and very distracting. I spent all of last weekend at this intense golf boot camp. I was so busy trying to remember all of the things the pro was telling me to do that the day flew by and I didn't miss Jess. Usually I find the weekends without her very long and lonely, but it was fine.'

'Well, if Harry's anything to go by, you'll become obsessed with it,' Julie said.

'Is he still playing as much?' I asked.

Julie shook her head. 'No. Since we had that big chat, he's agreed to play just one Sunday a month. He's really been trying and the boys are so happy to have him around more. They missed him. It's been lovely. I cooked us a late dinner last night and we actually sat down together and had a conversation. It's strange. It feels as if we're getting to know each other again.'

Sophie reached out and patted Julie's hand. 'That's great, Julie. You guys have a strong foundation. You'll be fine as long as you keep working at it.'

'He's taken my wanting to get a job very seriously. He's teaching me how to use PowerPoint and Excel and he keeps offering to set me up in a flower shop, a coffee shop, a boutique or any business I want.'

'And?' I asked.

Julie shrugged. 'I'm not an entrepreneur. I don't want to run my own business and have to deal with staff and wages and all that. I just want a part-time job I enjoy that keeps me busy, but still leaves me plenty of time to read.'

'And keeps you away from Facebook!' Sophie grinned.

'God, please don't remind me of that.' Julie shuddered.

'How's Pippa? Is she still being the wicked step-mother?' I asked.

Sophie sipped her wine. 'Jess said she was still grumpy but a bit nicer this weekend, and that when she started snapping, Jack took her and Robert out for a walk so Pippa could have a nap.'

'I wonder if Jack regrets getting involved with her now that she's not all young and bouncy,' Julie mused.

'I don't think so. I think he's just hoping this is a phase that will end when Robert starts sleeping through the night.'

Julie roared laughing. 'Good luck to him with that. My kids have only started sleeping through the night recently. After the baby stage you get the teething, then the bloody night terrors and then the bed-wetting.'

'Anyway, it's SEP, as Jess said the other day.' Sophie grinned.

'SEP?' Julie wondered.

'Somebody else's problem,' Sophie explained.

I went to pour more wine, but Julie stopped me.

'No, thanks. After the Dan fiasco, I realized I was drinking too much.'

I topped up Sophie's glass and mine. 'How is Dan? Any word?'

'Not since he texted to call me a prick-tease. In capital letters, no less.'

'What a total idiot.' Sophie grinned.

'He's such a tosser. Why did you ever go out with him?' I asked.

'I honestly don't know,' Julie said, staring into her half-empty glass. 'I suppose he was good-looking back then, but it's all a bit of a blur. I do remember now that he was always tight. I think that's why I broke up with him, actually. He never wanted to spend any money. He always wanted to stay in, drink cheap beer, eat toast and have sex. I just got bored.'

'He didn't come up in your big chat with Harry, then?' I asked.

'God, no!' Julie's eyes were wide. 'Harry does not need to know about it. Besides, it was just a load of hot air.'

'And throbbing members.' Sophie chuckled.

I put my fork down. 'Stop! You're putting me off my food.'

'Can we please change the subject?' Julie begged.

'How are you feeling?' I asked Sophie. 'You look great but are you able to manage work and Jess? You don't think you went back to the office too quickly?'

'No. I needed to get back to normal. Besides,

poor Quentin is so traumatized about what happened that he'll only allow me to do the bare minimum.'

'Well, if you need anyone to answer phones or help dress models, I'm free,' Julie offered.

I hadn't planned on telling them about it yet, because it was still early in the planning, but I figured now was as good a time as any.

'Actually, Julie, I need your help. In the research I've done into Asperger's and the whole autism spectrum, I've discovered that, because the health system in this country is such a joke, people who can't afford to be seen privately have to wait up to two years to have their child assessed. That's far too long and puts the child at a huge disadvantage. I've decided to do something about it. I'm setting up the Clara Devlin Foundation to help with early diagnosis. I need to get a lot of people on board – psychologists, nutritionists, nurses, doctors, carers, parents and anyone else who deals with or has experience with children on the autism spectrum. I want to create a safe place where parents can come for free advice, help and assessments. I'm going to tap my wealthier clients for funding and—'

Julie sat up very straight in her seat. 'I'll be happy to give you the money. It's no problem. How much do you need?'

I put my hand on her arm. 'Julie, I don't want your money. I want you to help me set it up and run it.'

'Really?' Julie looked shocked.

'Yes. You're brilliant with people and you'd be a great asset. It'll probably be very busy in the beginning, but you can work around the boys' schedule and—'

'Oh. My. God . . . Lou*iiiiiiiise!*' Julie burst into tears and cried loudly into her napkin.

'Hey, now.' Sophie rubbed her back.

Julie pulled the napkin down. 'I'd be honoured to help. I'm so touched, thank you. You really are the best sister. I promise I'll make this foundation the best foundation anyone has ever seen. I'll work twelve hours a day. I'll do everything I can. I'm so happy. I was thinking of going to stack shelves in Tesco just to get me out of the house, but now I'll be doing something brilliant and worthwhile. I promise I won't let you down. Thank you, thank you!' She threw her arms around me.

I hugged her back. 'Julie, I know you won't let me down. I have total confidence in you. I'm going to ask Gavin to help run it, too.'

'I feel left out now,' Sophie said.

'Sophie, you have a full-time job and you're a single mum. You have enough on your plate.'

'I'd like to help, though. I'll come in on the weekends.'

'That would be great, and I'll be looking for someone to organize a charity fashion show fundraiser, so I'll definitely need your help too.'

'I'd be delighted.'

'It'll be fun, all of us working together, and I'll

even be able to do pie charts for you on PowerPoint,' Julie said, as we laughed.

I explained that I had three premises in mind and I'd like them to view them with me. I wanted their input, not just as sisters but as mothers. I wanted the foundation to be somewhere that parents and children would enjoy coming to spend time.

I'd spoken to Mum about it and she had promised to help too. Dad had offered to do the books for me. It was going to be a family affair and, I hoped, somewhere for Clara to feel happy and safe, maybe even make friends.

I was determined for her differences not to stop her leading a full and joyful life. Clara's Asperger's had changed my life and made me look at things differently. I'd had to rip up my plans for her and start afresh. It was challenging but I was determined to make this new life-path as wonderful as I could for my little girl and me.

The motto for the foundation was going to be a Proust quote that I'd come across when researching Asperger's. It expressed exactly how I felt: 'The real voyage of discovery consists . . . in seeing with new eyes.'

CHAPTER 39

Julie

I unlocked the door and turned to Harry. 'Ta-dah!'

'Wow,' he said, taking it all in.

We had worked non-stop for three months to get the place ready for the grand opening.

'You've done incredible work. No wonder I've hardly seen you lately. The place is transformed. Well done.' He kissed me.

'I'm so happy, Harry. I haven't felt this fulfilled in ages. I really feel like I'm doing something that matters. I'm not just going to be working but helping people, too. It's brilliant. I feel alive again.'

Harry laughed. 'I can see that.'

There was a knock on the door. Harry opened it. Dad, Gavin and Jack were carrying cases of wine, followed by Mum, Sophie and Shania, with platters of canapés. Jess came in behind them, bearing napkins and tablecloths. After Jess, came Louise and Colin, who were hidden behind huge bunches of flowers.

Louise put her flowers on the floor. 'Thanks for

470

being here, everyone. Only two hours to go until the official launch. Can you believe it's actually happening?' She beamed.

We all cheered.

'How about a glass of wine?' Gavin suggested.

'Not yet! Too much to do,' Louise said. 'Right, if the men can sort out the wine, we'll set up the flowers and the food. Gavin, I need you to organize the sound system for my speech and presentation.'

I went over to help Sophie with the flowers. We made up six beautiful bouquets and set them around the room.

'Isn't this exciting?' I said. 'Louise really is amazing.'

'And so are you,' Sophie said. 'You've done so much work setting the place up. You've been a rock to Louise. You're so good at handling her when she gets all tense and bossy.'

I grinned. 'That comes from sharing a bedroom with her for sixteen years. Besides, I've loved working on this project.'

'You seem so much happier, back to the old fun Julie.'

I paused. 'I don't think I realized how lost I was.'

'Well, it's great to see you back to yourself.'

'Thanks. How are you? How was the date?'

Sophie wrinkled her nose. 'It was OK. He was nice, but not my type. I've got five more lined up over the next month. The thing I like about this dating agency is that you just go for coffee with the guy so it was only thirty minutes out of my day.'

'Are you talking about men?' Jack stuck his head between us.

'Yes.' Sophie laughed. 'I was telling her about my date.'

'Forget him. I've got a great guy for you. Nigel works in my office. I know you'll like him. He's like me but not as good-looking and three years older.'

Sophie rolled her eyes. 'Definitely not my type.'

'I know your type.'

'I've changed my taste since you.' Sophie swatted him with a white rose.

Jack laughed. It was nice to see them getting on so well. In fact, it almost seemed like they were flirting.

Jess came over and stood between them. 'What else can I do, Mum?' she asked.

'Could you help Granny with the food?'

'Sure.'

'Thanks, Jess, you've been great,' I said.

'It's fun.' Jess smiled and skipped over to her grandmother.

Jack's phone rang. He looked down. The screen flashed 'Pippa'. Without answering it, he put it back into his pocket.

'Jack!' Sophie scolded.

'I'll call her in ten minutes.'

'She might need you. Robert could be running a temperature or something,' Sophie said.

'More likely she needs a soya milk latte urgently from Starbucks.' He sighed.

'Be nice. Robert's still young – she'll be back to her old self soon.'

'Here's hoping,' he grumbled.

Sophie nudged him towards the door. 'Thanks for helping. Now go home to Pippa.'

Jack left reluctantly.

I turned to Sophie. 'You two seem to be getting on well.'

She smiled. 'Much better, since his worship of Pippa wore off. But I'm worried. He needs to make more of an effort with her – they're fighting a lot. I really don't want them to break up. It'd be bad for Jess.'

'Not if you got back together with him,' I said, looking at her sideways.

'Don't be silly.' Blushing, she scurried off to help Jess and Mum with the canapés.

Louise and Colin were deep in conversation about her speech. I heard Louise say, 'I want to talk about their special qualities and talents.'

Colin nodded. 'Absolutely. Why don't you take out that paragraph and move it there?' He pointed at the screen.

Louise frowned. 'No, because then *that* won't make sense.' She thumped her leg in frustration. 'Oh, God, it's all wrong. It has to be perfect.'

Colin took her chin and turned her face towards him. 'No, it doesn't. It needs to be heartfelt and passionate, which it is and you are. Now, stop fussing over every syllable and talk from your heart.' He kissed her gently on the lips.

I could see the tension melt away as Louise responded.

'Get a room!' Gavin shouted.

'Stop that,' Mum hissed. 'She's finally met a nice man who seems to like her *and* Clara. Under no circumstances is anyone to mess it up. I want to see Louise settled and happy, and Colin seems very suitable.'

'It's awesome to see Louise being like an actual woman and not just kicking arse,' Shania said.

'I agree with you there. I was worried if any man would be up for the challenge of being Louise's boyfriend,' Dad said.

'She's brilliant. Any man would be lucky to have her,' I defended my sister.

Gavin snorted. 'Dude, we know she rocks, but she's no picnic for a guy. She gives off this very I-don't-need-a-man-in-my-life vibe.'

'Well, Colin doesn't seem intimidated,' Harry pointed out, with a smile, as the loved-up pair continued to kiss.

At exactly six forty-five we were all standing in the reception area of the Clara Devlin Foundation building. Everyone was tired, but happy. The place looked wonderful. There was a feeling of anticipation and excitement, and we couldn't stop grinning at each other. It was a mixture of delight, relief and disbelief that we'd actually pulled it off.

474

Christelle had arrived with the triplets, Tom and Clara. We'd kept them away for as long as we could while we got ready. Harry had wisely brought an iPad for the boys to watch a movie on. Clara was talking to Colin about birds.

Louise tapped her glass to get our attention. 'Does everyone have a drink?'

We nodded.

'Well, before the guests and the press arrive for the official opening, I want to say a few words. None of this would have been possible without your help. I've been blown away by your enthusiasm, commitment and hard work. I wanted this foundation to be perfect, and because of you all, I think it is.' With her voice quivering, Louise turned to Clara. 'Sweetheart, you are the reason we're here today. Your amazing spirit, personality and courage inspired me to set up this foundation. You're such a wonderful little girl and I'm so proud to be your mum.'

I stifled a sob, then saw that everyone had tears in their eyes.

'I'm proud of you, too, Mummy,' Clara said.

Harry handed me a tissue.

'I don't want to single anyone out, but I do have to say two extra special thank-yous to Julie and Gavin, who have devoted themselves to this project. Honestly, guys, I'll never be able to thank you enough.'

'I'll take cash,' Gavin said, allowing us all a much-needed laugh.

Louise smiled. 'So, if you'd raise your glasses, please help me to toast the Clara Devlin Foundation!'

We cheered loudly and took a sip of our wine. I looked around at my wonderful, colourful, crazy, dysfunctional, warm, supportive, close family and felt so happy.

Our future seemed bright and filled with promise.